SHOT IN THE DARK

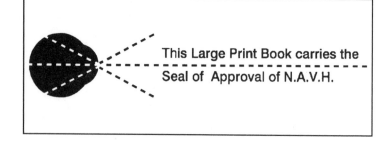

This Large Print Book carries the
Seal of Approval of N.A.V.H.

SHOT IN THE DARK

CLEO COYLE

THORNDIKE PRESS
A part of Gale, a Cengage Company

Farmington Hills, Mich • San Francisco • New York • Waterville, Maine
Meriden, Conn • Mason, Ohio • Chicago

LIBRARY OF CONGRESS CIP DATA ON FILE.
CATALOGUING IN PUBLICATION FOR THIS BOOK
IS AVAILABLE FROM THE LIBRARY OF CONGRESS

ISBN-13: 978-1-4328-5247-4 (hardcover)

Published in 2018 by arrangement with The Berkley Publishing Group, an imprint of Penguin Publishing Group, a division of Penguin Random House LLC

Printed in the United States of America
1 2 3 4 5 6 7 22 21 20 19 18

To our longtime literary agent,
John Talbot,
for his steadfast support.

Cheers to you, John,
for fighting the good fight — and winning.

ACKNOWLEDGMENTS

Shot in the Dark marks the seventeenth entry in our Coffeehouse Mysteries. Once again I thank my partner in writing and life — the talented Marc Cerasini. Though we met before the rise of dating apps, I "swiped right" from the moment I saw him, and we haven't gone wrong since.

The pleasures and pitfalls of romance in the digital age are depicted in this mystery with a fair measure of cheek, but also truth. Marc and I thank the many "Cinder-ellas" and "-fellas" who provided background material by sharing their dating delights and mishaps with apps.

New York City plays a pivotal role in this story, especially Hudson River Park (hudson riverpark.org), the longest waterfront park in the United States. We thank the Hudson River Park Trust for answering our questions and, more importantly, for their work in transforming our city's decaying waterfront into a priceless gift to the people of New York and the millions who visit each year.

A delicious shout-out for location research goes to the kind staff at Pier 66 Maritime (pier66maritime.com) on the Hudson River, where you'll find the Frying Pan lightship permanently moored, and a high-spirited outdoor bar and grill with a stunning view of the city's waterfront.

Our interaction with New York's Finest has been nothing but the finest, and we thank them for providing background, including information on the NYPD Harbor Unit. Deviations from doctrine are our doing with an age-old defense — in the service of fiction, rules occasionally get bent.

We thank our agent, John Talbot, to whom this book is dedicated, for his perseverance and professionalism. John in three words: a class act.

Caffeinated cheers to everyone at Penguin Random House's Berkley for their indispensable roles, especially Kate Seaver, whose keen suggestions strengthened this story. Cheers also to our new editor, Michelle Vega, for taking us on; and assistants Sarah Blumenstock and Jennifer Monroe for keeping us on track.

We applaud our longtime cover artist

Cathy Gendron for another dazzling cover for the original publisher's edition and gratefully acknowledge designers Rita Frangie and Kristin del Rosario; production editor Stacy Edwards; copyeditor Marianne Aguiar; and Tara O'Connor in publicity for their essential contributions.

To everyone we could not mention by name, including friends and family, we send our heartfelt appreciation for all the beautiful support you've shown us over the years.

Last but far from least, we toast our readers. Please know that we absolutely treasure the encouraging notes you send us via e-mail, our website's message board, and on social media. You inspire us to keep writing, and we cannot thank you enough for that.

Whether you are new to our world or a longtime reader, Marc and I invite you to join our online Coffeehouse community at coffeehousemystery.com, where you will find recipes, coffee picks, and a link to keep in touch by signing up for our newsletter. May you eat, drink, and read with joy!

— Cleo Coyle,
New York City

Three things in human life are important. The first is to be kind. The second is to be kind. And the third is to be kind.

— Henry James

"Will you have some coffee?" I asked. "It might make you human."

— Raymond Chandler,
Farewell, My Lovely

ONE

"Shot down again . . ."

My ex-husband dropped his hard body onto the soft stool at our crowded coffee bar, the thorny end of a long-stemmed rose still pricking his hand.

"Three strikes in one night," I said. "Does that mean you're out?"

"No, Clare. That's another kind of ball game."

"I hope you're talking about the Yankees."

"What do you think?"

"I think you should give up pitching woo and pitch in behind this counter . . ."

We were short-staffed this evening with every café table occupied, the coffee bar packed, and a line of customers spilling into the chilly West Village night. Couples who couldn't find seats were sipping their lattes on the cold sidewalk.

According to my young baristas, the reason for this bounty of business was a hot new "dating game" application for smart-phones. *Hot* was the operative word, since the app was called Cinder. This one included "user ratings" for the best public meeting places in the city, and we currently ranked in the top three.

Now that our landmark coffeehouse was a hookup hot spot for digital dating, my quiet evenings at the Village Blend displayed all the tranquility of a Times Square crosswalk.

"I'll work a shift," Matt told me. "But I'm not aproning-up until you caffeinate me."

"You want a single?" I asked.

"Make it a Red Eye."

The Red Eye aka "Shot in the Dark" was the barista's answer to the bartender's boilermaker, a jolty combination of espresso poured into a cup of high-caffeine light roast. It wasn't for the faint of heart. But then neither was my ex-husband.

A legend in the trade, Matteo Allegro was among the most talented coffee hunters in the world, as comfortable on a yacht floating in Portofino as in a muddy Jeep flirting with the edge of the Andes on Bolivia's infamous Death Road.

Adrenaline wasn't his only drug. During our marriage, he became addicted to cocaine while partying too hard below the equator. I helped him kick that deadly habit but failed to dent his other addiction — women.

Matt generated enough heat around the world's coffee belt to increase global warming, which is why I made the mature decision to put our marriage on ice. Even so, his behavior tonight seemed excessive. *Who makes three dates in one night? And how could Matt have possibly struck out on all of them?*

The very idea was (I had to admit) amusing. Not that anyone's rejection deserved to be mocked. On the contrary, I did my level best to suppress the surging wisecracks.

My raven-haired barista Esther, on the other hand, did not share my overactive conscience. From her perch at the register, she propped a hand on her ample hip and targeted Matt through her black-framed glasses.

"Did I hear right?" she asked. "The prince of passion was passed over? The sultan of seduction shunned? The archduke of desire dumped?"

"Hard to believe, I know . . ." With a smirk, Matt pushed his sweater's sleeves up tanned and sculpted forearms. "But even the best swingers foul out from time to time."

"I saw your first two dates vacate your

15

table," Esther said. "I lost track of the third. What was the reason for the last heave-ho? She's a vegan and you eat veal?"

"No. The vegan was Mindy, an hour ago."

"What about the redhead at eight thirty?"

"She said I reminded her of her ex."

"And the little blonde who just left? Why didn't she like you?"

"Actually, she did. I reminded her of her father."

"Ouch."

I tried not to laugh — and failed.

Matt noticed. "You're enjoying this, aren't you?"

"I'm sorry," I said. Hoping to make it up to him, I slid over his Red Eye. "Here you go, made with love."

Matt took a long hit and sighed. Then he laid his rosebud on the counter like a carnation on a coffin — and picked his smartphone back up.

"Hey! You agreed to help us back here, remember?"

Matt's focus didn't falter. "Just one more check of my Pumpkin Pot."

"Your what?"

Esther rolled her eyes. "He's talking about that stupid Cinder app."

With a deep breath for patience, I went back to work behind the espresso machine.

Three cappuccinos and two hazelnut mochas later, the man was still swiping.

"Enough!" I grabbed the phone.

That got his attention. "What's with the hostility?"

"I'm not hostile!" A few heads turned, and I lowered my voice. "Okay, maybe I'm a little hostile. This swipe-to-select coupling, and all these amped-up matches — it's like romance on Red Eyes. In my view, love should not be a sport."

"Not a sport, Clare, a game . . ." Snatching back his phone, Matt waved me closer. "Check this out —"

Like a little boy with a new toy, he showed off the screen. The word *Cinder* crackled in red letters, tongues of flame licking the edges. Below the logo were colorful animations — a glass slipper, fluttering fairy, and pulsing pumpkin — floating as innocently as Disney props.

Matt's finger stroked the tiny pumpkin. It jiggled and bounced, then grew and grew. Fairy dust fell from the digital sky, and the pumpkin transformed into a royal carriage with a purple banner reading —

TODAY'S CINDER-ELLAS!

Thumbnail images of a dozen women flew

out the carriage door and formed a grid pattern. Matt tapped one of them, and a profile opened, showing an attractive woman with a forced coquettish smile, bangs arranged over one eye with great determination.

"I just swiped this Ella into my Pumpkin Pot. If she swipes my profile right by midnight tomorrow, I'll get a Tinkerbell notification."

"A what?"

"It means she sent him a Glass Slipper, dear." The reply came not from Matt but from his mother — Madame Dreyfus Allegro Dubois.

The beloved octogenarian owner of this century-old family business was in fine form this evening, sporting tailored wool slacks and a cashmere sweater the color of textured latte milk. Her silk scarf, printed with Edgar Degas's *Dancers in Violet,* brought out that very hue in her eyes, which appeared livelier than usual in our shop's soft evening light.

As Matt greeted his mother with a kiss on both cheeks, I pulled her a fresh espresso. "What brings you here so late?"

"I have a rendezvous!"

"With Otto?" I assumed since she'd been seeing the gallery owner for some time. But she shook her head.

18

"Otto's consultation work in Europe is ongoing. He and I agreed to keep things loose. And you know I'll need an escort for your wedding — once you and your blue knight finally decide on a venue."

"Believe me, we're trying."

"So . . ." She waved her smartphone. "I'm swiping to meet!"

"You're using Cinder?"

"Don't be silly! I use the Silver Foxes dating app. That software allows either sex to make the first move."

Matt's eyebrow arched. "Maybe I should try it."

"Heavens no, it's not for children! The user age starts at sixty-five."

Esther snorted. "Hear that? In twenty short years, Mr. Boss will have a date."

Matt waved his phone. "More like twenty seconds."

Tinker-Tinker!

"See!" he said with renewed vigor — and thumb typing.

"What just happened?" I asked Esther.

"Cinder sent him a Tinkerbell notification."

"Of what? The approach of Captain Hook?"

"It's just a glorified text message," Esther explained, "telling him a woman wants to communicate with him. In Cinder-speak they call it a Glass Slipper. Only a Cinderella can send a slipper to a Cinder-fella. That's one reason the app has become so hot."

Matt nodded. "Contrary to the Connie Francis song, boys go *where the girls are,* and more women are on Cinder than any other app. They feel safer making the first move, and I'm happy to let them. Once they swipe me right, Tinkerbell alerts me, and we can set up a date to see if —"

"The Glass Slipper fits. I get it."

"And if it does . . ." Matt grinned. "We're on our way to the . . . *uh-hem* ball. That's Cinder-speak for going to —"

"I get that, too. But what happens if Ms. Pumpkin Pot swipes left on you instead of right?"

"Then we're done. Accept-Reject. Win-Lose. It's that simple."

"Simple? Or reductive? The decision to accept or reject a human being is being made on a few pictures and a paragraph!"

"So?" Matt halted his thumb-typing. "Look, it's no different than meeting a prospective partner in a bar or at a party. You check each other out, flirt a little, and you hit it off — or you don't. The app just makes the party bigger."

"One must keep up with the times, dear," Madame advised with a wink. Then she finished her espresso and tossed us a farewell wave. "My Silver Fox is in the coop!"

"I don't disagree with your mother," I told Matt when he finally joined us behind the counter. "Keeping up with change is smart — from a practical standpoint. But there are larger issues to consider."

"Like what?"

"Like change isn't always for the better, especially when it involves human nature."

Matt scoffed, but Esther countered —

"Ms. Boss ain't wrong. I read an article by a social scientist who believes these dating apps are artificially turbo-boosting the 'hit-it-and-quit-it' culture, devolving excessive users into the addictive cycle of Skinner box animals."

"See?"

Matt waved away my concern. As he tied on his apron, he pointed to his mother, who was already happily on her way out the door with her dapper-looking date. Then he challenged me to prove this "devolution" theory with a concrete example.

I couldn't. Not then. Within the hour, however, one of our customers did it for me . . .

I was sipping an espresso on a much-needed break when —

BANG!

The sound of a single gunshot tore through our upstairs lounge.

Looking back, I shouldn't have been so shocked. A new mate with every swipe meant the old one was tossed away. When it happens enough times, anyone's candy-store excitement could turn sour, even bitter. Binary code could connect continents, but it couldn't reprogram people, delete our fears and frailties. Or erase our potential for violence . . .

At the sound of that *bang* upstairs, everyone on the main floor quieted, the sea of faces going blanker than a dead smartphone screen.

Was that really a gun?

BANG! BANG! BANG!

With three more shots, chaos ensued. Freaked-out bodies stampeded the exit in unstoppable waves, and I bobbed amid the panic like a cork in the Atlantic.

"Clare!" Matt shouted, leaping over the counter. "Where are you?"

"I'm here!" I jumped up to show him and, on the next bounce, screamed a gentle suggestion to —

"Call the police!"

Two

As frantic patrons flowed around me, I noticed something disturbing (apart from the gunfire and mass exodus). Not a single person had come down from the second floor.

I pushed my way through the crowd until I'd reached the bottom of our spiral staircase. It stood like a wrought-iron sculpture, still and empty. Peering up, I saw no one and quickly climbed three steps for height.

Across the retreating sea of humanity, Matt was calling 911. When our eyes met, I pointed to the ceiling, my meaning clear —

I'm going up!

Matt's eyes bugged and he fervently shook his head.

I knew he wanted me to wait for the police, but I couldn't sit by and do nothing. One of my other baristas, Dante Silva, was up there, along with a floor of innocent customers.

Was this a hostage situation? Or someone's idea of a joke? Were people terrorized and injured? Or was this simply a misunderstanding?

Whatever was going down, I was determined to have a look, and (if possible) try to help. This was my coffeehouse, my staff, my responsibility.

"You take the service stairs!" I mouthed to Matt before starting my climb.

As I crested the top, I slowed my movements, entering the lounge in a crouched position. I spotted Dante's shaved head and tattooed arms in a small crowd of gawking patrons.

Finally, I saw who they were gawking at.

A slender woman stood near the middle of the room. She was about my daughter's age. Her white silk blouse looked virginal over her pink flowered skirt. Honey blond hair fell to her twenty-something shoulders.

I'd seen her several times in our coffeehouse. She seemed a shy type, always sat alone — though she sometimes conversed with Tucker Burton, my assistant manager. On those visits, her willowy arms had sported a fashionable handbag or tote. Tonight, those limbs appeared to be accessorized with a semiautomatic handgun.

"DON'T YOU EVER LAUGH AT ME

AGAIN. GOT IT?!"

Her shrill threat was directed at a man in his thirties. Cornered and cowering in a high-back Victorian chair, the guy appeared to be dressing for success in a designer skinny suit and open-collared shirt. His brown hair was threaded with salon-golden highlights, and the cut looked trendy — close-cropped on the sides with the thick, longish top slicked back.

I'd seen this man a few times over the past week — in the company of several different women — though I couldn't be sure, since his hands were raised in front of him and his head was turned at an angle that effectively hid his face.

"I'll shoot you next time instead of the ceiling! How would you like that? A bullet right into your heart. Or maybe your smirking mouth. Or better yet, how about down there?"

Wisely, Mr. Bullseye elected not to take the multiple-choice quiz.

"Maybe I should shoot you down there. Then you'll know how painful it is to be shot down!"

Tinker-Tinker!

The man's smartphone had fallen onto the ground and lay near his expensive loafers, along with a pen and a few bits of paper. When it sprang to life, so did he. In a stunningly brainless move, he lunged to answer it.

"No! Don't you touch that phone!!"

With a savage kick, the young woman sent the device flying. Then she slapped the man's head with her gun. He gave a yelp and curled back farther into the chair.

"I won't let you degrade another woman. I'd rather see you dead! Do you understand? DEAD!"

About then, I noticed something that alarmed me (even more than this mini Italian opera). My barista Dante began to inch closer to the female shooter and her loaded gun.

Bad idea.

This young woman hadn't shot anyone. Not yet, anyway.

Was she disturbed? *Yes.*

Homicidal? *Maybe.*

Enraged? *Absolutely* — at the guy in front of her, and that was the point. She was obviously reacting to some kind of rejection from this man, which made me certain that *another* man wasn't the answer to helping her see reason.

Dante, despite being dependable, creative, and kind, was the wrong gender for this task. Unfortunately, that didn't occur to him. So when he lifted his tattooed forearms to do something heroic — and possibly fatal — I quickly rose from my crouched position.

"Dante!" I barked in a bad-boss tone. "Your shift was over an hour ago. No more overtime. Clock out and leave this minute."

Shocked to see me, Dante froze, unsure what to do.

"Go," I mouthed.

"But —"

"Now!"

I pointed to the steps, and (thank goodness) he obeyed, heading down the spiral staircase.

The crazed young woman either didn't notice or didn't care about our exchange. She simply continued making verbal threats to her target.

Standing now, I got a better read on the crowd of people who had stayed to watch this drama. Many had their phones out to record the action.

That's when I reconsidered the situation, and the young woman's goal. This audience — and all those busy phone cameras — might be the whole point. If it was, the show was over.

"We're closing," I declared. "Everyone has to leave. Right now!"

My patrons shuffled in their seats. Then their phones disappeared as they collected their things and slowly headed toward me and the staircase.

I used the exit tide as an opportunity to move closer to the armed woman.

"Go ahead, finish him!" I heard a gruff voice call from somewhere behind me.

I would have liked to know who made such a crass and dangerous remark, but it wasn't worth taking my focus off that gun.

As the last of the customers hit our wrought-iron stairs, I heard a *psssst* sound across the room.

This time I looked.

It was Matt, peeking around the corner of the service staircase door. When our eyes met, he made a hand gesture, showing me he was ready to enter the room and help. But my ex wasn't the right gender for this task, either, and I shook my head, shooing him back before he was spotted.

I knew the police would be here any minute. I also knew the protocol for an active shooter, thanks to my fiancé, Detective Lieutenant Mike Quinn. *"When innocent lives are in jeopardy, Clare, we don't hesitate. We shoot to kill."*

This distraught young woman was bent on terrorizing the man in front of her. But did she realize her own life was in danger?

With a deep breath, I took a few more steps. I couldn't watch this young woman get gunned down or commit cold-blooded murder right in front of me. Not if there was a chance of talking sense into her . . .

"We're closing now," I said, my tone as gentle as I could make it. "Your audience is gone. Now you must leave. You and your friend —"

Poor choice of words.

"He's not my friend!" she raged. "He's a monster. A sick crusher who needs to be taught a lesson!"

While shouting at me, her gun stayed on him, but she turned a bit more in my direction. I noticed she'd taken great pains to make herself up for this performance: flawless foundation; perfect eyeliner; dusty rose blush and lipstick. Her jaw was proudly set, her small chin thrusting forward like a determined child. But her blue eyes looked wrong — frantic and darting one minute, then unfocused and eerily distant the next.

"If he committed a crime against you," I said softly, "you can go to the police. The Special Victims Unit will —"

"He didn't rape me. He lied to me. Said things that made me like him, trust him. And the next morning, I woke up next to a different person. He said awful things. Humiliated me. That may not be a crime, but it's inhuman, abusive, and I'm not the only one he's done it to!"

"I understand," I said. "You wanted him to listen to you. And he has. Now you need to stop."

"Me?" She waved the weapon. "*I'm* not the one who needs to stop! *He* needs to stop!"

"I'm certain he will." I glanced at Mr. Bullseye, quaking in his chair. "Look at him. He got your message —" As I continued to reassure the girl, I inched closer to that gun. "Now let's put it down, okay? I don't want you to get hurt. And that's what could happen if the police come up here —"

I told her *if,* but I knew they were coming, and we'd have no warning. Given the circumstances, they would roll up silently, no lights or sirens.

The thought of police arriving appeared to throw a bug into the girl's brain waves. Confusion overwhelmed her, and she froze up, eyes going glassy.

This was my chance.

A gentle tug was all it took to pull the gun from her hands. Before I knew it, Matt was behind me, taking the weapon away, and I was putting my arms around her.

Seconds later, uniformed officers of the NYPD stormed into the lounge from both flights of stairs, guns drawn.

THREE

Cuffed and Mirandized, Gun Girl was soon seated in the same high-back chair where she'd cornered her Cinder-fella. One police officer was posted by her side, while a half dozen more wandered around our upstairs lounge.

With its antique lamps and eclectic mix of furniture, our second floor had the look and feel of a bohemian apartment — and given the cramped state of most Village flats and NYU dorms, many residents actually did use our lounge as their living room.

This space is where Esther held her poetry slams; Tucker staged read-throughs and auditions for shows he was directing; and our community celebrated special events.

These historic walls (covered with works by artists whom Madame had cheered up, warmed up, or sobered up over the past six decades) had seen everything from band rehearsals to baby showers and bar mitzvahs. But tonight was no party. As of thirty minutes ago, this space had become a crime scene.

I recognized most of the uniformed cops milling around. They were all good customers, especially Patrolmen Langley and Demetrios. These long-time regulars on the Hudson Street beat were now updating the young detective on the scene.

"She never talked. Not even when I read her rights," Officer Langley said. "But I got her to nod that she understood, so it's legit . . ."

He was right about her despondency. When I'd hugged the young woman, I felt all the fight go out of her. Once the drama was over, she deflated like a sinking raft. Now her head was bowed, her gaze fixed on the floor, her loose honey-colored hair veiling an expressionless face.

Officer Demetrios lowered his voice. "I think she might be off her meds or something . . ."

I considered that observation. The way her manic performance instantly flatlined to dazed silence, she might have been off her medications — or on illegal narcotics.

"And this was the only weapon you recovered?" Detective Sergeant Emmanuel Franco displayed the gun, now encased in an evidence bag.

Langley nodded. "Funny, huh?"

Detective Franco frowned. "Not for her."

"You want me to wait?" Langley asked.

Franco shook his shaved head. "Take her back to the precinct and start processing her."

The two officers carefully helped Gun Girl out of her seat and led her away. Detective Franco stayed behind.

Another Village Blend regular, Franco had been nearby when the report of shots fired came over his police radio. As a concerned friend, he rushed to the scene — though the man was much more "friendly" with my daughter, Joy Allegro.

As ranking officer, he took charge of the investigation, which (no surprise) utterly annoyed my ex-husband.

Matt disliked uniforms in general and policemen in particular, the result of too many encounters with corrupt officials in developing countries that just happened to grow excellent coffee. But his animosity toward Emmanuel Franco went far beyond Matt's typical penchant for uniform scorn.

Franco had arrested my ex-husband — more than once.

Truth be told, he'd arrested me, too, but I got over it. Matt never did. Even worse,

Franco had captured the heart of Daddy's little girl. For that, I worried Matt would never forgive the man, whom he alternately referred to as a "mook" or a "slob," depending on his mood or the weather.

To be fair, Matt was spot-on about Franco's typical dress-for-distress wardrobe. Stained hoodies, old T-shirts, scruffy denims, and scuffed work boots were the usual attire for the young detective — job-appropriate choices since he spent most of his time on undercover work for the OD Squad (the nickname of an elite NYPD task force that focused on investigating drug overdoses).

But tonight was different.

Franco was put together like I'd never seen. A charcoal gray jacket, immaculately tailored, hugged his muscular frame. Sans tie, his ebony Egyptian cotton shirt was open at the neck. His biker boots had been replaced by upmarket footwear no downmarket cop should be able to afford.

"Going to the prom?" I asked.

He grinned and fingered the collar. "Nice, huh?" he said.

I waited for an explanation. He could see I was curious. But he offered none. Instead, after an awkward pause, he looked suddenly uncomfortable and turned away.

After directing officers outside to grab statements from witnesses still on the scene, he instructed me to take a seat in the lounge and wait for him to take my statement. Matt joined me, and together we both watched (and listened) as Franco spoke with the victim.

Richard Crest, an investment banker of some sort, was agitated. Not because of his recent brush with death. Crest was stewing because Gun Girl had cracked his phone screen when she kicked the device across the room.

"I should make her pay for damages," he griped, cursing as he tried to resuscitate his phone.

Franco gripped his elbow and directed him to a chair beside the woodburning hearth. In the flickering glow of the still-crackling fire, the two young men appraised each other.

Manny Franco's poker face betrayed nothing while Richard Crest's disparaging gaze took its time looking over Franco's new suit. Crest grudgingly approved. Only then did he begin to talk.

"The girl and I hooked up two or three weeks ago — through Cinder. We had a few laughs, went back to my place. I sent her packing the next morning, shook her loose, end of story — except she kept bugging me, so I told her she was a gold-digging whore, and I blocked her from my account."

Franco raised an eyebrow. "You called her a gold-digging whore?"

"Sure. I've got to be honest, right? A lot of these bitches see bags of money when they look at a guy like me, so I've got to be harsh to shake them off."

"But you *didn't* shake her off, because it didn't end there, did it?"

"It should have," Crest said. "But she started stalking me, ruining my new hook-ups . . ."

Holy cow, I thought. *In this guy's view, a "relationship" has a shorter shelf life than latte milk.*

On the other hand, I had to admit, our society didn't exactly discourage his way of thinking. God help the "so-five-minutes-ago" product, idea, news stories, or health food trend. Sometimes it felt as if half the population was mentally swiping, on a mad mission to continually discard a perfectly decent thing in favor of something else — and not necessarily better, just different, and seemingly newer. *Seemingly* because, once you'd taken enough laps around the sun, you knew there was very little new under it.

After Franco listened to Crest's statements, he scratched his shaved head. "You'll have to explain something to me. If you were trying to discourage Ms. Kendall's interest in you, why did you agree to meet here tonight?"

"Well, duh! She obviously tricked me. I didn't come to meet *her*. I thought I was meeting a twenty-two-year-old model, but all I got was that skank and a gun in my face!"

The interview went downhill from there. Franco finished the victim's statement, had the man sign it, and sent him into the night.

Franco sat back down and motioned me and Matt over.

"To be fair," I began, "she only shot at the ceiling and made a lot of threats. I don't think she meant to hurt him, or anyone."

"That's a safe bet," Franco replied, "since the gun is a showbiz prop."

"What do you mean *prop*?"

"The gun was loaded with blanks."

Matt smirked. "I knew I should have tackled her."

"Which begs the question . . ." Franco eyed him. "What were you doing while Joy's mother was heroically disarming the shooter?"

"Backup," Matt said flatly.

"How far?"

"Oh, for pity's sake! I was *acting as* her backup. And if you don't know what 'backup' means, you ought to watch a few TV police shows. You know, for some advanced training."

Franco opened his mouth. But before he could say something our daughter would regret, I cut between them. "Are you sure they were blanks? Those shots were so loud. So realistic."

"That's the point," Franco said. "Guns loaded with blanks are packed with more powder to give a louder bang for the camera or the audience."

"How did she even get a weapon like that?"

"Carol Lynn Kendall had several IDs on her, including a union card for the International Alliance of Theatrical Stage Employees and a temporary pass for the film studios in Astoria, Queens."

That certainly explained her friendliness with my assistant manager, Tucker. The thespian connection brought another thought, too . . .

"During tonight's incident, I got the impression Ms. Kendall was playing to the phone cameras in the room. Do you think this was some kind of publicity stunt?"

"Not according to the victim. But I would like to hear your side of the story — from the beginning. No theories, please. Only what you saw and heard."

"Just the facts?"

He nodded.

"Okay, Sergeant Friday, I'll do my best . . ."

I recounted everything, from the moment I heard the shots until I disarmed the shooter. I even repeated the crude remark made by one of the men as he was leaving the scene.

"I'm sorry I didn't see who he was . . ."

I paused, waiting for Franco to catch up with his note-taking. My requisite serving of "just the facts" was complete, but I couldn't stop myself from adding a *tiny* side of speculation.

"That man I mentioned with the nasty remark? I can't help wondering if he'd been goading the young woman on before I got up there. Maybe he was involved somehow, because I have a hunch what Ms. Kendall did here tonight was performance art. For reasons of her own, she was playing to those phones."

"We'll review any footage we find, but I wouldn't put much stock in that theory. At every suicide attempt or hostage situation,

40

you'll find some bonehead yelling for the poor slob to jump or pull the trigger." He shrugged the shrug of a New York street cop. "Human nature."

With that, Franco closed his notebook.

"Nice work tonight, Coffee Lady. No harm done, except to that poor girl's record. If she's lucky, a sharp attorney will get the felony charge pleaded down."

He cleared his throat. "One more thing. There's a news hound from the *Post* who's been haunting our stationhouse. If he gets wind of this, it's going to hit the paper."

"Let's hope he doesn't get wind of it," I said.

Franco studied me. "You're worried about bad publicity?"

"I'd hate to lose customers over safety concerns."

"What about the mobile phone footage you mentioned?"

I waved away that worry. "This world is an ocean of motion. With millions of people continually uploading videos, I doubt tonight's little incident will make a ripple."

FOUR

"Time to stress eat!" Esther announced an hour later.

By now, the police were gone, and I'd made an executive decision to close early. We locked the doors, cleaned the tables, and replenished supplies for the morning.

We also loaded most of our leftover pastries into the City Harvest van for New York's food banks and soup kitchens. I say "most" because after our rough evening, Esther, Dante, and Matt all wanted to nosh.

My own appetite had vanished with an adrenaline rush that was still making me manic. So instead of food, I steamed up a latte with a heavy dose of our Homemade Caramel Apple Cider Syrup, a comfort drink remedy for one stupendously uncomfortable night.

I insisted our snacking be done in the second-floor lounge — an earnest attempt to exorcise the evening's negative energy by eating with joy. And then I heard it —

Tinker-Tinker!

After all the drama, Matt was swiping again.

I wanted to scream. Instead, I gritted my teeth and civilly asked —

"What will it take for you to give your inner Peter Pan a rest?"

"Excuse me?"

"It's a syndrome. You can look it up on your smartphone — later."

As Matt waved me off and mumbled something about "just a quick check," Esther pursed her dark purple lips. "It's useless, boss. He's become hooked on the idea of hookups. And there are plenty of fish in that sea, which, come to think of it, is the theme of another of those shop-and-drop apps . . ."

As Matt's thumbs continued roving madly across his phone screen, Esther noticed my distress and elbowed the man.

"Be careful," she told him. "Or we'll think you're phubbing."

Matt's brow furrowed. "Phubbing?"

"An abbreviation for partner phone snubbing." Her thick black glasses slipped down her nose, and she peered over them like a goth psychoanalyst. "I should *also* point out that ignoring the people around you to check your phone isn't just rude. It's the first sign of cyber addiction."

My ex, who was (ironically enough) seated in Richard Crest's favorite high-back chair, flashed a smug smile.

"Okay, I'll shut mine off, if *you all* do the same."

When Esther and Dante quickly agreed, Matt's jaw dropped. He didn't expect two young baristas to welcome a phone-free break. But I'd shared enough shifts with them to know they were as tired as I was of Manhattan Phone Zombies.

Forced to go along with his own dare, Matt squinted with annoyance as he shut down his device and tucked it into his pocket.

Esther shot me a triumphant glance before pondering more important matters: whether to go for a melt-in-your-mouth Chocolate Soufflé Cupcake, one of our famous Banana Bread Muffins with Maple-Crunch Frosting, or another Birthday Cake Biscotti (long golden cookies baked with rainbow sprinkles and dipped in vanilla glaze with more sprinkles).

The decision was made for her when Dante grabbed the remaining two Birthday Cake Biscotti and Matt reached for the last Banana Bread Muffin.

With a shrug, Esther picked up a Chocolate Soufflé Cupcake. And since those beautifully airy treats were a light bite, she also grabbed a rustic wedge of our buttery, crumbly Espresso Shortbread before plopping into an overstuffed armchair.

"This evening made me feel really old," she announced, dunking her shortbread into her flat white.

"Old?" Matt responded. "You're not even thirty."

"Yes, but I can't get into this mobile phone culture," she said between satisfying chews. "I prefer the way it used to be — when people hooked up by chance at concerts, clubs, or poetry slams — which is where I met my Boris."

"Don't forget art galleries," Dante added, brushing confetti-laced crumbs from his T-shirt. "And museums, and sculpture parks, and street fairs."

"Sure, and bars, buses, and subways!" Esther said. "But my point is that people did things out in the world that interested them, where they'd be open to the magic of organic meetings. Now everything is techno-polluted. It's all phones and texts and swipes. It's not dating — it's *shopping*. You're a product. And you're judged, not by the depths of your soul, but by the artifice of Instagram appeal, job description, and some sort of cutesy ironic copy."

"It's true." Dante nodded. "You have a few seconds to capture interest. Like a human pop-up ad. Only you're selling yourself instead of an energy drink or cellular plan. It's no wonder so many of the connections are lacking in . . . you know —"

"Ubuntu," Matt finished for him, licking his fingers clean of Maple-Crunch Frosting.

Dante and Esther blinked. "What?"

"Ubuntu. It's an African term. Bantu, actually."

"But what does it mean?" Esther asked with her goth-eyed stare.

Matt tipped his head in my direction. "Ask Clare. She's an expert."

Now my two baristas were staring at me.

FIVE

My ex-husband surprised me. I wasn't the global coffee hunter, he was. The man had trekked across Africa more times than I'd been to Brooklyn.

"You're the one who taught me the term," I told him.

"But you put *ubuntu* into practice more than anyone I know — outside of the Nguni, anyway."

Esther threw up her hands. "So what does it mean?"

"It means *humanity*," I said.

"More than that . . ." Matt leaned forward. "*Ubuntu* is a deep-seated belief that humanity is something we owe to one another. How I act toward you is what defines me. Not what I have or what I wear — but how I treat you, how I interact with you."

"In Africa, it's also about sharing," I pointed out. "Generosity of spirit and community. An awareness that we're all interconnected."

"That's right," Matt said. "And that's why I actually *like* the dating apps —" He sat back, put his hands behind his head, and grinned. "I can *connect* with much more ease and frequency."

Esther snorted. "Too bad everyone swiping doesn't believe in *ubuntu*!"

"Forget humanity," Dante griped. "I'd settle for simple civility. Some of these girls are so arrogant. Right to your face, they start ticking off every single thing that's 'wrong' with you! Like you offended them by showing up and being less than their ideal. And then there's the potential danger of the instant hookup."

I frowned. "Danger?"

Dante nodded. "I swiped right on this one girl. She had a great smile and was lots of fun from the start — bubbly, flirty, totally into me. She asked to come back to my place, and I thought I was about to have the greatest night. We started kissing, and then . . ."

Matt's eyes widened. "And then?"

"She broke off the kiss and ran down a price list."

"A what?!" I was certain I'd misheard him, but he repeated —

"A price list."

"Yeah," Matt said, waving his hand. "That's happened to me."

Esther faced Dante. "So what did you do, Baldini? Bite the bullet and pay for it?"

"I told her to leave. That's when she freaked out and threatened me. Said if I didn't pay, she'd have her pimp work me over."

"I hope you called the police!" I said.

Dante shrugged. "At first I didn't want to — the situation was totally embarrassing. So I tried to reason with her, told her to leave or I'd call the cops. She had a kind of tantrum, kicked the furniture, damaged a painting I was working on . . . so I finally phoned 911. That's when she ran." He shook his head. "I thought it was going to be the best night. It was the worst."

Esther tapped her chin. "You know what, Baldini? I think you just gave me the subject of our next poetry slam."

"What? How I dodged a pimp beatdown?"

"No! Hookup Horrors. You know, Dating App Disasters."

Dante grunted. "Yeah, I can see it. Catfishing for Fun and Profit."

"Catfishing?" I frowned. "I don't suppose you're talking about the thing you do with a pole near a well-stocked river."

"Catfishing is luring someone into a

relationship using a fake identity."

The confounded look on my face spurred Esther into gleefully defining an entire list of terms from the dating app culture. There was —

Breadcrumbing: "When you send flirty messages (crumbs) to keep a person interested without committing to an actual date — the digital age's version of leading someone on."

Ghosting: "You end a relationship not by telling the person up front but by killing all contact. You ignore their texts and voice mails, block them from your social media pages, and expect them to 'get the hint.' "

Benching: "From the sports term, meaning being put on the bench. When a current love interest keeps texting and flirting with you to keep you around, just in case other 'better' prospects don't pan out."

More terms ensued: *Catch and Release, Cushioning, Haunting, Love Bombing, Slow Fade,* and *Thot,* aka *"That hoe over there."*

"Goodness." I shuddered. "We've come a long way from *ubuntu!*"

Shaking my head, I studied Matt, hoping he'd learned something from this conversation, but after decades tramping through the most dangerous coffee-growing regions of the world, he didn't scare so easily.

Instead, he looked distracted and was fidgeting in place — not unlike an addict who needed his fix.

"You know, Matt, after what happened to Richard Crest, you might consider giving swipe-right dating a rest for a while."

"Richard Crest?!" Matt cried. "How could you imply I have anything in common with that walking, talking asshole of a human being?"

"I only meant —"

"Mr. Boss is right." Esther shook her finger at me. "He's nothing like Crest. Last week the guy crushed an NYU grad student at the coffee bar, left the poor girl trembling and in tears. She was in such bad shape, Nancy brought her upstairs to calm her down."

"You saw this?"

Esther nodded. "Another time, he left a date so upset she threw her latte at his back."

"You hear that, Clare?" Matt pressed. "That's not me. I love women. All women. I treat them with respect and affection. The women I meet walk away on a cloud!"

"I know you have a good heart," I said. "But from what I've seen, you're swiping your screen like mad. You're tearing through women."

"I'm not tearing through women any more than they're tearing through me! I use swipe-to-meet apps, sure — to meet like-minded, sophisticated ladies of legal age who want to hook up, have a good time, and move on."

"And that sort of casual date makes you feel good?"

"It makes us *both* feel good. None of the women I've met has ever complained, and plenty want a repeat performance." He leaned back and crossed his arms. "If I'm not mistaken, one of them is in this very room . . ."

"Oh, please!" I said and changed the subject. (Matt had many shortcomings, and I knew from experience "performance" wasn't one of them, but his prowess in the bedroom wasn't the point.) "What do you even talk about on a Cinder date?"

"Food, wine, movies, our drinks, the waiter's mustache. It doesn't matter because the conversations never last long."

"And afterward?"

"We kiss good-bye and go on with our lives."

"No sharing of thoughts? No baring of souls? No intimacy?"

"Intimacy?" Matt laughed. "They don't want to know I'm twice divorced or live in a warehouse on the crap end of Brooklyn any more than I want to know about their skinflint boss or their backstabbing coworkers. That's not why we connected."

"Connected?" *What a word!* "How can two people truly connect without intimacy? Be honest, Matt, with your second marriage over, isn't this swipe-to-meet obsession your way of coping with loneliness?"

"Not everyone is looking for intimacy, Clare. People can enjoy one another's company without getting too personal, too invasive. Whether you like it or not, Cyndi Lauper's '80s manifesto is still true. Sometimes girls just wanna have fun. I'm happy to help them."

"And if you're not alone, you're not lonely, right?"

"Give it up, Sigmund, it is what it is."

I noticed he was still fidgeting. I crossed my arms. "You're just dying to check your phone, aren't you?"

Matt opened his mouth, but the sound I heard didn't come from him. The voice was female, and it came from the street outside.

A young woman was screaming.

Six

"PLEASE, ANSWER ME. I AM SO SCARED!"

For an awful moment, Matt, Dante, Esther, and I looked like newly chipped ice sculptures. Then we ran to the windows facing the street to find Nancy Kelly, our youngest barista, peering up at us, a ribbon of streetlight illuminating her wheat-colored braids and fear-filled eyes.

"ARE YOU ALL OKAY?" she shouted.

"ARE *WE* OKAY?" Esther boomed back. "OF COURSE WE'RE OKAY! ARE *YOU* OKAY?"

"YES!" Nancy assured us.

"THEN WHY ARE YOU ACTING CRAZY?"

"I'M NOT CRAZY. I'M WORRIED!"

"ABOUT WHAT?" Esther yelled. "ARE YOU DRUNK?"

"NO, I AM NOT DRUNK!"

"BOTH OF YOU, STOP!" I ordered, but

(of course) they didn't. The pair kept arguing — which, in itself, was far from novel.

To the rest of the world, Nancy was a perky, positive transplanted farm girl. To Esther, she was naïve to a fault, the polar opposite of her own acerbic, forever-urban persona.

Smaller than Esther but with a country-girl fullness to her face and form, Nancy had a Judy Garland "Dorothy" kind of innocence with perpetually astonished eyes and crushes on nearly every "Mr. McDreamy" who ordered a macchiato.

Esther, by contrast, was engaged to a streetwise Russian émigré who baked bread in Brooklyn by day and rapped poetry at night while she worked on a second master's degree.

Given their many differences, everyone was surprised (okay, shocked) when the two girls announced they were going to share an apartment in Alphabet City. Then again, the economic realities of New York real estate often made strange bedfellows.

Truth be told, my ex-husband and I had endured sharing the duplex apartment above our coffeehouse for a short (exasperating) window of time, long after our divorce — but that was another story.

Suffice it to say, these sisters from different misters had long ago dispensed with "polite" conversation, although tonight's bi-level shouting match was a first.

"Excuse me, ladies . . ." Matt interjected, attempting to take control of the situation with his Mr. Smooth approach. "How about we take this inside?"

"DID YOU HEAR MR. BOSS?!" Esther scolded. "HE'S PISSED THAT YOU'RE DISTURBING THE PEACE!"

"ME?!" Nancy's hands went to her hips. "YOU'RE DISTURBING THE PEACE AS MUCH AS I AM!"

Right about then two things happened: Dante began to laugh uncontrollably and our residential neighbors decided to join the conversation — with typical New York sensitivity.

"KNOCK IT OFF, MORONS!"

"PUT A SOCK IN IT!"

"I'M CALLING 311!"

Instead of taking the hint, Esther and Matt began yelling *back* at the neighbors — and with less than civil replies.

That's it, I decided. *Enough!*

With a two-handed tug I yanked both of them away from the windows, stuck my head out, and ordered Nancy to —

"GET IN HERE. NOW!"

SEVEN

Ten minutes later, we were all downstairs, sitting around the coffee bar.

Actually, Matt and my staff were sitting. I was behind the counter, whipping up our Koko-Mocha Latte to warm Nancy up — and calm her down. And, boy, did she need calming.

Nancy's eyes were giant saucers, her hands flying objects.

"After my Critter Crawl workout class, I checked my phone. When I saw the video, I freaked! Right there in the lobby of Equator Fitness! I couldn't believe I was watching an *active shooter* on our very own second floor. I tried all your phones, to see if everyone was okay, but *nobody* answered."

"We turned them off," Dante said.

"Mostly because of Mr. Boss." Esther jerked a thumb in Matt's direction.

"Hey, don't blame me! It wasn't my idea."

"Actually, it was," I reminded him.

Dante nodded. "You said if we turned off ours, you would turn off yours."

"Yes. But I didn't want to."

Esther glanced at her roommate and mock whispered, "He was phubbing us."

Matt folded his arms. "I can hear you, you know."

"Well, whatever the reason," Nancy continued, "I was desperate to find out if you all were still alive. And you didn't answer your phones, and I didn't see anything on the local news." Her eyes began to tear up. "You're like my family here — you're all I've got in this big city, and I was scared out of my mind, certain you were all shot dead!"

"Take it easy, okay?" I slid the Koko-Mocha across the counter and patted her hand. "We think of you as family, too. And you can see we're all just fine."

Nancy wiped her eyes and took a warming sip of the espresso mixed with our Dark Chocolate Syrup and infused with my lovingly steamed coconut milk. She thanked me with a shaky smile, but I could see she was still upset.

"She needs more carbs!" Esther pronounced.

Dante's brow furrowed. "Carbs?"

"Yes, Baldini! Don't you know what you

get when you spell *stressed* backward?"

Dante scratched his tattooed arm. "Desserts?"

"That's right! Carbs help raise serotonin levels!"

Esther quickly found a stray slice of my Amish Cinnamon-Apple Bread.

"Eat this!" she ordered with the fretting intensity of a mother hen. As Nancy obeyed, Esther turned to Dante.

"That'll help her feel calmer and more relaxed."

"So would a good stiff drink."

"Please." Esther showed him her hand. "The only thing worse than a hysterical Nancy is a tipsy Nancy."

Nancy rolled her eyes. "Will you stop talking about me as if I'm not sitting right here!"

"Excuse me," I interrupted, "but there's something I still don't understand. Nancy, how were you able to view that video? Did one of our customers send it to you?"

Mouth filled with sweet cinnamon-apple bread, she shook her head, then swallowed and announced: "I saw it on Chatter. It's a trending topic. It has a hashtag and everything!"

I rubbed my forehead. There were so many apps and online services, I'd lost track of keeping them straight. "I'm sorry. What exactly is Chatter?"

Nancy pulled out her phone and showed me a streaming timeline of posted comments with images, news stories, and videos.

"It's a new global social networking board. See the Trending Topics here along the side . . ." She pointed to the topic tags #VillageBlend and #CoffeeShot halfway down the list. She clicked on one of the tags, and a stream of comments appeared about the video, which had been shared multiple times.

"Would you play the video for us?" I asked.

"Sure!"

Gathered around Nancy's glowing screen, we watched the film begin — innocuously enough — as a video review of our coffeehouse.

". . . and here we are at the Village Blend in New York's West Village!" A perky young woman winked at the camera then turned the phone to pan our second-floor lounge. "Home of the famous Fa-la-la-la-Lattes and Billionaire blend!"

"But we didn't get either," said the filmmaker's female friend. This second girl held up her drink. "I got their new Turtle Latte with their special house-made Chocolate-

Caramel Syrup, topped with whipped cream and pecan praline syrup — it is soooo gooood!"

"And I'm trying the Cinnamon Dolce Cappuccino — cinnamon and vanilla bean syrups whisked into an espresso with foamed milk. They drizzled it with vanilla-caramel and sprinkled on Ceylon cinnamon. Super-mazing!"

"This *place* is even more super-mazing," her friend pronounced. "They do open mic poetry slams here once a week. Cool musicians perform here. And the actor Tucker Burton has worked here forever. He's had little guest parts in episodes of some of my fave TV shows!"

"He directs, too, mostly cabarets and Off-Off Broadway, but he uses this room for rehearsals, and they say famous actors sometimes stop by to —"

BANG!

At the sound of the first shot, the girl on the video looked confused. "What the — ?"

"I SAID DON'T MOVE OUT OF THAT CHAIR. I MEAN IT!"

"Oh, wow," said the girl holding the camera. "We got lucky tonight. Check out the performance art over there!"

As she turned the lens of her camera phone, Richard Crest came into view. There he was in his skinny suit and open-collared shirt, cowering in the high-back chair, hands shielding his face.

Standing in front of him was honey blond Carol Lynn Kendall in her white silk blouse and pink flowered skirt, waving her favorite semiautomatic handgun.

In the background, several customers were backed up to the wall; others had taken cover under tables.

"EVERYONE, LISTEN! I AM NOT GOING TO HURT ANY OF YOU! I'm here to make a point." Carol fixed the gun on Richard. "This piece of garbage needs to stop abusing women. And I'm going to make sure he does! DO YOU HEAR ME, NOW, YOU PIECE OF TRASH? I'm sure you'll hear this!" Pointing the gun at the ceiling, she pulled the trigger three more times.

BANG! BANG! BANG!

"Keep shooting," a voice whispered. The command wasn't for Carol. It was the girlfriend of the perky filmmaker. "If this is real, we could sell this footage!"

She wasn't the only one who saw dollar signs in snapping crime.

Multiple camera phones began rolling, and as Carol Lynn continued to berate Richard, even the customers who'd taken cover came out, their curiosity overcoming caution.

In the next few minutes, I arrived on the scene . . .

I winced, seeing myself on camera, playing the bad boss and ordering Dante and the rest of the customers off the floor. The two girls shooting this video kept filming as they followed the customers down our stairs and out the front door, showing the small crowd that formed outside, staring up at the second-floor windows.

When police cars pulled up and two officers began moving back the crowd, the video abruptly ended, and I asked Nancy to send me and Matt the link to it.

"Wow," said Dante. "That was intense."

"*Now* do you see why I was freaking?" Nancy asked.

Esther patted her shoulder. "That video was harrowing. I would have freaked, too."

"How many people could have seen it?" I wondered aloud. "Not that many, right?"

"Let's find out." Esther grabbed Nancy's phone and tapped the screen a few times. "Just as I thought. This video was uploaded to YouTube and shared from there."

"How many views?" Dante asked.

"Three hundred thirty in under an hour — and it's going up really fast."

I glanced at Matt and we both exhaled with relief.

"Thank goodness," I said. "Three hundred thirty people isn't that many."

Esther, Dante, and Nancy all stared at me as if I'd lost all sense of reality.

"Boss, I didn't mean three hundred thirty views period. I thought you understood — if it's on Chatter with two hashtags, it would have to be bigger than that. It's three hundred thirty *thousand*!"

"We're viral!" Dante declared. "How cool is that?!"

As the three young baristas hooted and bumped fists, Matt caught my eye again, and I saw my own worries reflected there.

Notoriety like this was nothing to celebrate.

Like far too many posts on social media, those hashtags delivered only part of the story to the scrolling public. To them it was a minute's entertainment, a momentary freak show.

To us — and our beloved century-old coffee business — I feared those hashtags meant disaster.

EIGHT

"It might be okay," Matt said unconvincingly.

"An 'active shooter' in our coffeehouse?" I wiped the table in agitated circles. "That video will destroy us . . ."

The two of us were back upstairs, cleaning the remains of our snacking. I told our staff to call it a night, and they headed out, still believing "going viral" was "awesome." Matt and I held our tongues — until we were alone.

"Do you think our regular customers will be put off?" he asked.

"Some will."

"I hope you're wrong. One thing I *am* sure of. We can kiss all that new swipe-to-meet business good-bye."

"That's certain. Who's going to set up a date in a coffeehouse where Crazy Cinderella goes gunning for Prince Piece-of-Trash?"

"I'm guessing our 'Most Romantic Coffee' in the Village ranking is history, too." Matt collapsed into his favorite high-back chair.

Too upset to sit, I took a fast walk around the floor, looking for stray cups or glasses. My baristas had done a good job busing the tables. The floor needed a more thorough sweeping, but that could wait for morning.

Morning. I closed my eyes and released a pent-up breath. What would the morning bring? *Will the press and media cover the story — and make things worse for us? Or will Gun Girl be old news by the break of day?*

With no crystal ball to tell me, I returned to Matt, who was back to staring into his crystal screen.

"After the night we've had, *please* tell me you're not looking for another Glass Slipper."

"Nope. Ordering an Uber. Unfortunately, the Broadway shows are letting out, so it looks like I'll have to wait for a car . . ."

As he continued tapping his phone, he slumped back and crossed his legs. That's when I spied a slip of paper stuck to the heel of his designer loafer.

I yanked it free, and Matt sat up. "What is that? A bill of large denomination would be nice."

"You're close." I skimmed the print on

the paper. "It's a bank withdrawal slip for — *wow,* ten thousand dollars."

"You're kidding?!" Matt dropped to the ground and searched for more paper under the chair. "Too bad, no cash. All I found was this ballpoint pen."

He tossed it onto the café table, and I told him where I'd seen that pen before. During tonight's awful scene, it had fallen at Richard Crest's feet, along with his phone and a few scraps of paper — this was obviously one of them.

"Why would Crest withdraw ten grand in cash?"

Matt shrugged and returned to his phone screen. I studied the paper in my hand. There was no name on the withdrawal slip, but the bank branch was listed along with the last four numbers of the account. There was an exact time for the transaction, too: almost five hours ago, 4:47 PM.

"What should I do with this?"

"Throw it away," Matt said.

"No, I think I'll hold on to it . . ." I tucked the paper into my apron pocket. At the very least, it would give me an excuse to talk to Richard Crest the next time I saw him. And I had to admit —

"Something about this bothers me."

"What?"

"In the age of credit cards and smart-phones, why would anyone withdraw so much in cash?"

"Maybe he had a craving for a diamond martini at the Blue Bar."

"Nobody orders that ten-thousand-dollar drink. It's a publicity stunt."

"I was kidding."

"Listen, do me a favor. Call up that video again."

Matt studied me. "Are you all right? You look stressed. Maybe you should go upstairs and get some rest, try to forget about what happened here, and —"

"Just do it!"

With tight lips, he tapped the screen. I leaned over and together we re-watched the video. When it hit a certain point, I pounded his shoulder.

"Matt, look at that!"

"Ouch! What?"

"Pause it." I pointed to the screen. "See that? Richard Crest's face is completely hidden from the camera. His head is turned to the side and down, his hands are up, and he keeps them there. Don't you find that strange?"

"Why? He obviously didn't want to be shot in the face."

"But look —" I tapped the screen to start

the video again. "Carol Lynn keeps trying to engage Crest, and he won't respond. Not one word. That's not natural. Most people in that situation would have tried to calm her down, reason with her, persuade her not to shoot. But Crest just sits there, not saying a word. And he never moves his hands away from his face."

"Well, when you put it that way . . ." As Matt watched more of the video, he began nodding his head. "Yeah, you're right. It's as if he doesn't want to be —"

"Recognized!" I finished for him. "Now why would that be?"

"Off the top of my head? He's married with children, and using the app to serially cheat."

"Wow. You came up with that in record time. Having a flashback?"

"Please. Let's not revisit ancient marital history."

"Fine . . ." I took a breath. "And you're right. Using dating apps to cheat isn't exactly uncommon in the swipe-to-*meat* market. Or maybe there's something else going on here."

"Like what?"

Tinker-Tinker.

I frowned at my ex. "I thought you said you were ordering an Uber?"

"I was, but the Cinder app never sleeps . . ." As his voice trailed off, he began typing a reply to the Glass Slipper message. Seconds later, he gave me a sheepish shrug. "Looks like I won't be going home alone after all. One of my earlier dates had second thoughts."

"Seriously, Matt, after what you witnessed tonight, I'm surprised at your judgment — or lack thereof."

"I told you already, I'm not Richard Crest. I don't mistreat women."

"That's not the point. You don't *know* these women."

"That's what the app is for, Clare, to *get* to know them."

"You mean in the biblical sense?"

"You trust my mother's judgment, don't you? She's probably having a wonderful evening with that Silver Fox date of hers."

"A man whose name you can't even tell me." I pointed at his phone. "And who is this Cinder-ella that contacted you? You said she had 'second thoughts.' What does that mean?"

"Remember the little blonde who said I reminded her of her father? Well, she texted me that she kept thinking about our conversation — even during her other dates tonight — and she wanted to see me again." The

Tinkerbell noise sounded. "That's her. She's rolling up now. Gotta go!"

Shaking my head, I pulled out my ring of keys. Against my own better judgment, I unlocked the door and once again set my ex-husband free in the concrete jungle of love.

A minute later, I watched him climb into an old-fashioned yellow cab with his smiling Cinder-ella giddily sliding over as he slipped into the backseat.

The petite blonde had a Millennial Marilyn Monroe thing going, complete with platinum glamour curls, false eyelashes, beauty mark, tight sweater, and (to trendify the whole look) rhinestone cat glasses.

With a mighty exhale, I locked the front door and set the security alarm. This night was awful, and I was glad it was over. But I wasn't ready for bed. I was agitated, wide awake, *and* getting my appetite back . . .

Just then, I noticed a long-stemmed rosebud on the espresso bar. The red petals were closed, the edges slightly wilted, but I couldn't bring myself to throw it out. That's when I remembered.

Matt brought this flower . . .

He obviously left it behind.

Inhaling the floral aroma, I filled one of our glass latte mugs with warm water. Taking care to avoid the thorns, I placed the thirsty stem inside — and found myself wishing Matt had stayed behind, too, just a little while longer.

He could have joined me for a bite to eat, helped me figure out how to deal with this disastrous publicity, and (okay, I admit) kept loneliness at bay.

My fiancé, who usually worked out of the nearby Sixth Precinct (where he supervised the OD Squad), had been putting in long hours on some special project at One Police Plaza.

Mike planned to crash at his East Village apartment late tonight, but I expected to hear from him soon — especially in light of our viral-video shooting.

With that thought, I pulled out my smartphone, turned it back on, and searched for any new messages from the man my body and soul still ached for.

There were three unread texts — all old ones from Nancy.

My heart sank a little until I saw the "urgent" new voice mail waiting for me. Unfortunately, the message wasn't from Mike Quinn. The caller ID read PIER 66 MARITIME, a popular watering hole on the Hudson River.

Who would leave me a voice mail from a

bar phone?

Curiosity piqued, I hit play —

"It's me, dear," cooed my octogenarian employer. "Please don't tell my son about this. You know how Matteo tends to over-react. That's why I'm contacting you. I hate to admit it, but . . . I'm in a pickle!"

NINE

By the time I got to Madame, she wasn't just "in a pickle," she was well on her way to being pickled.

"I'm stranded," she went on to explain in her phone message. "And my mobile refuses to recharge!"

Without the use of her phone, Madame couldn't order (or pay for) an Uber. She had cash, but at this late hour, yellow cabs seldom trolled for passengers along the desolate riverfront, and she didn't think it prudent to venture out alone.

I didn't think so, either, and quickly called her back on the bar's phone. When she asked me to order an Uber car for her and put it on the Village Blend's tab, I insisted on driving her myself.

"Then let's make the best of it, shall we? Meet me on Pier 66, and you can enjoy a late dinner!"

With my appetite back, I agreed and

(reluctantly) ended the call. I wasn't about to grill the poor woman on a public phone, but I was dying to ask the obvious —

Where in the devil is your swipe-to-meet date? And why isn't he seeing you home safely?!

Fifteen minutes later, my curiosity on steroids, I parked our shop's van under a streetlight on 26th Street.

I'd hastily spruced up before coming, brushing my Italian roast hair free of its ponytail and swiping on some lipstick. My new jeans and boatneck sweater were presentable enough, so off went the Village Blend apron and on went my wool peacoat. The night was temperate for fall, but temperatures would drop near the river.

Sure enough, as I crossed Twelfth Avenue and the city's Greenway, a frigid wind whipped off the dark water, sending my newly freed hair flying. I pulled the strands off my face and pushed on, shoving chilled fingers into coat pockets.

Despite the cold, I liked being outside. The brisk ocean air was invigorating, a fresh reminder that New York, though crowded and claustrophobic, was also a port city with a long maritime history. No matter how oppressive the city became, an escape to the peace of wide-open water was only a few miles away.

The very idea was mentally freeing, especially to hardworking stiffs like me — one reason city advocates labored to keep the West Side waterfront accessible to the public (not just multimillionaires). Over the years, broken-down docks were transformed into lush green parks, and sinking piers into grown-up playgrounds.

My destination was one such playground: Pier 66.

Formerly a loading dock for train cars, the pier was extended into the Hudson by way of an attached railroad barge, and the whole shebang converted into an outdoor bar and grill.

As my ankle boots thumped across the dock's stout wooden flooring, I couldn't help admiring the weather-beaten hull of the US lightship *Frying Pan,* now permanently anchored on the south side of the pier as an extension of its restaurant.

When I first heard the ship's name, I thought it was a food service gimmick, but I was wrong. For much of her life, *Frying Pan* had worked as a warning vessel, protecting the hazardous Frying Pan Shoals off the coast of Cape Fear, North Carolina. Once, she even sank into the sea, where she foundered for three years before being raised and awarded landmark designation.

Now the old red boat shined again, not as a floating lighthouse but a lively venue for happy revelers. My spirits lifted seeing the pulsing life on her restored topside, above the lower deck's rust and barnacles. Her tower light no longer shined as powerfully, but the bright sounds of laughter and conversation certainly lit up the dark.

In many ways, she reminded me of the redoubtable employer I'd come here to meet . . .

All her life, storms had battered Blanche Dreyfus, even as a little girl. Winds of war had swept her from a beautiful Paris home to a Lower East Side tenement. During that harrowing journey, she'd lost her beloved mother and sister, a terrible blow at such a young age. But she overcame it and worked to build a new life in the New World.

As a young woman, she found happiness again in the form of a handsome Italian American man with a thriving coffee business. When Antonio Allegro swept her off her feet, she thought her marital bliss would never end. But her vital husband's life was cut short, and she was devastated once more.

Instead of giving up and selling the business, she worked night and day to get the Village Blend through New York's toughest years — and her son through the grief of losing an adored father.

It was a blow, too, when my marriage to that son fell apart. Without a mother of my own, Matt's had become one for me. As a pregnant art school dropout, I badly needed one, and she gave me her unwavering support — through not only those first nine months, but also all the rocky years of raising Joy.

She also taught me everything she knew about the coffee business. And she remained a cherished part of my life, even after the divorce papers set her son free.

I still cared deeply for my former mother-in-law. I admired her grit and respected her wisdom. Madame had seen and done so much in her life, and she was darn fine company, too. Another reason I quickened my steps down the pier . . .

When I finally reached the authentic fire-engine red caboose — a less-than-subtle reminder of the converted railroad barge beneath my feet — the hostess greeted me, and I made my way through a gauntlet of crowded tables. Despite the chilly breezes off the water, patio heaters kept the exposed dining area surprisingly comfortable.

I found Madame regally relaxing at a table, admiring the magnificent view. Up and down our side of the riverbank, Manhattan's towers lit up the sky, while across the water, Hoboken's smaller structures shimmered in the Hudson's black glass.

Blanche seemed to shimmer, as well. Her violet eyes looked bright, and her silver-white pageboy appeared to reflect the glow from the string of lights above us. Though the heat lamps kept us cozy, she left her chic Italian leather jacket on, parted enough to reveal the elegance of her latte milk sweater and *Dancers in Violet* scarf.

Like me, she had applied fresh lipstick, but not blush — she didn't need to. Her gently wrinkled face, which was usually pale, tonight displayed a pronounced rosiness.

I gave her a hug and barely sat down before she lifted her half-empty highball glass and declared —

"You *must* try one of these!"

"What is it?"

"Rum, ginger beer, and a dash of lime."

Aha, I thought, *the mystery of those flushed cheeks is suddenly solved.* "You're drinking a Dark and Stormy —"

"Not exactly. Here they mix things up their own way and call it Troubled Waters."

Considering my evening, either name seemed appropriate.

While Pier 66 featured casual self-service from a center bar and grill, Madame had arranged for waiter service. (She always did have a knack for negotiating special treatment in this town, and I certainly wasn't going to refuse a little pampering.)

"So?" I said after giving our waiter the order. "Are you going to tell me about it?"

"My date?"

"Yes. What happened to your Silver Fox?"

"Wrong animal. Albert was more of a Slimy Snake."

TEN

For a moment, I thought she was joking. The look on her face told me otherwise.

"A snake?" I repeated. "But you seemed so happy when you met him at the Blend."

"Oh, he was charming enough, though not as interested in art or culture as he claimed in his profile. The real estate market was what he enjoyed talking about, and he did — all night long . . ."

She waved her hand. "Albert brought me here for after-dinner drinks, just so he could point out all the structures on the Jersey skyline that he and his financial institution had bankrolled over the years."

"Well, I'm sure you learned something."

"Oh, I did. The lesson came when I visited the women's room, where I was confronted by my escort's irate sister-in-law —"

"You mean his brother's wife?"

"No, dear, I mean his spouse's sister."

"Albert is married?!"

Madame nodded. "He was using the app to step out on his young wife."

"Excuse me, did you say *young* wife?"

"As the snake hastily explained to me — his sexy new wife enjoyed his money and gave him plenty of physical gratification, but out of bed she was a complete bore. He couldn't talk to her, he said, and he enjoyed the romance of taking mature, accomplished women like me out on the town."

"I guess that's flattering."

"It's ridiculous! I sent him on his way, refusing even a ride home. But with pride cometh the fall." Madame patted her page-boy and looked away. "My phone went dead."

"Well, it's over now. And we're making the best of it, right?"

"Indeed we are!" She finished her drink and raised her empty glass.

Just in time, the waiter appeared with a cocktail for me, and fetched a new one for her.

I could see why Madame was feeling no pain. Troubled Waters wasn't so bad in highball form. The bubbly mix had a citrus-sweet tang and peppery ginger beer sting. It tickled my nose and packed a head-spinning punch. But its powerful effect didn't deter me, and when the waiter returned with our food, I asked him for a refill.

Since Madame had dined earlier, she ordered dessert (apple strudel).

I, on the other hand, could have consumed every item on their "Octoberfest Celebration" menu. Resisting all-out gluttony, I settled on the Chicken Schnitzel Sandwich with Bavarian Beer Cheese Sauce, braised red cabbage, and a side of German potato salad.

The white meat chicken was pounded as thin as a deutsche mark, the bread crumbs sautéed to crunchy perfection. The seeded bun was fresh, and the beer cheese was an inspired touch that added a creamy richness to the simple sammie. The cabbage brought back savory memories, as did the Hot German Potato Salad — it was the kind with bacon and vinegar that a local church in my Pennsylvania hometown served during their Octoberfest, and I forked the tangy, smoky bites into my mouth with a contented sigh.

"You know, Madame," I said between unladylike mouthfuls, "yours isn't the first bad dating-app story I've heard tonight, and it certainly isn't the worst."

"I can roll with the punches."

"Honestly, I don't know if I can stand it anymore. I'm sorry, but I'm beginning to despise this 'swipe-right' culture. I can't understand why women and men are continually putting themselves in situations where they can be humiliated, betrayed, or worse."

Madame raised an eyebrow. "It sounds as if you have personal experience."

"I do."

"You surprise me, Clare! You're engaged to a perfectly wonderful and chivalrous man. Why are you using a dating app?"

"Not me! My 'personal experience' involved two customers . . ."

I briefly gave her the skinny on Gun Girl and her Crusher, including the unfortunate news that a video of the event had gone viral on the Internet.

"The Village Blend's image is taking a beating," I lamented. "And I don't know how to turn it around . . ."

Madame's reaction surprised me. She didn't appear upset. In fact, she seemed amused.

"I am sorry for that poor girl and that foolish boy. Both clearly lack maturity, good judgment, and the most basic tenets of civil behavior. But what happened tonight could prove to be a positive thing."

"Positive? I'm sorry, but I can't see a silver lining to this particular Dark and Stormy."

"Perhaps a little perspective might

help . . ."

"What do you mean?"

Madame's violet gaze moved over the river. She tipped her head toward a slow parade of working barges. Some floated by us in silence, others with bright blasts of their air horns.

"I've watched the years pass like those barges, Clare, some quiet as death, others with earsplitting changes. I've seen shops open and close; buildings rise and fall; trends come and go. Through it all, new generations always tried to break through boundaries. Out with the old, in with the new! But there's very little new when it comes to human behavior. That's why a single crime can change everything."

"A *single* crime? In this town?"

Madame nodded. Then she leaned forward and fixed her eyes on mine. "Tell me. Have you ever heard of the Groovy Murders?"

ELEVEN

"The Groovy Murders?" I shook my head.

"It was 1967. They called it the Summer of Love. But all that peace, love, and understanding didn't last long . . ."

Signaling for another cocktail, Madame went on with her story, her gaze going glassy as her thoughts traveled back to the 1950s and early '60s.

She and Matt's father were young shop owners, working hard to keep their business afloat in a neighborhood of modest means. Meanwhile, all around them, struggling poets and writers, avant-garde artists, and urban folk musicians were driving the counterculture movement.

Greenwich Village became synonymous with bohemia, birthing experimental theaters and art galleries, radical small presses and cutting-edge clubs.

During those years, Blanche and Antonio Allegro served strong coffee and Italian and

French pastries to some of the country's most influential iconoclasts — from Willem de Kooning to William S. Burroughs; Jackson Pollock to Jack Kerouac; Andy Warhol to Allen Ginsberg; Joan Mitchell to Johnny Allen (aka Jimi) Hendrix and Bob Dylan.

"It was a liberating time, full of new ideas and boundless possibilities . . ." A little smile brightened Madame's face, but it slowly faded. "By 1967 the culture began to shift. Beatniks, poetry, and bongo drums gave way to hippies, free love, and psychedelic drugs . . ."

In Madame's view, it was a slow devolution.

"Artists, writers, musicians who came to the Village in the past worked very hard. They took odd jobs to survive while they focused with ferocity and passion on producing and evolving their art. This, my dear, was the hidden bedrock beneath our little bohemia."

"What do you mean *hidden* bedrock?"

"From distant shores, bedrock is invisible. That's why naïve eyes see bohemian life as romantic. While the Village continued to attract serious artists and committed activists, it also attracted those who heard only the siren's call to mere pleasure seeking."

She shook her head. "Unfortunately,

throwing off societal constraints amounts to nothing if it produces nothing; and a life of aimlessness is far from a triumph of the human spirit. That's what I'd like you to keep in mind before I tell you what took place that summer."

"In 1967, you mean? The Summer of Love?"

" 'Turn on, tune in, drop out' became a slogan that lured scores of impressionable young people to our neighborhood. What concerned me most were the teenagers — children, really — who fled middle-class homes to chase the bohemian ideal. By that summer, the streets and parks in and around our neighborhood were teeming with young runaways, drifters, panhandlers, and phony gurus . . ."

Madame's third Troubled Waters arrived, and she took a melancholy sip. "Some were girls from sheltered families, who made themselves available to men who used 'free love' as an excuse to take the worst sort of advantage of their naïveté. I knew the family of one of these young women. By the end of 1967, every New Yorker knew Linda's story."

"Linda?"

"She died a teenager in the dingy basement of a Greenwich Village flophouse. But she was born to a well-off Connecticut clan whose great-great-grandfather started a coffee importing business after the Civil War. Antonio knew the owners. Their daughter, Linda, entertained dreams of becoming an artist. She dropped out of an exclusive boarding school to live the kind of romantic lifestyle that she believed would lead to making her great. And so, at eighteen years old, she moved to the Village."

"Her family allowed it?"

"Linda convinced them she was serious about pursuing her art, and her doting parents sent her money every week. Of course, they had no idea how she spent it. The girl lied to them, claiming she was living with a female friend, 'Paula,' but her roommate turned out to be 'Paul,' a man, and she had relationships with a number of men. She told her family she had a job when she didn't. She wasn't studying. She wasn't producing any art. Most of the money her parents gave her was spent on drugs, which she shared with friends. In the end, all those lies and all those drugs finally caught up with her.

"One afternoon, Linda took some of the cash her parents sent her, hooked up with a young man — a gentle neighborhood character we knew as Groovy — and together they went looking for drugs in Tompkins Square Park. That decision prevented Linda from seeing her nineteenth birthday. A few hours later, she and Groovy were dead, murdered in the boiler room of an East Village tenement. The papers shied away from the bloody details, but they soon leaked . . ."

Madame suppressed a shudder. "Linda was drugged, sexually assaulted, and her skull bashed by a brick. The perpetrators were a local drug dealer and his accomplice, well-known in the hippie community . . ."

On the river, a barge horn released an unsettling blast, and Madame fell silent. As we both stared somberly at the dark water, I couldn't help thinking of my own daughter. Despite the pier's heat lamps, a shiver went through me.

"Linda's parents must have been devastated," I whispered.

"They were. We all were. That brutal crime affected the whole neighborhood. It changed the culture."

"What do you mean?"

"Those murders shook awake the youth camping out in the Village. They were shocked into a realization: Peace and love may be worthy ideas, but the real world is no Garden of Eden. It's a perilous place with dangerous predators."

"They didn't know that already?"

"Not the sheltered ones. To them, 'concrete jungle' was a literary term — not a literal one. They came to the Village wanting freedom from rules and expectations. But while conventional living requires standards of behavior, it also provides a blanket of security. Those murders hardened hearts and sent a bone cold chill through most of those vagabond children. They suddenly realized how exposed they were, and they wanted that blanket back. Within a few weeks, most of the runaways gave up on their bohemian playtime and returned to their homes. The drifters drifted, and attitudes changed. The Groovy Murders were the beginning of the end of an era . . ."

As Madame's voice trailed off, I couldn't help thinking of *ubuntu* again, how human beings should treat one another.

"The hippie ideals weren't wrong," I pointed out.

"No — but it takes work to make a vision come true. You can't simply wish things into being." Madame squeezed my hand. "This phone app culture with its swipe-to-meet ethos, I must admit, is seductive, too. There's someone out there who's perfect for you. Someone who will finally complete you, make you happy. You simply have to *keep swiping, keep shopping.* With all this new technology, and all the potential matches out there, it's easy to believe . . ." Her eyes shined with amusement. "Even I wanted to believe it of my Silver Snake. But it's a fad, that's all. In time, it will float down the river, like all the others."

"I don't know. This phone culture is so pervasive. I can't see how this genie goes back in the bottle."

"I'm not saying people will stop swiping, my dear. Our modern culture rewards novelty — and, unfortunately, disposability. But as young people age, most of them will grow bored with games. That's when they'll stop shopping and start working on real relationships. Sooner or later they'll understand that shared experiences over time are what create true intimacy and steadfast love."

The waiter brought the check unasked — a signal that the restaurant would soon be closing. Madame sat back in her chair and drained yet another cocktail glass.

"Perhaps the incident at our coffeehouse tonight will alert a few young people — girls and boys — of the risk they take in too hastily trusting complete strangers. And that's a start."

I wished I shared Madame's optimism,

but I didn't see how one bad date gone viral would change the way millions of people behaved on a daily basis.

On top of that, I couldn't get the grisly image of poor murdered Linda out of my head. Even now I could almost see her body, lying on the dirty floor of a dingy boiler room, head crushed.

The vision was so strong, I thought for a moment I actually saw a dead woman floating in the rippling waters of the Hudson River.

I sat up in my chair.

My God. I'm not imagining it.

There really was something in the water. Or someone . . .

TWELVE

Rising from our table, I leaned over the railing.

Madame sensed my alarm.

"Clare? What is it? What do you see?"

I wasn't sure, but in the dark water below, a human figure appeared to be pushed along by the white-water wake of a passing barge.

"Do you see a body down there?" I whispered.

She squinted at the river and frowned. "It's all a blur. I admit vanity is to blame. I left my glasses at home."

A second look made me doubt my own eyes.

Is it a mannequin? A life-size display standee?

Oddly, it appeared a flotation device of some sort was ballooned beside the figure's head, obscuring my view of its facial features. As I watched, the sudsy wake from another passing vessel swept the figure closer to the pier. But I still couldn't tell what it was.

"Shall I summon the hostess?" Madame asked.

"No. I'm not sure what's down there. I need a closer look."

"Should I go with you?" Madame began to rise when her eyes went wide and she sat back down. "Oh, my!"

"Are you all right?"

She laughed. "I'm feeling no pain. It's all those Troubled Waters. They're finally making waves!"

"The drinks are hitting you. Just stay put. I'll be right back . . ."

I asked our waiter to bring Madame a pot of coffee. Then I hurried out of the restaurant.

Away from the space heaters, the cold was biting. I buttoned my coat as I walked past the lightship. Its festive bar sounds faded as I moved toward land.

Back on the riverbank, I searched for the entrance to another dock, which I noticed ran parallel to Pier 66. No more than a collection of planks, it was really more of an observation deck, offering water-level views of activities on the river.

I found its entrance easily enough, on the north side of the restaurant pier. But at this late hour, the area was shuttered, its overhead lights turned off.

Luckily, a single chain was all that blocked my way, and I was short enough to duck under it. Then I proceeded with caution. I had to. With no exterior lighting, this deserted dock was nearly pitch-black — *nearly* if not for the residual glow from the antique light tower atop the *Frying Pan* on the other side of the big pier.

Silently thanking the scrappy old girl for her lofty light, I continued on. Sounds of life faded as I moved out over the river. Water gurgled and growled as it lapped the worn wood piles under my feet. But the omnipresent thunder of Manhattan was muted and distant.

The farther my low boots walked, the blacker my surroundings. Windows of riverfront buildings became little more than pinpoints of plasma, light-years away.

With growing unease, I reached into my shoulder bag and pulled out my key chain's mini flashlight. Its weak power barely penetrated the gloom as I approached the railing at the far end of the platform.

It took me a moment, but I spotted the floating figure again. It was close to the edge of the dock, practically bumping the wooden planks, and once more, I noticed a balloon-like object attached to its form.

I aimed my flashlight at that ballooning bulge.

Though it appeared black in all this darkness, my little light unmasked its true color — bright red with the trademark name *Patagonia* printed in bold letters. At last, I knew what it was.

A waterproof backpack!

I dropped down to all fours and reached through the railing bars. The wood dug into my knees, the cold leeched through my jeans, and the gap was so narrow the steel bars pinched my upper arm. But I strained as hard as I could to grab that pack.

For all my groping, my fingers merely brushed it, and I ended up nudging the figure farther out of reach!

With a soft curse, I despaired — until another wake, this time from a passing party ship, pushed the figure toward me again. My fingers quickly closed on a strap, and I held on tight. Still on my knees, I tugged at the heavy form with one hand while I directed the flashlight with the other.

The figure slowly turned in the water. Faceup at last, there was no more doubt. My hand was holding the strap of a backpack worn by a human corpse.

Biting back a scream, I gritted my teeth and forced the flashlight beam over the woman's face.

She was cold and still and appeared to be young — early to mid-twenties. Shoulder-length blond hair with brightly dyed streaks of hot pink floated around her head like rays of light from a center sun.

I noticed a visible gash high up, on the left side of her forehead. And there was something on her face. I steadied the little flashlight for a closer look.

Finally, I saw what it was: a tiny heart-shaped tattoo inked on her left cheek. The sight struck me like a blow. I remembered that tattoo and the girl wearing it.

She was a Village Blend customer.

THIRTEEN

Breathing hard, I released the backpack and crab crawled backward, until my spine pressed against the opposite railing.

The dead girl slipped back into her watery grave, and I watched her slowly twirl. Her blue eyes were half-open. She seemed to be watching me, too.

I couldn't take it. I had to turn off my flashlight.

My hands trembled as I dialed 911. In the low glow of the smartphone's light, I gave my name and reported my discovery to the emergency operator. She told me to stay on the line and put me on hold.

I got to my feet, clutching the phone like a lifeline.

I felt very alone and vulnerable — and that's when I heard another sound.

Footsteps! Coming closer . . . and closer . . .

I held my breath as I peered into the darkness. The mobile phone's light obscured my night vision, but I could make out a human figure moving toward me.

Skin prickling, I fumbled for my key chain's flashlight again, barely swallowing a scream when —

"Clare! Clare!"

I steadied my little light. "Madame?"

"Clare! I can't see! What happened?"

"I called the police."

"Police!"

"Why did you follow me? It's dangerous out here."

"You seemed so agitated, and . . . I was curious."

And more than a little tipsy, I noticed.

Madame's gaze shifted to the body in the water.

"Is that . . . ?"

"I'm afraid so."

For a moment, she shuddered, then quickly steeled herself. "What can we do?"

"She's beyond our help. But there is something we can do to help the authorities. Here, take this —"

I handed her the flashlight. Then I activated the camera on my smartphone. "Shine that beam on her face while I take a picture."

Madam's eyes went wide. "A picture! Whatever for?!"

"She was a Village Blend customer. I can't ID her. But one of my baristas might know her name . . ."

As I shot the photos, a shiver ran through me.

The red tattoo on the dead girl's cheek sent my mind back to the first time I'd seen that little heart. It was a frigid winter afternoon, many months ago, during the frenzy of the holiday season . . .

The Village Blend was dressed in its festive best and packed with last-minute shoppers, all needing the warmth of our fireplace and energizing caffeine from our coffee before pushing on to the next store.

I was at the machines, pulling espressos and mixing drinks. Esther, in a floppy Santa hat, worked the register.

"Cool tattoo," she noted as she rang up a young woman's purchase.

"Thanks! Some people wear their hearts on their sleeves. I prefer mine on my cheek. It's my way of telling the world it's right here, and you can't break it. Ha!"

The young woman wore her blond hair in a severe pixie cut. Her eyes were bright blue, her good cheer infectious. Esther and I caught the bug, laughing along with her.

"I have a tattoo like that," Esther confided.

"But if I showed it off, I'd get arrested for public indecency!"

While they laughed and chatted, teenage twin sisters began arguing in the line behind the girl with the heart tattoo.

"I can't pay. I'm out of cash," the first twin told her sister. "I gave you everything I saved up. Don't you have any left?"

"Hardly anything. Grandma's gift cost way more than we thought it would. Maybe we should have bought her something else."

"How can you say that? You know she's going to love it! I can't wait to see her face when she opens it. But we still have to buy a nice card and some pretty wrapping paper —"

"We don't have enough money for that today. And I only have two dollars left. Maybe we should leave."

"No. I'm really cold and want to warm up. Here's all my loose change. Count it up. We can't afford the fancy holiday lattes, but we can share one small drink before we head home. You decide . . ."

Overhearing the exchange, Heart Girl winked at us and laid a twenty-dollar bill on the counter.

"We've all been there, right?" she whispered. "This should get them whatever they want — with change to help pay for Grandma's card and wrapping paper. Just don't tell them it's from me."

"Your secret is safe with us," Esther told her.

"And your heart is a lot bigger than that little tattoo," I added.

Heart Girl lit us up with her smile. Then she wished us both a happy holiday and went on her way . . .

Now my own heart sank as I snapped image after image of a beautiful life snuffed out.

It was too late to save this sweet girl. But I could help her parents, her friends, her family — by bringing to light who she was and what in the devil had happened to her.

"I'm sending these photos to my baristas now . . ."

I included a warning that the images were disturbing and they were to remain *private,* but I urged my staff to reply with anything they knew.

"Sent!" I took a breath, hoping I'd hear from them soon.

Madame hugged herself. "Shall we go back now?"

"I'm supposed to wait for the police. I called 911 a few minutes ago, but I don't see any sign of them . . ."

I tensely scanned Manhattan's Twelfth Avenue. No emergency vehicles, no sirens, just sparse traffic, rolling along without urgency.

Then a muted voice called, "Ma'am? Ma'am?"

It was the 911 operator who'd put me on hold.

"I'm here!"

"Officers are on the scene. You should see them now."

But Twelfth Avenue looked no different. "Where are they? I don't see any —"

Madame tapped me and pointed at the river. Flashing emergency lights lit up the mirror-black water. Then a sleek police boat burst into view. Powerful engine rumbling, it streaked toward us.

Of course!

I'd been expecting the authorities to arrive by car, but in this town, the river was a road, too. And it was served by an elite force —

The NYPD Harbor Patrol.

FOURTEEN

The blue and white fast boat named *Martin Morrow* decelerated as it approached us.

The vessel was fifty feet long with an enclosed bridge. A high mast behind the cabin carried the emergency lights, which stopped flashing when the engine was cut.

Avoiding the corpse in the water, the boat floated up to the dock, lightly bumping the wooden planks. Immediately, a figure in a shiny wet suit leaped from the deck and hit the river with a splash.

As he swam toward the dead girl, a young cop in a blue formfitting uniform hopped over the rail and landed in front of us. His badge read *Burns.*

"Hello, sailor!" Madame said with a wave.

"Ahoy, there," Officer Burns replied.

We watched as he tied off the boat. Then he pulled a wrench from a utility belt and worked the safety railing. In under a minute, Officer Burns unbolted a section of the railing and set it aside, giving the crew full access to the dock.

"Which one of you is Ms. Cosi?"

I waved my hand.

He jerked his blond head in the direction of a male silhouette inside the shadowy cabin. "Our sergeant will need your statement, so stick around, okay?"

"Like glue," I assured him.

Suddenly, a voice called from the water. "Give me a hand, bro!"

Burns donned waterproof gloves. Then he and the man in the wet suit moved the body onto the shadowy dock. As the diver climbed out of the river, Burns detached the dead girl's red backpack and set it aside. Kneeling, he looked up at his partner.

"You're the EMT, Hernandez. What do you think?"

Hernandez ripped the dripping snorkel-mask from his head to reveal curly black hair and liquid brown eyes. With obvious irony, he said —

"I think she's a goner."

"Yeah, sure, but do you think she's the jumper they're looking for upriver?"

"She's fresh enough, I guess."

Hernandez then leaned in for a closer look, but he didn't need to lean far. He wasn't much taller than I was, though his skintight wet suit revealed all muscle under the neoprene.

"I see maceration on the extremities." Hernandez glanced at me. "That's wrinkled skin, ma'am. There's not much rigor mortis, but cold immersion slows the process, so there's no gauging time of death from that."

Hernandez wiggled the water out of his ear with a stubby finger.

"Low tide and wakes from river traffic could have swept the jumper down here. I mean, it's definitely possible —"

"Excuse me," I interrupted. "What jumper?"

"We received a report of a female going into the water at the Boat Basin on 79th Street," Officer Burns replied. "The scuba team went in after her, but no joy. They knocked off their pattern search up there a couple of hours ago. They'll be back at it in the morning."

"When did this woman jump?"

"Sixteen hundred hours."

My civilian mind translated: *four o'clock in the afternoon.* "You said the jumper went into the water. Did she fall?"

Burns shook his head. "Eyewitnesses claim it was a suicide. They saw her jump. It was very deliberate."

Madame sniffed. "If you think this might

be the same woman, why were divers search-ing where she jumped in? Clearly, the cur-rent moves objects up and down the river, depending on the tide. I'm just a taxpayer, but it seems like a terrible waste of resources to me."

Burns's reply was diplomatic.

"Ma'am, when a body drowns, its lungs fill with water and the corpse sinks. It's only after gases build up in the stomach that it becomes a floater, and that could take days."

"Then why didn't *this* poor child sink?" Madame asked.

"Her backpack. It contained enough air to keep the body buoyant."

"I'm sorry, but that doesn't add up," I said. "Why would a girl jump into the river to commit suicide with what amounts to a flotation device strapped to her back? If this girl was so determined to kill herself, wouldn't she have filled her pack with rocks or something equally heavy?"

Hernandez and Burns exchanged glances but offered no answer.

"And what about that wound on her head?" I pointed to the visible gash.

Hernandez found his tongue. "Could be postmortem damage. Bad stuff happens in the river. She could have hit a rock or a pier, or been clipped by a passing boat. She definitely got knocked around. I mean, look at her. She's even missing a left shoe . . ."

It was true. The dead girl wore a single slip-on sneaker on her right foot, hot pink to match the streaks in her blond hair. The pockets of her skinny jeans were turned out, too. They looked like stunted angel's wings against the saturated denim.

Burns faced the corpse. "Let's find out who she is."

Still on his knees, his gloved hand rifled through the pockets of her cropped jacket but found nothing.

"Looks like the tide took everything," he said glumly.

"Check out her backpack," Officer Hernandez suggested.

The gloves made it a struggle, but Burns managed to get the zipper undone. Inside he found three sealed plastic containers that formerly held food but now carried only air.

Madame cocked her head. "Did you find any rocks among all that buoyant Tupperware, dear?"

Ignoring her, Burns tossed a small plastic box to Hernandez.

"There's something in the backpack's other compartment."

He opened the second zipper and reached

inside. A moment later, Burns displayed what he'd found.

Madame gasped at the sight.

In his gloved hand, the Harbor Patrol officer clutched a thirty-two-ounce stainless steel thermal mug. The logo branded on its side was a familiar one —

The Village Blend.

FIFTEEN

Burns shook the thermos. "It's still half full."

"Please, open it," I said. "I'd like to smell the coffee inside. I may need to see it, too."

Burns blinked. "Excuse me?"

Hernandez scratched his head. "Why would you need to do that?"

"Because I'm the manager of the Village Blend, where that thermos was purchased. We refill those with our 'daily specials' for a discount, and regular customers stop in often."

Hernandez shrugged. "So?"

"So if this young woman came to my shop for a refill today, the coffee inside that thermos will tell me when she bought it. That information should help you narrow down the time of death."

Burns and Hernandez shared dubious looks.

"Coffee is coffee," Burns said. "It's stale

or fresh, and that's the end of it."

"Sorry, Officer Burns, but you're out of your depth."

Hernandez snorted.

"Let me elaborate," I said in a more patient tone. "Between seven AM and noon today the Village Blend offered a single-origin from Ethiopia. Those beans carry a floral aroma with notes of apricot and honey. I roast them light, which better preserves the delicate flavors as well as the caffeine content. At noon, we changed our special to an estate Panama, with notes of berry and vanilla. My roast for that is City — that's medium. At six, I switched to a blend we call Fireside. Sumatra is the star, and it's not a coffee we source from a big estate. Our coffee hunter buys it out of the backyards and gardens of small farmers in Indonesia, and the semi-washed processing gives it a distinctive earthiness with power-ful notes of chocolate and spice. I give those beans a Vienna roast, medium-dark, less caf-feine for after-dinner enjoyment."

I rested my hands on my hips. "So, are you going to open that thermos now?"

For a moment, Burns and Hernandez stared at me with slack jaws. Then a force-ful new voice broke the silence.

"Let the lady smell the coffee!"

We all turned to face the man who'd spoken. It was the boat's commander. He'd finally emerged from the bridge.

Lanky and lean, legs braced against the rocking deck, the sergeant was at least two decades older than his crew. There was a hint of gray at his temples, but the rest of his head was jet-black — the patch covering his right eye was black, too.

Madame's violet eyes grew wide at the striking mocha-skinned figure. "Yo-ho-ho, and a bottle of rum!" she declared with a giggle that (unfortunately) came from consuming a tad too much of that very libation.

With an embarrassed swallow, I reread the name painted on the bow, *Martin Morrow,* and concluded the obvious (or what I *thought* was obvious).

"You must be Sergeant Morrow?"

Officer Burns winced. Hernandez dipped his head and stifled a laugh.

"This *boat* is the *Martin Morrow,*" the commander replied. "All NYPD vessels are named after fallen officers."

Okay, color me mortified. "So your name is?"

"Sergeant Jones."

Madame giggled again. "*Davy* Jones?"

"No, darlin'. Leonidas Jabari Jones."

Burns and Hernandez exchanged surprised glances. "Leonidas?" they mouthed to each other.

I cleared my throat and introduced myself to the sergeant, stressing again that I was sure I could help. The sergeant nodded and instructed Burns to open the thermos with his gloved hand.

"Don't touch it, okay?" Burns warned me. "It's evidence."

"I'll just take a sniff," I assured him.

Balancing it on one knee, Burns held the container aloft like a consecrated offering.

I lowered my nose to the opening and inhaled deeply. I raised my head and slowly let the air out of my lungs before I sniffed again. There was nothing floral, delicate, or fruity about this coffee. The bold spice and rich chocolate were unmistakable — this was my darker-roasted evening offering, the Fireside blend.

"I'm sorry, Officers, but this woman isn't your jumper. I know this coffee, and it wasn't brewed and sold until after six this evening. You told me eyewitnesses saw your jumper go into the river at four, right?"

Hernandez nodded.

Officer Burns closed the thermos and set it beside the backpack. Then he gently closed the victim's eyes and covered her body with a plastic shroud.

Sergeant (*not* Davy) Jones stepped off the deck and approached me. Now, I'm not much over five-two, even on a big-shoe day. And though I'm quite used to my near-munchkin status, I couldn't help finding the eye-patched sergeant intimidating. It was more than his height. Jones had the commanding presence of a battleship. Even his voice projected the power of an air horn.

"You're sure about the time, Ms. Cosi?"

"I'm sure."

Thankfully, Jones stopped looming over me — to loom instead over Hernandez. "What's in the plastic box Burns tossed you?"

"Something to do with her work, maybe . . ." Hernandez displayed a bright red memory stick with a USB plug-in.

"It's possible that storage device contains her suicide note," I said, pointing to the red stick. "If she *is* a suicide."

The sergeant fixed me with his good eye. "So why do you think she wouldn't simply write a note on a piece of paper like everybody else?"

"Maybe she did, but I'm convinced she did not float all the way down from 79th Street . . ." I pointed across Twelfth Avenue to the Manhattan skyline. "That whole area is an extension of the Flatiron District's original Silicon Alley. Tech companies like Uber, Google, Microsoft, and Thorn, Inc., have East Coast headquarters close by. I know because I've catered their events."

"What's your point, Coffee Lady?"

"I think this woman may have been a tech company employee. And I don't think she killed herself. But if she did, it's likely she would have digitized any final message to the world."

"Let's find out." Sergeant Jones turned to Burns. "Grab my laptop on the bridge and bring it here."

"Why, Mr. Jones . . ." Madame giggled. "Are you sure he shouldn't check your *locker?*"

The sergeant arched a dark brow over his one good eye.

Oh, brother. "We better get some coffee into you," I whispered to Madame.

"Well, don't use *that* thermos," she declared. "It's *evidence,* you know!"

Meanwhile, Burns scrambled aboard the *Morrow* and returned with the computer — an older-model laptop scuffed and grimy from use. He inserted the drive into a USB port, then glanced at the screen.

"It won't read."

"Wiggle the drive in the socket," Hernandez said. "That's what I do."

As they struggled to activate the drive, my smartphone vibrated.

I quickly checked the caller ID, hoping one of my baristas was getting back to me about the identity of this poor girl. But I was wrong.

It was the police who were calling, or rather one very special police person — my long-lost fiancé, Detective Lieutenant Michael R. F. Quinn.

With a deep breath, I answered the phone.

"Hi, Mike," I said, forcing my voice to sound light and carefree. (It wasn't easy.) "Where are you?"

"Where am I? In front of your coffeehouse! I stopped by your shop for a surprise visit, but I got the surprise. Where are *you*?"

Sixteen

I'm standing on a cold, damp dock ready to scream!

That's how I wanted to answer the man, and I wouldn't have stopped there. I would have spilled everything, all my fears and frustrations, all my shock and anger and sadness.

But now was not the time.

"We had a bit of a problem," I said. "I'll tell you about it later —"

Quinn quickly cut off my equivocating. "If you're talking about the shots fired from a prop gun, I already heard about it . . ."

Not exactly a shocker. While Quinn wasn't the kind of guy who kept up with viral videos on social media, he almost always got the word on local police incidents.

"Franco?" I assumed.

"He let me know about fifteen minutes ago. That's why I left work early and came to see you —"

"Is that your man on the phone?" Madame called through her cupped hands. "Blow him a kiss from me. Just like Dinah Shore!"

She blew a tipsy kiss and threw out her arm, smacking Sergeant Jones on his shoulder. Thankfully, the big guy appeared more amused than annoyed.

I lowered my voice even more and informed Quinn: "Madame invited me out for a late meal at Pier 66, and a few too many rum cocktails —"

"So I deduced."

"Got it!" Officer Burns cried at last. "Okay, here we go. I see a bunch of video files on this memory stick. One, two, three — five of them."

"Play one," Officer Hernandez urged.

"We'll see if this antique can do it."

"What's all that chatter?" Quinn asked in my ear. "Are you still in the restaurant?"

"No, dinner is over."

"So you're taking Madame home?"

"Not this minute. We kind of got jammed up."

"Jammed up?" Quinn's tone sharpened. "How?"

"We're at a crime scene, actually."

"What!"

"Relax. We're just witnesses."

"Except I left my glasses at home, so I didn't see a thing!" Madame announced.

Quinn went silent a moment. "Clare, is your former mother-in-law soused? At a crime scene?"

"No comment."

"I got one of the videos going," Burns said. "Looks like a woman waving a gun. Let me turn up the volume . . ."

"EVERYONE, LISTEN! I AM NOT GOING TO HURT ANY OF YOU! I'M HERE TO MAKE A POINT . . ."

I froze in place.

This video wasn't a suicide note. It was the same viral video I'd viewed with my staff earlier this evening. Like that Village Blend travel mug in the dead girl's backpack, this downloaded video was connected directly to my coffeehouse.

What I didn't understand was why.

Why was my former customer carrying a digitally saved version of Gun Girl's active shooter show? Did she know Carol Lynn Kendall? Or Richard Crest?

Given Crest's aggressive approach to meeting random women through Cinder swipes, the latter seemed more likely. Could this dead girl have been one of Crest's many shop-and-drop women?

I had zero evidence of this, of course, and

I knew what these Harbor Patrol officers would say if I started blathering wild speculations.

They would say I had no proof.

They would tell me there was no need for a crime scene unit because *the body* itself was the crime scene and any gathering of forensic evidence would take place at the morgue.

They would argue time of death alone doesn't prove she was murdered. Even if she wasn't the four o'clock "jumper," that doesn't mean she didn't also commit suicide.

They would tell me I didn't even know this girl's name, and her possession of a viral video seen by tens of thousands of people meant absolutely nothing.

But with everything I'd seen and heard tonight, I strongly suspected there was something to these connections. These officers would agree if only they were in my shoes.

I blinked. *Shoes* . . .

"Clare? Are you there?"

"I'm here."

"Is everything all right?"

"No, it's not . . ." I stepped away from Burns and lowered my voice to a whisper. "Could you come to the pier? I may need your help."

"To get Madame home?"

"No. To find a missing shoe."

SEVENTEEN

"This is nice."

"Nice?" My fiancé ran a hand through his short sandy-brown hair. "And here I thought we were on some sort of investigation —"

"We are. But I can't remember the last time we took a walk in the park."

"Neither can I." Quinn's arctic blue eyes peered down at me. "Although I'm fairly sure it was daylight . . ."

At almost two in the morning, Hudson River Park felt desolate. Though the place officially closed at one AM, it was too big and too accessible to close in any literal way. While the tennis courts and playgrounds were locked up tight, the bike and pedestrian paths were open to anyone willing to venture along shadowy grounds in an under-patrolled urban area.

Fortunately, for tonight's venturing, I had a police escort. And not just any police escort, a decorated narcotics detective with years working anti-crime on the streets of New York.

I elbowed my bodyguard's solid chest. "Come on, admit it. This is nice."

"I'll admit that being alone in the dark with you is giving me ideas." By the glow of a distant streetlamp, I saw actual signs of warmth lurking in Quinn's typically glacial gaze. "Why don't we start our investigation over there on that bench?"

"I'll be game for that kind of activity *later.* Right now, we need to concentrate on business . . ."

Quinn was good at business. Too good. His track record of closing challenging cases, along with his leadership abilities, and experience in Washington's Federal Triangle, had made him one of the most popular officers in the department. It also made him a trusted one for "special" (i.e., impossible) assignments.

That coffee stain on his gold tie, the slump of his posture beneath his sports coat, and the five-o'clock shadow morphing into late-night bristles told me the weight of too much responsibility had fallen on his shoulders again.

Since we entered this shadowy park, however, a noticeable spring had boosted his steps, which told me he was enjoying tonight's little foray into the kind of nitty-gritty police work he missed — and still loved.

I knew these things because I understood my fiancé's hard-to-detect disposition better than anyone, an intimacy that hadn't come easily or quickly. What Quinn and I shared had grown over years.

The first time I saw him, he strode into my coffeehouse looking like a man in need of caffeine. A rumpled trench coat hung from his broad shoulders, his blue eyes were bloodshot, his expression haggard. He'd been overworked, sure, but what really wore him down were the kinds of personal burdens I'd once carried.

I would find out more about those burdens over time. During our first meeting — a routine follow-up after one of my baristas had been hospitalized — Quinn was all business. As we talked, I convinced him of two things: my employee's "accident" was no accident, and my premium, meticulously made coffee was profoundly better than the stale dregs of the cheap cups he'd been drinking for years.

Quinn was suitably impressed with my persuasive abilities, as well as my coffee, and kept coming back for more.

We became friends, then confidants, until finally he convinced me to look past the poker-faced policeman and see the caring man behind the stoic mask.

After years dealing with my ex-husband's hot-blooded outspokenness, Quinn's cool, enigmatic ways took some getting used to. For one thing, I had to learn a whole new language — how to read the man.

But I loved what I read.

Where Matt had been short-tempered, argumentative, even thickheaded, Quinn was patient, understanding, and perceptive. But then a good detective would have to be.

Take tonight. With no more than a simple request, Quinn had met me at Pier 66. Explanations weren't needed. I asked him to come, and he was there.

After I'd given my statement to the Harbor Patrol and a team from the medical examiner's office took the girl's body away, Quinn even helped me pour a woozy Madame into the shop's van and see her home safely.

She was extremely chatty on the ride — mostly about that "intriguing" boat patrol Sergeant (not Davy) Jones. "How do you think he lost that eye? I'll bet *he'd* make an interesting dinner companion. Not like that *awful* man I had to listen to all night, droning on and on about the New Jersey real estate market!"

As soon as I got Madame up to her penthouse, I helped her change for bed. And (thank goodness) the moment her head hit the pillow, she was out.

I borrowed her kitchen to press some Ethiopian light roast, poured the eye-opening brew into paper cups, and Quinn and I returned to the riverfront. On the way, I filled him in on Gun Girl's bang-up performance in our second-floor lounge; the awful video-gone-viral; and my discovery of one of our young female customers floating in the Hudson.

"I know it sounds crazy," I admitted. "But I believe this girl's death is connected to what happened tonight in our coffeehouse."

Quinn's mask never cracked. "I think you're right."

I sighed with relief, until he added —

"It does sound crazy."

EIGHTEEN

I stopped walking.

Quinn studied my face and softened his tone. "What I mean is: *without evidence,* it would sound crazy to an investigating officer." He folded his arms. "I assume you have a theory?"

"I do."

"I'm listening."

"When Carol Lynn Kendall terrorized Richard Crest tonight, she claimed it was because he charmed her into sleeping with him and instantly treated her like dirt. This is a pattern for Crest."

"A pattern based on what?"

"Nancy and Esther witnessed him emotionally abuse at least two other Cinderellas at our coffeehouse. Even Crest's own statement to Franco corroborated his behavior."

"And the statement was?"

"Something along the lines of: 'A lot of

these bitches see bags of money when they look at a guy like me, so I've got to be harsh to shake them off.' "

"What a prince."

"I know. That's why I think our dead customer was yet another Richard Crest horrible hookup. I think she arranged a meeting to confront him, just like Carol Lynn Kendall did. But something went wrong, and he threw her body in the river, thinking it would look like a mugging. Or suicide . . ."

"Go on."

"For her body to have ended up at Pier 66, she would have gone into the water somewhere north of the pier, and this park seems a likely place for two people to meet."

"But how do you know the deceased girl met with Crest? Did the Harbor Unit recover her phone?"

"She had no ID or phone. Her pockets were emptied, which makes me think Crest took it all with him —"

"Slow down, Clare. Your theories are getting way ahead of the facts. I have yet to hear you connect the dead girl in any provable way with Richard Crest."

"Didn't I mention? I sent the victim's photo to my staff. Before you arrived at the pier, Esther texted back. She didn't know the young woman's name, but she remembered her as a customer because of the heart tattoo. She also remembered the last two times she saw her. Earlier this evening, she refilled her travel mug. She also saw Heart Girl about two weeks ago, sitting and talking intensely with Richard Crest."

Quinn frowned. "You realize that doesn't prove anything."

"I'm not finished. The victim had a memory stick in her backpack containing five different recordings of tonight's Gun Girl incident. I didn't even know there were five. I only saw one. But she found and collected all five, each from a different website or social media platform, which she labeled on every video file. That's what the officers from the Harbor Unit told me."

Quinn scratched the rough stubble of his unshaven jawline. "If she was astute enough to locate and download all those videos that quickly, she likely worked around here in Silicon Alley."

"That's what I thought."

"So you believe our Jane Doe may have met with Crest to confront him, just like Ms. Kendall did in your coffeehouse. They argued and then what? It's your theory. Keep it going —"

"He might have struck her. Maybe he

panicked when he realized how hard he'd hit her. Instead of calling for help and giving paramedics a chance to save her, he could have taken her phone, wallet, and ID, making it look like a robbery. Then he dumped her unconscious body in the river. Or maybe she was dead already from his blow; the autopsy should tell us. Either way, I do think Crest is contemptible — and dangerous. If he was responsible for my customer's death, I want to prove it."

"What about that memory stick? The one with the viral videos. Why didn't Crest take that, too? It connects him to the victim, doesn't it?"

"My guess? In his haste or panic, he missed it. The same reason he misjudged her backpack."

"What do you mean?"

"The pack was bulky. At a glance, anyone would think it was also heavy and would drag her body down. But it was filled with empty Tupperware and a half-empty Village Blend thermos. The pack was also waterproof, so it acted as a flotation device, which is how I spotted her."

Quinn's gaze drifted toward the overcast sky, where thick clouds were finally beginning to break up.

"So where are we going, Detective Cosi?

131

And what exactly are we hunting for?"

Quinn already knew the answers to those questions. But after years of training rookies, Socratic habits die hard.

"We're looking for a crime scene," I stated with patience. "Somewhere in this park. We should stick close to the water and move north, because the victim floated south with low tide."

"And? If you think the killer took her phone and wallet, what are we looking to find?"

"Whatever else she might have had in her pockets that can be connected to her. An ATM receipt or sales slip with credit card number. A Post-it note with her handwriting. A key chain or charm — she had a thing for hearts. Whatever proves she was here."

Quinn scanned the waterfront around us. "I can see why you wanted to do this in the middle of the night. Sanitation is going to sweep this place in the morning, and anything like that will be gone. But I have to warn you, those things wouldn't prove much. It's pretty tenuous."

"Maybe. But don't forget the primary reason we're out here — the item I mentioned on our call."

"Sorry, but I don't recall . . ." He scratched his head. "Drop the other shoe."

"Funny you should put it that way."

"Why?"

"Because our departed Cinder-ella was only wearing one."

Nineteen

Finally, Quinn saw the light — metaphorically speaking, because the deep shadows around us were as daunting as ever. But he had to agree with me. Locating the dead girl's missing shoe would be a brilliant find.

"If we actually discover it, I'll call Night Watch myself," he promised. "They can create a perimeter and get CSU down here to look for additional evidence — blood, hair, prints, fibers, whatever they're able to recover. But I have to be honest, Cosi, I'm not optimistic."

"You're here, Mike — and after a long day of work. That's optimistic enough for me."

At that, he gave me a little smile. Then together we began casing the concrete walkway along the river.

Every few feet, Quinn directed his heavy Maglite to aid my shadowy search. I carried a flashlight, too, a standard one from my shop van's glove compartment. But he insisted on bringing his Mag, and I knew why.

For years, the weight and solidity of the long-handled design allowed street cops to use the Maglite as a defensive weapon. It wasn't a pleasant idea, but it certainly was a practical one when venturing down dangerous alleys, approaching suspicious vehicles, or (in our case) entering dark, desolate areas of an officially closed park.

As we searched under trees, around bushes, and near every bench, we encountered others daring enough to enter the deserted green space.

A few bicyclists raced by quickly, to avoid being ticketed by random patrols. We also found a pair of homeless men — one older, one younger — camped out among the greenery.

Despite the autumn chill, the weather wasn't bad enough to drive the two into city shelters, but soon enough winter would come. Feeling a sudden sting from winds off the water, I remembered the frigid day I'd taken a walk along the icy river and found a homeless old man frozen to death beneath a blanket of newspapers.

I shook off the tragic memory as Quinn and I spoke with the bearded pair. Quinn initiated the conversation. Then I gave a general description of the dead girl and asked if they'd seen her.

They both shook their shaggy heads.

Before we left, Quinn shared a few more concerned words with the men, passing each a small card from a special pocket. I already knew what was on those cards: the addresses of shelters and food banks in Lower Manhattan.

As we walked on, he silently handed me the Maglite and pulled out his phone. I knew why he'd done that, too. The HOME-STAT app would allow him to report the men — not for arrest, but to get them help via the city's outreach program. A Street Action Team would arrive within the hour to evaluate their situation, and (hopefully) help the pair into transitional or permanent housing.

As we continued along the riverfront, checking bushes and benches, I couldn't help thinking back to my dinner with Madame — and what this park might have looked like if it had existed during the Summer of Love.

"Those camped-out men we saw. They got me thinking . . ."

"About?"

"Something Madame brought up at dinner. Do you remember the Groovy Murders?"

"Sure. They were way before my time, but senior officers talked about them, back in my Academy days."

"I know the facts surrounding the victims. But what about the two killers? Were they ever caught and convicted?"

"They were."

"How?"

Quinn shrugged his broad shoulders. "No Sherlock tricks, if that's what you were hoping to hear. Just meat and potatoes police work."

"What? Detectives canvassed the neighborhood? Questioned residents?"

"They did that. They also put the squeeze on their only witness."

"There was a witness?"

"Experienced officers know that the person who 'finds the body' is sometimes responsible for the crime, and the 'discovery' is simply a ploy to hide his or her involvement. In the case of the Groovy Murders, the man who reported the dead teens was the building's janitor. He used the basement boiler room — the location where the female victim and her friend, Groovy, were killed — as a place to crash."

"The janitor wasn't involved in the crime?"

"That's what he claimed. But the detectives were suspicious, so they grilled him. While he was in custody, a woman reported being assaulted that same day, in that very basement. A little too coincidental, right? She identified the janitor, and they used that assault charge to put pressure on him for the names of the killers."

"He knew?"

"He knew because one of the killers lived in the building. The other was the petty drug dealer who led the two victims to the basement with the promise of selling them LSD. The two killers were high when they did it, passing the murder weapon — a brick — back and forth."

I shivered. "So evil. So awful."

"Both of the killers died in prison."

As Quinn's voice trailed off, his gaze scanned the brush and walkway. This time, I could tell, he wasn't looking for a shoe or scraps of paper. The Groovy discussion seemed to make him more wary of our vulnerability.

"As police work goes, Cosi, solving that murder was pretty routine, though the aftermath wasn't."

"You mean the fear on the street when everyone learned about those murders?"

"That was part of it. But you have to

remember, with all those kids bunking in parks, alleys, and doorways, and openly using drugs, the business owners and eventually the entire city expected the NYPD to do something about it. Those Summer of Love kids also had parents who were looking for them. The old-timers said not a day went by without some poor mother or father showing up at a local precinct desperate for news about a lost child. Or just wanting someone to explain to them how their child died — usually from an overdose."

"Oh, God."

"After those murders, the public expected police to do more than catch criminals after the fact. They wanted us to start addressing the underlying conditions that lead to crime."

"Madame was right then."

"She usually is." He smiled. "What was she right about this time?"

"She said the Groovy Murders changed the Village culture. But they did more than that, didn't they? They started to change the NYPD."

"That's true, I guess. Although when it comes to policing, some things never change . . ."

Quinn's last enigmatic comment became all too clear a few minutes later, when we

139

passed more men along the waterfront. Only these guys weren't homeless, or quietly camped out in the brush.

Perched like roosters on the riverbank railing, this rough crew was loudly laughing and cursing. Their tan overalls were identical, displaying the name of a nearby West Side warehouse.

Three of the six young men were smoking, and all of them held cans or bottles tucked inside wrinkled paper bags, a popular method of avoiding a citation for consuming alcohol in public.

I could tell Quinn was going to ignore the raucous group, until a few made loud, lewd remarks about yours truly.

That did it.

"Good evening, gentlemen."

"Good evening, asshole!"

The young man's reply cracked up his five friends.

Quinn didn't blink. "Not just any asshole," he coolly returned. "An asshole with a badge."

TWENTY

One flash of his gold shield and the cackling stopped. When Quinn spoke again, his tone was dipped in steel.

"My partner here has a few questions for you. If you're smart, you'll give her your full attention — and respect — because this park is legally closed; from the smell of it, you're not drinking soda pop; and I can have backup here in less than five minutes . . ." As Quinn finished, he casually opened his sports coat, just enough for them to glimpse the butt of his brand-new Glock nestled in its shoulder holster.

For a few seconds, the young men shared uneasy glances. Then they all stared at me, Quinn included.

"You're on," he whispered.

I cleared my throat, lowered my voice, and in my best imitation of "just the facts" Sergeant Franco, asked —

"Any of you see a young woman tonight?"

I went on to describe the dead girl; what she was wearing; height, weight, etc. But they all shook their heads.

"We didn't see nothin'."

"Hell, we just got here fifteen minutes ago."

"We didn't know the park was closed."

"Yeah, we didn't know."

"Okay, gentlemen, we're done. Move along. Out of the park . . ."

Quinn's sweeping Maglite showed them the way.

Alone again, I noticed the edges of his lips were quirking upward.

"That was fun for you, wasn't it?"

He arched an eyebrow. "You're the one who said I should enjoy our little walk in the park."

"I'll enjoy it when we recover something to help that poor girl I found floating in the river . . ." I thought of the Groovy Murders again, all those families and parents waiting for word on their lost loved ones. "This is so frustrating."

"I know, Cosi. I've been there — a thousand times. That's police work. If you want to get anywhere, you have to be willing to make friends with the three *P*'s."

"Permits, parades, and parking violations?"

He laughed. "Painstaking patience and persistence."

"Believe me, Lieutenant, I'm willing."

"Good. Then let's keep at it."

Ten minutes later, Quinn stopped at an overflowing trash bin.

"You're not —"

"I am . . ." Reaching inside his jacket, he grabbed a pair of gloves. "You don't know how many times I've found incriminating evidence tossed into the trash and forgotten."

I plucked the gloves from his hand. "Must I remind you, this is my investigation?"

"Clare, I don't want you going through —"

I moved the gloves out of his reach, and quite a long reach it was, given Quinn's height.

"Listen, Mike, half the job of managing food service for the public is managing the garbage they leave behind, which makes me the expert here. Besides, you don't even know what the shoe looks like. If it's in this bin, I'll find it."

I slapped my flashlight into his hands, pulled on the gloves, and was about to dive in when we were interrupted by a loud clattering. We looked up to find a noisy shopping cart coming toward us, pushed by a rail-thin gray-haired man wearing a tattered tuxedo.

Neither Quinn nor I was surprised.

From the guitar-carrying Naked Cowboy of Times Square, to the strange, slick-haired Snare Drummer sticking out famous solos in his red velvet smoking jacket, to the break-dancing Santa, who used to frequent my shop, the variety of New York eccentrics was never-ending.

But then this city has always been a haven for oddballs and misfits, and (honestly) I hoped it always would be. In my view, everyone had a freak flag. Some of us just flew it higher than others.

The gentleman coming toward us tonight was a particular genus of street life: the rolling junk collector. This one had painted his rickety shopping cart in a rainbow of colors. He pushed it with pride in his natty tux, the squeak of its wheels joining the clomp-clomping rhythm of the stacked heels on his red and black snakeskin boots.

Halting the cart beside us, he gloated —

"Too late, kiddies. I got all the good stuff out of that one. You got to be fast if you want the good stuff!"

Playing along, Quinn nodded solemnly. "I guess you're right. You were too quick for us. Did you happen to find a shoe?"

"A bright pink slip-on sneaker," I quickly added.

"Nope. But I do have a pair of flip-flops in here somewhere." He squinted down at Quinn's legs. "Too small for Big Foot here, but they'll fit you easy, girly. Want to try them on? I'll sell 'em to you cheap."

"We'll take a rain check. But we are interested in one thing, if you have it — a little information . . ."

Quinn's glance told me I was "on" again, describing the girl with the heart tattoo.

"Ain't seen nobody like that. Saw a six-foot lady of the evening with a tiara, yellow wig, and ball gown. A BMW picked her up on Twelfth and drove off." He scratched his chin. " 'Course my eyes ain't so good these days. Can't be sure she was a she."

"Right. Well, thanks for your trouble," Quinn said, slipping the man a fiver. "You have a good night."

"Oh! Thank you, sir! Bless you both!" Tipping an imaginary hat, the man with the cart trundled away. "Good luck finding your girly friend!"

Our next encounter came quickly after that, but it wasn't nearly as cordial . . .

We reached an area across from 28th Street called Habitat Garden. The name had to be ironic since there was nothing garden-like about it — no flowers or plants — though the small concrete plaza did feature a few eccentrically sculpted habitats.

There was a square pavilion, made of metal, with permanent chairs built into the supporting poles like seats on a bizarre merry-go-round. A few yards away, a massive, oddly shaped slab, with seats cut into it at irregular intervals, looked like a breakfast nook from the Bronze Age.

Both "habitats" were uninhabited at this hour, but we approached them with high hopes. These were just the sort of landmarks people might use to arrange a meeting.

As we entered the deserted area, I noticed a male silhouette swiftly detach itself from beneath a cluster of trees. Without a word, the man fell into step behind us.

I leaned into my fiancé. "I think we're about to be mugged."

No smile this time. Quinn's lips were tight as he replied —

"I know."

Twenty-One

"Hey!"

The call was sharp, the voice low and gruff.

We turned to find a youngish man, early to mid-twenties. The stranger's face was unnaturally pale, his eyes close-set. A scraggly goatee sprouted from his recessed chin, and an oversize jacket crawled around on his skinny shoulders.

"Give me your phones and wallets. I got a knife . . ."

"What are you hooked on?" Quinn quietly asked as he nudged me behind him. "Heroin? Oxy . . ."

The signs were there, and Quinn had seen them countless times. The emaciated physique, the sickly look. Dark circles under eyes with extremely small pupils, even in this shadowy light.

"You don't need to do this," Quinn pressed. "I can get you help."

Shaking with agitation, the mugger stepped closer. "Give me your phone and your money. Hers, too. Or I'll cut you both!"

Despite the threat, the mugger's hands remained in the pockets of his black denim jacket.

Quinn's grip tightened on the Maglite. "Show me your knife first."

"You'll see it when I stick you in the gut and cut your girlfriend's throat!"

"Naw, I don't think so. Not after I show you my gun and shield."

The mugger's eyes went wide when he realized his mistake. But as he turned to flee, my fiancé's Big Foot hooked the punk's ankle, tripping him.

Our mugger hit the concrete with an audible "Oof!" Then in a move practiced more times than a Yankee infielder's double play, Quinn tossed me his Maglite with one hand while whipping out cuffs with the other. Before the dazed kid could react, he was shackled and on his knees.

"Call 9—"

"Doing it!"

To free my hands, I quickly pocketed my flashlight and bent to set down the Maglite. Suddenly, I heard Quinn curse.

In a last burst of defiance, our mugger put up a struggle. I jumped out of the way as

Quinn subdued him. Now the kid was flat on the ground with Quinn's knee in his back.

"Stay down. Stop moving," he ordered.

As I talked with the 911 operator, Quinn continued speaking with the kid on the ground. No more orders. He was back to being the social worker, getting him to come clean about his addiction, his identity. Where was he from? Did he have any family? What drove him this low?

With the police on their way, I knew our shoe searching was over for the night. It seemed pointless now — even dangerous — to continue.

I was sorry, but grateful to Quinn for backing me up. Proud of him, too, for helping those homeless men and this lost soul. His promise to get this kid help for his addiction wasn't idle. I knew he'd do it.

After the weak whine of police sirens grew stronger, and the 911 operator assured me that help was on the way, I moved to retrieve Quinn's Maglite, which had rolled away during that last scuffle.

As I bent to pick it up, my gaze absently followed its stabbing light. The golden column reached across the concrete walkway, toward the railing along the riverbank.

What I saw there made me blink — then

shout!

Beneath a low bench, spotlighted by the flashlight's glow, was a pink slip-on sneaker, lying on its side.

TWENTY-TWO

"Breakfast or dinner?"

It was a valid question at 4:35 AM.

"I could go for either," Quinn replied between sips of my smooth and soothing low-caffeine dark roast. "Dinner, breakfast, glorified snack, whatever you like. You decide."

We were back in my duplex apartment above the Village Blend. Dawn would soon be lightening the dark canvas outside my kitchen window, signaling the start of a new day. For me and Quinn, it was also the end of a very long one.

True to his promise, after I'd found my deceased customer's missing shoe, Quinn had called his contacts in Night Watch. Once a patrol car took our mugger away, my newly discovered "crime scene" became an NYPD social scene.

Hand shaking and backslapping increased as more uniforms and CSU detectives appeared. Fellow officers, whom Quinn hadn't seen in months or even years, congratulated him on our recent engagement.

That's the way things were on the street. Whenever cops came together, they caught up with one another, talked about the Job, shared personal news.

As for business: NYPD tower lights went up, along with a perimeter of crime-scene tape, and the search for forensic evidence began. A female Night Watch officer took my statement, which (Sorry, Franco!) included not only the facts, but my theories about Richard Crest, and my strong suggestion that the police question the man as soon as possible.

As I expected, the officer told me the case would be assigned to detectives who would follow up with me in the next few days.

When we finally left the chilly gloom of Hudson River Park, my long-suffering lieutenant had offered to warm me up and "reward my good work" with a carb-fest at Veselka — a twenty-four-hour East Village diner that had been stuffing New Yorkers with stuffed cabbage and other Ukrainian soul foods, from cheese blintzes to potato pierogi, for over sixty years.

But I turned him down.

If I could stay awake a few more hours,

I'd be able to open my coffeehouse on time and arrange coverage of the shop while I got some sleep. Given my goal, descending two flights of stairs from my apartment would be a lot easier than drowsily driving twenty blocks from Quinn's East Village neighborhood.

Sure, a plate of warm blintzes was tempting, but I knew what would happen with my last bite of cheese-stuffed crepe. Quinn would start whispering sweet ideas about his king-sized bed — and that would be the end of my conscientious manager plan.

Instead, as we left the cold waterfront, I suggested he come home with me. I needed to feed my two furry roommates (Java and Frothy). And I had enough adrenaline left in my system to fix a human snack, too.

In fact, Madame had given me a wonderful recipe for Blueberry Blintzes. She'd gotten it from (of all people) the legendary abstract expressionist Jackson Pollock — another painter who loved the art of cooking. No doubt he also loved the splatter of blueberries on the blank canvas of folded crepes.

The question was: Did I have the ingredients for this foodie work of art? The answer came with a quick inventory of my fridge.

Pollock used a combination of cottage and

cream cheeses for his blintz filling, neither of which I had. Farmer's cheese would have been a good substitute (that's what Veselka used), but I didn't have enough.

So what did I have?

Italian cold cuts — check.

Mild provolone — check.

Flour tortillas — check.

"Okay," I announced, "we're on!"

"We are?" Quinn raised a lecherous eyebrow. "You're ready to join me upstairs?"

"Behave, Lieutenant — at least a little longer — because I have all the ingredients for my famous Italian Sub Quesadilla."

Intrigued, Quinn loosened his tie, sat down at my table, and stretched his long legs.

"In that case, I'll wait."

TWENTY-THREE

Ten minutes later, Quinn's eyes were closed in ecstasy.

No, we were not in the bedroom. We were still in my kitchen, where coffee-furred Java and fluffy white Frothy were feasting happily on Fancy Feast, and the good lieutenant was tearing hungrily into my crazy Italian-Mexican concoction.

"Cosi," he said, between satisfying chews and swallows, "how did you ever come up with this?"

"Necessity is often the mother of foodie invention."

"You were out of queso blanco?"

"Close. Back when I was married to Matt — and he was actually home — he liked to make traditional Puerto Rican–style pernil. One weekend, those amazing pieces of roasted pork were all gone, and a nor'easter was raging. I remember my Joy was only a few years old. She was so scared of the thunder that Matt convinced her it was nothing more than a big drum being played by a giant parading around in the sky. He had her marching around the apartment, pretending to play her own drum. 'Boom! Boom! Boom!' You should have seen the two of them — they were pretty adorable."

"I'll bet."

"We didn't have much cash for takeout, and I didn't want Matt going out into the deluge, so I invented these." (It was a cinch, given the stack of tortillas on hand for the pernil and my years helping my grandmother make subs for her little Italian grocery.)

"I know my squad would love them. Easy to make, right?"

"Sure, just a few tricks to keep in mind."

"Which are?"

I suppressed a laugh. The only thing cops liked to talk about more than the Job was food.

"Tell them to warm the cold cuts first. Some of that luxurious, buttery fat will melt out of the meat and into the pan, which will boost the flavor."

Quinn dipped the edge of a second quesadilla into the small bowl I'd filled with olive oil, vinegar, and herbs. "Mmm . . ." He closed his eyes again. "This salad dressing dip is inspired, too."

I nodded. "A classic Italian sub comes with a drizzle of salad dressing. So I thought, why not turn it into a dip for the quesadilla? The bright tang perfectly complements the unctuous richness of the meats, don't you think?"

He licked his fingers. "What meats, exactly?"

"Whatever *salumi* you like: prosciutto, salami, soppressata —"

"Super-whatta?"

"It's what you're eating, buddy: dried Italian sausage."

"Well, it's delicious, even if I can't pronounce it." He smiled. "What else am I eating?"

"Mortadella — that's basically Italian bologna. It's made with big chunks of fat that will melt like a dream in your hot pan . . ."

He raised an eyebrow. "Are you trying to turn me on, Cosi? Because if you are, it's working."

I laughed. "After your cold cuts are warm, take them out of the pan, drizzle in a little olive oil, and heat it through. Then you're basically making a meat-stuffed grilled cheese, except you're using tortillas instead of bread."

"Got it — except the cheese. What kind? Mozzarella?"

"Thinly sliced provolone. Not the aged kind. You want the young, mild version. It melts as beautifully as mozzarella but has more flavor . . ."

As I spoke, Quinn took another bite. Strings of oozing cheese trailed from his lips. With sensual sounds of gustatory joy, he used his tongue to recapture those warm, delectable strands.

It was surprisingly erotic, and my mind paused a few seconds, contemplating what else the lieutenant might do with his tongue.

"Sweetheart? You okay?"

No, I wanted to say. *I'm tired. I'm in love with you. And I'm ready to melt, too. Let's go upstairs . . .*

But I didn't say that. Instead, I gritted my teeth against my weak flesh and checked my watch. I had responsibilities, even if my libido didn't.

"Any dessert?" Quinn asked, licking his fingers clean.

Forcing my attention away from the man's mouth, I did a quick dessert recon and came up with victory. The last two squares of my Italian Cream Cake.

Despite its "Italian" moniker, the cake was an American specialty (some say) invented by an Italian baker living in the South. That's why the recipe I'd made came not from my *nonna* but Tucker's Granny Chestnut in his native Louisiana.

I added a few tweaks for smoother texture; adapted the layer cake ratios for a sheet pan; and slathered the frosting on wickedly thick.

Quinn was silent as he ate, inhaling the final blissful bite with closed eyes, then licking the last bit of sweet, creamy frosting off his fork.

"Marry me."

"Already said yes."

As I got up to clear our plates, he gently captured my wrist and pulled me close.

"So when are we going to set a date?"

TWENTY-FOUR

It sounded simple enough.

Find a place for the ceremony and reception. Look for a weekend in the future that wasn't booked — and didn't conflict with major commitments in our busy lives. Oh, yes, and be sure the cost of the whole thing didn't send us to debtors' prison.

"Believe me, I'm trying."

"Everyone's asking at work. You sure you don't want my help?"

"Food and beverage service are my expertise, not yours. I want to take care of this. Madame offered to help, too. She's as excited as anyone, even started experimenting with dating apps just so she could line up an escort for our big day . . ."

The question remained: When would it be?

I'd been looking for a place that was large enough, affordable, and in our hemisphere. With the population density of New York, popular spaces were booked far in advance, some for close to a year.

Quinn thought a moment. "How about a venue along the Hudson River?"

"That's an idea. There are lots of new event spaces and restaurants on the waterfront now . . ."

"Picture it. We could get married in late afternoon, have the reception as the sun goes down over the river. Sounds pretty, right?"

"Yes, and romantic, and memorable . . . and expensive."

"I know . . ." Quinn got up to refill his coffee cup. He noticed the rosebud in the glass latte mug sitting next to the coffeemaker. "Where did this flower come from? One of your customers?"

"Oh, that's Matt's."

"Allegro won't ever give up, will he?"

"What are you talking about? That rose wasn't for me. He bought it for a Cinder date then forgot it on the counter." The poor forgotten bud perked up nicely after its little drink. The petals were even starting to open.

"I was happy to give it a little TLC . . ."

"And Allegro was happy to leave it behind for you to find."

"That's crazy."

Quinn didn't think so. "He's always on the make, that guy. And he's still in love with you."

"Oh, please. Matt's in love with any woman who smiles at him. I can't believe you're bothered by a little rosebud!"

Quinn sat down heavily. "It's not Allegro. Not really . . ." He shook his head. "You deserve roses, Clare. Dozens of them. And you deserve more attention than I've been giving you lately."

"Don't start that again. I know very well what your job demands, and I'm proud of the work you do. I'm not your ex-wife. Please try to remember that . . ."

Like me, Mike Quinn had married young and quickly — too quickly — with the disintegration of the union happening slowly, over many years. He'd tried to make it work, again and again, but his wife had been too unhappy.

When she'd first moved to Manhattan, Leila Carver had been a beautiful young woman, excited by the prospect of life in a big city. She'd dabbled in modeling, but didn't have to work. Her wealthy parents had footed her bills. Mostly, she'd partied, shopped, and courted male attention. Eventually, she attracted the wrong kind.

Mike had been in uniform back then, a

handsome cop who'd saved Leila from an attempted rape. She'd been beaten and terrorized in the attack. In fear and gratitude, she'd clung to Mike. Her doe-eyed adoration had bowled him over. She was gorgeous, classy, and viewed him as her savior knight. He bought a ring, and she said yes.

Too late, she realized what she'd done: anchored herself to a quiet life in an unglamorous part of town with a "square-jawed bore" of a husband and two crying babies. She asked him to quit his job, but Mike was the Job, and she quickly grew to hate it.

Police work in New York was gritty, stressful, and often heartbreaking. She didn't want him bringing those burdens home, so he stopped talking about work and the vocation that absolutely defined him.

In time, Leila missed her old life: the parties, the shopping, the lavish vacations, the trendy bars and male attention. She began to cheat to get it back. By then, Mike had made detective, and knew exactly what she was doing — and when and where she was doing it.

Mike never thought much of himself compared to her. He figured she deserved better. When she'd cheat and return, he always took her back. (I knew how he felt.)

Divorce was never something Mike thought of as an option, especially with two kids. But he had to face reality. Leila was unhappy to the point of irrational and erratic behavior. It wasn't good for their two kids, let alone her well-being — or his. Things had to change. And they did.

After his divorce, our friendship blossomed into something more, though it took time. I still remember the guardedness in his eyes whenever I asked about his police work — and the flash of happy relief when he remembered I was genuinely interested. At last, he was with someone who wouldn't throw a fit or tantrum. Who actually wanted him to open up and talk.

To me, it was much more than talk.

I wanted to be a supportive partner to him. Not abstractly, but in the day-to-day ups and downs he faced. I understood his dedication, not just to the ideals of justice, but also to the real-world work of keeping people safe and trying to make their lives better.

Maybe I understood a little too much . . .

Sometimes I was compelled to right a few wrongs myself, which (I got the feeling) astonished, even amused him. Our "walk in the park" tonight, for example, was something his ex-wife would never have considered, not in a thousand lifetimes . . .

Now, sitting in my kitchen, Mike gazed at me with disarming tenderness as he said —

"I can't wait to marry you."

"We could speed things up, you know, go to City Hall."

"No." The tone was firm. "That's what you did with Allegro. We're doing it right. I want all our friends and family there —"

"And half the NYPD?"

"Of course! And don't forget my kids."

"They could come to City Hall with us."

He shook his head. "Jeremy expects to be an usher, tuxedo and all. And Molly's got her heart set on the flower girl role. You promised both of them, remember?"

"Of course I do. I'm thrilled they're excited about being involved."

"So am I. Our wedding will be a great *céilí* — a happy, dancing celebration of life and love. The world needs more of those, don't you think?"

"I do."

"Remember that line. I'll want to hear it again soon."

"Good." I traced his lips then tasted them. "Hold that thought . . ."

He did more than that. He pulled me close, moved his mouth over mine, and engaged that tantalizing tongue in a deep, soulful kiss, until —

Bzzzzzz. His smartphone vibrated.

Reluctantly, almost painfully, we parted.

"Work?" I assumed.

He nodded as he read the text. "Franco's confirming receipt of a message I sent about our mugger. I asked him to follow up with the case."

"I knew you would make good on your promise."

"If the guy's record is clean, no violent crimes, we can help him. We'll see."

As Mike typed a reply, I checked my watch.

"I better get downstairs. Bakery delivery."

His face fell. "You aren't coming upstairs with me?"

"I'll be there soon. I promise . . ."

TWENTY-FIVE

Two hours later, I was finally headed for bed.

My ex-husband had agreed to take over downstairs. *Thank heaven for small favors.* Matt really was a good guy — especially after he'd had great sex — and his night at the "*uh-hem* ball" with his Cinder-swiped Millennial Marilyn had given him enough take-on-the-world energy to cover my entire shift.

Lucky for me, my lieutenant was off the NYPD clock until the second tour (3:00 PM). Before he hit the sack, he said he'd set my alarm for early afternoon, so we could both get some rest.

Now I was freshly showered and ready for shut-eye. Shuffling my slippers across the bedroom rug, I was glad to see Mike had already closed the drapes against the dawning sun. He'd also set a fire in the hearth. But by now it had burned down to embers and a creeping chill filled the darkened room.

I noticed his sports jacket hanging on the chair by the closet. The straps of his leather holster were wrapped around his weapon, which he'd placed on the nightstand next to his wallet and Catholic medal — St. Michael, patron saint of police officers.

Mike had carried that silver charm since his early years, when he kept it tucked into his uniform hat. These days he kept it in his breast pocket, next to his heart.

My own heart was aching to be near him again. When I'd left to open the shop, the disappointment in his expression had been almost painful. Like me, he was sorry we'd missed a chance to make love.

Now, as I approached the bed, I could hardly wait to cuddle up to his big, warm body. Unfortunately, my feline friends had beaten me to it. The purring pair had curled up beside the man. As I slipped beneath the covers, I gently nudged Java and Frothy to the bottom of the four-poster. They mildly complained, but I wasn't buying it.

Shoo, girls, he's mine!

Mike had showered before sacking out, his bare skin betraying faint aromas of clean soap and citrusy aftershave. Inhaling deeply, I closed my eyes, still grateful to him for staying by my side through the night, helping me find the evidence that (I prayed) would stop the dangerous game of a monstrous young man who'd made a sport of hurting and humiliating women — and possibly even murdered one.

"How can I thank you?" I quietly asked Mike's sleeping form.

I could still see the disappointment on his face as he'd headed up to bed. After all he'd done, he didn't deserve to end his day that way. But what could I do?

Inspiration struck when I recalled the words he'd used to subdue that mugger in Hudson River Park . . .

With renewed purpose, my hands and lips gently roused my fiancé. His sleepy blue eyes came slowly awake, then quickly gleamed with hungry interest.

As he pulled off my nightshirt, delicious sounds rumbled from his throat. Then his mouth and hands began to roam, exploring new ways to make me melt . . .

But this was my collar!

I didn't have handcuffs, but I did have strong hands, so I captured his wrists the old-fashioned way before moving my body over his. A thrilling gasp escaped him when he realized my intentions. Then a slow smile spread across his face as I put my lips to his

ear and whispered his favorite order —
"Stay down. Stop moving."

TWENTY-SIX

"Boom! *Boom! Boom!*"

My eyes were closed, everything was dark, and a little girl was laughing. It sounded like Joy! I felt the light weight of her body in my arms . . .

Where are we?

I open my eyes. The sun is shining. The weather is lovely. Looking up, I see a soaring archway of Tuckahoe marble — Stanford White's arch.

I'm in Washington Square Park!

A band is playing. The crowd around me is young and beautiful. Women are barefoot, wearing flowing summer dresses, proud of the flowers in their hair. Men are peacocks in expensive suits and polished black shoes. They're dancing together, but in the strangest way.

Couples pair off. They bow with formality. Then they swing each other with wild abandon. Suddenly, they stop and switch partners.

Switch, switch, switch . . . again and again and again!

It's an ugly dance, jerky and graceless.

"Mommy, I want to dance, too!"

"I don't know, honey —"

"Pleeease!"

I have so much love for my baby. I want her to be happy. So I put her down, watch her twirl in front of me. Her dark hair lifts. Her little yellow dress billows on the breeze.

As she spins, she begins to grow taller and older. Before my eyes, she turns six, then eight, and twelve. A few more turns and she's a gangly teen. At last, she's a fully bloomed woman, spinning away . . .

"Wait! Where are you going?"

I try to stop her, but she disappears into the crowd. Pushing bodies aside, I finally see her across the park. A man approaches. He has a scraggly goatee and a black denim jacket. The face of this man looks familiar to me. He's been in my coffeehouse.

It's Richard Crest!

"No!" I shout. "Not him! Get away from him!"

But the sounds of the crowd swallow my words.

I feel a sharp tap on my shoulder. Madame is behind me, shaking her head. "You're too late, Clare. Linda is gone. You can't save her."

"I have to try!"

As the young pair leaves, I follow, hurrying out of the park and into the streets. I pass dear little shops and quaint cafés; historic town houses and landmark buildings with Italianate flourishes and Federal lines. This is the Village of Henry James, the only one Linda's family knew.

But there is another Village, one with a basement and boiler room, a dark place, haunted by a brick and bloody fingerprints.

In this Village, the streets are dingier. Cement cracks open, paint peels, weeds sprout from broken sidewalks. I reach the very edge of Manhattan, but it doesn't look right.

This isn't the East River!

Suddenly, I'm on the West Side, in Hudson River Park . . .

A young woman is crying. I hurry toward the sound. It's my daughter! Joy is sobbing at the Bronze Age table in Habitat Garden. Her yellow dress is gone, replaced by a pink flowered skirt and virginal white silk blouse.

"What's wrong?" I ask.

"Boom! Boom! Boom!" she shouts, pretending to fire a gun at the sky. She rants and rages, yelling at thin air. Then she runs toward the river and jumps in!

Horrified, I scream and race after her. A foot trips me. I fall to the concrete. Looking up, I see Richard Crest. He's back in his designer skinny suit — and laughing at me.

As I try to rise, he grabs my arm, pulls me to the railing. I punch and kick, but he's too strong. Like a bag of refuse, I am picked up and thrown away. I drop forever, then splash into the water.

The waves are choppy, but I swim and swim, desperate to save my daughter. Barges float by like silent giants, indifferent to me. I thrash and try, but the harder I swim, the more I sink, and as the surface recedes, darkness swallows me . . .

TWENTY-SEVEN

"Clare, wake up!"

"What is it?!"

"You were thrashing around, calling out."

My heart was still racing. "I was swimming, getting nowhere, starting to sink."

"Yeah . . ." Mike rubbed his eyes. "I've had dreams like that. Your mind's processing all the stress, trying to work things out."

"I guess."

He touched my cheek, his blue eyes looking worried. "You okay?"

"I'm fine. I'm glad you're here. What time is it?"

He stretched and smiled, leaned in close. "Time for breakfast."

Clearly, the man was hungry, but not for food. His kisses were sweet at first, trailing along my jawline and shoulder. Then his hands got busy and both our passions quickly rose. I was relieved when he pulled me beneath him. After the awful things in that nightmare, I needed to feel something good.

Eventually, we made it to the kitchen.

Wanting to spoil Mike, I brewed a fresh pot of Tanzanian peaberry. Full-bodied with sweet notes of fruit and a finish of bright citrus, it was a heavenly cup, like having dessert for breakfast.

Unfortunately, I was all out of actual dessert — and much of everything else. The coffeehouse had been so busy lately, I'd been working extra hours, and my kitchen cupboards were nearly bare.

I let Mike know.

"You don't have to cook. I'll treat you," he said, renewing his Veselka offer, but I wanted to stick close to home.

Frankly, I was worried. The Village Blend's early-morning opening had gone well. I even served a new customer: Sergeant (not Davy) Jones from the Harbor Patrol. "You described your coffee so nicely last night," he said, "I decided to try some myself."

The sergeant downed a free sample and left with our largest refillable travel mug.

Many of our regulars stopped by, too, none of whom mentioned the viral video. Then Matt had arrived, and I went to bed. Now I couldn't stop hoping: *Is the Gun Girl story over already? Is our business safe from repercussions?*

I was anxious to find out.

"You shower and get dressed," I told Mike. "I'll fix us something to eat."

"I thought you said your cupboards were bare."

"*Nearly* bare. Trust me . . ."

A little scrounging produced one red pepper, the heel of a breakfast sausage, four eggs, and a hunk of mild cheddar — all I needed to make my big, beautiful sausage-and-pepper-stuffed omelet for two.

When the omelet was done, I brought the pan to the table, cut my fluffy, cheesy, overstuffed handiwork in half, and plated it with the last slices of my Amish Cinnamon-Apple Bread (toasted and slathered with Irish butter).

As Mike and I inhaled our afternoon breakfast, his phone buzzed. It was Franco again, but this time he wasn't texting. He wanted to talk.

I cleared the table and listened in — or tried to. Mike's end of the conversation betrayed nothing, except at the close of the call. (And this was a shocker.) He actually smiled.

"Good news?" I asked.

"You remember our mugger?"

"How could I forget?"

"Well, Adam Thomas — that's his name — is also an addict."

"Didn't you already deduce that last night?"

"Yes, and Franco confirmed it. He's been interviewing this kid for three hours. Thomas has no record, and he's flat broke. But he has something extremely valuable to offer us."

"Information?"

"Key information, something we've been after for weeks. I guess small favors really can give up big rewards — at least in this case."

"So you're happy?"

"Happy? Sweetheart, I don't know how to thank you for bringing me to that park. If this kid's story turns out to be true, he could be the Rosetta Stone of Styx."

TWENTY-EIGHT

Styx.

Not the "Come Sail Away" retro rock band Styx or the River Styx of Greek mythology. This Styx was a dangerous new recreational drug. Chemists called it by its long, technical name. Law enforcement described it as a synthetic opioid, one that gave users a floating high like heroin.

Styx was so new that none of Mike's regular informants had a clue about it. The drug wasn't being distributed on street corners or through Internet sites. Yet it was showing up in clubs and bars, and no one seemed to know how it got there. "I bought it from a guy who bought it from a girl" was the typical story. Its popularity was spreading fast; sadly, so were the overdoses.

"They're off to the underworld," was how Franco put it.

Since the discovery of Styx, the OD Squad even nicknamed their naloxone kits "Hercules." Fitting enough, given their goal of dragging lost souls back to the land of the living.

Styx was particularly alarming because it came in powder form and was being sold like old-fashioned Pixy Stix candies in a rainbow of straw-shaped wrappers. It hadn't reached the school yards yet, but Mike feared it would — and that fear is what fueled his overtime.

Every day now, Mike was camped out at One Police Plaza, working with the NYPD's database to get a picture of sale and usage via reports filed by the city's narcotics, gang, and precinct detectives. The port of entry for this drug appeared to be New York, and he'd been poring over toxicology reports, consulting with the DEA, and conducting conference calls with his counterparts across the Northeast.

In the meantime, Sergeant Franco had been taking care of the day-to-day aspects of the OD Squad, including stakeout operations and stings. His dedication had freed up Mike to work on the larger, regional investigation — putting pieces together to get a bigger picture of the problem and form a strategy to solve it.

"Thank goodness for Franco," Mike said. "I'll head over to find out more directly.

But it looks like we've got a genuine crack in the case."

"I hope you do — and I'm happy to hear Franco's promotion is working out so well."

"He's become my right-hand man, and he's been doing an outstanding job."

"I'm not surprised. Despite what Matt thinks of him, I'm relieved he and Joy are a couple. I think Franco will make a great husband."

"Hypothetically," Mike said.

"What does that mean?"

"Nothing."

I narrowed my gaze. "You have something on your mind? Or is there something you know that I don't? Come on, spill it."

"I just think . . ." Mike shrugged, his expression looking far too skeptical. "The issue with your ex disliking him — and that's an understatement — isn't going to make life peachy for them as a couple. And living in different cities isn't easy on any relationship."

"We managed it."

"We're older."

"Please!" I held up my hand, Esther-style. "Do not mess with my mother-of-the-bride fantasy of seeing my daughter married to a good man like Franco. I'm sorry, but I'd like to think of her as settling down soon. If

181

she were unattached and using those dating apps, I'd worry myself sick, especially after that dream of mine. Did I tell you about it?"

"Just the swimming part."

"Well, before I ended up in the river, Joy was dressed like Gun Girl — same blouse and skirt — and pretending to shoot the sky in Hudson River Park."

"You're kidding."

"I wish!" I went on to describe the rest of the dream. "Mostly, I was trying to save my daughter from running off with Richard Crest, descending into an East Village basement, or drowning in the Hudson. It was horrible."

Mike rubbed his chin. "Mmm."

"What?"

"Just that . . . it's not helpful to your peace of mind to see your daughter in these victims — or these victims as your daughter."

"But that kind of thinking is natural for any parent. When you work so hard to get drugs off the street, aren't you thinking of Jeremy and Molly? There, but for the grace of guardian angels, goes my baby."

"Except Joy has a mother who's fiercer than St. Michael when it comes to protecting her child."

"I wish I could protect her — and all of these young women. But our world is far from a Garden of Eden; that's how Madame put it. These days, I think we're closer to that concrete Habitat Garden, filled with bizarre man-made structures of social interaction. And someone is always lurking in the shadows with dark intentions."

"Like our mugger?"

"Like the killers in that boiler room. Or Richard Crest."

"Even so, Clare, you can't let your fears shake you." Mike pulled his patron saint medal from his pocket and held it up. "Do you remember how that little prayer goes?"

"What prayer?"

Mike smiled. " *'Angel of God, my guardian dear. To whom God's love commits me here. Ever this night, be at my side . . .'* "

I hesitated then finished — " *'To light, to guard, to rule, and guide.'* Yeah, I guess I do remember."

"So there you go. You're not alone. Not even when you face those dark nights of the soul."

"And what about dark souls? What do you do when you have to face them?"

He dropped St. Michael back in his pocket. "Sometimes you have to fight them, before you can help them."

■ ■ ■ ■

After one more pot of coffee, Mike was kissing me good-bye. When he headed for the door, I heard his phone going off again.

Suddenly, he was back.

"What is it?" I asked, worried.

"Another text from Emmanuel Franco — about you."

"Me?"

"Take a look . . ."

Tell the Coffee Lady to turn on her phone.

"Why? What's wrong?"

"I don't know, but I've got to run —" Mike tapped his watch. "Maybe you should take his advice."

The moment I powered my smartphone back on, it vibrated like crazy. I checked the caller ID — my daughter! She was trying to reach me.

"Joy, what's the matter? Are you okay?"

"That's my question for you, Mom. Manny swore to me that you were fine, but I just saw the video of you and that girl with the gun — and I'm freaking!"

"I'm okay, honey. Calm down. Did you see it on Chatter?"

"No, on cable news! All the networks are playing it, every one!"

For a moment, I was speechless.

I'd expected that video to be history by now. But it wasn't, which meant the Village Blend hadn't dodged this bullet. The shot was simply delayed. Now it was headed straight for the heart of my beloved coffeehouse.

Twenty-Nine

Two days later, I was once again standing behind my shop's counter. Sunlight streamed through our wall of French doors, its golden rays gleaming on the spotless plank floor. A fire crackled in the hearth, dispelling the chill of the autumn afternoon. The espresso machine perfumed the air with freshly brewed ambrosia.

Too bad there were few customers to enjoy it.

At two o'clock on a hectic Manhattan weekday, my coffeehouse had precisely two patrons.

At the window, a brunette twenty-something in a pleated skirt and pastel tee tapped away on her laptop, a rolling Pullman parked by her side. She chewed her pink lips with intensity — probably a traveling graduate student who hadn't checked in with the outside world in days.

Sitting by the fireplace, a big guy with a

curly red beard nursed a cappuccino and glowered at our neglected front door, obviously waiting for someone who had yet to arrive.

I knew how he felt. I was impatiently waiting, too — and not just for more customers.

By now, detectives would have been assigned to investigate the case of the dead girl in the river. I had plenty to say to them, mostly about Richard Crest, but they had yet to contact me.

Quinn warned me it would take time. The police already had my statement. What they really needed was a ruling by the medical examiner on cause of death. An autopsy report and any forensic evidence collected by the CSU would give them more hard facts than I could.

Even my baristas weren't able to tell me the girl's name or where she worked, and only Esther recalled seeing her with Richard Crest. I had yet to hear back from my assistant manager, Tucker Burton, who was out on vacation. But I assumed he received the group text message I sent about "Heart Girl" and would have contacted me if he had any information.

When the bell over the door rang, I looked up expectantly. It was only our mailman. I gritted my teeth. Just two customers in an hour meant I had more staff (and newly arrived bills) than patrons, not the best business model.

The trouble began, as I guessed it would, when the cable news started playing that viral video. Next our local news showed it. Then newspapers picked up the story with glaring headlines:

Espresso Shot of Hot Lead
Gunplay at a Village Café
You're "App" to Get Shot at This
Coffeehouse

Most of the articles were reprints of a single wire service report, which relied on the police blotter for facts. The new Cinder app was a prominent part of the story's background, since it brought shooter and victim together; and users of the app had rated the Village Blend a favorite hookup hot spot. But the articles failed to inform readers that the "bullets" were blanks until the very last paragraph!

If that weren't bad enough, Nancy called from her Critter Crawl workout class to tell me the video on Chatter was "even more viral than ever," now with over one million views.

Nancy thought it was "awesome free publicity."

It was, but not the good kind.

The public was not intrigued by Gun Girl's story; they were alarmed and disturbed. Dating app users wanted a safe space to meet, not one that attracted a gun-wielding banshee, and the result was a devastating down-turn in customer traffic.

By last night, business went from dire to disastrous. Though we managed to stay open the entire evening (no weaponized tootsie to close us this time), the City Harvest food pantry ended up with more pastries than we'd sold.

With all those leftovers, I didn't need the end-of-day receipts to know business was in *la toilette.*

Today was even worse. Both the morning and lunch rush were duds — so bad I cut tomorrow's bakery order in half, and the dairy order by a third. Another week like this, and I'd be forced to lay people off.

The good news was our coffee brand hadn't suffered, and probably wouldn't. We still had an excellent business supplying our beans to select restaurants and hotels.

From Joy's reports, our store in Washington, DC, was also doing fine. Only this landmark location had been damaged by the bad publicity. While I didn't expect this boycott to last forever, I feared it would go on long enough to threaten our financial viability. If traffic didn't return soon, this century-old shop could end up shuttering.

Madame's heart would certainly be broken, and I couldn't live with myself after disappointing her. It was almost too horrible to contemplate, but the business had to be saved, even if our flagship store couldn't be.

Esther was perceptive enough to sense the storm brewing (pun intended), but she glumly chose to catch up on chores in our basement roasting room rather than face this empty room.

Dante was getting a clue, too. With a dearth of NYU co-eds to charm, he doodled a dozen artistic ideas on napkins before sending himself to the pantry to inspect our porcelain cups for chips and cracks.

The part-timers I usually employed for busy afternoons and evenings were already sent home.

Sadly, the only staff member I felt comfortable discussing this problem with was missing in action — and, boy, did I miss him.

Tucker was my rock-steady right hand and the best American barista I had ever known.

Personable, capable, and trustworthy, he was also a beloved fixture of our Village shop. His showman's wit and Southern charm were as embedded in these walls as its exposed red bricks.

For the past week, however, Tuck had taken a well-deserved leave to practice his second career as a thespian. He and I usually arranged his Village Blend hours around his theatrical schedule, but this was something different.

Tuck had landed a speaking role in a feature film now shooting at Astoria Studios in Queens, and his part required him to be on set sixteen hours every day.

I hadn't heard a word from him since he'd started the gig, so I was shocked when the bell jangled and he walked through the front door. Elated, I raced around the counter and gave him a tight hug. He stiffened unnaturally as I wrapped my arms around his lanky form.

"I was just thinking about you! Did your shoot end early? How have you been?"

Only then did I notice the dark circles under his eyes and deep frown on his usually cheerful, boyish face.

"Tuck, what's wrong? You look terrible . . ."

Avoiding my gaze, he ran a knobby hand

through his floppy brown hair. "The production isn't over. But I've been given a few days off, along with the cast and most of the crew. The shooting schedule is a mess because of the police investigation."

"What police investigation?!"

"Clare, I came here today to explain — and apologize."

"For what? What's this all about?"

As Tucker's narrow shoulders slumped, his gangly frame seemed to shed inches. "It's about what happened with Carol Lynn."

"Carol Lynn Kendall?"

He nodded. "What happened in our upstairs lounge, that whole awful scene? It was my fault."

THIRTY

"Are you talking about Gun Girl?"

Tuck's brown eyes widened. "Oh, God! Is that what they're calling her now?"

At his anguished cry, the young brunette by the window stopped tapping and peeked over her computer screen.

Time for privacy!

I hustled Tuck to the empty coffee bar, sat him on a stool, and pulled him a fresh espresso. Then I slid the demitasse in front of him, rested my elbows on the marble counter, and quietly commanded —

"Tell me what's going on."

For the first time in recent memory, Tucker Burton refused to meet my gaze.

"Oh, Clare, I wanted to help Carol Lynn, that's all. I never imagined she'd do what she did, right here in our Village Blend."

"I still don't understand. I knew you were acquainted with Carol Lynn, but —"

"More than acquainted!" he cried, rattling

the demitasse. "She's a friend. And a wonderful, generous person! She's also vulnerable and lonely and a walking pharmacy —"

"A what?"

Tuck raised a hand. "All prescribed by her psychiatrist. She has a few emotional issues. But mostly she's just naïve to the ways of this big bad town, like you were —"

"Me?"

"I took the girl under my wise and seasoned wing, like I did with you —"

"Me!?!"

"Of course. You both needed advice and guidance when you arrived in Manhattan, and I was happy to provide it."

"Let's stick to the present, shall we? How exactly did you meet Ms. Kendall?"

"She did seamstress work for Punch. Those cabaret gowns are a bitch to take care of, especially the sequined numbers, and she did a fabulous job. So I hired her to do all the costuming for my superhero charity show. She's a whiz at mending spandex, too, let me tell you! That's how she got noticed by the costume designer on the movie I'm in. After she was hired to assist in wardrobe, she told me about a late casting call for an actor who dropped out. Carol Lynn is the whole reason I got the part!"

"I don't even know the name of your

movie."

"*Swipe to Meat.* That's *Meat* with an *A.* It's the story of a New York chef turned serial killer who hooks up with his beautiful victims through a dating app, kills them in the throes of passion, and bakes their hearts into meat pies — kind of a *Sweeney Todd* meets *He's Just Not That Into You.* I play the genial doorman who keeps helping the killer with his garbage bags and wondering why there are so many of them. I catch on eventually and have the greatest death scene! It's just spectacular — on paper. They paused the production before we shot it!"

I shuddered. "I don't know if I could take seeing you killed, Tuck, even as a fictional character."

He patted my hand. "Honey, I don't blame you. Frankly, if the producer was an exploitation ham like William Castle, he'd probably use Carol Lynn's viral video for publicity." Tuck sighed. "But instead he's going to help defend Carol Lynn. He feels very bad about what happened with the gun —"

"Gun?"

"The weapon she loaded with blanks —"

"Oh, now I see. Carol Lynn took the gun from your set."

Tuck lowered his voice. "The gunsmith left the set early with the weapon unsecured, which is a big no-no. Carol Lynn 'borrowed' it, and you know the rest." Tuck's shoulders sagged again. "I'm so sorry, Clare."

"But you're not responsible. Not for any of this."

"You don't understand. Carol Lynn started using Cinder on my advice. She's such a shy person, very private. She had little experience with the opposite sex, but she confided that she was lonely. With daydreams of romantic dinners and strolls through Washington Square Park, she asked me and Punch if we knew any nice guys around her age. The only straight young men we knew were already in relationships, so I advised her to use Cinder — I thought it would be totally safe for her. Its users are supposed to be screened for legitimacy. No make-believe profiles. And she would be in control of making first contact; no unwanted pervy messages, like women get with other apps. I was also the one who told her to meet her dates here at the Village Blend. I *convinced* her it would all go fabulously!"

He seized the demitasse and drained it in one gulp. Finally, his eyes met mine. "So you see? What happened here the other night is completely my fault."

"You're wrong, Tuck, you only tried to help her. If anyone's to blame, it's Richard Crest. Did Carol Lynn tell you about him?"

"Are you kidding? She poured her heart out to me after he shredded it."

"Didn't she check him out first?"

"She did. His social media looked legit, and in line with how he described himself. And the 'Cinder Chat' forum comments had entries for Crest that were totally complimentary — *'He's a real gentleman.' 'What a nice guy . . .'* When I heard that baloney, I told Carol Lynn to put up her own comment, tell the truth to prevent Crest from hurting another unsuspecting Cinder-ella. And report him to the app administrators for abuse!"

"Did she?"

"I read what she wrote before she tried to post it. Carol Lynn was articulate and detailed. But the comment never posted. First, an auto-reply claimed it was 'awaiting moderation.' Then her comment was deleted, without any message explaining why. The administrators ignored her abuse report, too. They just allowed Crest to keep on swiping."

I was outraged. *How could they do that?!* Before I could say as much, Tuck dropped a bombshell on my head.

"I've made up my mind, Clare. Because of my actions, I hurt a friend and this wonderful coffeehouse. I let Madame down and especially you. That's why I'm resigning. Today. Without a two-week notice. You can keep my final paycheck, too. I don't deserve it."

"Tuck, no! You can't do this. We need you —"

"You don't. Look around! I did this." He shook his head and stepped off the stool. "I know you'd never fire me. You'd keep me here, paying my salary while your coffeehouse died. But I am not going to put you through that —"

Tears in his eyes, he bolted. Before I could get around the counter and across the shop, he was opening and closing the front door.

"Good-bye, Clare!"

Undeterred, I hurried forward. If I had to chase Tucker all the way to Hell's Kitchen and drag him back by his floppy hair, I would!

Pulling open the door, I was ready to go when a wall of humanity hit me. In a tidal wave of pastel tees and skinny jeans, the female swarm crowded my entrance and flowed in, carrying me along with it!

THIRTY-ONE

As my shop's welcome bell jangled relentlessly, the army of women surged through my coffeehouse door.

My solitary male customer wanted no part of it. Faster than you could say "suffragette," Red Beard fled the female incursion, an expression of mortal terror on his furry face.

My only other customer, the twenty-something brunette in the pleated skirt and pastel tee, stood up. Instead of fleeing, she opened her luggage to reveal the guts of a technical device. Then she hurried to join the swarming pack.

That's when I realized the brunette's T-shirt displayed the same graphic emblazoned on all the others. No words, just hearts on fire — the same icon as the Cinder app!

"What is this?!"

"Hold still!" the brunette in the pleated skirt commanded, and aimed some kind of advanced digital camera at my face.

I tried to move away, but the group wouldn't have it. Like tigresses in booties and ballet flats, the twelve young women surrounded me — not unlike predators separating the weakest prey from its protective pack.

"Back off!" I cried, loud enough to bring Dante running from the pantry.

"Need help, boss? What's going on?"

"I'm not sure yet."

Dante rolled his shirtsleeves up his strong, tattooed forearms and leaned against the counter, wary eyes on the young women — who didn't appear to mind. Wetting their glossy lips, the pretty tigresses looked over my resident fine arts painter as if he were a fresh piece of meat.

In the meantime, I looked *them* over. Most were well under the age of thirty. Despite a diversity of race, body type, and hair color (which ranged from curly black to light blond with pink neon streaks), they each had the same pixie haircuts, including the camera operator.

"What is going on here?" I demanded.

The answer came from a thirteenth tigress, the oldest one. Her perfect elfin features were caressed with a slick blond pixie as shiny as polished plastic. She stepped out of the throng and right past me. Flashing a brilliant smile, she gazed into the digital camera.

"Hi! I'm Sydney Webber-Rhodes, founder and CEO of Cinder!"

Her perky tone matched her cheer girl demeanor. "My Tinkerbells and I are here in New York City, at the legendary Village Blend coffeehouse, to get to *The Heart of the Story* —"

"You can't film here!" I told her.

Sydney's megawatt grin switched off like stadium lights. As her elfin face went dark, her cherry lips pouted, and she thrust her left pinkie finger into the air.

For a second, I thought she was flipping me off in a hip new way, until I spied a tiny microdot set in the middle of her glossy crimson fingernail. The instant she raised her digit, the camera stopped.

"Stand by, AJ," she told the photographer, who nodded her brunette pixie with grave obedience. Then Sydney turned back to me.

"We're not filming, Ms. Cosi. We're time-delay *streaming* to all users of my Cinder app. But since you've put the *delay* in time-delay, it would help if you stepped over here. I just realized how much better the light is near the window . . ."

She curled a too-familiar hand around my

wrist and leaned close, her hazel-bronze tiger eyes staring me down in an expression as sharp as my daughter's favorite chef's knife.

"And one more thing: I would appreciate it if you didn't interrupt me."

Clearly, this woman was used to bulldozing her way through life — not to mention being in total control. She didn't even trust her own photographer to operate the camera!

Well, unfortunately for Sydney Webber-Rhodes, I learned how to block bulldozers a long time ago. And I was pretty big on control myself, especially when it came to the Village Blend.

Her tiger eyes widened in surprise as I jerked my wrist from her grasp. "I decide what is or isn't streamed in my coffeehouse."

Though not much older than my daughter, she tossed back her slick blond pixie with the testiness of an exasperated parent. "Given all these empty chairs, I doubt this place will be yours much longer."

I met the woman's assured stare with my own. "That was uncalled for. The Village Blend has survived two World Wars, a Great Depression, and a Great Recession or three. We'll find a way to weather this storm, too."

The salesgirl smile returned. "Why

weather a storm when you can reap the whirlwind?"

The Tinkerbells nodded in expressive agreement. Apparently, they'd heard this snappy bit of faux Sun Tzu before.

"Why are you here, Sydney?"

"For one reason, Clare. To save your business and mine."

THIRTY-TWO

I folded my arms and stared with stark skepticism. Sydney didn't flinch. Instead, she dropped her voice, along with her bulldozing bull.

"Look," she said, "that debacle the other night did as much damage to my brand as yours. But I've devised a smart strategy that will save us both."

She did sound sincere — if not entirely sane. "You're here to save my business?"

"And mine. But we have to work together."

"Please explain."

"Right now, your Village Blend and my Cinder app are generating a lot of buzz —"

"Yes, bad buzz."

"It's bad," Sydney agreed, glancing away. "But it's also the kind of media exposure you can't buy for any price. Which means we have to hack it — take control of the story and tweak it until it fits the narrative we want to tell."

"That sounds vaguely dishonest."

"Please." She waved her hand. "All of advertising is vaguely dishonest."

"I don't know if I'm comfortable with this."

"I respect that. But don't you agree that the viral video and the news reports didn't tell the whole truth?"

"Yes."

"So why not tell everyone the whole story? Tell it our way? All you have to do is participate in this interview. You do not have to be dishonest in any way. Just follow my lead. This will benefit both of our brands. I promise." Sydney locked eyes with mine. "We can turn this ship around if you'll let me steer."

My mind raced. *Should I actually cooperate with these Silicon Alley Cyber-Sirens, or have Dante toss them into the street at the end of this so-called interview?*

The latter option was far more appealing, but I wasn't convinced it was the correct one. While I didn't trust this arrogant girl-child or her streaming scheme — and frankly, her staff of Tinkerbells gave me the willies — I could see that Sydney was an ambitious woman who would employ every trick in her social network arsenal to save her own business. I also knew that she would execute her strategy with or without my consent or cooperation.

But if I'm on board her ship, I'll at least have some control over the direction, right?

Madame once told me that getting through difficult times sometimes coupled you with bizarre bedfellows. This appeared to be one of those times. So . . .

Despite my misgivings, I mentally swiped right and accepted this Cinder match for the Village Blend, praying I wouldn't end up ranting about this Horrible Hookup at Esther's next poetry slam!

Turning to Dante, I asked him to serve coffee to our guests.

Sydney took my hospitality for assent, retrieved her electric smile, flashed that magic pinkie, and addressed the camera.

"As you know, *The Heart of the Story* is a weekly forum for sharing the experience of an Ella or Fella who's found empowerment in taking control of their social life through our Cinder app. Well, today's story is going to be a little different, a little disturbing. But the good news? It stars one awesome fairy godmother, and I promise there will be a happily ever after."

Sydney laid her pale hand on my shoulder. "Most of you have seen the viral video featuring this legendary coffeehouse and this amazing woman . . ."

Accompanied by nods and gentle applause from her Tinkerbells, Sydney continued to chatter to her audience of heaven knew how many Ellas and Fellas.

Finally, she faced me and asked: "So tell us what happened here the other night."

I briefly related the basic events to the camera. But Sydney did not look satisfied. "Surely, the story doesn't end there!"

I blinked as the camera went for a tight focus of my face, and I'm pretty sure a deer in a pair of headlights would have looked less startled.

"You evacuated the upstairs lounge," Sydney coaxed. "And now you're alone with an armed individual and her victim. What did you do next? What's the *Heart of the Story*?"

"Well, um, my main concern was getting my customers out of harm's way. After that, I didn't do much."

"That's not true!" Dante suddenly blurted. "She did way more than that!"

"Dante —"

"You did!"

Sydney's expression lit up with glee. Then she twirled her magic finger and AJ, the digital photographer, spun with it. Now all eyes, including the camera's, were focused on my *artista* barista.

THIRTY-THREE

"Clare did plenty," Dante went on. "She talked the distraught woman into giving up her gun, so that by the time the police arrived, it was all over — without anyone getting hurt."

"I understand the police response was quite rapid," Sydney said.

"It was," Dante replied, folding his tattooed arms. "The Sixth Precinct isn't very far. A lot of the cops are regular customers."

Sydney nodded. "So I've heard! Your coffeehouse must be one of the *safest* places for anyone to meet a Cinder date! So let's talk about the Village Blend. Since we brought Cinder to New York City, this landmark coffeehouse has been rated as *one of our most popular meeting spots.* Here's one reason why . . ."

Sydney pulled a note from the pocket of her tight jeans. "Brenda, an Ella from Park

Slope, posted about a date gone wrong on our message board — we've all been there, right?

"Anyway, Brenda was involved in a public scene right here in the Village Blend. But before it turned ugly, she was rescued by one of the staff's baristas. They say the baristas here have the same insight into human nature as good bartenders. And Brenda testified to that. Ms. Cosi's barista saw how upset Brenda was and took her upstairs for complimentary coffee and tender loving care."

Sydney tucked the note away and looked at the camera.

"That's some Fairy Godmothering from you and your superior staff, Clare Cosi." As Sydney spoke, a hand covered her heart. "And in case you're wondering why this place is so famous —" The Tinkerbells all lifted the coffee Dante served them and made yummy sounds. "The house blend is amazing."

Sydney stood beside Dante. "And so, for superb coffee, inventive lattes and pastries, a barista staff that delivers so much more than caffeine, eye candy like this dude" — she winked and AJ gave a little whistle — "but especially for a fairy godmother of a manager who would risk her own well-being to keep her customers safe, Cinder declares the Village Blend the Number One spot for Happy Hookups in all of New York City!"

Sydney and her Tinkerbells applauded and hooted. Even Dante joined in, turning on his most magnetic smile.

"I urge every Ella and Fella in the tristate area to come down to the Village Blend in New York City this weekend. It's Cinder approved! And now you know *The Heart of the Story . . .*"

A twirl of her pinkie and the photographer lowered the camera and rushed to her rolling luggage, still open to reveal the portable digital streaming system, which fascinated Dante almost as much as he appeared to fascinate the photographer.

As he and AJ began to talk (okay, flirt), Sydney exhaled, sounding as relieved as I felt that the streaming event was over. Then came a loud, intrusive voice —

"Happy Hookups, huh?"

We all turned to find Esther Best coming around the counter, shaking her raven head. She'd been in the basement when Sydney and her Tinkerbell posse arrived. I wasn't certain how much of the streaming Esther witnessed, but I gave her credit for maintaining radio silence. Now that the camera was off, however —

"What about the *Horrible* Hookups?" she challenged. "The Dating App *Disasters*?"

Sydney's tiger eyes narrowed into slits. "Who is this person?"

"This is Esther," I said, "one of those dedicated baristas you mentioned."

"That's right." Esther stood next to me. "I'm one of the people who consoles the not-good-enough 'rejects' on your lousy app."

"Does she need to be here?"

"Absolutely," I said.

THIRTY-FOUR

"You want the *Heart of the Story,* sure," Esther challenged, "as long as they're not the broken ones."

"That's not true," Sydney replied.

"Then why do you delete negative comments in your Cinder Chat forum? And ignore abuse reports on users?"

"That's crazy!"

"Not so crazy," I said.

Sydney turned on me. "And what would you know about it, Clare? I thought you were engaged to be married to a rather delicious police lieutenant."

"How do you know about my personal life?"

"I always do my research. For instance, I know your daughter is a Paris-trained chef working at your Washington, DC, location. And you're running this coffee business with your ex-husband, a coffee broker who owns a warehouse in Red Hook, Brooklyn

— full of amazing beans he sources himself. Anyway, with a fiancé like the one you have, what are you doing using my Cinder app?"

"I'm not using it. A reliable source told me that Carol Lynn Kendall filed an abuse report on Richard Crest for his appalling behavior, but your administrators allowed him to continue using your app. She tried to warn other women about him, but your Cinder Chat moderators deleted her negative comments."

"Your 'reliable source' is badly informed. I created this app to protect women from abuse, not encourage it. My Tinkerbells would never do what you've described. They couldn't if they wanted to. We have backup systems in place for review and protections embedded in our coding." She snapped her fingers. "Right, AJ?"

"Um, excuse me?" AJ tore herself away from Dante and hurried over.

"This is AJ, the temporary head of my development team."

"Temporary?" I said. "What happened to your permanent head?"

"Gone," AJ replied.

"Haley Elizabeth Hartford was a real whiz, and a real loss, I have to admit. Until recently, she oversaw all of our coding, but she's gone off to spearhead development of a new app; and we wish her well, don't we, AJ?"

"We don't hold grudges," AJ said almost robotically. "We like happy endings."

"You see? That's why your charges are totally bogus," Sydney reiterated. "Tell them, AJ."

"Tell them what?"

With that familiar head-toss of parental exasperation, Sydney explained: "These ladies have been led to believe that Cinder ignores abuse reports and deletes negative comments in its forums."

"That's crazy!" AJ echoed. "We encourage our Ellas and Fellas to tell us about abuse of any kind so we can keep all our users safe and happy!"

Sydney folded her arms. "You see, Esther, we strive for happy endings. Not broken hearts."

"I don't believe you."

"Well, that's your malfunction, not ours."

Sydney tried to wave her away. But Esther stepped up, right into the CEO's space. Before she could utter another word, one of the Tinkerbells rocketed out of the group and blocked my barista, forcing her backward.

"Hey!" Esther and I objected together.

"Stand down, Cody," Sydney ordered.

A golden-tanned siren with a brownish blond pixie, athletic build, and square-jawed scowl, Cody looked like the girl most likely to be flagged for an offensive body check in Ivy League Lacrosse.

Like a good Tinkerbell (or German shepherd), she did as her mistress ordered, but not before glowering a warning at Esther. Then she took a position to the right of Sydney, her hand poised over a bulging pocket the way I'd seen uniformed officers anticipate a gun draw.

"Is she carrying a weapon?" I asked in alarm.

"Cody is my head of security," Sydney replied, "and she's licensed to carry a stun gun and other forms of protection. She'll be here Saturday night with Team Tinkerbell, so you'll have no worries."

Saturday night? I exchanged glances with Esther and we both blurted: "Why Saturday night?"

Sydney glanced at her cyber-posse and snapped her fingers. "Is everything on schedule?"

A beautiful African American Tinkerbell with a curly black pixie raised her smartphone. "The crowd has been hired. Not as couples, of course. They'll hook up in the coffeehouse for the cameras."

"Thank you, Tanya."

Crowd? Esther and I exchanged glances again: "What crowd?!"

"We've arranged for a rent-a-mob," Sydney replied. "A lot of trendy young people will be hanging around the Village Blend Saturday evening. Two hundred or so will be coming, starting around six PM until you close."

"But I don't need a fake crowd," I said. "I want real customers."

"They will be real, paying customers. They've got a one-night expense account, and they're urged to spend generously. They will all be young and attractive, too, and they are all bona fide users of my Cinder app. You don't see the symmetry here?"

I scanned the tigresses around me. "Yes, and a fearful symmetry it is."

"Oh, don't get all apocalyptic on me, Clare. The crowd we put in place will do the trick. They'll be posting on social media with images of your drinks, your pastries, and their attractive Cinder matches — all of the people coming are alphas with plenty of followers. And their activity will attract legit customers. The whole thing will provide the perfect background for our *Post* story. We have a reporter and photographer coming Saturday night."

"The *New York Post* is coming Saturday?"

"The *Washington Post.* We're taking this story national."

"But —"

"Do you have tables you can set up outside?" Sydney asked. "It would be great if it looked like people were clamoring to get in."

"But we can't even fill this space —"

"You will. And you'll need those tables outside, too."

Dante stepped forward. "Boss, do you want me to haul up the outdoor café tables and heaters from the basement?"

"I guess so." I turned to Esther. "You better call our part-timers to see who's available for tomorrow evening."

"Oh, I'll be doing much more than that!" Esther promised with a mad poet's gleam in her eye. (I was afraid to ask.)

Luckily, Cinder's CEO took her words literally.

"Then we're set!" Sydney declared. "You'll see, Clare. I always deliver. Your Happy Ending — and mine — are on the way."

Just then, my welcome bell jangled, and two women walked in. I knew these customers. They were NYPD detectives. And from the look in their eyes, they weren't here to deliver a Happy anything.

Thirty-Five

Detectives Lori Soles and Sue Ellen Bass arrived with their game faces on.

Tagged the "Fish Squad" by their peers, Soles and Bass cut through the pack of pastel tees like a couple of hammerheads parting a school of rainbow fish.

In their mid-thirties, the two tall women — one blonde, one brunette — reminded me of an old married couple, together so long they could read each other's thoughts (and twang each other's nerves). The pair even dressed alike. Today's ensemble consisted of sharp-creased slacks and battleship gray blazers. The only dash of color came from the gold shields clipped to their belts.

When the sister skyscrapers halted in the middle of the rainbow pack, all conversation ceased. Then CEO Sydney announced —

"Good afternoon, Detective Soles, Detective Bass."

The officers nodded. "Ms. Rhodes."

The greeting surprised me. *Since when did these three know one another?* Sydney's next words gave me a clue.

"The Cinder account information you formally requested has been sent to you. What more could you possibly require from me or my business?"

Sue Ellen Bass tossed her dark ponytail — pulled so tightly that no wrinkle would dare crease her forehead. "We're not here about the Carol Lynn Kendall case. We're here to speak with Clare Cosi on another matter."

I stepped forward. "Is this about the young woman in the river? The one I found?"

Lori Soles's head bobbed, along with her loose blond ponytail. "You're on our interview list."

"Then we'll be going," Sydney said, snapping her fingers for her posse to follow.

Sue Ellen blocked her exit. "Not so fast. Since you're here, we'd like to speak with you, too. You're also on our list."

"What do you mean? How could I be on your list for a woman found in the river? Unless —" Sydney's frown deepened. "Was she a Cinder user?"

Sue Ellen jerked a thumb toward the fireplace. "Take a seat over there. Let's talk in private."

"Must we do this now?"

Lori cocked her head. "We must."

The CEO followed the two detectives across our wood plank floor. Like a loyal guard dog, Cody followed a few steps behind, lingering close enough to eavesdrop while the Fish Squad questioned Sydney.

They talked too quietly for me to overhear — other than Sydney's insisting, "No, I'll stand," after the Fish Squad again requested that she take a seat.

Instead, Sydney anxiously checked her smartwatch and folded her arms. As the detectives continued to speak, her impatient expression completely froze then morphed into one of obvious shock.

Dropping into a café chair, Sydney looked with distress to Cody, who crouched by her side. The pair whispered back and forth. After a minute, Soles and Bass sat down across from Sydney, and Cody stood behind her.

As the detectives continued their questioning, the Cinder CEO grew increasingly agitated, aggressively shaking her sleek blond pixie. Finally, she rose and tapped her watch. Soles and Bass glanced at each other, appearing to reach an agreement to let Sydney go.

When the Cinder CEO rejoined me and her curious Tinkerbells, her voice sounded scratchy and much weaker.

"Clare, I'm due for a meeting back at our Chelsea office. I trust you'll be ready for our Saturday night action plan?"

"We'll be ready."

"Good. Where's your phone?"

"Why?"

She tapped hers then waved it. "I have my contact information for you." She transferred it with a warning. "That's my *private* information. Get in touch anytime if you need my help. But don't share it."

"I understand."

"And *do not* forget to set up those outdoor tables," she ordered, the perky power already back in her voice. "Trust me, you're going to need them!"

Finally, Sydney squared her shoulders, and with a wave of her magic pinkie, she and her pastel army marched into the chilly autumn afternoon.

Only AJ lingered behind, apparently to "pack up," but she appeared more focused on flirting with Dante.

Sue Ellen Bass, on the other hand, was more interested in the activity outside our French doors, where the Cinder-ellas were piling into Uber carriages.

"They certainly seem motivated," she told her partner. "Maybe I should give Cinder a try."

Lori exhaled hard. "Do us both a favor, Sue. Stick with cops."

"You're just saying that because you married one."

"I'm saying that because nine out of ten civilian males can't handle you."

"Based on what?"

"You know what. I can barely keep up with the Italian opera that is your love life."

"I told you a thousand times. Nick stabbed *himself* while peeling an avocado."

"In the groin?"

"*Near* the groin. And there was no permanent damage."

"Excuse me, Detectives," I interrupted. "You did come here to interview me, right?"

The Fish Squad turned around, cop faces back on.

Thirty-Six

Sue Ellen wasted no time: "Three nights ago, you told Sergeant Jones and his River Rats that the girl in the water was a regular here at the Village Blend, correct?"

"That's right."

"Tell us what you know about her," Lori commanded.

"Not much. We spoke only once. I didn't even know her name or exact age —"

"The victim was twenty-six," Sue Ellen read from her notes. "Single. She lived alone at 1 Horatio Street. Her name was Haley Elizabeth —"

"Hartford!" I blurted. *Of course,* I thought, *now it made sense.* "She was head of the development team at Cinder, wasn't she? But she left three weeks ago — under some sort of a cloud, by the sound of it."

Sue Ellen scowled. "I thought you said you didn't know anything about the dead woman."

"Sydney Rhodes made a few comments about her former employee. I just now made the connection."

Lori flipped through her notes. "In your statement, you name someone who you claim is a 'strong suspect' for Ms. Hartford's killer. Did that information happen to come up in your conversation with Ms. Rhodes?"

"Only the fact that her company appeared to ignore abuse reports about him. That may be how Haley Hartford ended up murdered."

Sue Ellen and Lori exchanged skeptical looks.

"What?" I pressed. "You don't think she was murdered?"

"Oh, it's definitely murder," Sue Ellen said. "Ms. Hartford did not die of drowning. The amount of river water in her lungs was minimal."

"The official cause of death is blunt-force trauma," Lori added. "She was struck once, on the side of the head, and was likely dead before she hit the Hudson. According to the ME, it was a blow with a small object from a right-handed perpetrator. We also found blood near her shoe. DNA testing is still out, but the type matches the victim. The weapon has not been recovered. No surveillance footage to speak of — DOT cameras were too far away."

"And private cameras in the area gave us zilch," Sue Ellen said. "Park foliage blocked views of the scene, and the forensics recovered thus far gave us no hits with known offenders."

"I assume you interviewed the usual suspects?"

"If you mean neighbors, friends, and family, yes," Lori said. "We always look for romantic or personal angles."

"Would you mind sharing what you found?"

The pair hesitated, and I thought fast.

"The details might, you know, jar my memory of Haley — as a Village Blend customer . . ."

After mulling this over in silence, Sue Ellen and Lori gave each other consenting looks. Then Lori consulted her notes.

"Ms. Hartford's parents are deceased. They died in a car accident on Long Island five years ago. We spoke to her only sibling, a younger sister, studying medicine at Stony Brook. We also interviewed her ex-boyfriend, a graduate student at Cornell. Both seemed genuinely devastated, and both have solid alibis. Her current employer is a Mr. Ferrell, who was at his place of business, with plenty of witnesses, until midnight the evening of Ms. Hartford's murder. No one knew of enemies or animosities. By all accounts, Haley Hartford was a good-natured young woman, described as kind, intelligent, thoughtful, and hardworking. You just saw us interview her previous employer, who had nothing to add, just a routine statement for the file, similar to all the others."

"And what about my statement?"

Again, the detectives exchanged glances. Then Sue Ellen folded her arms. "Okay, Cosi, get it off your chest."

For the next five minutes, I reviewed all I'd learned the other night, including Esther's recollection of seeing Haley in an intense discussion with Richard Crest two weeks ago, and Crest's abusive pattern of behavior toward women.

"I think Haley may have been one of Crest's horrible hookups. I believe she could have recognized him in that viral video and may have decided to confront him, just like Carol Lynn Kendall. She could have arranged a meeting at Habitat Garden — or maybe Crest set the meeting place. It may have been an accident during an argument, but I believe he could have tried to make it look like a mugging or random assault by taking her wallet, smartphone, and any identifying information."

When I'd finished, a long silence followed. Finally, Lori spoke.

"We can see you're honestly trying to help. Unfortunately —"

"There are giant holes in your theory," Sue Ellen cut in. "Including one the size of a South Bronx subway rat."

"I'm not wrong about Crest. I'm sure he's involved. You've got to interview him, at least."

"We tried," Lori said. "Based on your statement, we gave it a shot."

"What do you mean, you gave it a shot?"

"All of Richard Crest's identifying information was available to us based on the crime that occurred in this coffeehouse. We went to his apartment and his place of business —"

"And?!?"

Sue Ellen shook her head. "The man doesn't exist. There is no such person as Richard Crest."

THIRTY-SEVEN

Nothing much surprised me anymore, not after working New York food service — and parenting a teenage daughter. But Sue Ellen's statement knocked me back a step.

"How can a man who was assaulted in my coffeehouse, and became the star of a viral video that's wrecking my business, not exist?"

Soles and Bass provided no answers. They simply made it clear that if I had nothing else to add to the Haley Hartford case file, they were done listening to "my half-baked theories" — as Sue Ellen so diplomatically put it.

Before I knew it, the two detectives were headed for the door. But they couldn't leave, not yet; I had too many questions. *Think, Clare, think!*

I needed to lure this Fish Squad into staying, reel them in long enough for me to grill them. What I needed was bait . . .

"Before you go, Detectives, how about some fresh, hot coffee? We're about to brew a single-origin Rwandan. Its creamy body and caramel finish pair perfectly with our *Maple Pecan Sticky Buns . . .*"

Sue Ellen's long legs halted, mid-stride. Slowly, she turned. The grim cynicism in her gaze had morphed into a gluttonous gleam. *Success!* Unfortunately, her partner was still wavering. So I gave her a little push.

"It's on the house."

A few minutes later, the detectives were settling into chairs at a center table in my empty upstairs lounge. Esther delivered the promised goodies, and the women began eating and slurping with work-break contentment.

After a deep breath, I revived our interview — nothing intense, just a casual conversation over coffee . . .

"You know, it's funny. I watched Sergeant Franco check Richard Crest's ID the other night, and I was sure the man had a valid driver's license. The sergeant was, too."

"It looked like a valid license —" Lori paused to swallow. "From what Franco told us, he also had business cards with his name and the logo of a real investment firm on Wall Street —"

"Forgeries," Sue Ellen declared, mouth

still full. "Much better than the laminated crap you get at the back of a bodega in Jackson Heights, but still phony."

I stated the obvious. "Since we know this man used the Cinder app under the name Richard Crest, can't you check to see if Haley Hartford ever hooked up with him?"

"Slow down, Clare," Lori said, vainly trying to clean the sweet maple-stickiness off her fingers. "Just because we don't have Ms. Hartford's phone doesn't mean we haven't already accessed and reviewed its contents."

"You looked at her backed-up data?" I assumed.

Sue Ellen nodded. "And her Cinder activity and messages. After we got a warrant — and a cyber-forensics analyst on the case."

"And?"

"Haley Hartford didn't have a date with Richard Crest, because she didn't date — not since the breakup with her boyfriend two months ago. She did have the Cinder app on her phone, but never arranged any meetings. She appeared to use it only to test functionality."

"Haley must have communicated with someone prior to her murder. Didn't she make a phone call or send a text? Something?"

"The girl was a workaholic," Sue Ellen

said. "She was holed up in her apartment, focused on developing a new app. There's no social contact with anyone in the forty-eight-hour period leading up to her death, except two delivery calls to that vegetarian joint on Christopher Street."

"She did have a few back-and-forth calls concerning the new app she was developing," Lori mentioned. "Part of a start-up fitness business."

"Didn't she use any other dating apps besides Cinder?" I asked. "Maybe she and Crest hooked up through —"

Lori silenced me with a raised hand. "Sorry, Clare, let it rest. Your theory is shot to hell."

THIRTY-EIGHT

The detectives were getting restless, and I was getting frustrated. Despite their opinion of my theory, I still felt my suspicions had merit, even if I couldn't pull out hard evidence to back them up. "Richard Crest" (for want of his real name) stank like shark scum at low tide, and I had plenty more questions about Haley Hartford's murder.

But the pastry was eaten, the coffee cups empty, and Sue Ellen began pushing away from our table. I feared all was lost — then Esther arrived. Balancing fresh cups of Rwandan and two more sticky buns (warmed this time), she flashed me a wink as she set down the small tray. The warm buns were fragrant with sweet yeasty goodness; the coffee rich, nutty, and enticingly aromatic from this morning's roasting.

Note to self: give my barista a bonus!

Both detectives immediately reached for seconds. My Fish Squad was back on the hook! And I resumed my grilling . . .

"So let me get this straight," I said with feigned incredulity. "You're telling me that all you know about Richard Crest is what he looks like?"

Sue Ellen confessed: "We're not even sure about that."

"How is that possible? I thought you reviewed his dating profile?"

"We did, but the guy is devious," Lori said. "Most of his social media photos are group shots where he's half hidden. And he's usually wearing sunglasses and a hat, or in a pose that obscures his facial features. He's also big into pushing the affluent lifestyle impression. The pictures were taken on fancy boats or around expensive convertibles or at resorts —"

"That's because he's pitching himself to the ladies as a rich beach bum," Sue Ellen cut in. "Translation: he wants hot bodies. All of his matches are with women who post bikini shots."

"What about his profile photo?" I asked. "You must have been able to tell what he looked like from that!"

But the detectives shook their heads.

"It's a typical 'love-my-bare-chest' dude shot taken on a beach," Sue Ellen said, "but at a distance."

"And with a slouchy hat and sunglasses," Lori added. "I mean, a guy could rob banks like that."

Sue Ellen snorted. "Don't you remember? We busted a scumbag who did just that!"

"I remember him! He was wearing a shirt, though —"

"And he had a lot more chest hair!"

At their mention of banks, I suddenly remembered something — Richard Crest's ten-thousand-dollar bank withdrawal slip that I'd picked up off this very floor.

The night of the Gun Girl incident, I had dropped it into my apron pocket. Then Madame phoned with her upsetting call, and I hurriedly hung up my apron and forgot about it.

Now it was too late. I didn't bother checking the pantry. I already knew. The last batch of aprons, towels, and rags were picked up last night for laundering at Matt's warehouse.

I quickly sent text messages to both of the guys on his day crew, but I didn't hold out hope. That receipt was probably long gone.

As the Fish Squad continued to laugh about their old cases, I remembered one more thing: how desperate Richard Crest was to hide his features on that viral video. But he wasn't able to hide them from me.

"I think I can solve your ID problem," I suddenly declared to the detectives. "My barista Dante is an excellent artist — and I have a fraction of talent left over from my art school days. Together, I'm sure we can create an accurate sketch of Richard Crest, facial features and all. You could use it for an all-points bulletin."

Lori and Sue Ellen exchanged uncomfortable glances. Then Lori put on her diplomatic hat.

"Clare, we would never use a sketch like that for an APB. You would have to sit with a police artist for it. And we'd never get that authorized because Richard Crest is not a suspect in Haley Hartford's murder."

Sue Ellen agreed. "The guy wouldn't be on our radar at all, except he had a gun pointed at his head in this coffeehouse, which officially makes him the victim of a crime, not the perpetrator of one."

Lori nodded. "Face it, there's no evidence Crest is anything more than —"

"A scumbag," Sue Ellen spat.

"— a cruel confidence man who is also a person of interest in a minor assault investigation, but as a *victim,* not a suspect."

I quickly considered another angle. "Doesn't the DA's office need this man for testimony against Carol Lynn Kendall?"

"Sure, if the case were going to trial," Sue Ellen said, "but it's a nothing burger. Kendall's attorney already accepted a plea deal."

"Okay, fine." I sat back. "Then who do you believe killed Haley?"

"We think she was the unfortunate victim of circumstance," Lori said. "A robbery gone wrong —"

"Or an attempted sexual assault. There's been a string of both in that area of the park." Sue Ellen locked her gaze on mine. "Of all people, Cosi, you should know that's a dangerous spot. You and Quinn collared a mugger there."

"Yes," I said, "and I agree that looks like an obvious theory. But what was Haley doing there? And with all those downloaded viral videos in her backpack, the ones starring Richard Crest?"

The two detectives glanced at each other once more; this time they practically rolled their eyes.

"What Ms. Hartford put on her memory device is immaterial — a distraction. The most likely scenario for the deadly assault against her person is obvious to us, as well as our commanding officer. And it should be to you, too."

"A mugging gone wrong?" I assumed.

They nodded.

"Then how do you plan to solve it?"

Sue Ellen shrugged. "Standard police work. Over the next week, we're supervising a sting, using decoys to lure any muggers operating in the area."

"Even if we don't find Ms. Hartford's killer," Lori said, "we'll take a few perps off the street — and out of that park."

Sue Ellen's eyes lit up at the prospect. "If we squeeze hard enough, we might get a lead or even a confession out of one of them . . ."

Yeah, I thought, *when it comes to policing, some things never change.* They were Quinn's words, and he was righter than ever.

"Can you at least share anything else you know about this Richard Crest character? What do you think he's doing with these abusive games?"

"It's clear enough to me," Sue Ellen said. "He gets his kicks from screwing women and then screwing them over."

"Then why won't you help me stop him?"

"Because our commander wants the park cleaned up and Haley Hartford's killer caught," Lori said. "That's our priority."

Sue Ellen nodded. "Crest may be an asshole, and his bad-boy act is vile. But, so far, it's not a crime."

"Giving a false statement to a police officer is," I pointed out. "And so is using a fake driver's license."

"You're right," Sue Ellen finally agreed. "And if the man walks back into your coffeehouse, give us a call. We'll pick him up. We'll find out his real name and run it through the system. We'll question him — and charge him on the fake ID and false statement stunt. Otherwise . . ."

"Otherwise, he gets a pass? Walks away free and clear?"

"Sorry, Cosi, like my partner said, we have our priorities." Sue Ellen drained her cup and rose. "Right now, our job is to find a guy who breaks heads, not hearts."

THIRTY-NINE

As the detectives headed for the spiral staircase, I automatically stood up to bus the table — then sat back down.

The facts the detectives revealed were "just facts" in conversation. Now that the conversation was over, those facts became anchors, depressing enough to sink my spirit.

Haley Hartford's last moments on Earth were horrific. Someone had bashed that poor girl in the head hard enough to cause fatal brain damage. Because I discovered her body, I knew it didn't end there. While she lay dying, the killer coolly emptied her pockets, and then hefted her into the Hudson, full backpack kept in place with the likely hope it would drag her into oblivion, leaving her loved ones forever tortured by unanswerable questions.

This person — this murderer — was a monster.

The detectives knew it. I could see it in their impatient glances. And I didn't doubt their determination to catch this cold-blooded killer. They could hardly wait to set their riverside trap.

The only trouble was — I still believed they were setting it in the wrong place, and for the wrong person.

"Hey, boss?"

I looked up to find Esther Best staring at me from across the lounge, still pretending to clean a perfectly clean tabletop.

"For what it's worth, I think you're right."

I leaned back. "You were eavesdropping?"

"No, I was just —"

"It's okay." I waved her over. "I'd like another perspective. Tell me what you think."

She shrugged. "I think the detectives mean well, but their theory makes no sense to me."

"Why didn't you speak up?"

"Because you already said everything I was thinking." Standing beside me now, she lowered her voice. "Look, when you first sent out those photos of Haley in the river, I was really upset —"

"I'm sorry, Esther. I wasn't trying to upset anyone. I was hoping someone could help identify —"

"Hold on! I know why you sent them. I would have done the same thing. I was upset because I knew Haley — as a customer, I mean . . ."

I gestured for her to join me at the cluttered table. When her Rubenesque hips were settled in, I started my own interview.

"Tell me what you remember about her."

"Nothing that could have helped the detectives. I didn't even know her real name. I used to greet her as Heart Girl because of the tattoo on her cheek. That's mainly what we talked about — tattoos. And coffee, of course. She *loved* our coffee. And she did not strike me as stupid."

"What do you mean?"

"You heard Soles and Bass. They said on the day Haley was killed, she was holed up in her apartment, working on a new app. They described her as a workaholic with no social life. So why did she stop working to download five viral videos of the same incident, within hours of it happening, put them all on a memory stick, and take them to Hudson River Park — alone, at night?"

"It's baffling. I agree."

"The other thing that bothers me is the fake ID stunt this Crest creep pulled. I mean, catfishing is fairly common — you know, creating a false online identity. Crest may have even Photoshopped himself into some of those resort pictures. But why go to the trouble of creating fake IDs? Who does that?"

"A criminal might."

Esther nodded. "That's why I think you're right about Crest. He reeks of bottom-feeding. The guy's guilty of something."

"Soles and Bass agree. But they don't believe he killed Haley, and they think his fake IDs are small potatoes. They're throwing all of their energy into proving the mugging theory with that sting operation in the park."

"So why don't we conduct our own sting? A coffeehouse sting?"

"That's a thought." I leaned forward. "How would we do it?"

"Have Dante sketch Crest, like you suggested he do for the cops. We scan it and send it to the phones of everyone on staff."

"Like a Barista APB?"

"Exactly! The moment Crest walks into the Village Blend, he's made. We call the Fish Squad, and the lady cops reel in the creepy catfish on the fake ID charge."

I thought it over. "It's a good plan. But how do we even know Crest is still swiping?"

"Oh, he's still swiping!" Esther waved her

hands. "This guy is a textbook addict. I'm sure of it."

"How can you be?"

"Behavioral science. One of my professors cited a case study. Ever heard of Hookster?"

"You mean streetwalkers? Ladies of the evening?"

"No, not hookers — *Hookster.* It was one of the early swipe-to-meet dating game apps. A couple of frat boys brainstormed the idea over spring break in Florida . . ."

I reflexively recoiled. But I steeled myself just the same. Dating app culture was part of the urban fabric. It had affected my business — first positively, now negatively. It was time I learned more about it.

"Go on," I told Esther.

She did, describing how the Hookster app marketed itself to college guys as having the "hottest" women. But the app was shut down when attorneys representing a group of users brought a multimillion-dollar class action suit against the app's owners, charging fraud.

"The app's software pushed profiles of real women to the bottom of the pile," she explained. "At the top, where users swiped first, the app was packed with fake profiles of girls in bikinis."

I shook my head in astonishment. "Where

did they get all these photos for profiles?"

"Young women, lots of them. They were happy to be paid flat fees and sign legal releases. So anyway, these bikini photos were programmed to come up first on the app, and if a young man opted to 'chat' with one of the fake profiles, he would be connected to a paid operator at Hookster's offices."

"But how could they get rich from that? Aren't these dating apps free to use?"

"To a point. On Hookster, three free messages to the girl were allowed before the app put up a paywall. So a user would have to pay premium dollars, which he gladly did to stay connected with some babe who said she was hot for him."

"It sounds like one of those old 1-900 phone sex lines."

"Exactly, but posing as a legit dating app. It worked, too. The Hookster creators spun off ancillary products and sold native advertising to sponsors. They became millionaires."

"But, Esther, what happened when one of these young men wanted to meet with the fake girl?"

"That's the beauty of it. Most of them didn't want to meet."

"I don't understand. Isn't that the whole

point of a swipe-to-meet dating game app?"

"You would think so, wouldn't you? But swiping is an end in itself for a lot of users — like looking through a catalog of cool things you might want to buy someday. It's aspirational to look. And then there's the chatting, which fulfills the Skinner box need for affirmation pellets."

"Affirmation of what?"

"That you're attractive, wanted, liked. Some women say they use dating apps daily because they like the attention from random guys — compliments, come-ons. It's a boost to the ego. Some men say they get off on the flirting or sexting. And that interaction, that 'feeling' of romantic connection through app chatting is satisfying."

"You make it sound like a drug."

"It certainly acts like a drug. You get a high that you want to feel again and again — which also makes it addictive. The Hookster app banked on that. They pocketed plenty of dead presidents from users looking for pretend girlfriends."

"And if one of them *insisted* on meeting?"

"Apparently, plenty of meetings were planned but never happened. The girl would always be canceling at the last minute for some reason. Meanwhile, guys could send endless obscene phone shots of their junk,

246

without ever getting into trouble."

Good Lord. "Not exactly Austenland, is it?"

"More like Moby Dicks."

"Or mobile ones . . ." I thought over Esther's story. "Is that why you were so hostile to the Cinder staff? You don't think they're legit?"

"That's not it. Cinder is nothing like Hookster. Sydney's app is creating legit matches. But that doesn't mean they're clean as new snow. I'm sure they're using algorithms to rate users and push up the more 'appealing' ones — in their opinion — and push down the children of lesser Greek gods. That's what really pisses me off: the invisible techno-Darwinism that's going on."

"So you don't trust them?"

"I don't." She pushed up her black-framed glasses. "And I don't think you should, either — or allow them to take over the 'narrative' for our Village Blend."

That comment brought to mind Esther's earlier crack to Sydney about doing "much more" on Saturday night.

"So what's your narrative?" I asked. "What are you planning to spring on the prepaid Cinder crowd?"

"Planning?"

"I mothered a teenage daughter, Esther. Don't waste your clueless puppy-dog eyes on me. I know you're preparing some stunt for tomorrow."

"Stunt?"

Folding my arms, I gave her my super-serious boss stare.

"Okay, okay." Esther put up her hands. "Don't *Deadeye Dick* me . . ."

And with that obscure literary reference, my resident slam poetess explained her own action plan — the Esther Best Op — and her reason for staging it.

I was fine with it. More than fine. I thought her plan was brilliant.

"You have my blessing," I told her. "And you're right. Sydney may be 'taking control of the story.' But this is still our coffee-house."

"Oh, thank you, boss! I just know it won't suck!"

Rising from my chair, I almost laughed. Almost. But the memory of Carol Lynn Kendall's arrest, Haley's cold corpse, and Tucker's resignation kept my chuckles at bay.

Esther gestured to the clutter before us. "I'll bus your sticky-bun-bribery table. You should head downstairs, because we might get a new customer, and Dante is otherwise engaged."

"AJ is still here?"

"She and Dante obviously made a love connection. And they didn't even swipe to meet. Imagine that!"

As I headed for the stairs, I was imagining a few other things, too, mainly questions about Haley's work for Cinder. There were still plenty of missing pieces in this fishy puzzle. Maybe AJ could float a few into place.

FORTY

When I reached the shop's main floor, I found the Village Blend was still a customer-free zone. Dante, God love him, had moved behind our counter, just in case one happened to show up.

AJ was now perched on a barstool across from him. Her pleated skirt fell to the side to reveal long legs, tightly crossed, the one on top bobbing up and down like the handle of an excited water pump.

Their private smiles and flirtatious glances quickly disappeared as I approached.

"Hey, boss, are you finished upstairs?" Dante asked, suddenly all business.

"Done," I told him. Then I faced AJ. "Did Dante help you pack your equipment?"

"He's been a perfect ten —" she said. "I mean gentleman!" Her cheeks blushed rosy. "I mean . . . he's keeping me company while I wait for my Uber car."

"So, AJ," I began, hoping I sounded

casual. "I understand you worked under Haley Hartford. She was your supervisor?"

AJ frowned. "For a while."

"What did you and Sydney mean about not holding grudges? Did Haley leave under some kind of cloud?"

AJ shifted uncomfortably. "I really can't talk about that."

"Can you share anything about Haley's new job?"

"She was developing an app for a start-up fitness company."

I nodded. "The detectives mentioned her new boss was a Mr. Ferrell. But there's something I don't understand . . ." I made a show of scratching my head, doing my best to look innocently perplexed. "Why would Haley quit a full-time position at a successful company like Cinder for an untried business that might fail?"

"Money, that's why!" AJ blurted, her leg pumping faster. "Three weeks ago, Tristan Ferrell instantly doubled Haley's salary and gave her a ten-thousand-dollar signing bonus — in cash."

"Cash? Why?"

"Off the books. No taxes. Haley was helping her little sister through medical school. She was always looking for a way to earn."

"Tristan Ferrell?" Dante murmured.

"Hey, I know that name! Tristan Ferrell is Nancy's other boss."

"Nancy Kelly? *Our* Nancy?"

"That's how she keeps her membership at the Equator fitness club. She couldn't afford it otherwise."

"I thought that foreign exchange student from Dubai bought her a membership."

"A one-month pass," Dante said. "He's already moved on to a new conquest, but Nancy found another way to extend her gift, and make a little cash on the side."

"Well, I hope Tristan Ferrell doesn't steal Nancy from us the way he stole Haley from Cinder." I turned back to AJ. "I wonder . . . was Haley doing that other job on the side before she took it full-time? Was that the source of the tension? Is that why she left?"

The leg was pumping so fast now that I feared AJ was going to lurch off her stool. "There were . . . other issues," she confessed.

Unfortunately, that's all she confessed. An alert on her smartphone ended our conversation.

"Oh! Sorry, gotta go. My car is coming."

As I waited for Dante to help the less-than-talkative Tinkerbell load her equipment into the hired car, I couldn't help wondering about the "other issues," and I made a mental note to find out. Tomorrow night Team Tinkerbell was coming back to the Village Blend. With a little luck, one of them might enjoy gossiping about office politics — or at least have looser lips than AJ.

By the time Dante returned, Esther had joined me behind the counter.

"What?" Dante said, seeing our hopeful stares follow his every step across the shop. "Did I do something wrong?"

"We have an action plan," Esther announced.

"And this involves me?"

I nodded. "You're the best artist on staff."

A grin of pride split his face.

"Don't get all peacocky, Baldini, you're no Leonardo."

"I wouldn't be, would I? Da Vinci is not among my influences."

"Let's hope the 'Code' part is," I said. "Because we need you to decipher your memory of a face, and reconstruct it as a sketch. Esther and I will help . . ."

After I explained our Barista APB idea, Dante said he understood what we wanted, but we would have to decide "which version" of Richard Crest he should draw.

Esther blinked. "What do you mean, which version?"

"There's the one we saw the night Gun Girl confronted him, when he was trying to hide his face. And there's the one I saw last night."

"Last night!" Esther and I cried together.

"At that new gastropub on Bleecker. I saw him swiping through women on his phone. Fifteen minutes later, he was drinking with a giggling NYU undergrad. She was practically in his lap . . ."

I exchanged glances with Esther. She was right. Crest was still swiping. I turned back to Dante.

"You said he looked different?"

"Changed his hair. It was much darker. The top wasn't slicked back anymore. It was shaggy and kind of tousled. The skinny suit was gone, too. He wore jeans and a hoodie. And he had lots of jaw shadow, you know, celebrity stubble."

"Draw both versions of him. Right now."

While Dante went to work in our upstairs lounge (sketching Village Blend *wanted* posters), Esther took over the empty counter, and I went to the basement to roast coffee.

In the heat of our vintage Probat, I stewed.

My staff would soon be ready to ID Richard Crest. And Soles and Bass assured me they'd pick him up when he walked in.

But what if Crest never walked in?

What I needed was something to entice the man back into my coffeehouse. Unfortunately, my expertise was culinary, and this guy wasn't the sort who'd be seduced by sticky buns — not the kind we sold, anyway.

So what would tempt him?

As the light dawned, I pulled out my smartphone. To reel in this catfish, I would need the proper bait. And no one knew more about alluring lures than my ex-husband.

Time to consult the king of hooks — and (pickup) lines.

"Hello, Matt? Can I come over?"

"To my place? Hey, anytime . . ."

FORTY-ONE

"I want you to help me set up a Cinder account. I want you to do it as soon as possible. And I want my profile to attract as many men as possible."

For a frozen moment, my ex-husband stared at me, slack-jawed. Then he howled with laughter. "At last, you've come to your senses! You finally dumped the flatfoot!"

It was nine o'clock in the evening. I was sitting on a couch in the newly built man cave of Matteo Allegro's Brooklyn warehouse, and I wasn't wearing my own clothes.

To cover my top, Matt had lent me an old flannel shirt (with buttons missing in all the wrong places). As for my bottom, it was (barely) covered by a pair of his skimpiest nylon gym shorts.

The wardrobe change hadn't been part of my plan when I'd called the man, hours ago, to arrange this meeting. After leaving Esther on duty at the Village Blend, and receiving no answer from Tucker after five voice mail messages, I climbed into my hired car and rode to Red Hook. The next thing I knew, I was having a near-death experience . . .

It was seven o'clock and the sky was already murky-dark when my Uber car pulled up to Matt's coffee storage facility. Surrounded by eight-foot-high chain-link fencing, the blocky structure sat on the edge of New York Bay.

Fog was rolling in off the water. Its cold dampness seeped through my light jacket, and I shivered under the only visible streetlight. As my low boots clicked along the cracked sidewalk, the lonesome call of a ship's foghorn made the deserted area seem even more desolate.

Next to Matt's warehouse, a burned-out auto garage, which had once been a mafioso chop shop, was now leveled and would soon be the site of the Village Blend's brand-new roasting facility.

The Uber driver had taken off before I had time to punch in the keypad code that would unlock the warehouse's gate. As I began to enter the string of numbers, a flash of light drew my eyes to the street.

Typical of urban residences in residustrial neighborhoods, the old row houses around

Matt's warehouse appeared abandoned. Doors were blocked by iron gates, windows by jailhouse bars.

There was only one vehicle on the block — a wine red SUV parked beside the roastery construction site.

I knew Matt employed a two-man day crew at the warehouse. They helped with things like transporting coffee and supplies, and odds and ends jobs like our shop's laundry. But I didn't recognize the vehicle as one of theirs. I also knew Matt liked to meet with his architect every Friday, and wondered if this was his SUV.

Maybe Matt and the architect are at the site now.

I walked toward the high plywood fence. This blighted area, where Matt had set up shop, was notorious for poor drainage. On the way, a broken sidewalk and massive mud puddle forced me into the street.

That's when I heard it — the SUV's engine turned over, its loud roar shattering the stillness. Then powerful headlights snapped on, blinding me.

Before I could take a step, the SUV lurched forward, fishtailed on the damp pavement, and headed right for me!

I tried to get out of its path, but slipped in the mud instead and, with an ugly splash, landed on my padded posterior. The SUV surged through the puddle's edge, sending a cascade of freezing, filthy water over my head as its wheels missed me by inches!

I cried out, but the SUV kept moving down the block. Then it skidded around the corner and disappeared.

Five minutes later, I was stumbling through Matt's warehouse door.

"Clare, are you okay?!"

My ex-husband's expression went from surprise to concern to barely suppressed laughter, the latter after I reassured him that my muddy, dripping self was perfectly fine — and hopping mad.

"What happened?"

"Ask your architect!"

"What are you talking about? He left hours ago."

"Well, *someone* nearly ran me over, and then just drove off, leaving me like this on the ground!"

Matt took a step backward. "I can see that — *phew* — and smell it."

Between the delayed shock, and the fact that Matt liked to keep his storage facility temperature on the cool side, I began to shiver. My ex quickly wrapped me in his jacket, and guided me up the wooden stairs to his newly built living space.

"Let's get you out of those wet clothes and into a hot shower. I guarantee my new spa heads will sooth your troubles away."

"What about the jerk who nearly killed me?! If he wasn't your architect, what the heck was he doing, lurking there in the dark?"

"Are you sure it was a guy? There's a nice view of the bay between the buildings — the lights are really pretty at night. Sometimes couples park around here to make out. You might have spooked them in the act."

"You really have a one-track mind, don't you? There are no 'pretty lights' out there tonight. The bay is covered in fog! Why don't you make sure that wasn't some burglar, casing your warehouse to rob you? Maybe he thinks there's a safe in here!"

"Take it easy. Geez, Clare, talk about a one-track mind. That flatfoot of yours has you thinking every gomer on the street is a major crimes suspect."

"That's not fair. This *is* New York City. Any man who drives away from the scene of an accident shouldn't be taken lightly."

"Fine." He pushed me into the bathroom. "Calm down, clean up, and I'll check it out."

The bathroom was small and bare-bones

basic, with one of those fiberglass floor-to-ceiling efficiency showers that you'd find in a bargain motel.

I wasn't surprised at the Spartan accommodations. Matt Allegro spent half his life in low-rent hotels, glorified shacks, or even tents — places where air-conditioning and hot running water were not part of the amenities. He learned to live with less and make do with what he had.

That said, on his hunt for exotic coffees, Matt might go days or even weeks without a shower or shave; yet when he returned to New York, he insisted on comfort, even luxury. Take this bathroom. The design may have been utilitarian, but it had plenty of steaming hot water, and no less than three stacked showerheads with eight glorious spa settings — and, yes, I tried them all.

Matt's soaps, shampoos, and scents were top-of-the-line, too. I used a tiny cake shaped like a rose petal (made by Fragonard of Paris, no less) and left the steamy shower feeling clean, refreshed — and nicely perfumed.

In the tiny bathroom, I slipped into the old flannel shirt Matt had hung on the towel rack. He'd done it ten minutes ago, when he'd interrupted my showerhead sampling with a suggestive offer to "wash my back."

I not-so-suggestively told him to "back off."

He did.

He also failed to return with clothing to wear *below* the waist — an innocent oversight, I'm sure.

FORTY-TWO

I crept into Matt's bedroom to dig up something for coverage down under and found him sitting on his king-sized bed with his laptop open.

The screen displayed grainy security footage of the vehicle that almost ran me down. Matt had frozen the image so I could see the driver, a youngish man with a beard, caught in the act of opening the SUV's door.

"So that's the flash I saw? His car's interior lights?"

Matt looked up and I tightened my grip on the towel around my waist.

He smiled — actually, he suppressed a laugh. "You want to borrow a pair of shorts?"

"Please."

"Come here first. Take a look. The SUV that nearly ran you down was parked by my warehouse for almost an hour. The driver got out and disappeared behind his vehicle.

My guess? Nature called. Then he saw you coming toward him and took off."

"Don't you think that's suspicious behavior?"

Matt shrugged. "The roastery construction site is locked tight, and this warehouse has obvious security cameras. I think the guy was just innocently looking around, curious about the area. Maybe he wants to build here . . ."

As Matt went on, I stared hard at the screen and realized I recognized this man. The photo was grainy and black-and-white, so I couldn't tell the color of his beard, but I was sure that facial fur would be dark red — just like the man's SUV.

"I've seen that bearded man in our coffeehouse!"

Matt looked closer. "Yeah, he does look familiar. I think I've seen him in the Village, too."

"So what's he doing parked for an hour in front of your Brooklyn warehouse?"

"Could be a coincidence."

"I spooked the guy, Matt, so much so that he fishtailed to get out of here and nearly killed me — without slowing down to find out if he did. That doesn't sound innocent."

"No, it doesn't . . ." Matt moved through the footage again. "I can't make out his vehicle's license number. But I see the warehouse camera did get a nice shot of you landing on your beautiful round behind. Would you like to see?"

"I'll pass."

"Look, I'll share the footage with the local precinct, but that's about all I can do — other than confront the guy if I see him again."

I considered the possibilities. "Do you think he could be a private investigator?"

"What would he be investigating?"

"You."

"Me?!"

"Yes. Using dating apps to cheat is not uncommon in the swipe-to-meet world — you agreed to that fact three days ago."

"I'm not married anymore!"

"No, genius, but one of your conquests might be."

"I don't sleep with married women, Clare. It's asking for trouble. And before you say it — *yes,* I can spot when a woman is married and posing as single."

"Really? You have mind-reading vision, do you?"

"End of discussion." Matt closed the laptop. Then he handed over a skimpy pair of nylon gym shorts. "Best I can do."

"And here I thought you'd forgotten."

Matt looked me up and down. "I figured you didn't really need them. That shirt is long enough to cover your sweet parts, yet it's the perfect length to show off your legs. It also looks better on you than it ever looked on me."

I rolled my eyes. My ex-husband was the only man I knew who could find sexual overtones in an old flannel shirt.

"Can I get dressed now?"

"When you're done, join me in the kitchen. We'll have a bite to eat before we sample the new coffee."

"New coffee?"

"Isn't that why you're here? To try the East Timor cherries I sourced on Mount Ramelau?"

"Uh, sure," I replied. "But I also need your help with something else. Something important . . ." (I neglected to mention this "help" I needed involved setting a trap for a murder suspect.)

"You can talk to me about it in the kitchen," Matt said over his shoulder. "Dinner's almost ready."

FORTY-THREE

Though he'd left to give me privacy, the bedroom didn't feel very private. Matt's living space was nothing more than partitioned-off areas of a long, high loft — a simple wooden platform, really, built fifteen feet below the warehouse roof.

Each "room" had three walls. Where the fourth wall should have been was a railed open space that framed a view of the sealed, temperature-controlled coffee bean storage facility one floor below.

The loft didn't have a proper kitchen — just another partitioned section of the high platform, with a sink, a refrigerator, a hot plate, and a few small appliances. There was a storage cart with a butcher's block top, and a table barely big enough for two.

From the creamy-spicy-smoky scents wafting through the building, I knew Matt was cooking up something spectacular.

He was stirring a thick pink sauce with his

shirtsleeves rolled up when I arrived. Only then did I realize he'd changed his look. His shaggy dark hair was cropped, and his beard trimmed to a shadow of its former self.

"Heat up the tortillas," he commanded.

Matt had a million kitchen hacks he'd learned on the road — crazy, even goofy cooking techniques. He could make poached eggs in a drip coffeemaker, for instance, as well as ramen noodles, instant oatmeal, and broccoli (not all at once, of course). I'd seen him make crispy hash browns in a waffle iron; cook up a grilled cheese sandwich with aluminum foil and a clothing iron; toast bagels on a coffee burner; and cook a small steak sous vide-style with a bucket of boiling water and a sealed plastic bag. In a pinch, Matt could even use a simple French press to froth warm milk for a latte.

Remembering his favorite way to warm flour tortillas — even in a conventional kitchen — I cut four of the small circles in half. After folding them into foil, I plopped them into his wide-slot toaster, setting the time long enough for the inside of the packet to steam. As long as the foil stayed sealed, I could move the tortillas to the table and they'd keep perfectly warm until we were ready to nosh them.

"So, what's on the menu?"

"Barbecued chicken with creamy chipotle sauce."

"That's some 'bite to eat.' "

I glanced around the improvised kitchen. "How the heck did you barbecue chicken, Matt? You don't have an oven, and I didn't see a grill in the parking lot."

"I have a tent set up on the roof, with two charcoal grills, a wine cooler, folding chairs, and blankets. You should see it, there's a spectacular view of the bay."

I double-checked the man's trim waist and firm tush. "Obviously, you don't cook like this every night."

"Actually, this was supposed to be dinner for two. Marilyn and I had a date for eight, but she bailed on me — working late. So you're in luck!"

"Are you talking about that Millennial Marilyn Monroe you matched with on Cinder?"

"Is that what you call her?" Matt thought it over. "Yeah, I guess that platinum blonde thing is Monroe inspired — and her name really is Marilyn. Marilyn Hahn."

"This was supposed to be your second date?"

"Third."

"Wow. On Cinder that's like a long-term relationship."

"Ha-ha," he said. "Anyway, it's not like that."

"What's it like, then?"

"Why do you want to know? I thought you didn't care for the swipe-to-meet scene. You've made your disdain pretty clear."

"Not disdain, Matt. *Distrust.* Have you ever heard of Hookster?"

He snorted. "You're kidding, right?"

"No. Esther just told me about it."

He waved his hand. "I dumped that thing after I read the terms of service agreement."

"You actually read those?"

"I do. And the Hookster fine print, which went on forever, included the 'understanding' that the app was a form of interactive entertainment and employees of Hookster would be compensated for conversations on the app."

"So the users were warned it was a fake?"

"They were."

"I'm surprised you remembered all that."

"The *Wall Street Journal* just refreshed my memory last week with their coverage."

"Coverage of what?"

"The results of the Hookster civil litigation. The trial finally ended."

"Did they win or lose?"

"Both. The jury sided with the users, believing Hookster employed deceptive business practices."

"So Hookster's owners did lose?"

"Not entirely. The jury found the users were at fault, too, for not reading the terms of service. So there were no punitive damages awarded. But Hookster does have to give back all the monthly premium payments they collected."

"Then they're finished."

"They are — although, given the app's ancillary earnings, the owners might be able to retain a few million or so."

"Pretty nice payday for dealing out dating app addictions."

"There's that disdain again."

I took a breath — and let it out. "Believe it or not, Matt, I honestly am interested in learning more about swipe-right dating. I need to know, actually . . ."

"Fine," Matt said with a shrug. "Let's have dinner first. I'm starving. Over coffee, you can tell me why you're suddenly so interested in something you detest so much — and while you're at it, you can give me a clue how I'm supposed to help you with some mysterious 'important' thing."

"They're actually the same thing."

"What does that mean?"

"I think the answer will go down better when you're stomach's full. Let's eat."

FORTY-FOUR

I rolled the warm tortilla in the creamy pink sauce and captured the last morsels of juicy chicken between its folds.

The medley of flavors tangoed on my tongue — from the charcoal-grilled meat to the smoky goodness of the brick red chipotle peppers, their mild heat beautifully balanced in the rich cream sauce.

Matt once told me he'd created this recipe to punch up the blandness of plain cooked chicken. Lacking a stove, he took the recipe to a lip-smacking new level.

My plate wiped clean, I pushed away from the table, sated. "That was spectacular. I couldn't eat another bite."

"Good, because all I have for dessert is chilled champagne."

"I'd better not."

Ten minutes later, the French press was primed, and we moved along the loft floor to the sectioned-off space that served as

Matt's living room. A typical man cave, it included a leather couch, easy chairs, a big-screen TV, and a high-end sound system. It simply didn't have a fourth wall.

Soon the aroma of fresh-brewed coffee filled the air and wafted across the railing that overlooked the cavernous warehouse. That's when I realized this makeshift shotgun apartment was the perfect habitat for a peripatetic coffee hunter who balked at the very idea (literal or romantic) of being boxed in.

"I roasted the sample a little too dark," he said, filling my mug. "But you can experiment. I'll give you a package to take with you, so you can officially 'cup' it when you have time. Tonight I just want you to enjoy it . . ."

We clinked our mugs. Then I closed my eyes, took a sip, and immediately knew Matt's latest find would pay off, especially with our restaurant and hotel clients.

The East Timor coffee was richly layered — earthy and herbal with charming cocoa undertones, and the mouthfeel was extraordinary. "Even dark, these beans retain an exciting effervescence, yet the finish is nearly as creamy as your chipotle chicken."

Grinning with coffee sourcing *and* culinary pride, Matt made a promise. "Next time I'll grill steaks for you, with Brandy Mushroom Gravy."

The description almost made me hungry again, but gluttony could be a punishment in itself. So I curled up on the couch, content with my personal digestive philosophy: enjoy one meal at a time.

With my legs in Matt's too-short shorts feeling uncomfortably naked, I looked around for cover — and found it in his *ruana,* a wool poncho from the Colombian Andes. The region was famous for not only fine coffee, but also the criminal gangs who grew coca leaves to make cocaine. (Given Matt's past, I continued to pray I'd never find any of the latter in this warehouse again.)

More of Matt's exotic treasures were displayed on the exposed brick wall. I recognized most of them. A piece of artwork made from thousands of lacquered Kona beans and laced with pearly seashells was a gift from Matt's good friends, the Waipunas, a coffee-farming family in Hawaii. A traditional Ethiopian *gabi,* its edges expertly embroidered in blue and green threads (the blue signifying peace and progress; the green representing the rich fertility of the land), hung protected behind glass. A co-operative of African farmers had presented the handwoven garment in gratitude for Matt's help financing a badly needed irrigation system.

Then I noticed something new. "When did you get that crocodile tapestry? It's gorgeous."

"It's a *tais* from my last trip to Southeast Asia," Matt said. "See the design? It's supposed to depict a classic legend of the country. Once a boy did a good deed for a crocodile, and the animal thanked him by transforming into a beautiful island that the boy could live on, along with all his future generations — the island of Timor-Leste."

He shook his head. "Unfortunately, the croc I ran into was not so friendly. I had to save a little kid from becoming his lunch."

"Oh, my God, is the child all right?"

"He's fine. I was snorkeling in Dili when it happened. All I did was get the croc to chase me instead of the boy. Then I screamed like a little girl and climbed a tree. I nearly lost a leg; but, hey, I saved the kid — and got a pretty cool wall hanging out of it, right?"

He grinned as he refreshed our mugs. Then he leaned back, content in his La-Z-Boy. "So you liked my chicken and loved my new beans. Now are you ready to tell me the 'something important' you need my help with?"

Like a novice diver, I took an extra-deep breath and said it —

"I want you to help me set up a Cinder account. I want you to do it as soon as possible. And I want my profile to attract as many men as possible."

Matt's howling laughter (after his frozen shock) echoed through the warehouse. "At last, you've come to your senses! You finally dumped the flatfoot!"

I set him straight. "Mike and I are still very much engaged and very much in love."

My ex scratched his dark beard. "So if you're still feeling all warm and fuzzy about Detective Drugstore Cologne, why do you want a Cinder profile?"

I brought Matt up to speed on our murdered customer; Sydney and her Tinker-bells; Tuck quitting; and the fact that the Crusher, with the fake name Richard Crest, appeared to be responsible for all of it — including crushing our shop business.

Then I laid out my plan to reel in the creep with a provocative Cinder profile, and explained why I had to attract as many Fellas as possible — because I didn't know what new identity the former Richard Crest would be using.

"Matt, you and I both know there's something very wrong with this guy. He's got to be stopped."

My ex-husband's reaction was predictable.

"You're crazy, Clare, and so is your plan. Crazy and dangerous."

"No, it's not. All I want to do is lure him to our coffeehouse and keep him there long enough for Soles and Bass to take him in. The Village Blend is a public place. I'll be perfectly safe."

Matt shook his head. "That's what Tucker thought. Then he and his friend Carol Lynn found out different, didn't they?"

I could see Matt was moving into guardian mode, a trait that emerged after our daughter was born. But it hadn't stopped there. His recent run-in with a crocodile to save a young child was classic Matt. Unfortunately, this mule-stubborn protective streak had a downside, too — his longtime feud with Joy's boyfriend, for instance. Once my ex was locked in, arguing was useless.

To win on this, I would have to change tactics.

"Okay, then," I said with a shrug. "I guess we're done."

"You're giving up?"

"If you aren't confident you can help me —"

"Huh?"

"I understand creating a winning Cinder profile is a tricky endeavor. Don't feel bad about not knowing how."

Matt laughed. "Oh, please. That is not the problem."

"I probably should consult with someone younger. Hipper. Dante maybe?"

"Dante?! I know more than that kid about creating a winning profile!"

"Maybe you can do it for yourself, but I doubt you can do it for me."

"You don't know how wrong you are."

"Really? Why is that?"

"Because, according to PopCravings.com, I'm a certified expert. In fact, you're looking at their newest in-house *sexpert.*"

"Excuse me?"

"I've been hired by Pop Cravings as a freelance contributor to their Digital Libido and Sexpert Advice sections, read by millions of app daters all over the world."

I blinked. (It took a minute for that to sink in.)

"I told you before," Matt went on. "Marilyn and I aren't really dating. Well, we are dating, but hot sex is not the reason we're hanging out together. Okay, not the *only* reason . . ."

"What's Marilyn got to do with your new

sexpert status?"

"She's a content editor for PopCravings
.com. Turns out I impressed her enough on
our first date that our second was really an
audition. She liked my ideas for articles;
thought my sample answers to advice column questions were clever; and tonight she
wants me to meet Pop Cravings' executive
editor at a midnight event in Williamsburg
—"

"I thought you said this job was a done
deal."

"It is. She's hired me already."

"And you have time for this?"

"Oh, please. I've got tons of downtime in
airports. Writing for the web will be a
pleasure. Not to mention easy money."

"Okay. Then prove to me you're a sexpert
by creating my winning profile."

Matt folded his arms. "To attract a confirmed sadist, misogynist, and possible
murderer? And you call *me* reckless."

"Think of it as another audition. Who
knows? You may get a feature article for Pop
Cravings out of it."

"Fine," Matt said. "But only if I'm part of
your sting. When you meet up with this guy,
I insist on being in the same room — preferably armed with a scalding pot of coffee,
aimed at his lap."

"It's a deal. Now let's get to work, before your new boss sweeps you away to that midnight party."

FORTY-FIVE

Matt cracked his knuckles. "We'll start with the basics by looking at the perfect Cinder profile. That would be my own."

Settling down on the couch beside me, he pulled out his smartphone. "I tap the app and —"

I frowned. "An advertisement?"

"An offer. I'm a premium member of Cinder, so I have a Treasure Chest."

"A what?"

Matt explained that basic Cinder use was free. But premium members, who loaded "Cinder dollars" into their "Treasure Chests," got perks — special deals on dining, clothing, event tickets, bars, and clubs.

Because you could "allow" Cinder to access your social network accounts, the marketing was very target specific, and very effective.

"I get it, one-stop shopping — and a lucrative ancillary business for CEO Sydney. Now can we please create my Cinderella profile?"

He asked for my phone. I unlocked it, handed it over, and he downloaded the Cinder app.

"You're using a fake name, I assume?"

"I can get away with that?"

"As long as it's a free account. Once you go premium, you'll need to use a credit card. And if you want to attract a lot of men, you'll want a premium membership. It's like paid placement in a retail store. You'll get better exposure."

That made me pause. "Do you think Richard Crest had a premium account?"

"To get as much action as he did, I'd say so."

My heart beat faster. "Then Cinder's administrators know his real name, his real identity! Not to mention his billing address!"

Matt doused my excitement with three words — prepaid credit card.

"There are plenty of ways to pay online without revealing your identity. The prepaid credit card is only one."

"Are they hard to get?"

"You can buy them at almost any drug or grocery store."

"Then a fake online identity isn't difficult

to create."

"Not if you're motivated. There's even an Internet rumor that guys set up fake female Cinder accounts so they can read the comments their dates make about them."

"I'll keep my gender, thank you, but I do want a false name. I always thought Rafaela was pretty."

Matt rolled his eyes. "Who can pronounce that? You want to use something simple, but not mundane. Exotic, but not silly."

"What if my name really *was* Rafaela?"

"Here. Look —" He pulled out his own phone, activated the Cinder app, and showed me a screenshot of a woman straining to look natural in an obviously posed shot.

"Her name is Bernadette. Now, she knew enough to shorten her moniker for her profile, but she should have used more imagination."

"Why?"

"Because no straight man wants to cry out, 'Yes, Bernie, yes, Bernie,' in that most intimate of moments."

I buried my face in my hands. "I give up. You win."

We finally settled on Kara C. The C was because the app didn't display last names, unless you specifically chose to use one, which I didn't. As for social media platforms, I told Matt to connect Kara C.'s profile to our Village Blend accounts. Later tonight, I'd simply add "Kara" to our barista staff list.

"Okay, Clare, now you have to mention your interests and likes. Are you fun-loving? Do you like long walks in the park?"

"Only when they lead me to forensic evidence."

"Excuse me?"

"Forget it," I said. "Likes . . . let's see. I like coffee. Art. And the art of cooking. Live music. Theater. River walks. Sunsets. Swimming. Roses. Cats. New York history. I like trying new restaurants —"

"Good, all good."

"I also like eating . . . almost everything. Pasta. Pastries. Candy —"

Matt groaned. "Stay away from liking 'candy.' It's code for drugs."

"Drugs? You mean like Styx? Is that why it was made to look like candy?"

"Styx?" Matt's brow furrowed. "That's one I haven't heard of. What the hell is Styx?"

I told Matt everything I knew about the new party drug — courtesy of Mike Quinn and his OD Squad. How it came in powder form and was packaged like the old Pixy

Stix in colorful, straw-shaped wrappers . . .

"So please be careful, okay? I still worry."

"Clare, I'm never going to touch drugs again. And I stay away from people who use them, especially women."

"You do drink."

"Not to excess, and never on the road. Believe me, alcohol I can handle. Drugs and I are finished. You can trust me on this."

"Easier said than done."

"Oh, it's done. *A fully grown tree cannot be bent into a walking stick.*"

"What's that supposed to mean?"

"It's a Kenyan proverb. Basically, it means strength and wisdom come with maturity."

"So you're saying you're mature?"

"Hey, I may not be the Dudley Do-Right your flatfoot fiancé is, but I'm not a stupid kid anymore, either . . ."

Matt studied my still-worried face.

"Listen, I became a husband and father before I knew what it meant to be either. At this age, I know what I lost. But I also know what I still have. I'm not going to risk my life; or screw up my business; or hurt you and Joy and Mother. Not ever again."

That I did believe. "So who told you that proverb?"

"The smartest man I know — a truck driver in Kenya."

"Did he teach you anything else?"

"Yeah, that *a donkey's thanks is a kick.*"

"I don't get it."

"You should. You're doing a good deed trying to catch this psycho, but you're likely to get kicked in the process."

"You know what? I can take it — along with my so-called 'round behind.'"

"Your beautiful round behind."

"Hey, we could put that in my profile."

"The description or the photo?" Matt rubbed his beard. "We could do both."

"For heaven's sake, I was kidding! Let's get back to work . . ."

With a shrug, Matt turned back to his Cinder app and began swiping left through random women. In the interest of creating the "perfect profile" for me, he stopped every so often to make a comment.

Pearls of wisdom followed. They were made of paste, but they had their uses just the same. I only remembered a few . . .

"This girl is frowning. That's a red flag. If she's not smiling on her profile picture, she never will.

"This one posed in front of her framed diplomas. She'll probably keep reminding you that you're no rocket scientist.

"This one likes 'harness racing.' Sorry, darling, but I couldn't get into *Fifty Shades of Grey.*

"She loves children. That's code for 'I'm not looking to hook up with a guy. I'm looking to *hook* a guy.'

"Oh, my. Tiffany says she's a waitress, but all her pictures have her in expensive Prada lingerie. Tiffany is a prostitute.

"This one loves to go to the ball." Matt paused. "Wow. She has a nice smile."

"The ball?"

"Yeah, give me a second, will you? I need to swipe right."

FORTY-SIX

"Almost finished," Matt said fifteen minutes later. "All you have to do is enter your credit card information, add a few pictures, and you're official."

I entered my real credit card number with my real name. The app didn't seem to mind that it didn't match my profile. Sparkles appeared on the screen, and my smartphone suddenly played a royal fanfare, the welcome greeting for a newly minted Cinderella.

"You are now officially Kara C.," Matt announced.

"In Cinder-land, anyway. Would you send me a list of other dating apps you think a guy like Crest might use? I'll set up more Kara C. profiles after I leave tonight."

"Sure. But what are you going to use for pictures?"

"I was thinking we could use those old photos you took of me in Hawaii . . ." Matt once brought me along on a sourcing trip for Kona, and we made a romantic vacation out of it. "Do you still have the pictures?"

"The sexy bikini shots?" He nodded. "I still have them. But why those? I thought you were embarrassed by them."

"I was, but Richard Crest has a thing for bikinis. Did you ever digitize the photos? Or do we have to dig them up and scan them in your office downstairs?"

Matt brought his laptop to the coffee table, sat beside me on the couch, and tapped a few keys. I was surprised how fast he found the photos. He knew exactly what folder to look in. He didn't even have to search.

On-screen, a slide show appeared with a dozen shots of me in a skimpy string bikini, taken over two decades ago on the beach in Maui. Together we silently watched the images appear and disappear, like bittersweet ghosts.

"I remember that first sunset," I said with a pang. "We were alone on a secluded beach with chilled champagne, and that succulent pineapple pork."

"I remember what happened after dinner. It was pretty memorable, too."

"Yeah, it was . . ." I swallowed hard. "You know, I can't believe you talked me into wearing that string thing. I always wore one-piece bathing suits —"

"Until you met me."

"You were always a bad influence."

"And you loved every minute of it."

"No, Matt. Not *every* minute."

"You look pretty happy in these pictures."

"I can't believe how young I was —"

"And hot."

"I'm a different person now, in so many ways. I'll never be that young again."

"Maybe not . . ." He smiled. "But you will always be hot."

Matt's hand moved to my thigh. I gently removed it.

"I appreciate the compliment. I do. But there's only one man I want to think of me as 'hot' now."

Matt sat back. "So why aren't you married to him yet?"

"We'll be tying the knot soon. I'm still looking for the right venue."

"I don't get why you don't just go down to the courthouse. The groom is a cop. He should feel right at home among prison guards and perps heading off to trial."

"Mike Quinn is beloved in the NYPD. His entire precinct wants to attend our wedding. He's got a big Irish family, too, and with his work downtown, half of 1PP will expect invitations."

"Then why not choose someplace really spectacular and be done with it?"

"Sticker shock. You would not believe the prices."

Matt snapped his fingers. "You know what? One Police Plaza is lovely in June. You could hang flowers from the guardhouse at the gate, and drape white silk over the bulletproof glass."

"Ha-ha."

"Seriously. What are you looking for?"

"Seriously?"

"Yes, all kidding aside. I promise."

"Mike and I talked about a place overlooking the Hudson River with an afternoon wedding and reception, so we can enjoy the sun setting over the water. But it's too much money. We have to think more practically."

"Well, that's something you've always been good at, Clare — and I mean that as a compliment. You'll find a way . . ."

Matt's gaze drifted back to the never-ending slide show, now displaying a full-body shot.

"Wow." He paused it. "Look at you."

"It's perfect!" I cried. "I'm using this one for the Cinder profile."

Matt agreed. "If that doesn't attract the guy, introduce him to Tucker."

I took a closer look at the photo. "You know, I haven't seen photos of me this young in years. It's uncanny how much I resemble Joy."

"What? No way . . ." Matt leaned in. "Oh, God, you're right." He threw up his hands. "Why did you have to bring up our daughter? Now you ruined it for me!"

"Speaking of Joy, I should text her about your new beans. If all goes well with my sample roasting, I should have a shipment ready for next Saturday's delivery to our DC shop . . ."

While I texted Joy in Washington, Matt sent me the slide show of photos. Then he went to the kitchen to press us more of that superb East Timor. As he returned with two steaming mugs, Joy replied to my text. But it wasn't about single-origin coffee.

Can we talk later tonight?

"Something's wrong," I murmured.

"What?! What's wrong?" Matt's protective mode was back.

I showed him the phone screen.

"She wants to talk?" He nodded tensely. "What else does she say?"

"Nothing. She doesn't have to. I can tell something's wrong from this."

"Five words? Your daughter wants to talk to you, Clare. Maybe it's *good* news."

"It's not. I can tell. A mother knows."

"Well, let *me* know if I can help, okay?"

"Okay."

"And it better not be a problem with that mook cop or I'll turn his shaved head into a boccie ball."

"You'll do no such thing. Really, Matt, it's time you got on board with Emmanuel Franco. He's a good man. Loving, loyal — he would never cheat on Joy."

Matt grunted. "He's no saint. I'm sure of it. And she could do better."

"She could do worse, and you know it —" I tapped the burning heart on my phone and waved the match game at him. "Without Franco in her life, a date from hell could be in our daughter's future. Think about that!"

Before Matt could mutter a reply, a loud buzz echoed through the loft.

"Marilyn is here. I'm going downstairs to let her in."

While he was gone, I uploaded my bikini photos, and — speaking of dates from hell — wondered if there was a direct way of connecting to Richard Crest. I noticed Cinder-ellas were provided with a name search. So I typed in his full fake name to see what came up.

A moment later, Crest's profile filled the screen, but with a big red INACTIVE bar across it and some fine print: *Under review for violation of terms of service.*

The pictures were just as the Fish Squad described. I found the heart-shaped button that led to user comments about this "Fella." I would have loved to read them, but that button had been deactivated, too.

I stared at the screen, trying to pick out Richard Crest from the crowd around him. I found the beach bum photo and enlarged it.

"You'll want to stay away from that SOB if you know what's good for you . . ."

Though deep and throaty, the voice belonged to a woman — Marilyn Hahn. She greeted me warmly. "You're Clare, right? Matt's ex-wife?"

"And current business partner." I rose and shook her hand.

"Matt's told me all about you," she said. Her platinum blonde hair was still retro-styled in sleek waves, but the young woman had ditched the cat glasses, her large eyes enhanced by Prussian blue eye shadow. Her full, glossy lips frowned as she pointed at the screen. "Take my advice, steer clear of him."

"You know this guy?"

"Dick Crest?" she spat. "Yeah, I know him. He's a —" The expletives that followed were more suited to a burly sailor than a young professional in a strapless Ferragamo dress.

In the interest of hearing more from her (other than four-letter words), I hedged: "Matt did already warn me that some men would be sexually aggressive in their messages, even send obscene photos —"

"Not this guy. And that's why you have to be careful. Richard Crest will *act* like a perfect gentleman. He'll listen to you talk, because nice guys listen, right? He'll take you somewhere really nice to impress you with his money. He'll act reluctant to suggest a first-date sleepover, insisting he respects you too much for that. And by the end of the evening, you'll melt into his gentle postfeminist arms because you can't help yourself . . ."

She shook her platinum locks. "Yeah, it's all a dream until he gets into your panties. After that, it's a nightmare. Sleep with that guy, and next morning you're no better than the dirt under his Fendi penny loafers."

"Did you know that a woman pulled a gun on Crest?"

Marilyn's eyebrows rose. "Did she kill

him?"

"The pistol only had blanks."

"Too bad," she said.

I lowered my voice. "What did he do to you, exactly? It must have been bad."

A shadow crossed her pretty face. "It was," she rasped. "Very bad."

Before she could say anything more, Matt came around the corner with chilled champagne and three glasses. "Great," he said. "You've met."

My ex-husband's timing could not have been worse. Marilyn instantly changed her demeanor, plastering on a sunny smile for Matt. I gently tried to resume our conversation, but she refused to talk any more about her experience with Crest in front of her current Cinder-fella.

"Let's toast to an amazing evening!" she insisted instead.

I declined the champagne. After some small talk, I could tell three was a crowd. So I ordered a car, borrowed Matt's London Fog trench coat, and left the fired-up Cinder matches to their midnight party plans.

Forty-Seven

On my ride back to Manhattan that night, I officially joined the ranks of New York's smartphone zombies. Door to door, my gaze never left the mobile screen.

First, I replied to my daughter's text, telling her to call me anytime.

Next, I checked for any reply from Tucker to my many messages, pleading with him to reconsider his resignation, found nothing, and feared my beloved assistant manager was (in the parlance of the digital domain) "ghosting" me!

With a sigh, I scanned a new note from Matt:

Told Marilyn about your mission 2 find & unmask Crest. She is all 4 it. Suggested 3 more dating apps 4 U . . .

I downloaded the new swipe-to-mate apps and set up "Kara" profiles on all of them.

Then I returned to Cinder to get comfortable with its glittery bells and whistles.

By the time my car pulled up to the Village Blend, I was feeling confident about my first steps into this sparkly new digital dating world. Then I pushed the door open to the depressing state of my real one.

As the welcome bell echoed through my near-desolate shop, I took in the sad customer count. Three NYU students sat by our wall of French doors, and an older couple faced the fireplace — a far cry from the packed house we usually had on Friday nights.

At least we've got a plan, I thought. *Two, actually, if you count Esther's scheme. After tomorrow, if things don't turn around, I'll try something else — because, I swear, if our Village Blend goes down, it's going down swinging . . .*

As for tonight, Esther was still behind the counter, so bored she was reading a book of poetry to pass the time. When I took a seat at the empty espresso bar, she set it aside.

"Hey, boss lady! Take off that trench coat and stay awhile."

"I can't take it off. I'm practically naked under this thing. I had to borrow it from Matt —" When Esther's eyes widened behind her glasses, I realized what that sounded like. "No! It's not what you think . . ."

After my story of a near-death experience with an SUV the color of a young cabernet, Esther shared her own news.

"Our Barista APB is activated! Dante's sketches are now on the phones of everyone on staff. And I hung his originals in the pantry. That goof is so proud of them, he even signed them."

"Dante's no goof when it comes to art, Esther. He's very talented. Those sketches might be worth a pretty penny one day."

As Esther rolled her eyes and cracked wise about "Baldini's Rogues' Gallery," I considered giving Dante another assignment — drawing that man with the red beard who nearly ran me over. But I quickly talked myself out of it.

What if Red Beard actually turned out to be a PI, sent to catch Matt *in flagrante* with a married woman? The public revelation would be beyond embarrassing. No, my plate was full enough, and Matt said he would handle it.

"So what's our next step?" Esther asked.

"I start the manhunt by swiping right on the most likely suspects. I plan to invite them to 'ask for Kara' at our shop tomorrow night —"

"Tomorrow? But that's our big event night."

"Exactly. With a large crowd here, Crest will feel comfortable, believing he can blend in. He won't know our entire staff will be on the lookout for him."

"Smart," Esther said with tiny applause. "This is going to be fun. Can I help you swipe through suspects?"

"I was counting on it."

"Stimulation first!" she declared. "An espresso?"

"For plowing through peacocks? I'm going to need something *much* stronger. Make it a Shot in the Dark."

While Esther got busy dropping a shot of espresso into a black pool of high-octane brew, my finger got busy swiping on one of Marilyn's recommended apps.

Eesh. Talk about a rogues' gallery!

I paged through the profiles with hope, but out of the whole muscle-flexing, back-packing, dog-smooching, naked saxophone-playing bunch, not one had Crest's MO.

Suddenly, in the midst of my swiping, a sound distracted me, the full-bodied alto of a mature woman's laughter.

Madame?

Turning in my seat, I took a longer look at that older couple facing the fireplace.

301

When I'd hurried in, I barely noticed the violet beret and matching jacket of the female in the pair. Now I realized the hat was sitting at a jaunty angle on a familiar silver pageboy.

But if the woman was Matt's mother, who the heck was the lanky, mocha-skinned gentleman giving her the giggles?

Must be another "Silver Fox" date, I assumed, admiring the man's jet-black hair and distinguished gray temples. But I was wrong. In mild shock, I suddenly recognized Madame's sixty-something companion —

"Sergeant Jones?!"

At my cry of surprise, the older couple turned in their chairs. It was Madame, all right, getting cozy with Leonidas Jabari Jones of the NYPD Harbor Patrol.

"Clare!" she exclaimed. "I didn't notice you arrive. My goodness, dear, whatever are you wearing?"

FORTY-EIGHT

Gathering my barely clothed dignity, I tightened the belt on Matt's oversize London Fog and made my way over to the couple's table. The sergeant gallantly rose.

"Good evening, Ms. Cosi."

Though he was out of uniform, the man's spine was still flagpole straight, his legs braced as if our floor's wood planks were a boat deck. His shoulders were squared under his tweed jacket, and the black eye patch was still in place. But the hard-nosed cop face was gone, replaced by an easy grin.

"As I was telling your charming employer — after I stopped by the other day to try your delicious coffee, I realized I'd been here before. Many years ago —"

"Lee and I are practically old friends," Madame said, her violet gaze glistening in the firelight.

As I sat down with the pair, Esther brought my Shot in the Dark, and Madame asked her to brew something exceptional for "Lee and our special reunion." Esther quickly returned with her order — a French press primed with our most sought-after (and insanely expensive) coffee, one we kept in rare reserve.

While the coarsely ground Billionaire blend beans were steeping in filtered hot water, Madame urged Sergeant Jones to tell me and Esther the story of how they first met.

"I'm sure these young ladies don't want to hear me reminisce —"

"Don't be silly!" Madame jabbed him playfully with her elbow. "It's historic. They'll love it."

"If you say so, darlin'," Jones said with a wink of his good eye. "It was decades ago, a lifetime, really. I was no more than a punk-ass kid running wild in the Village with my friends. Suddenly, I see my idol, Jimi Hendrix, entering this very coffeehouse. I burst through the door, ready to charge right up to him."

"But I stopped him," Madame said. "Jimi dropped in every so often, and sometimes even played upstairs. Onstage he was riveting, a genius musician, but offstage he was fragile and shy. Encounters with his fans often ended badly, so I tried to be protective of his privacy."

Madame patted Lee's arm. "But I couldn't bear to disappoint this handsome young man. So when I served Jimi's coffee and pastry, I quietly introduced him to one of his youngest fans."

"That *is* historic!" Esther cried as she pressed and served the Billionaire blend. "What did the greatest rock guitarist in history say?"

"You mean after I greeted him with something incredibly stupid?" Jones replied.

"It couldn't have been that bad," I said.

"I told Jimi that I wanted to play guitar *just like him*. Oh, man. He set me straight. 'Kid,' he told me. 'I've been imitated so many times I've heard people copy my *mistakes*.' Then Jimi told me I should live my own damn life and make my own damn mistakes. That's the only way I would find my own song. I didn't understand what he meant. I was too young to know how valuable those words would be."

Jones paused. "Not long after that, Jimi died of an overdose. Jump ahead in time, and I've got no job, no future, taking every drug I can lay my hands on. One day I overdose. While I'm recovering in the hospital, I hear 'All Along the Watchtower' on the radio. That's when I understood what Jimi was trying to tell me, and I knew if I didn't change my life, I'd end up imitating the worst mistake of his . . ."

The sergeant went on to tell us about his favorite uncle, an ex-navy man, who visited him during recovery and encouraged him to join the service.

"He warned me to get away from the music scene and all the drugs or I'd start using again. And if I died, he'd never forgive me, because it would kill my mother — his only sister. I knew my uncle was right. I was broke and broken. So I held my breath and jumped into a new world."

"That's a big change," I said. "Didn't you have trouble adapting?"

"Plenty, at first, but . . . I liked the camaraderie of the navy, the traveling, the ocean at night. I liked the structure of knowing what I had to do each day and what was expected of me. I kept playing music, too, formed a little band on the ship. I'll tell you, no one was more surprised than I was, but I stayed clean on the water."

"Only you're not in the navy now," Esther pointed out.

He laughed. "Blame it on Fleet Week. I fell for a wonderful woman here in New York, and we started a family. That's when I left the service, to be closer to them. It was my late wife's father who helped me get into the NYPD and then the Harbor Unit, and there you go — that's my song. So far, anyway. I'll be forced to retire soon, and I'm sad to say that part of my life will be over . . ."

While Lee Jones turned his attention back to Madame and sampling our Billionaire blend, I exchanged glances with Esther. I could tell she was still bubbling with excitement about the Hendrix connection to our coffeehouse.

Though I was never a big fan of his music, I knew Hendrix had a passionate following, which gave me an idea. I'd have to research it upstairs in the attic, where we kept the old photos and memorabilia that Madame had amassed over the decades. But if it worked out, the Village Blend might benefit.

There was another part of the sergeant's story that impressed me even more than the Hendrix meeting. And that was the grit he showed in overcoming his addiction.

Now, as Sergeant Jones raved to us about our "Billionaire" beverage, I couldn't help considering the coffee hunter who'd made the cup possible. Like Jones, my ex-husband had kicked his drug habit. Unlike the sergeant, however, he hadn't changed much else in his life.

Matt was still hooked on the partying that led to his downfall in the first place. Despite all his assurances, I'd never stop worrying that in a weak moment, with the wrong crowd — or the wrong woman — my daughter's father might end up making the worst mistake of his life, too.

My grim meditation was interrupted by a tiny royal fanfare, the signature alert for female users of the Cinder app, telling me that a pack of potential princes had been pumped into my Pumpkin Pot.

Sergeant Jones overheard it and laughed. "Is Queen Elizabeth on deck?"

I pulled the smartphone out of my pocket and did my best to explain why a grown woman, engaged to a loving man, had four dating apps on her mobile screen.

FORTY-NINE

The sergeant listened with amazed interest as I told him about my "fishing expedition" for a man I believed was connected to the murder of Haley Hartford — the young woman his crew had pulled out of the Hudson.

"You wouldn't have any new insights, would you?" I asked.

"I'm flattered you'd like my input," he said. "But until you told me, I didn't even know that girl's name."

I was surprised. "Soles and Bass never spoke to you?"

Jones shook his head. "The Harbor Unit pulls people out of the water all the time — the living and the dead. We're almost never involved with the investigation into how they got there. We fill out reports and let detectives take it from there."

"But you know the Hudson River, right?"

"Better than I know myself. I've worked

on that stretch of water for going on thirty years."

"The detectives said there's no camera footage they can use. But now I wonder — what about outside New York's jurisdiction? Could there be cameras on the New Jersey side that captured Haley's murder?"

"The Hudson is over a mile wide. Standard security cameras shoot five hundred feet, at best. Even if you found a camera aimed at the right area of the riverbank with no river traffic in between, best you would get is a blur."

My hopes sank.

"But," he added, "since the Tappan Zee Bridge accident several years ago, insurers have been pressing for crash cameras on all commercial vessels. I know for a fact that a lot of the barges on the river that night were equipped with cameras."

"Really?" I leaned forward. "Could you request access to the footage?"

"Warrants would be involved, because the cameras are on private vessels. And there's going to be a lot of footage, too. But I can make a few informal queries; contact some of the captains who were on the river that night. When they hear the circumstances, they might want to volunteer their help. I'll see what I can come up with . . ."

"That's very good of you, although it sounds like it may take a while."

"A week, at least, maybe longer."

"Then we better not cancel the Barista APB," Esther advised.

"The barista what?" Madame asked.

"It's part of the fishing expedition . . ." Esther pointed to the pantry, inviting her to check out Dante's sketches.

Madame's eyes widened. "I see the game is afoot. Count me in, too!"

With the moral support of everyone around me, I finally opened my Cinder Pumpkin Pot — and gasped. The little digital count told me no less than 380 men in the tristate area had swiped Kara into their own Pots as a desirable match.

"Good grief, Matt was right about that bikini photo!"

"Target the newbies first," Esther suggested. "Filter for guys who are new on the app. Unless our shark had more than one identity, he probably started using his new profile in the past week."

I applied the filter, and the profiles narrowed down to around sixty. Finally, I started swiping, looking for photos with telltale signs of a fake identity.

Sergeant Jones helped plenty on that score.

"That's a doctored photo." He pointed at the screen. "A boat that size would capsize if it had that many girls on it."

"Great!" Obvious duplicity. I immediately sent that Fella a message.

"Look at this one." Jones laughed. "He claims he's the #VegasKing. But those trees behind him aren't desert palms, they're Florida palms."

"I'll bet that's a spring break photo . . ." I sent him a message, too. Within ten minutes I'd sent out a dozen Glass Slippers, reaching out to every questionable or dishonest profile we could find.

Despite the lateness of the hour — or more likely because of it — responses dropped into my box immediately. Given the dubious nature of the men I'd contacted, these replies tended to be "adult" in nature (not to be confused with *mature*).

"Goodness," Madame cried when I displayed the first message. "That invitation doesn't sound very comfortable —"

"Or anatomically possible," Jones added.

I hit the next message. "This man wants to show me a picture of his bedroom." I displayed the image.

"Looks more like a hardware store," Esther said with a snort. "I get the dangling chains, but what's with the John Deere rid-ing mower?"

"Now here's a man who's rather hand-some, despite his obvious toupee," Madame said of the next suspect.

"Hmm . . . he wants to 'reveal his true self,' " I said, reading his text. "And in the interest of openness, he wants me to look at the picture he sent."

I tapped the screen and blanched.

"Oh, my," Madame said. "Is the poor man completely bald?"

"He sent you a shot of his junk!" Esther cried. "What is it with these dirtbags? If I wanted to look at sausage, I'd go to a German restaurant!"

Madame wasn't laughing anymore. She was fuming. "Why are young men so crude these days?"

"Not so young." I pointed to his profile age. "Mr. Toupee-Wearing Reveal His True Self is pushing forty."

"He must think it's something women want to look at," Madame reasoned.

"Let's take an informal poll," Esther announced. "Out of the three women present, how many of us want to look at that? Show of hands. Okay, none!"

"Then who can explain it?" Madame asked in all seriousness.

The women at the table automatically

stared at the only chair occupied by the opposite sex.

"Oh, no, you don't!" Sergeant Jones waved his hands. "I'm a widower with two grown, single daughters, who constantly worries that my beautiful babies are being subjected to this kind of disrespect."

"You know what," I said. "I honestly don't know if it is disrespect."

"What else would it be?" Madame asked.

"Complete cluelessness," I reasoned. "Lack of experience on what appeals to women."

"Sorry, boss," Esther said, "you forgot to insert the word *real* before women."

"What's the alternative?" I asked. "Plastic women?"

"In a few years, when sex dolls become affordable? Yes. Until then, from a behavioral science perspective, the issue is *pixilated* women."

"Video games?"

"Internet porn. Their brains have been pickled by it. And, no doubt, plenty of them have absolutely no clue what to do with an actual, real woman."

"Oh, this is depressing," Madame said, sitting back.

"Don't be depressed," Esther cajoled. "We're talking about an odd subset of a rarified culture. Believe me, my Boris knows what do with a real woman!"

"Dante knows what to do with them, too," I said, then choked on how that sounded. "What I mean is: he's a charming young man who respects women and has a clue what to do with them — you know, romantically." In the awkward silence that followed, I glanced at Esther. "Don't tell him I said that!"

Esther cackled.

"We all know what you meant, dear," Madame said, patting my shoulder.

"You know what?" I said, clapping my hands and rising. "I think it's time I called it a night."

FIFTY

"Are you in bed?"

It was Mike Quinn's warm voice in my ear, calling around midnight.

By now I'd fed, petted, and brushed my Java and Frothy into purring paradise, done a few chores around the apartment, dealt with another crop of Cinder Fellas (even more unsettling than the previous), and left another voice mail message for Tucker.

I was tempted to call Joy, too, but didn't want to rush her.

Our DC coffeehouse, which featured live jazz on its second floor, was crazy-busy on Friday nights. Joy usually closed the kitchen around eleven and was free by midnight.

"I'm waiting up for Joy's call," I told Mike. "She wants to talk."

"Okay to talk with me in the meantime?"

"Sure, what's up?"

"Are you in bed?" he asked again, but this time his voice had gone all low and throaty, and I sensed a mischievous tone in it.

"I'm in the bedroom," I told him, "changing into a nightshirt."

"Can I watch?"

"That depends," I said. "Where are you exactly?"

"In a conference room at One Police Plaza."

"Are you alone?"

"Not if you count the dozen other senior officers from the Joint Operations Anti-Narcotics task force. But they're *very* distracted, and I'm in a corner by a window."

"Mike, I am not engaging in phone sex with you while you're on the job!"

"Really? That's a new rule."

"Consider it an addendum: only when you're totally alone. Like that stakeout you were on forever and were bored because there was absolutely no action and your fellow officers left for a meal break. But that's it!"

He laughed. "I was missing you, sweetheart, that's all. Can I come over tonight? I'll just slip into bed."

"That would be nice." Now my voice was going all low and throaty. "Yes, I'd like that. Very much."

"Good. I'll see you soon . . ."

Mike signed off, and I climbed into the

antique four-poster. The night had gotten colder, and the bedroom felt chilly, but I was too tired to light a fire — and, honestly, though Mike's call was short, it succeeded in getting me sufficiently hot and bothered. As I drew the bedcovers over my legs, my furry feline roommates cuddled up.

"You can stay," I told the pair, scratching their purring heads. "But when the big guy gets here, you better make room for him . . ."

Yet another royal fanfare sounded on my phone. I muted the Cinder alert, but kept the device on. Joy should be ringing any minute.

I couldn't help recalling what Sergeant Jones said about the worries he had for his single daughters, out there on uncertain waters, trying to navigate their way through the "hit-it-and-quit-it" dating app culture.

More than ever now, I was glad my Joy was in a loving, committed relationship with a good man. With a yawn, I put my head on the pillow, staring at the phone on my nightstand, waiting for that special ringtone, "Always Be My Baby."

But my daughter's call never came.

Instead, a text alert sounded. I scanned the phone screen to find another cryptic message from her.

2 tired 2 get into this by phone.

Let's talk tomorrow.

I collapsed against the pillows. *Get into what exactly? What on earth could be wrong?*
My ex-husband would say I was being ridiculous, overthinking two simple messages — but I knew my daughter.

Though I would always think of her as my baby, Joy was a tough young woman with remarkable resilience and strength. I knew because I'd suffered with her through every heartbreak, every costly mistake, including the shame of being expelled from culinary school. Thank goodness, Joy refused to let it break her. Instead, she dug deep and applied herself to a demanding apprenticeship in a Paris kitchen. First, she learned. Then she soared. Her culinary ideas even helped earn the restaurant its first Michelin star.

Now, Joy had the best kind of confidence, born of experience, and it made her bold and frank when it came to discussing any issues with me or her grandmother about our business. She was a great manager, a superb cook, and got along wonderfully with everyone in DC — which is why I doubted this "talk" was going to be about her work.

Whatever was wrong, I'd have to be patient, just like I was when Joy was a teenager, all quiet and sullen, reluctant to open up about some problem at school or fight with a friend, until I pulled it out of her.

With my mind working overtime — not just about my daughter but about my flagging business downstairs and my assistant manager going AWOL — I turned to face the wall.

Beautiful artwork hung there, part of Madame's large collection, but it gave me no comfort tonight. The room was too dark. All I could make out were grim shadows of swaying tree limbs, crawling across the frames like the crooked arms of a looming monster . . .

Monster.

The word brought a chill that had nothing to do with the cold state of the room. It was a monster who ended Haley's days, emptied her pockets while she lay dying, and threw her body away like trash.

I wanted to see Heart Girl again, smiling at our counter. But I never would. Not even in my memories. The only image I could dredge up was the one still on my smartphone. A corpse in the water, hair floating around her, bloodred tattoo on a cheek pale as death.

Tears rose in my eyes, and I took a breath, let it out. Mike would be here soon and I was glad. I needed to see him.

Fearing nightmares, I fought against sleep. But the day had been long and my worries weighty. Instead of keeping me awake, they pulled me down, making my eyelids heavier and heavier, until I slipped beneath a wave of black.

FIFTY-ONE

Am I dreaming?

The room felt warmer. Soft sounds of crackling ascended from the hearth as a deep voice tickled my ear.

"Mmm, your skin smells nice . . ."

I opened my eyes. A golden glow now bathed the beautiful wall of artwork I faced. Strong hands sweetly caressed my body. Soft lips tasted my bare shoulder. I moaned and turned over to find the top buttons of my nightshirt undone — and I didn't mind one bit.

"You're here . . ." I touched his bristly cheek. "It's not a dream."

"I'm here," Mike said. "And you smell different."

"It's the soap. A pretty little rose petal soap from Paris."

"That's funny . . ." He propped himself on an elbow. "I didn't see anything like that in the bathroom."

Forever the detective, I thought. Even in the shadowy light, Mike's blue gaze was sharp, searching my face for answers. I didn't blame him. After years living with a wife who frequently cheated, he'd learned to look for clues and signs, like a different soap when she cleaned up at some posh hotel.

Well, I had nothing to hide, not where my faithfulness was concerned. "I took a shower at Matt's warehouse," I told him straight. "And before you ask, there was a perfectly good reason."

"I'm sure there was."

I explained how a red SUV nearly ran me over and left me freezing in a muddy puddle. "Matt took care of me, let me clean up in his bathroom and warm up in his warehouse."

"Are you okay?"

"I'm fine — bruised ego, that's all."

"So how's Allegro's loft coming along?"

I paused. "I didn't know you knew about that."

"Why?" he said. "Because it's a building code violation?"

"I *think* he used a licensed architect — the one designing our roastery. And I have to admit, it's the perfect living space for a 'don't fence me in' guy like Matt. None of his rooms have a fourth wall; he can sleep with his beloved coffee; and when he misses the bush, he's got a tent on the roof with two charcoal grills."

"So there's a fire code violation?"

Oh, brother. "Forget I said anything. Please? The way things are going with our shop downstairs, he can't afford citations."

"Don't worry. I'm not out to stick the guy . . ." Mike leaned back, put his hands behind his head. "But I do like having something on him — just in case he gets out of line."

"Can't we all just get along? Strive for family harmony?"

"Harmony's okay by me, as long as Allegro understands that you and I are an exclusive duet."

"He does." I leaned closer. "And when he doesn't, he gets a swift mental kick of a reminder."

Mike smiled at that. "I'll give Allegro credit for one thing. He has good taste in soap."

"He does, but it's not *his* taste I care about at the moment . . ."

I didn't care about petty arguments, either. With everything going on in our lives, discussions about my ex-husband were a waste of precious time.

"We're together now," I told my fiancé, "and I can think of much pleasanter preoccupations . . ." Then I finished unbuttoning my nightshirt and Mike's smile grew wider.

FIFTY-TWO

"What's in the bag?"

Mike was nuzzling my neck again, only this time he was the one who smelled of soap. All freshly showered and shaved, he curled an arm around me as I stood at the kitchen counter, unpacking morning treats from downstairs —

"I've got hot cups of Breakfast blend and Blueberry Cream Cheese Scones with Vanilla-Lemon Glaze."

"I was hungry for something else," he growled in my ear. "But now I'm thinking —"

"Let's eat," we agreed together.

The day was humming along nicely. I'd opened the coffeehouse to a slow but steady stream of our neighborhood regulars. Then Dante and one of our part-timers arrived, and I left the front to check inventory for our big event this evening.

I also checked my phone for contact from

Joy, but there was nothing. So I set aside my mother-hen worrying. (It wasn't easy.)

"Ahhh . . ." Mike's sounds of bliss as he chewed and sipped brought my attention back to our little breakfast, and I dug into my own.

The warm scones were tender and flaky with bits of lemon zest in the vanilla glaze perfectly balancing the sweetness of the glazing sugar and bursting blueberries.

I licked my fingers, enjoying the pastry as much as the rare sight of Mike out of suit and tie. His long legs, which always seemed to go on forever in my cozy Village kitchen, were clad in comfy NYPD sweatpants while his still-damp hair rained tiny droplets on his worn gray T-shirt. He looked homey and relaxed — and sexy, too, with his broad shoulders squaring off the tee's thin material and his biceps straining the short sleeves.

"Thanks for letting me sleep in," he said.

"I could see you needed it."

"Yeah, yesterday was a long one. But for good reason . . ."

As Mike paused to drain his cup, I was about to tell him that I'd had a long day, too, and was anticipating another. But before I could bring him up to speed with our Barista APB or our big event tonight, he dropped his own news . . .

"I'm going to London."

"London, *England*?!"

He nodded. "For a week."

"Why, for heaven's sake? You had a mad impulse to watch the Changing of the Guard and eat fish and chips?"

"Not quite, although I'd never say no to fish and chips . . ."

According to Mike, a senior officer in the Joint Operations group was scheduled to give a presentation at an NCA conference. But the officer's wife went into early labor.

"Most of yesterday, I was briefing the man for his presentation," he said. "Now I've been ordered to deliver it."

"Wait, back up," I said. "What is NCA?"

"The National Crime Agency. It's a UK law enforcement entity that focuses on organized crime, including drug trafficking. They've got more data on Styx than we do — it's been in the UK much longer. We still have no leads on how it's being trafficked into this country. So we're going to share information. The DEA is sending an agent, as well."

"When are you leaving?" I asked.

"Soon . . ." He checked his watch. "I've got to pack and get to JFK by three. The conference begins early Monday, and I'll need to get settled in at the hotel."

"Call me when you can, okay?"

His blue eyes smiled. "At night, when I'm all alone in that big hotel bed, you bet I'll be calling."

"Don't forget, you'll be five hours ahead."

"Yeah, you're right . . ." He rubbed his jaw in thought. "How do you feel about planning a few late afternoon breaks this week? You know, for a sexy bubble bath or change of clothes in your bedroom?"

I raised an eyebrow. "With the phone camera pointed in my direction, I suppose?"

"Of course."

"We'll see . . ."

FIFTY-THREE

Since we only had time for one more cup of coffee together, I decided to make it count and use the East Timor beans Matt sent home with me last night.

"Tell me something," I called as I searched the next room for my handbag. "Is our mugger from the park going to be part of your presentation?"

Mike laughed at the "our mugger" phrasing, but confirmed he was indeed part of the presentation. "The information he gave us cracked the online codes that the Styx dealers are using to sell their product in the New York area . . ."

I remembered Matt's warning not to say anything about liking "candy" in my Cinder profile. According to Mike, Styx had its own peculiar hashtag codes, which included liking #rainbows or listing #RainbowParty or #Like2BChill among other codes.

"Now we're following the money," Mike

went on. "Using those codes to connect with dealers, we're building a case against a big fish for distribution — though we still have a long way to go on stopping the manufacturing and international trafficking."

"I guess following the money is never a bad strategy."

"It worked in this case. The payments we're tracking are all being processed the same way — and providing the very best bread crumbs to the big cheese . . ."

"Big cheese? Is that the official term?"

Mike laughed. "I thought you'd appreciate the foodie reference."

The money reference, as it turned out, was the one I appreciated more as I opened the bag my ex-husband had handed me last evening.

Inside, I found a sealed package of East Timor beans, which I expected. But there was something else in there, something Matt forgot to mention: a small, sealed envelope with "Clare" scrawled on it and a yellow Post-it note in his handwriting —

My day crew guys found something U wanted from the laundry? DK??

DK likely meant that Matt didn't know

what was inside the envelope. I quickly opened it to find out — and shouted with glee!

"Clare? What is it?"

"A bank withdrawal receipt!" I waved it in the air. "I left it in my apron pocket and thought it was gone for good."

"Is it yours?"

I shook my head.

"Then who does it belong to?"

"That's what I'd like you to find out . . ."

Over cups of the excellent East Timor, I told Mike about Soles and Bass, Richard Crest's fake identification, and our Barista APB. (And, yes, I left out the part about posing as Kara to bait Crest — because no sane person would be happy about his romantic partner swiping a dating app for *any* reason.)

While Mike had no time to follow up on investigating the bank slip himself, he had a plan: "Since Soles and Bass aren't sold on your theory, I'm bypassing them for now. Monday, I'll put Franco on this. He's the one who took Crest's original statement, so he should request the warrant."

"Wait," I said. "You're putting Franco on it Monday?"

"He's off this weekend. And last I spoke with him — at our morning briefing yesterday — Franco was heading to Washington to see Joy."

My jaw went slack as I wondered why Joy needed to "talk" with her mother when her boyfriend was visiting, a boyfriend she was mad for — at least, the last time I'd checked.

Mike finished his coffee and rose. "So, first thing Monday, I'll send him these account numbers from London . . ." Noticing the stricken look on my face, he misjudged the reason.

"We have to go through proper channels, Clare. We can't do it any faster, and I should also warn you that the bank may not even have this man's real identity. Creating a bank account under a false name is not that difficult for someone who's motivated. Locating him may take a lot more steps and a lot more time."

Mike checked his watch again, and I kissed him good-bye. Though I wanted to keep talking about Franco and the bank withdrawal slip, this was not the time.

One thing I'd learned from loving cops: when duty called, you let them go. And this one was already heading for the door.

"Sorry, sweetheart, I've got to run. I'll miss you."

"I'll miss you, too. Stay safe — and call me!"

FIFTY-FOUR

"Following the money is never a bad strategy . . ."

I thought about that as I descended the back service stairs, entered the coffeehouse pantry, and found myself face-to-face with Dante's sketches.

The two likenesses of Richard Crest stared silently at me. And I stared back. I could see why all those young women were eager to believe Dick's "good guy" act. His features were chiseled, classically masculine, with a squared-off chin and perfect nose.

Maybe too perfect? Plastic surgery?

Folding my arms, I asked the man why he wanted to abuse women. For a thrill? A sense of superiority? You obviously think well of yourself. And you appear to have money. Few people can afford to casually withdraw ten thousand in cash.

Ten thousand in cash . . .

It was a neat sum and a familiar one. Too

familiar.

Just yesterday, I heard AJ mention it: *"Tristan Ferrell doubled Haley's salary and gave her a ten-thousand-dollar signing bonus — in cash."*

She said that happened three weeks ago.

Richard Crest's bank withdrawal slip on the day of Haley's murder was for the exact same amount.

A coincidence? Or a connection?

Detectives Soles and Bass said they interviewed Haley's new boss, "Mr. Ferrell," even checked out his alibi the night she was murdered. But they also admitted not knowing what Richard Crest looked like.

Could Ferrell and Crest possibly be the same man?

I went back upstairs, found my laptop, and called up the Equator website. The top of the site was a video loop of tanned and toned bodies smacking a giant globe around like an Atlas volleyball team. Suddenly, a young woman appeared with a tennis racket, batting words at me —

Equator
World of
Luxury
Fitness &
Innovative Workouts!

Names of the "Innovative" classes followed as I scrolled. Slick photos showed fit bodies intensely engaged in each of them.

Cyclone Cycling
Extreme Kickboxing
Global Volleyball
Cardio Badminton
Ping-Pong Flow
Non-Confrontational Dodgeball
The Critter Crawl® by Ferrell Fitness

I stopped scanning when I saw Tristan's signature workout. *Now where's the staff page?*

The name "Tristan Ferrell" was listed, but his picture was no help. His sinewy body was posed on all fours, prowling in a forest setting like a jungle cat. But his head was off to the side with camouflage paint over his face o match his skintight animal-print bodysuit.

Below the bodysuit photo was his bio.

Tristan Ferrell
Creator of The Critter Crawl® Workout

Tristan has quickly become one of Equator's most popular fitness instructors. An innovator in bodyweight training and fluid movement, Tristan has developed multiple programs for Equator — including our most in-demand workout class, The Critter Crawl®, which celebrates natural movements of the human/animal body. The president of Ferrell Fitness, Tristan is a respected personal trainer to celebrities and athletes. He created The Critter Crawl® Workout and Critter Motivational Flow and Well-Being Program® after traveling to the rain forest of Brazil, which taught him . . .

I stopped reading. If I wanted to learn anything about the rain forests of Brazil, I would ask Matteo Allegro.

Frustrated with no image of Ferrell's face, I turned to a general search engine, typed in "Tristan Ferrell," and was surprised by the results — or lack thereof.

The few photos of Tristan I found were body-focused, much like his Equator staff photo. Either that or he wore primitive masks to mimic the animal poses of his fitness workout.

What are you hiding, Tristan?

Just then, my phone lit up and belted out Donna Summer's "She Works Hard for the Money." I wanted to clap with glee. It was Tucker's favorite song — and his ringtone.

My AWOL assistant manager was finally returning my calls!

FIFTY-FIVE

"Clare!"

"Tuck?"

What followed was a very un-Tucker-like stream of Spanish, going by way too quickly for my rudimentary skills to *comprender.*

"Punch, is that you?"

"Give me a minute, Clare. I have to catch my breath . . ."

Tucker's boyfriend, Punch, was a gifted dancer, a skilled martial artist, and one of the most popular drag performers in New York City. He wasn't usually that excitable, so I was getting worried.

"Is something wrong with Tucker?"

"I'll say. He's gone *loco en la cabeza!*"

"Crazy in the head? Why?"

"Tuck's decided to move back to Louisiana to work in his cousin's coffee shop —"

"No!"

"You have to do something, Clare. I can't live down South. I'm allergic to okra, and I can't stand grits!"

"Calm down. You and I need a plan —"

"Yes, please, talk some sense into him, because he's too hardheaded to listen to me. Convince Tucker to stay in New York —"

"Punch, I can't even convince him to return my calls. He's ghosting me!"

"You have to try again, for both our sakes. Moving will surely end his showbiz career, and mine. You know I don't do Scarlett O'Hara. Carol Burnett ruined that whole Southern belle shtick with that curtain rod. And I'm way too svelte to impersonate Dolly Parton!"

"So what do I do? The last time I tried to speak with him in person, he ran away."

"That's why I called. Tucker and I are going to some trendy, expensive gym this afternoon. The producer of *Swipe to Meat* is footing the bill for the cast as a morale booster after the police investigation shook everyone up."

"You're in *Swipe to Meat,* too?"

"Tucker got me in as an extra. No lines, but I have some nice on-camera moments prepping veg for the Killer-Lover Chef. Anyway, listen! There's a juice bar at this club. I'll take Tucker there after our class, and we can *just happen* to run into you. Okay? Together we can force Tuck to listen to reason."

"Okay, which club?"

"Equator — that luxury gym by Chelsea Park."

Oh, brother. "I'm not a member of Equator, Punch. I can't afford it."

"I'm just a guest myself. So I can't get you in. How about your barista? You know, the little fresh-faced farm girl with the Judy Garland Dorothy braids —"

"Nancy Kelly?"

"That's the one! Tuck told me she works there part-time. I'm sure she can sneak you by their muscle-bound bouncers. Please come. For your sake, and mine — Oh, no! Tuck's out of the shower. I've got to run! Remember, we're in the noon Critter Crawl Workout class. Equator at Chelsea Park. We'll see you at the juice bar at one!"

I checked my watch.

Things were slow downstairs, preparations were in hand for this evening, and Esther would be here within the hour.

I was planning to squeeze in a nice swim at my YMCA to work off those scones. But if I could convince Tucker to come back to the Village Blend, it would be worth my time to have a smoothie at Equator. And since I would be in the gym, anyway, hmm . . .

Would Nancy be able to get me into that workout class, too?

It would give me a chance to check out Tristan Ferrell, "creator of The Critter Crawl." According to AJ, he'd bribed Haley well to lure her away from Cinder. I'd like to know why, and whether or not this guy had an alter ego named Richard Crest.

Tucker and Tristan: time to kill two critters with one call.

And I placed it to Nancy.

FIFTY-SIX

I entered the exclusive gym in the most unglamorous way — through a Dumpster-lined alley and a dingy back door.

"Welcome to Equator: World of Luxury Fitness!" Nancy chirped, without a trace of irony.

"Are you sure I'm not going to get you into trouble?"

"We're good. The security camera above the door has been broken since I started. Nobody reports it because the instructors like to duck out to smoke."

"There are fitness instructors here who smoke?"

"Or vape." Nancy shrugged. "Hey, I don't judge."

I followed her wheat-colored braids into a long, dark hall. Fortunately, she was easy to track in her formfitting, tiger-striped Day-Glo orange leggings and X-back sports bra.

"All of Tristan's spotters wear glow-in-the-dark animal prints," she explained. "It makes us easier to *spot* in the dark!"

"The dark?"

"You'll see."

As we rode the service elevator to the top floor, along with a giant bin full of towels, Nancy gave me an encouraging smile.

"Don't look so worried. You'll be fine."

"Your boss won't mind someone crashing?"

She waved her hand. "He won't even notice. The Critter Crawl is always in high demand. Tristan accepts up to one hundred people in his Saturday introductory class. With that many bodies, it will be easy for you to blend in."

"A hundred in one workout class? That doesn't sound like very personal training."

"It's Darwinian. You know? Survival of the fittest."

"What? You have to *survive* the class?"

"Um, forget I said anything. You swim regularly — that's sort of exercise. You'll be fine!"

We exited the elevator and crossed to another door.

"Give me your jacket, and I'll check it. Then go through here and I'll meet you inside."

"Nancy, one more thing," I said. "I'd like

to speak with Tristan Ferrell after class. Is that possible?"

"So you're interested in his Critter Motivational Flow and Well-Being Program?"

"Sure!"

(Okay, so I told a white lie. But I didn't want Nancy to fret about my real objective. At best, to ask Ferrell about his relationship with the late Haley Hartford. At worst, to expose him as the real Richard Crest.)

As it turned out, I didn't need to worry.

"I think Tristan will want to meet you, actually. And Madame, when it can be arranged."

"Really?"

"He says it's his mission to seek connections with successful people in every walk of life. He's throwing an Angel Party, too. If you speak with him today, I'm sure you'll get an invite."

"Angel Party?"

"He's looking for investors. That's part of my job as a spotter. I'm supposed to spot wealthy candidates who want to back Tristan's new app, the Critter-a-Day Motivation and Exercise Calendar."

"Great," I said. "Can't wait."

Nancy leaned close. "Tristan always stops at the Euclid after class, just to network."

"Is that some hipster bar in the neighborhood?"

"Oh, no! Tristan doesn't drink alcohol! The Euclid is a juice bar in the lobby —"

Good, I thought, recalling Punch's plan to ambush Tucker there.

"After class, get a drink at the bar, and I'll introduce you to my boss . . ." She giggled. "I mean my *other* boss. Now give me that jacket; I've got to run or I'll be late."

I stripped off my outerwear, to reveal black leggings and a matching exercise bra under a baggy *Caffeine Is My Co-Pilot* T-shirt that was anything but formfitting — and hopefully covered most of my well-cushioned assets.

A moment later, Nancy was gone and I stepped "into a world of perfect fitness, balanced wellness, and all-around good health" — or so said the light-board scrolling around the equator of an enormous chrome globe dangling from the ceiling.

Now, I've got nothing negative to say about the bare-bones weight room at the McBurney YMCA, but Equator's facilities were on a whole different level — like beluga caviar was on a different level from frozen fish sticks.

Okay, so the circular atrium wasn't as large as the Coliseum, and its ceiling wasn't quite as high as the dome at St. Peter's, but this was certainly an impressive space. Tall glass walls offered a spectacular 360-degree view, with scores of ultramodern exercise machines set in a Stonehenge circle facing the glass.

The floor was padded to absorb shocks and mute the unpleasant echoes that typically plagued a hardwood gymnasium. Instead, New Age music flowed from invisible speakers. Neat rows of exercise mats had been arranged around a circular stage set under the giant globe.

Nancy entered with a dozen young men and women wearing the same garish animal prints.

"Come with me," she said. "I found you a spot beside the movie people in the front row."

The "movie people" had yet to arrive, so I did some stretches on my mat while scanning the crowd.

There was no sign of Tucker, but I did spot one familiar face: Cinder's head of security, Cody, her muscular frame Amazonian — and a little intimidating — in green camouflage leggings and matching sports bra.

CEO Sydney's loyal guard dog had apparently slipped her leash, for there was no sign of her boss. And if the toned member of

Team Tinkerbell noticed my presence, she pretended she didn't.

Then the gentle music began to fade. Automatic blinds descended over the windows, to block out all light, until only the stage was visible, bathed in a weird green glow. Meanwhile, the raucous sounds of the jungle poured from the sound system — wild animal chirps, barks, grunts, roars, and screeches. The cries rose in volume and intensity until the noise became earsplitting.

Suddenly silence descended and the room went completely black. All I could see were the ghostly forms of the glow-in-the-dark Critter spotters.

Slowly, a golden spotlight came up on the sculpted body of a near-naked man at center stage. Shirtless, pecked, and six-packed, his muscular arms were outstretched, legs braced wide. The man was shoeless, too — in fact, he wore nothing more than animal-print spandex trunks. From my front row perspective, they outlined more of the man than I cared to see!

"Welcome to my jungle, Crawlers! My name is Tristan Ferrell . . ."

With no mask or camo paint, Ferrell's face was now clear to see and not even close to Richard Crest's. Where Crest's bone structure was square, Ferrell's was triangular with features that were more refined, almost delicate — pointier chin, smaller nose, and sunken cheeks with prominent cheekbones.

"Please consider me a friend," the fitness guru told the class, "and call me Tristan, although my Critter Name is much more primitive. Would you like to hear it?"

Everyone nodded with interest.

"My Critter Name sounds more like this —" The crazed banshee screech that followed rattled the blinds and the crowd. Ferrell seemed to love this.

"That's right," he said with cocky confidence, "I like to scream. Screaming is good, and it's good for you, too. You won't hear a lot of grunts or groans in my fitness class, but you will hear a lot of screaming."

Uh-oh, I thought. *That can't be good . . .*

FIFTY-SEVEN

The tardy movie crew arrived as Tristan Ferrell was wrapping up his introductory remarks, telling us how a painful failure in "the business jungle" drove him into a real one — the Brazilian rain forest — where he regained "balance and wholeness and wellness."

As the *Swipe to Meat* cast filed past me to take their positions on the reserved mats, Punch spotted me, gave me an excited wink, and maneuvered his lanky, floppy-haired partner close to me.

Tucker seemed oblivious to his surroundings, locked in a whispered conversation with a pudgy, balding man wearing retro tennis shoes and white socks that ended mid-calf. I pegged him as the producer.

Soon their conversation ended, but my plan to catch Tuck's attention was thwarted when the lights dimmed again, until only the garish green stage was visible.

"I want you to come back to that night with me," Tristan said, "when I rediscovered my core. I became balanced. Whole. At peace with everything and everyone in the universe. Alone and naked, I could feel the jungle teeming with life. Tiny insects. Big cats. Long snakes. Short worms. Buoyant bats. Heavy hedgehogs. Then the revelation struck —"

Ferrell paused to smack his own head. "It didn't matter their size or shape, whether they flew or swam or slithered or crawled. Critters don't worry about fitness!"

Good grief.

"Critters *are* fit. And in that moment, The Critter Crawl was born."

Honestly, I nearly lost it at "long snakes" and "short worms," but the crowd was eating it up. Some even oohed and aahed. While Tristan continued his preamble, I tried to get Tuck's attention.

"Psst! Psst!" I hissed. But it didn't work. The only attention I caught was the teacher's.

"I hear the call of the slithering snake," Ferrell said with an approving nod. "Someone has been in my class before!"

Tristan then informed us we were about to learn our first position — the Boa.

"I want you to throw your arms back and

thrust your chest out. Snakes don't have arms, so I really want you to toss those useless old limbs away . . ."

A sudden scream marked the first wardrobe malfunction. A sports bra in flight slapped Tuck's producer in the back of the head, while the bosomy actress it belonged to covered herself and bolted for the exit.

As things turned out, she was the lucky one. The rest of us were compelled to lie on our stomachs in the dim green lighting and slither like boa constrictors.

With the animal soundtrack turned back up and everyone busy flopping around in the faux jungle, I squirmed on over to Tucker's long body. He was deep into method acting — he really *was* that snake — when I bumped him out of his trance.

"Clare Cosi! What in blazes are you doing wiggling around on an exercise mat?"

"That's a question we should all ask."

"Slither! Slither!" Ferrell cried. "I want to see you contort those stiff spines."

A howl of pain signaled a slipped disc. Two animal-print musclemen rushed to the scene and hauled the agonized man off in a luxury stretcher.

"Oh, my," Tuck fretted. "Now I know why they made us sign those releases!"

Several people threw up the arms they

were supposed to pretend they didn't have and headed for the exit. I longed to join them, but my mission here was not yet finished.

"Come on, Tuck!" I said, my plea muffled by the gym floor's padding. "You have to come back to the Village Blend. We need you. Now, more than ever."

Tuck tossed back his floppy brown hair and peeked nervously at the pudgy, balding man, who was earnestly boa constricting with the best of them.

"Clare," he whispered. "I'm here on business. Could we talk personal later?"

"Only if you promise you *will* talk to me."

"I promise."

"Right after class. Downstairs in the juice bar."

"Yes, yes," he replied, still wiggling.

"I'll be waiting."

As I Critter Crawled back to my mat, I heard Punch's exasperated groan. "This is horrid, humiliating, and no fun at all! I'll take my mother's favorite workout over this, any day."

"What did she do, jumping jacks?"

"No. Richard Simmons's *Sweatin' to the Oldies.* It was awesome! Everyone sang along — and wore nice comfy shorts and tees. None of this pinching spandex. Why can't I find a workout like that anymore?!"

"I don't know about *Oldies,*" Tuck said, writhing with effort. "But if you can find me a workout called *Sweatin' with Donna Summer* . . . and the *Village People* . . . and the *Bee Gees* . . . and *KC and the Sunshine Band* — I'll be the first one to sign up."

"OMG, Tuck. You just created *Sweatin' with the Seventies!*"

Tuck froze, mid-slither, as it hit him. "OMG, Punch, we *have* to produce that!"

Punch nodded like crazy, put up his palm, and the two high-fived each other.

"You there! No hands! No hands!" Tristan yelled. "You're a boa. The Monkey Climb comes later!"

The jungle guru's words were punctuated by another embarrassed cry as a man squirmed right out of his shorts.

FIFTY-EIGHT

Forty-five minutes later, The Critter Crawl had come to its grueling end. I was perched on a stool at the chrome-plated counter of the Euclid, the tony fitness club's minimalist juice bar.

I pondered why a juice bar would be named after the father of geometry, a science that took us into space. After I arrived, I decided it was because of the *astronomical* prices — eighteen dollars for a banana smoothie?!

(And, yes, no one knew better than I the need for retailers and wholesalers to pass along costs of importing produce and necessary labor — to, for example, pick, process, ship, and roast quality coffee beans. But, last I checked, even organic bananas were less than a dollar a pound. So unless their "World Famous Banana Smoothie" included Plantation rum, I'd be getting globally hosed on that one.)

At last, true to his word, Tucker arrived with Punch. Their evening slate was suddenly clear — since dinner with the cast had been postponed due to the producer's torn ligament.

Punch shuddered at the memory. "Those monkey moves were next to impossible, and I'm a trained dancer."

"But it was the Yellow Kangaroo that did him in," Tuck replied.

Over (twelve-dollar) Sparkling Pear Pick-Me-Ups — icy cold, fruity, honey-sweet, and nicely refreshing after all that exercise — Tuck and I finally talked.

I pleaded with my former assistant manager to rethink his relocation, and return to his job at the Village Blend. After fifteen minutes of relentless cajoling, I was halfway to victory. Tuck still refused to "burden my failing business with his salary," but he did come to the conclusion that returning to Louisiana would be a mistake.

"I have good reason to stay now," he said. "Punch and I came up with a brilliant concept for a fitness program, and we've decided to convince the McBurney YMCA to sponsor it."

"I call it exer-tainment," Punch said. "Mostly because enter-cise sounds vaguely indecent."

Not wishing to press Tuck too hard, I switched subjects to the message I'd sent him after Haley Hartford's murder.

"I'm sorry, Clare. I didn't even open your text. I was in makeup for hours, starting at four AM. Then we heard about Carol Lynn's arrest, and before we knew it, the police came and questioned the entire cast and crew about her, the prop gun, everything! Things were too frantic."

I opened my smartphone and displayed the grim image. "Tell me now. Did you know this woman?"

Tucker gave the photo a hard look then turned away.

"I know her face but not her name — honestly, I recognize that heart tattoo more than anything else. I do remember that she was in the coffeehouse the day Carol Lynn pointed out Richard Crest."

"You're certain?"

"I'm certain because Crest was sitting with the heart-tattoo girl. At the number three table by the window."

Finally, a second witness! I felt like cheering.

"What else do you remember about their tryst?" I pressed.

"It wasn't a tryst. It was more like a business meeting. Heart Girl showed Crest something on her laptop, and he passed her an envelope. Then they both left, but not together."

"Was it a big envelope? Little envelope?"

"Just a regular envelope, kind of bulky."

A new wrinkle. *Was Haley doing work for Crest, too? Or was there something else besides money in that envelope?*

I held up my smartphone to ask Tuck another question.

"Oh, that ghastly photo again!" a familiar voice cried.

Tuck, Punch, and I turned on our stools, to face Tristan Ferrell, Nancy by his side.

FIFTY-NINE

I was relieved to see the fitness guru had put more clothes on.

"Did we interrupt something?" Nancy asked.

"Not at all," I replied, extending my hand. "I'm Clare Cosi, and I know who you are."

Ferrell took my hand, then gripped my wrist, bro style.

"Great to meet you, Clare. Nancy has told me so much about you. She says your ohm is pure."

"Wow, that's, uh . . . comforting."

Up close, Tristan Ferrell's strong and sinewy physique was even more impressive. Not one molecule of extra fat on this guy. He wasn't very tall, standing only a few inches above me, but he seemed to radiate power, a Napoleonic sort of energy.

"Would you join us for juice?" I asked. "This Pear Pick-Me-Up is delicious."

Tristan made a face. "No sugar for me —

of any kind. Even honey can disrupt the purity of my detoxed and defragged system."

He glanced at my bottom. "You might consider cutting out a few forms of sugar yourself."

"Uh-huh." I held up the phone. "So you recognize this image?"

"Of course. That's a picture of Haley Hartford. The police detectives showed me a different one. They were two powerful women with aquatic totems. Do you know them?"

"Soles and Bass? Yes, I do."

"It's terrible what happened to Haley. Bad karma for the dude who did it."

"How do you know it was a man?"

Ferrell shrugged. "The police said it was a mugging in the park."

"Tell me . . ." I called up Dante's sketches. "Do you recognize this man? He's not a mugger. He goes by the name Richard Crest."

Ferrell hardly glanced at the picture. "I don't know any Richard Crest —"

"Look closely. You might know him by another name. He's wanted for questioning."

Ferrell took another look and exhaled. "Clare, there are so many people in my classes. It's possible he's attended — that's all I can tell you. What are you? Some kind of freelance private investigator?"

"More like a freelance concerned citizen."

"I see. And if you have to make a citizen's arrest, you're in shape for that?" He lifted a skeptical eyebrow as he looked me over again.

"Sometimes brains are a better weapon than brawn." With a smile, I lifted my smartphone. "Why wrestle a suspect when you can call 911 and have trained officers do it?"

"Why don't we discuss something more pleasant — and lucrative. Nancy tells me you own the Village Blend, the coffeehouse and the brand."

"Not quite. I have some equity. Eventually, I'll inherit partial ownership. Until then, my employer, Madame Dubois, owns and controls the brand and the shops —"

"Amazing real estate," Ferrell interrupted. "But I understand Mrs. Dubois is getting rather long in the tooth." He leaned close as if confiding a secret between us. "I know it's a bitch waiting for her to, you know, check out. Believe me, I sympathize. I'm in a similar position. But I'll bet it's nice to know that when the old lady kicks, you'll be sitting on a gold mine."

I was too appalled to reply. Ferrell took

my silence for agreement.

"So would you like to come to my Angel Party? I'm looking for investors in my new Critter-a-Day Motivation and Exercise Calendar app. It's going to be major, Clare. Big payoff for anyone who gets in early . . ."

He insisted we exchange contact information, which we did.

"I'll invite your employer, too. She'll enjoy the party — it's a venue Uptown, near the Boat Basin, where I keep my Riva."

He waited for me to be impressed. I forced a frozen smile. Then I tried to turn the subject back to Haley. I asked how he came to hire her.

"Sorry, Clare. I have an advanced class in Soho, and —" He pointed to Equator's wall of global clocks. "I'm running late in every time zone. Ha-ha! Nice meeting you. See you at my party!"

As the fitness guru vaulted away, my smartphone vibrated. It was Esther. Anticipating the reason for her call, I turned up the volume so Tucker could hear.

"We need more hands on the caffeinated deck," Esther said. "I texted Mr. Boss with a reminder on the supplies we need from his warehouse. And Dante and I could use help with the outdoor tables and heaters."

"We're on our way," I replied.

Ending the call, I faced Tucker.

"That hardly sounds like a failing business, does it?" I quickly told him about our big event. "So come back, Tuck, please? And start tonight? You'll break everyone's heart if you leave us, including, *and especially,* mine."

Tuck finally agreed, and we hugged tight. Then he and Punch left to get their coats, and I looked around for Nancy.

I spotted someone else instead, a woman on the other side of the bar, her eyes like a predator's, bright and sharp and intensely focused on me.

It was Cody, Sydney's head of security — with a banana smoothie mustache.

How long has she been watching me?

"Here's your jacket," Nancy said. "I'm coming with you since I'm all done here at Equator. And I just got an 'all-hands' text from Esther!"

As we headed out, one more call came in, the one I'd been waiting for . . .

"Joy?"

"Mom? Where are you?"

"What do you mean, where am I? I'm in New York."

"So am I. But you're not at the apartment or the shop. They said you went to some gym?"

"Forget the gym. What are you doing in the city?"

"I told you. I need to talk."

Uh-oh, I thought for the second time in two hours. *This can't be good.*

"Stay put, honey, I'll be right there . . ."

SIXTY

By the time I arrived at the coffeehouse, Joy was downstairs helping with the outdoor tables and heat lamps. I hugged her hello and went up to my apartment to change.

After my shower, I entered my kitchen for a quick bite to eat — and found all the evidence I needed of my daughter's distress.

Joy had shopped for fresh ingredients and made us sandwiches for lunch. But not just any sandwich. She'd made *le jambon-beurre* (literally, "the ham-butter"), a deceptively simple French classic, consisting of a baguette sliced in half, generously buttered, and layered with thinly sliced ham.

During Joy's first stressful months of her culinary apprenticeship in Montmartre, she had lived on these sandwiches, not just because they were one of the most popular in Paris, but because they reminded her of the sandwiches I'd made for her as a little girl — just as my grandmother had made for me.

My *nonna* had used salami instead of *jambon* and spread her butter on slices of crusty Italian bread, instead of French-style baguettes. But the culinary concept was the same: a simple sandwich that brought crunchy, salty, unctuous comfort.

And, yes, I inhaled mine in record time.

After assuring me everything was on track downstairs, Joy fell silent as she chewed her own sandwich. I filled the awkward quiet by bringing her up to speed on Sydney's (and Esther's) plans to give our customer base a boost.

"So . . ." I said at the end of my update. "You came here to talk?"

She cleared her throat. "I'm not sure how to say it . . ."

I glanced at the kitchen clock. "Joy, you're not a teenager anymore. Don't make me drag it out of you."

"I'm sorry," she said. Then her face contorted, as if she were choking on something, and she spit out the words like a piece of spoiled fruit —

"I think Manny is cheating on me!"

Oh, God.

As distressing as it was to see my daughter in pain, my instant reaction was to assume she was overreacting. I could not believe

Emmanuel Franco would do such a thing.

"Joy, did you actually see Manny with another woman?"

"No."

"Did anyone tell you Manny was cheating?"

"No."

"Then what makes you believe —"

"He was supposed to come down to DC for the weekend. We had firm plans. Then he canceled at the last minute. He said he had to work, but I think he was lying . . ."

I held my breath, remembering what Mike had said about Franco's schedule. He was off this weekend, which meant he did lie to Joy. I told her what I knew, but quickly added —

"It could have been a simple white lie. Maybe Franco was tired and needed rest, but he didn't want to hurt your feelings —"

"There's more."

"More?"

"Mom, I heard something at the end of our phone call. That stupid *Tinker-Tinker* alert. Do you know what I'm talking about?"

Unfortunately, I did.

"I think Manny has a second phone, one he keeps away from me. He's obviously installed that Cinder dating app on it. I'm *sure* he's using it to cheat on me!"

"Slow down, Joy. You can't be sure of anything yet. That Cinder alert may not have come from Manny's phone. It could have been a colleague's phone nearby."

"He was at his apartment when he called — I mean, I think he was."

"You see? You're jumping to conclusions."

"That's why I came up to New York. To surprise him, and set my mind at ease. But he's not at his apartment. I used my key to let myself in. And when I phoned him, he didn't pick up or respond."

"Okay, so we have ourselves a little mystery here. We just need to clear up what's going on with him. Then I'm sure you two will laugh over these simple misunderstandings —"

"It's not just the phone call. I *know* Manny. He's more comfortable in a Kevlar vest than a suit and tie, but he was wearing a really expensive suit when he came down to visit last weekend. He said he did it to impress me, but then he pulls a Louis Vuitton man-bag full of rich-guy stuff out of his duffel."

"Define 'rich-guy' stuff."

"The kind of cologne Dad used to get from his ex-wife's fashion clients, emollients and lotions I'd never seen him use."

"Maybe he's trying to spruce himself up,

you know, now that he's been promoted."

"Mom, I caught him slathering Crème de la Mer on his shaved head like it was Vaseline. It's like a thousand dollars for an eight-ounce jar! Where did he get the money for *that*? I'd like to know."

Me too, I thought, leaning back in my chair. *If it were anyone else in the NYPD, I'd think corruption — but Franco?*

"There must be some explanation," I continued to insist.

"Yeah, there is one. I was cleaning up the bathroom after he left, and I found a note crumpled in the trash bin."

"What kind of note?"

"Handwritten, in big bold capital letters, it said: 'FOR MANNY' and it was signed, '— JOAN.' "

"Joan?" I sat forward again. "Who is Joan?"

"I don't know! I was planning to ask him when we were together again this weekend, and then he canceled, pretended he had to work, when it's clear he lied to me. Now I don't know what to do. Mom, you've got to help me find out what's going on with him."

"Me?!"

SIXTY-ONE

"You're brilliant at snooping," Joy declared. "And I'm certainly not going to hire a private investigator. Manny's a cop, for heaven's sake. That would be a disaster. So I want you to find out who this Joan person is. She's obviously loaded. I think she's showering Manny with expensive stuff to buy his affection. I need to know how serious it is —"

She must be an older woman, I thought, but didn't dare say. It would just confirm Joy's worst suspicions.

"Slow down," I warned. "There could be an innocent explanation . . ."

As soon as I said it, my mind flashed back to the skeptical look on Mike's face when I said Franco would make a good husband. Then I recalled his discouraging words: *". . . the issue with your ex disliking him — and that's an understatement — isn't going to make life peachy for them as a couple. And living in different cities isn't easy on any relationship . . ."*

At the time, I had brushed off Mike's remarks. Now they weren't so easy to dismiss. *Did Mike suspect Franco was cheating on Joy? Did he actually know it for a fact — maybe even know this Joan person?*

"I'm sorry, Mom . . ."

I let out a breath that I didn't know I was holding. "Sorry for what? Joy, you have a right to be confused over Franco's behavior. And I'm glad you came up to talk this over. Believe me, I know how you feel."

"That's not what I'm sorry about. I never knew, not *really,* how awful it was for you all those years ago. How much it hurts — like a slice through your soul — when you love someone, as much as you loved Daddy, as much as I love Manny, and that love is betrayed."

Tears welled up in my daughter's green eyes. Then the dam broke . . .

"There's no crying on the line in a Paris kitchen," she once told me. *"The staff would crucify me!"* But she was crying now. It was full-out, ugly crying with fat drops streaking her ruddy cheeks, and her heart-shaped face contorting into a mask of pain and confusion.

Sliding my chair over, I pulled her into

371

my arms, and urged her to let it all out. Clearly, she'd been bottling up these worries for days.

When the sobs finally slowed, I stroked her dark hair. "Joy, do you remember that terrible storm years ago, when you were afraid of the thunder?"

"N-no . . ."

"Your father co-opted a few world myths and told you the thunder was just a big giant, beating his drum in the sky."

"Oh, y-yes." She wiped her nose. "That's right."

"Boom-boom-boom . . ." I reminded her. "You and Daddy marched around the apartment, pretending to beat your own drums."

"I remember. I actually *wanted* the thunder to boom again, so I could beat my drum even louder."

"When something frightens us, we try to make sense of it, get control of it, fight back in our own way. It's human nature."

"But, Mom, there never really was a giant in the sky —"

"No, and Franco's not a bad person. If you love him, you have to sit down with him, confront him, face the truth — and *know* that you'll be okay, whatever happens. It's easy to let yourself domino your worries, tell yourself that if you lose Franco, you've lost love forever. But that's just the thunder, honey, terrible noise to scare you. Look at your grandmother and all her heart has been through. You know what she always says? 'Survive everything, and —' "

" '— do it with style.' I know." She exhaled hard. "It's just not . . . it's not easy."

"No, it isn't. And leaving me to 'snoop' out answers will only make it harder, build up your fears and anxieties. That's why I want you to sleep here tonight. Then put on your big-girl pants tomorrow, face Franco, and find out the truth. I'll be here for you, no matter what happens."

Joy took a breath and let it out. Finally, she nodded. "Okay, Mom, I'll stay."

"Have you arranged coverage in DC?"

"Everything's set in Washington. And I can help you downstairs tonight. Sounds like you're going to need it . . ."

As my daughter swiped her wet cheeks with the backs of her fists, a flood of memories flowed over me, and I saw my daughter in grade school again, crying over scuffed knees; in middle school, nursing bruised feelings; and through all those teen years with social fears and heartbreaking crushes. We'd spent so many hours together in the kitchen, just mother and daughter, talking things over.

If only she were that little again, I thought, *and her problems were as easy for me to solve.*

But who was I kidding? It was never easy. No matter how much any parent tries, every childhood is a series of hardships and humiliations, anxieties and terrors.

"How about a 'Mommy and Me' cookie?" I found myself asking. "We have time. Would you like that?"

Joy actually smiled. "Do you remember the ingredients?"

"By heart . . ."

2 tablespoons melted butter, 1 teaspoon vanilla extract, pinch of salt, 1 egg yolk, 2 tablespoons granulated sugar, 2 table-spoons light brown sugar, 1/4 cup flour, 1/8 teaspoon baking soda, and 2 1/2 tablespoons mini chocolate chips . . .

My daughter and I mixed the dough and baked our favorite cookies — large rounds of buttery-caramel goodness with the perfect crispy-chewy texture and laced with just the right amount of chocolate. We ate the warm treats with satisfaction, washing them down with glasses of cold milk. And for a brief, innocent gap of space and time, love became simple again.

Sixty-Two

"See, Clare, I told you I'd deliver!"

Hours later, Sydney Webber-Rhodes was sitting at my crowded coffee bar in a pastel pink sweater and tartan skirt, her elfin features looking smug as a general reviewing her lockstep troops. Smartphone in her manicured hand, the Cinder CEO closely monitored her prepaid parade of trendy and beautiful people as they "hashtagged" happy comments to thousands of social media followers.

As for my part, the shop was in stellar shape. Joy and my baristas were diligently working to serve drinks and pastries as swiftly and cheerfully as possible — while keeping things tidy upstairs and down; inside and out.

Sydney had been right about those outdoor tables. They were as packed as the ones inside. The customers looked satisfied and relaxed, enjoying the cool jazz flowing through the sound system and the blazing hearths on both floors.

"My strategy is working," Sydney declared with a wink of one hazel-bronze tiger eye. Then her pink fingernail swiped away, showing me the photos and videos being uploaded about our shop: from smiling selfies to images of coffee and pastries to GIF loops of our crackling fireplace.

"Notice how the crowd is changing?" She tipped her shiny blond pixie toward a large group of newcomers. "Those people are obviously *not* part of my alpha group, yet here they are — real customers!"

When the motley crew of vastly different ages and body types, most clad in down-market fashions, ordered drinks and headed directly upstairs, I knew Sydney was right *and* wrong. These new customers were "real," but she was wrong about why they'd come. It wasn't because of social media endorsements.

They were here because of Esther.

For the past few hours, I'd tried to spot the *Washington Post* photo-journalist whom Sydney had mentioned was coming. I wanted to provide some background on Esther's ongoing urban outreach work and her extensive experience with poetry slams. But so many people were taking pictures that I pretty much gave up the guessing game.

Anyway, I had another fish to catch, and so far, my net was empty.

Then something intriguing happened.

Cody arrived in an agitated state. Hurrying through our front door, the athletic woman plowed through the crowd like a rugby forward barreling toward a goal. It was the first time I'd seen Cinder's square-jawed head of security since our encounter at Equator — which surprised me because Team Tinkerbell had arrived early with Sydney. Its members were now wandering around in their pastel shirts. Only Cody had been absent. Now she rushed up to her boss, tossed back her brownish blond pixie, and whispered almost frantically into Sydney's ear.

The CEO's satisfied grin morphed into an eye-blinking frown. When she realized I was staring, she checked her reaction and asked —

"Clare, is there somewhere I can go for a private conversation?"

"Of course, the pantry should be quiet. I'll show you."

As Sydney and Cody moved through the crowd to get behind the counter, they crossed paths with AJ, who'd been recording video interviews with happily Cinder-matched couples. Sydney tapped her shoulder and motioned for her to follow us.

Unfortunately, our pantry wasn't bare. Vicki Glockner, one of my part-timers, was desperately looking for more paper cups.

I turned to Sydney. "You'll find more privacy in our back alley."

I pushed open the back door. Sydney barely hit the cold pavement before she placed a call on her smartphone. I was hoping to eavesdrop, but she, Cody, and AJ moved too far from the exit.

Stopping in the middle of the alley, they began their conference right next to my coffee roaster's venting pipe — *a whole other kind of wireless communications device!*

After telling Vicki to break open the boxes that Matt had hauled from his warehouse, I hurried down the steps to our basement roasting room, unscrewed the wing nuts on our wall vent, and placed my ear to the opening . . .

Sixty-Three

The women's voices echoed strangely through the aluminum pipe, but I could make out every word. And though I'd missed Sydney's phone conversation, I quickly got the gist of it.

"I warned you that someone's been tampering with our app," AJ said, "and I told you it wasn't an outside hack!"

"You claimed it was Haley, and you were right," Sydney returned. "She created a backdoor and buried it so deep it took a week for my digital forensic investigators to find it. I hired the best in the business, and they still can't tell me who used it, or why."

"Well, I can't ask Haley. She's dead."

"I don't need excuses, AJ. I need solutions."

"Hey! If I hadn't figured out that those user complaints and abuse reports were being deleted, you'd still be in the dark. I'm doing my best to help your investigators find a digital trail that leads to the saboteur —"

"I've got my own suspicions about that," Sydney said bitterly.

"Who?"

"Someone from my past. But that doesn't concern you. Just do your job. I want that backdoor closed. *Permanently.*"

Finally, Cody spoke. "The backdoor is the least of our worries. None of this explains the account surpluses. More than one hundred seventy thousand dollars — and it's still coming in. I've spoken to a few users, and I don't like what I'm hearing. This is far more serious than deletions of abuse reports. I think someone is setting us up for —"

"Enough!" Sydney said. "We're not going to solve anything tonight in this alley. Let's put our game faces on and get back to the party."

Slapping brick dust off my apron, I raced back up the stairs.

By now, Vicki was gone from the pantry, leaving Dante's sketches in clear view. And that's where I found Sydney, frozen in place, staring at those portraits.

Sydney's "game face" was nowhere in sight. She looked positively livid with her fingers gripping her smartphone so tightly that I thought the quartz face would crack.

Cody appeared confused but concerned. And poor AJ seemed completely clueless. None of them noticed me, so I waited a moment, hoping somebody would say something. Finally, I asked —

"Do you recognize him?"

Sydney's tiger eyes remained on the sketches. "What are you doing with these, Clare?"

"This guy is the one in the viral video with Carol Lynn Kendall, the mystery man who started this mess. He's wanted for questioning by the police for giving them a fake identity. He's been abusing women he meets on your app. And I think he has something to do with Haley Hartford's death."

Cody's expression turned fierce. "What makes you think so?"

"One of my baristas saw this man sitting with Haley, having some kind of meeting. She showed him something on her laptop, and he handed her an envelope."

Sydney's face went white. Then she locked gazes with Cody.

"What is it?" I asked. "What's going on? Did this man hire Haley to sabotage Cinder?"

Suddenly, Matt burst into the pantry, pulling Joy behind him. "Clare! Clare! Oh, *there* you are. We have to talk. Now!"

As Matt moved toward me, Sydney and her Tinkerbells fled, leaving my question unanswered. Determined to corner Sydney later, I turned to deal with my bellowing ex-husband.

"What?" I said, throwing up my hands. "What do we have to 'talk' about?"

"Dad's acting crazy," Joy said. "I don't understand why he's freaking out. It's no big deal."

Matt shook his head. "This is a big deal, Joy, bigger than you think. Now tell your mother. Go on, tell her what just happened to you."

Baffled, Joy faced me. "Some guy mistook me for someone else. That's all. He thought my name was Kara."

Sixty-Four

Matt was right. This was a big deal!

I grabbed my daughter's arms. "What guy approached you? Describe him!"

"An older guy with glasses and a bad toupee. He acted like I knew him. He was kind of sweet, actually."

Relieved, I let go of Joy's arms.

Then Matt grabbed mine. "Did you hear that?! Some creep was looking for Kara. And I doubt he's going to be the only one. You've summoned a dozen dating app lowlifes and put them on the prowl for our daughter!"

"Mom? Dad? What are you talking about?"

I held my head. "God, you're right. Joy looks like me in that old photo. But she wasn't supposed to be here!"

"Well, she *is* here. And now she's a target. I'll bet that was Mr. Reveal His True Self out there propositioning her, too."

"How do you know about that?!"

"Mother called me. She never actually said the words, but I could tell she was concerned that I was behaving like that pervert. I assured her the only people who got pictures of my *hoo-hah* were working airport X-ray machines."

Joy threw up her hands. "Dad, what do I have to do with some old photo of Mom? Or with a picture of your — what exactly is a *hoo-hah*?! Will one of you *please* tell me what's going on?"

"What's going on, young lady, is you're grounded." Matt pointed to the ceiling. "You are going upstairs right now and locking the apartment's door behind you."

Joy laughed. "Dad, you can't 'ground' me anymore. I'm an adult!"

But he has the right idea, I thought. "For your own safety, Joy, you have to go upstairs. We have plenty of help down here."

Joy eyed us both. "Since when do you two agree on anything? Sorry, I'm going back to work."

Matt blocked her path. "Let your mother explain the situation first. Maybe you'll change your mind when you realize the peril she put you in."

I didn't want to involve Joy in this, but it was obviously too late. So I quickly shared the story behind the Barista APB. No surprise, Joy was undaunted.

"Count me in! I'd love to help put a lying, cheating heartbreaker under arrest!"

Every bit Madame's granddaughter, she was all for catching the stinky fish, which prompted Matt to suck air. For the next five minutes, he tried to talk her out of it — and failed.

"Fine," he relented at last. "You can stay. But" — he barked at me — "if our daughter is going out there to hunt for a predator, she's not going alone!"

"What does that mean?" Joy asked.

"That means, all night, I'm going to be on you like, like . . . like birds on a hippopotamus!"

Joy's mouth fell open. "A hippo? *Really,* Daddy? I've gained *a few* pounds since the last time you saw me, but a hippo?!"

Turning on her heel, she headed back to the front of the shop, Matt hurrying behind.

"Baby, that's not what I meant! It's just an expression — in Africa, the birds love the hippos. It's a mutually beneficial relationship. They keep ticks and parasites off their backs —"

"Eew!"

Sixty-Five

As I watched my ex-husband chase after our daughter, I felt a measure of relief — not total, but enough — because when Matteo Allegro vows to protect his baby (hippo or not), no male parasite on the planet stands a chance of getting near her.

And, yes, the vulture-like proximity of my ex-husband could scare off the likes of Richard Crest, but Joy's safety came first. Besides, my whole staff was on the lookout for the man; and, after years of hearing Quinn's war stories, I knew there was more than one way to catch a creep.

For instance, take this new wrinkle with Sydney Webber-Rhodes.

She recognized the face in Dante's sketches, and that recognition obviously upset her. *Why?*

It looked to me like this Richard Crest character had paid Haley Hartford to do work for him. And from what I overheard in the alley, Haley had set up some kind of digital "backdoor" to the Cinder programming.

Had Crest paid Haley to create that door so he could manipulate the app? Was he the one who remotely erased abuse reports and negative comments? If so, why did he want to sabotage the app? What would he gain by doing it?

Cody mentioned something about money, too — over six figures of deposits *into* the Cinder treasure chests that couldn't be accounted for. That made no sense, either. Extortion typically involved robbing a company of money, not adding to its coffers.

As I returned to the front of our shop to find Sydney (and attempt to get some answers), I noticed the cool jazz on our sound system was lowering in volume. Suddenly, Esther's voice poured out of our speakers —

"Good evening, and welcome to the Village Blend! We are about to begin tonight's open mic poetry slam in our upstairs lounge. Join us right now for some rap with your frap and wit that won't quit. Plus an important unveiling. Come on up and see what the talk of the Village will be!"

The buzz of conversation grew louder as

curious customers swarmed our spiral staircase. Across the room, Sydney's gaze found mine. *What the hell is going on?*

I pointed upstairs, wanting her to see for herself.

Immediately, she typed into her phone. The pastel Tinkerbells got the message and joined their boss at the crowded base of the spiral stairs.

Meanwhile, I hurried back to the pantry, climbed the empty service staircase, and slipped onto the packed second floor. Esther tossed me a wave. I flashed a thumbs-up, and she mounted our temporary stage.

Apron gone, my zaftig barista pushed up her black glasses, pulled the microphone off its stand, and took on her role as tonight's MC.

"All you Ellas and Fellas, you princes and princesses, and *especially* you paupers, peons, and peasants who seldom get invited to the ball, lend us your ear! And, if you're so inclined, lend your tongue for our first round of slam fun . . ."

I noticed Sydney and her posse cresting the steps. The large room was packed, every café table filled, but they quickly found standing room near the back.

"Which brings us to tonight's special theme . . ." Esther continued. "May I have a table drumroll, please?" She held the mic out to the audience, and they lightly pounded our tabletops.

"Dating Disasters and Horrible Hook-ups!"

As the crowd lit up with laughter, the Tinkerbells frowned, and Sydney's megawatt game face went dark.

Sixty-Six

Give it a chance, Sydney, I texted to her from across the room. *Keep an open mind . . .*

"If you're unlucky at love, you've come to the right space," Esther declared. "Planet Earth!"

The crowd laughed.

"Too big? Too broad?" she continued. "Then you will applaud when we narrow it down to this room, *this lounge!*"

Hearing his cue, Dante stepped onstage and pulled a string that unfurled his handmade banner against the back wall.

WELCOME TO THE VILLAGE BLEND'S
SHOT DOWN LOUNGE

As the whole room laughed and clapped, Dante swept his hand over the banner like a game show host and a few females in the audience added wolf whistles.

Esther rolled her eyes. "You're a hit, Baldini."

Going with the flow, Dante mugged a Mr. Universe pose, and more women (and even a few men) whistled at his tattooed flexing.

"So join us up here," Esther urged the audience, "if you're shot down some night, for live music, karaoke, or slam poetry *lite*. If you're not a poet, no worries, just share your woes in standard prose — and *smile* 'cause we're streaming to the digi-globe!" She pointed to Nancy, down in front, who waved at the crowd from behind a camera. "For those doing free verse, you can make it terse — or take the full three minutes before you quit it. And now . . . let's hit it!"

As more folks packed into the standing-room-only lounge, mobile phone cameras came out, and our amateur poets lined up near the stage. There were women and men, some in their twenties, a few in their thirties, customers we saw every day — a bank teller, a paramedic, an accountant, an office manager, a waitress, a programmer, a nanny, and a graphic designer, all waiting their turns to rap out their dating disasters. Finally the first poet, a young woman, approached the mic . . .

Un-Related

I matched an older dude, but he was still
    hot.
We met at a bar and he smiled a lot.
He said, "You look like her," and I asked,
    "Who?"
"Your cousin. We were married in 2002."
They'd split by now and weren't even
    speaking.
Too young to remember, I couldn't stop
    freaking!
"You want me, I know," he said with a wink.
I covered his head with my two-for-one
    drink.

Class Mate

I was sixteen at the time (six years in my
    past)
when a girl friended me and began to chat.
She was cute and funny and I thought she
    was cool.
She said she went to a nearby high school.
But nobody knew her, and I couldn't see
why she never FaceTimed or wanted to
    meet.
When I got her number, I ran a check.
Reverse directory made me a wreck.
She wasn't a scam-bot or dark-web

creature,
the "girl" of my dreams was my history
teacher!

The Wrong Divorcée

ForeverLoveWithYou.com matched my
ex-wife with me,
five years *after* our divorce.

Clueless

Slamming shots of tequila, she started to cry
about her ex-boyfriend and how she lost a
"great guy!"
With tears streaming down, I thought she
might drown,
and I'd feel like a skunk, if I left her
half-drunk.
So I listened for hours about her lost man.
Then I poured her ass into an Uber van.
Next day, she texts "thanks" for my
"hospitality."
Wants a second date! Are you kidding me?!

Hazardous Hookup

Greatest date ever! (I thought.)
We talked and laughed and went back to
his squat.

Made love and passed out. Then I had to
   pee.
Swung in the wrong room — and what did I
   see?
Guns and ammo and Semtex galore.
I even saw bulletproof vests on the floor!
I hurried home and called the cops.
Then got drunk on peppermint schnapps.
Three months later, I get a text from his
   brother.
"My bro is in prison for one reason or other.
He'd like to see you. Here's the lockup's
   process . . ."
I changed my phone number and blocked
   his address!"

Sliced

"Let's meet for pizza," she said, once we
   matched.
They say to meet quickly, and she was a
   catch.
So I bought the pie. We shared it and
   talked.
I worked hard to be charming, didn't think
   I'd get blocked
when I asked for her number. But she said,
   "Naw, I'm good.
Just wanted free pizza. See you in the
   hood!"

Catfished

"I can't decide what's more beautiful.
Your name or that smile."
He was so romantic. Had class and style.
It was three years ago, when I was
    eighteen.
I matched with him, and he spoke like a
    dream.
Said he was twenty, and looked it, too —
in the photos he used on social media
    views.
After weeks of messaging, we declared our
    love.
I wanted to meet, sure we'd fit like a glove.
He proposed that we kiss and take a long
    drive.
That's when I found out — he was fifty-five.

Empty

I swipe and type and fly like a kite
when he picks me from the dating app tree.
But my photo is shopped, and my texts are
    all copped
from a clever blog I know.
So who is he picking? And who am I
    kidding?
Welcome to the robot show.
Hi, wassup? Hi, wassup? A thousand times

a day.
One likes my smile; another, my wit,
but it's all a big pile of —

The poet tipped her mic to the audience,
who called out the missing word.

Fingers and thumbs, tapping and rapping
Feels like a party (where no one came)
So many guys. But after some time,
these dates all sound —

"The same!" cried the room.

This wireless connection is pretend
    affection.
The screen is a mirror, but I *need* its —

"Reflection!" the people shouted.

So it's back to the swiping, the selfies and
    liking,
back to the love less real.
Hold the phone, there's another entry!

The poet paused to uplift her phone like a
holy grail. Then she brought it down, her
voice going quiet . . .

My hands are full,
but my arms are empty.

The crowd had been warmly applauding every poet brave enough to approach the mic. But this last one must have hit a chord with the app users, because she got the biggest hand of all. Some women even stood up to applaud her.

As the next poem began, I noticed Sydney had heard enough.

With a snap of her fingers, she summoned her Tinkerbell posse and headed for the stairs.

I did, too, the *back* stairs.

Muscles still aching from that ridiculous Critter Crawl, I forced my feet to take two steps at a time. Then I burst out the back alley door and raced around the corner — just in time to catch Sydney Webber-Rhodes storming out our front door.

SIXTY-SEVEN

"You ruined everything, Clare. This is a total disaster."

"No, it isn't. The crowd is enjoying the show. And did you notice, after the poets came off the stage, people were eager to speak with them, wanting to share their own bad experiences —"

"Bad experiences?! Are you an idiot? My app delivers *happy* endings! That's the narrative. That's the message!"

"I know that's what you're trying to sell, but there's a bigger picture here to consider. Just listen a minute —"

"I'm leaving."

I blocked her path on the sidewalk. "*Please,* one minute?"

She folded her arms and gave me a look that felt like it plunged six inches into my chest. I sucked in air and plowed forward.

"Believe it or not, we all want the same things. Even Esther —"

Sydney scoffed, but I kept talking.

"Tonight we officially launched our second floor as the 'Shot Down Lounge' for my customers and yours. When their swipe-to-meet dates don't work out downstairs, they can move upstairs, into a community of people who are looking to find connections — and another chance at those 'happy endings' you claim to want so badly for your app's users. Esther and I already talked it over. We'll have live music, karaoke, and fun icebreakers for customers, like the open mic poetry slams —"

"More poetry? Like those awful ones tonight, you mean?"

"They weren't awful. I thought they were truthful and human — and remarkably brave. Don't you see? Esther's idea to dedicate the lounge is a kind of *ubuntu,* a gesture for the community. It's the best of both worlds, digital and physical, maybe even a chance for the worst app addicts to regain some self-worth, instead of desperately seeking it through swiping. Wait, don't go!"

But she was already gone, her Tinkerbells trailing after her.

When I spied AJ's brunette pixie in the exiting group, I impulsively hooked the girl's arm. "Hold on, AJ. I want to ask you something. It's important."

With worried eyes, she nodded, and I lowered my voice. "When Sydney saw those sketches in our pantry, she had an extreme reaction. How does she know that Richard Crest character?"

AJ's body tensed. "He's someone from her past," she whispered. "That's all I know."

I tried asking about Haley, but she broke away. Then she was gone, too. I considered chasing after her — as embarrassing as that would have been — but my way was suddenly blocked by a skinny, freckle-faced youth wearing a backward baseball cap and enough faux gold chains to open a hip-hop jewelry emporium.

"Yo, lady! I'm here for a hookup. A hottie named Kara wants to bump fuzzies with me. If you'd just point her out, I can induce the magic."

"Kara?" I looked him over. This freckle-faced teen was definitely *not* Crest. "Sorry, Kara is, uh . . . underage, and her father's in there lecturing her. I wouldn't tempt fate. The man's got a temper, and I think he's packing."

"Damn!" The kid couldn't flee fast enough. "Peace out, lady!"

SIXTY-EIGHT

AS the wannabe gangsta departed, I sat down heavily at an outdoor table and massaged my temples.

So far tonight I'd scored a big fat zero. The Cinder bash was a bust, as far as the company's CEO was concerned. And our Barista APB had come up empty. I'd like to say the night was young, but it was already past eleven PM, and there was nary a sign of Richard Crest.

At least Esther's poetry slam was a hit with the customers. Everyone seemed to enjoy it — well, everyone but the Tinkerbells.

Was the Shot Down Lounge a naïve idea? Sydney's extreme negative reaction (or maybe just my aching Critter Crawl muscles) put a pin in my optimistic bubble.

With two hours left until closing, there wasn't much more that could upset me, or so I thought — until I sat back in the café chair and caught sight of a familiar-looking red SUV parked across the street. It was the color of a young cabernet. I *might* have doubted it was the same vehicle that almost ran me down, if I hadn't seen the mud splattered on its grill and wheel wells.

I hurried into the coffeehouse to track down Matt. He'd promised to deal with Red Beard the next time he had the chance. And that time may have come.

I found Joy, but to my surprise, there was no sign of my ex.

"Where's your father?"

"He had to go, Mom. His date — Marilyn something — got a headache so he walked her home."

"I can't believe he left you alone."

Joy shrugged. "I think Daddy is *finally* acknowledging that I'm an adult and perfectly capable of taking care of myself."

As she moved to bus another table, Dante followed close behind.

"Don't worry, boss," he whispered. "Matt *ordered* me to keep a close watch on her — something about birds on a hippo?"

I suppressed a laugh. *Yeah, that was Matt.* "Have you seen any sign of Crest?"

"No. And no one's hit on Joy since I started looking after her. The Barista APB looks like a bust. I think the dude slipped our dragnet . . ."

Dante's words stayed with me for the rest of the evening. I kept watching for Crest, and Red Beard, too, but didn't see either.

Near closing time, we got busy again — a last call for coffee brought a surge to the counter, our supplies ran low, and our pastries ran out. Finally, we closed the doors.

I sent Joy upstairs. She'd been on the go since the crack of dawn and didn't argue. I told Dante and Nancy to take off, as well. Tucker agreed to handle closing duties with me, and Esther insisted on helping, claiming she was too keyed up from the slam to go home.

So, while Tuck policed the lounge and Esther cleaned the kitchen area and loaded the dishwasher, I headed outside with a broom, a dustpan, and a wheeled trash can.

The night was cold, and getting colder now that the outdoor heaters were turned off. Traffic was light on Hudson, and pedestrians were scarce.

As I began to sweep, I saw that Red Beard's SUV was (thankfully) gone. That's when I noticed a man passed out at the farthest table.

No big deal. I'd seen this sort of thing before, usually in the late spring or summer. Some college kid or bridge-and-tunnel partier would have one too many at a nearby bar and try to sober up with our coffee before heading home. They seldom gave us trouble, but I hung back, anyway, hoping he'd wake up and move on.

But ten minutes later, the man was still slumped over the table. I continued to sweep until I reached him. A coffee cup lay at his feet, its contents spilled onto the sidewalk.

"Hello!" I called, sweeping as I moved closer. "Are you okay?"

I was about to shake his shoulder when I was rocked by twin shocks. The coffee wasn't coffee; it was blood. And the man sprawled across the table was Richard Crest.

Sixty-Nine

Once again, my coffeehouse was a crime scene.

Outside our front door were four squad cars, two vans from the Crime Scene Unit, a truck from Traffic Control, an FDNY ambulance, and an SUV from the medical examiner's office. Hudson Street was so clogged that officers in reflective vests were redirecting traffic away from the area.

Yellow police tape blocked all the sidewalks around our shop, too, even though most of the action — and the bright tower lights — were concentrated in one small corner, at one table, around one very dead body.

Esther, Tucker, and I had been told to wait at a table "until detectives arrive to question you." A rookie officer was also stationed inside the shop to make sure we stayed put. As of now, we'd been here for nearly an hour — a conscience-stricken sixty minutes as Esther and I pondered our role in this mess.

Did I lure this man to his death?

Esther wondered the same thing, though Tuck pooh-poohed the notion, stopping just short of declaring that the dead man had it coming.

Guilty feelings aside, it was a question I was certain the detectives would also be asking — if not tonight, then after they cracked the victim's phone and found a message from bikini babe "Kara," inviting him to the scene of his demise.

I dreaded what was to come as the Fish Squad pushed through the front door. Soles and Bass were grim faced as they crossed the polished plank floor, though Sue Ellen's hard expression was softened somewhat by her loose hair, flowery skirt, soft sweater, and dangly earrings.

They were accompanied by a grizzled sergeant with a beer belly, and another policeman in a yellow NYPD Traffic vest, bearing an industrial-strength laptop.

The sergeant went behind our counter and looked around. Soon he disappeared into the pantry. Meanwhile, the traffic officer set the laptop on the marble coffee bar, turned it so we couldn't see the screen, and began to type. Soles and Bass watched for a few minutes, sometimes whispering instructions to the cop.

The sergeant's alarming two-word call — "Back here!" — interrupted them.

Soles and Bass strode into the pantry, where they lingered for a few minutes. When they came out again, the two detectives walked right up to our table, shaking their heads.

"Nice catch, Cosi," Lori Soles said. "Looks like you were right when you said this guy was trouble."

"I don't think we're going to get much out of him, though," Sue Ellen cracked. "Not after someone took the *trouble* of whacking him."

"Did you find out his real name?" I asked.

"He's got IDs for one Harry Krinkle," Sue Ellen replied, "but that identity might be as phony as the last one."

I brought out my phone and showed the detectives the photo I took of the man's bank withdrawal receipt. They asked me to send it to them forthwith. Then Lori's hands went to her hips.

"You know, you're lucky we were running a sting in Hudson River Park. We understand what you were trying to do here, but the Night Watch might have come to some *wrong conclusions* once they took a look at those two wanted posters in your pantry."

Sue Ellen sent a chuckle in my direction. "Dead or alive, eh, Sheriff? So does the shooter collect the reward?"

"You know that's not what I wanted," I firmly stated. "But if you think I'm guilty, arrest me alone. Please leave my staff out of it —"

Lori silenced me with a raised hand.

"Relax, Cosi. We've got our suspect. A traffic camera captured the actual murder. We'd like you and your people to look at the raw footage. It's disturbing, but maybe one of you can ID the woman in question."

"Woman?!" Tuck cried.

"That's right. Like I said, it's disturbing. So if any of you would rather not watch the —"

"We'll watch it!" Tuck, Esther, and I practically shouted together.

Lori pointed to the counter. "Okay, let's do it."

SEVENTY

We gathered around the computer. Then the traffic cop rolled the footage.

The screen time read 12:33 AM, twenty-seven minutes before the Village Blend closed. Despite the late hour, the nearby LED streetlight, along with our own exterior shop lights, provided good clarity and color to the picture, which was shot from a high angle.

At 12:34 the man we knew as Richard Crest stepped into the frame and sat down at the corner table — the farthest from our door. His chair was flanked by open sidewalk on one side and the redbrick wall of our shop on the other. Crest thumbed his smartphone, ignoring his surroundings. A few people walked by on the sidewalk, and all the tables near him remained empty.

Six minutes later, a slender woman stepped into the frame holding a blue paper cup and shouldering a large tote bag. She wore baggy sweatpants, a pulled-up hoodie, and a large, loose jacket. A scarf was coiled around her neck and lower face, and gloves covered her hands. Though her facial features were hidden, strands of honey blond hair spilled out from under the hood.

The man's attention was focused completely on his smartphone. As he crouched in his chair, typing into the device in his hand, she pulled an object from her jacket pocket.

Moving quickly, she placed the blue coffee cup on the table in front of Crest. In the split second it took for him to notice the cup being set down, the killer stepped behind him. Using her large tote bag to block the street view of the weapon, she shot Richard Crest in the back at close range. The victim jerked, and blood gushed from an exit wound in his chest. As he slumped forward, his dying spasms knocked the killer's blue coffee cup off the table.

By 12:41, Crest was obviously dead, and the killer was calmly walking away, taking the victim's smartphone with her.

Lori asked the traffic officer to run the footage again, while the two detectives provided commentary.

"The victim was shot once, through the heart. From the wound on the body, it was likely a .38 caliber handgun," Sue Ellen said. "Though we can't see it, the gun had some type of silencer attached, because the ShotSpotter in the area never picked up the blast, or sent an alert to the precinct."

"The Crime Scene Unit recovered the coffee cup," Lori said. "The killer wore gloves, but they hope to lift a fingerprint or two."

The words *coffee cup* spurred my memory. "Wind it back," I said. "I want to watch the victim die again."

"Whoa, you're a cold one," Sue Ellen joked.

"Freeze it right there!" I said at the moment the killer set down the blue paper cup. I stared at the screen, then shook my head.

"This can't be right. The cup —"

Lori squinted. "It's a Village Blend cup. I can make out the design."

"That's my point." I reached behind the counter and grabbed one of the *white* cups that we'd been using most of the evening. "This is our catering cup. We only use these white cups at events outside the Blend. Never here. But we were forced to use these cups tonight because we ran out of our standard blue Village Blend logo cups —"

"When?" Sue Ellen asked.

"About eight o'clock. Shortly after my barista Vicki opened a box of replacements in the pantry, I realized Matt had brought the wrong cups from the warehouse —"

"But you did use both cups tonight?" Lori countered.

"Sure. But don't you find it strange that the killer walked around the party with the same cold cup in her hand for over four hours — or kept a disposable paper cup from a previous visit? It's not normal behavior."

"Neither is shooting someone dead at a corner café," Sue Ellen pointed out. "Nevertheless, Cosi's got a point."

"Okay, noted," Lori said. "Let's move along."

As we watched, various street cameras followed the killer slowly walking up Hudson. After a right turn onto Barrow, her trek ended at a redbrick prewar apartment building at the corner of Barrow and Bedford.

"She used a key or was buzzed inside," Sue Ellen said. "The front entrance wasn't tampered with according to the CSU team over there now."

"It would help if any of you recognized this individual," Lori said. "A lot of people live in that building, and she may only be a visitor or a guest. Have you ever been to this place before? Do you know anyone connected with this apartment house?"

Esther and I shook our heads.

Tuck stared at the screen in tense silence.

Finally, I apologized to the detectives for our lack of help.

"No worries," Lori said as the traffic officer closed the computer. "With what we already have, we should be able to make an arrest within twenty-four hours — maybe less. There's so much evidence that it's only a matter of time."

"And I should thank you, Cosi, for pulling us away from decoy duty in the park," Sue Ellen said as she flipped her flowery skirt. "You don't know how much I hate dressing like a drag queen."

Then the Fish Squad wished us a nice night and headed out.

The detectives appeared chipper for good reason. They would soon have a killer in custody and a quickly solved homicide. But, as I sent my people home and locked the front door, I couldn't share their enthusiasm or their certainty. And — as heartlessly mercenary as it might sound — I went up to bed worrying what kind of impact this violent crime would have on our coffeehouse.

A few fake gun blasts nearly torpedoed our shop. How were we going to survive a real shot in the dark?

SEVENTY-ONE

"Mom?"

Hearing my daughter's voice, I shifted under the bedcovers.

"Wake up, Mom. I'm leaving . . ."

With a yawn, I opened my eyes to find Joy sitting on the edge of my big four-poster, sipping from a travel mug of coffee. She was fully dressed, her chestnut hair pulled into a no-nonsense ponytail, her eyes wet and bloodshot, her nose red as Rudolph's.

"Honey, what's wrong?" I quickly sat up, much to the dismay of Java and Frothy, who'd been cuddling up to me for some extra warmth during the cold autumn night. "Were you crying again?"

"I'm flying back to DC this morning . . ." She scratched Frothy's fluffy white neck as she spoke. "I want to relieve Chef Bell in the afternoon. I'd rather work than waste any more time blubbering over my stupid love life problems."

"They're not stupid . . ." I rubbed my eyes, then ceded to Java's feline demands to rub her soft brown ears, as well. "I thought we decided this yesterday. You're going to stay and speak to Manny. You have coverage in DC, and —"

"I don't want it anymore. I want to go."

"Why? What's changed? Don't you want to work things out? You love Manny. And I'm sure he loves you."

"After that awful video, I'm not sure at all."

"Video? What video?"

"You haven't seen it? Dad sent it to both of us. Here . . ."

She handed me my phone from the night-stand. I powered it on and tapped the e-mail app. A message had come in from Quinn. I bypassed it and opened the one from Joy's father.

I started by reading Matt's text . . .

After I walked Marilyn home, I was feeling beat, too, so I grabbed a cab and headed back to Brooklyn. On the way, I shot this footage. You both need to see this . . .

I played the five-minute video.

I could see Matt had captured it while traveling through Soho, on his way to the

Williamsburg Bridge. The streets in this area boasted the greatest collection of cast-iron architecture in the world, and one of the highest-priced real estate markets in the city.

The neighborhood's nightlife was equally expensive, and one of the hottest spots in Manhattan at the moment was the trendy new Soho Lounge. Tucked between another of those Equator luxury gyms and a gallery for digital art, the Lounge served craft cocktails and a menu of posh noshes from Royal Ossetra caviar to truffle beignets.

Matt panned the camera over a stylish downtown crowd, loitering in front of the exclusive watering hole. And that's when I spotted the reason for my ex-husband's attempt to channel Martin Scorsese.

Joy's beloved boyfriend, Emmanuel Franco, dressed for success in a gorgeously tailored business suit, was talking and laughing with a stunning brunette. A strappy black dress hugged her perfect curves, and Franco's big arm was hooked around her waist.

After exiting the Lounge's double glass doors, the pair strolled along the crowded sidewalk and paused at the corner, where Franco helped the woman into her coat.

Matt obviously shot this footage while stuck in a traffic jam. As the cab slowly moved down the block, he kept the camera on the young sergeant and his chic date.

"Make a left here," Matt's voice sharply told the driver.

"I thought you were going to Red Hook —"

"I'm taking a detour. Make the turn and go slow."

Matt continued to shoot the pair as they walked, arm in arm, into an exquisite residential building with an attentive doorman, who appeared to greet them with friendly recognition.

Off camera, I heard Matt call Franco a few choice names. Then, with disgust in his voice, he told the driver, "Let's go. Take off . . ." And the video ended.

"Mom, I can hardly believe it . . ." Joy's voice was weak, her lower lip quivering. "That he would do this to me . . . to us . . ."

I knew how she felt. And yet . . .

"Joy, you still need to *speak* with Franco about all this. You need to do it in person. He owes you answers."

She shook her head. "It's too humiliating."

"Have you tried contacting him?"

"Yes, of course! I left several messages, asking him to call me back. He replied twice by text. 'Busy working. Will get back to you soon. Love you.' Yeah, right."

"I'm sure he does love you."

"So what am I supposed to do? Track him down at this Joan woman's multimillion-dollar Soho apartment? Or go over to his place later and find her answering the door in his NYPD T-shirt? I can't. I can't . . ."

I couldn't blame her for wanting to run away. This news was crushing, the video evidence irrefutable. It broke my heart, too.

Still, I tried to argue with my daughter, convince her to stay, but it was no use. She had made up her mind. Like her father, there'd be no changing it.

After a quick, tight hug good-bye, my Joy was gone.

Seventy-Two

It was too early on this tense Sunday morning to be staring at fish and chips, but that's exactly what was displayed on my smartphone screen when I finally opened Mike Quinn's message — *after* a long, sad shower and a desperate double espresso.

London was five hours ahead of New York, and Mike had sent me a photo of his lunch. The man's voice mail message was cheerful, but I was hungrier to hear him speak than view his midday meal.

"I was hoping to hear your sweet voice before I listened to bureaucratese for the next five days, but I guess 'please leave a message' will have to do for now. I'm due at Scotland Yard for a meet-and-greet with our NYPD liaison officer. I'll call again later."

Pause.

"Oh, I was thinking about our wedding, and I visited a place this morning that would be perfect. It's called Westminster

Abbey, and it just might be big enough to accommodate my family. Think about it, okay?"

Another pause.

"And if it's too much trouble to contemplate our wedding, then use the power of suggestion to imagine we're having this delicious pub lunch together. And your Peanut Butter Cookies. Your shop always has them on Sundays, and I think I'm addicted. They don't have them here," he relayed with sweet disappointment. "Well, anyway, I'd better go. I miss you."

I missed him, too. So much. Unfortunately, he didn't send a selfie, just a pic of the fish and chips, and all that did was remind me of the Fish Squad and make me worry again how last night's crime scene would impact our business.

By now, I'd decided *not* to discuss Sergeant Franco's personal behavior with Mike while he was in London. I didn't want him to be distracted. And I still wanted answers from the horse's mouth — even though Franco appeared to be acting like the horse's other end. So I sent a curt message to the man, asking him to stop by the Village Blend for a talk.

If Joy was too humiliated to confront her boyfriend, I certainly wasn't. I planned to show the sergeant Matt's video and demand an explanation. At the very least, I expected him to be straight with me and my daughter.

This lying and cheating was beneath any man of decent character. I would demand he break things off with Joy in a civilized manner and give her the closure she deserved.

As depressing as *that* prospect was, the morning's business wasn't much better. For a Sunday, we were abnormally quiet, other than a few neighborhood regulars and NYU students stopping for coffee while they read the papers.

Tucker and I eagerly devoured the news, too, relieved to find that last evening's shooting only made one late edition — a police blotter paragraph with no pictures, no mention of the Village Blend, and the victim's name "withheld pending notification of next of kin."

Ironically, Carol Lynn Kendall's fake gun caused a bigger bang in our world than a killer's real one. With no one uploading mobile phone videos or spouting hashtag opinions on social media, the result was a crime committed in relative silence, and (for the moment) I dared to breathe a sigh of relief.

With Richard Crest gone, could the worst be

over?

By eleven AM, it certainly seemed that our luck was turning. Business became brisk and steady. By eleven thirty, more than a few people had come in asking for the pastries or coffee drinks photographed by Sydney's prepaid crowd and uploaded to the interweb.

About an hour later, there was a mini-rush, with many of the customers climbing the spiral staircase to the upstairs lounge after making a purchase. By one PM that rush became an avalanche — the Village Blend was so busy I pleaded with Esther to come in early to take up some of the slack. A quick text brought Dante here to set up the outdoor tables and heat lamps — because we desperately needed them, despite the chilly afternoon.

As I whipped up drinks behind the espresso machine, I was starting to think Sydney's plan had actually worked. It wasn't until later that I learned the real reason for the Village Blend's revived popularity, and it had little to do with the schemes of Sydney Webber-Rhodes and everything to do with Esther Best.

But I'm getting ahead of myself.

It was around three o'clock when Tuck and I neared the end of our break, and moved downstairs to get back to work. Suddenly, Tucker cried out and threw his lanky arms wide.

"Carol Lynn Kendall!"

SEVENTY-THREE

As Tucker wrapped his arms around his friend, I approached the pair.

Carol Lynn looked relaxed in denims, a soft blue sweater, and a quilted blue jacket. Seeing me, she smiled shyly and extended her slender hand.

"Ms. Cosi, right?"

A table was vacant, and I grabbed it while Tuck went off to bring some coffeehouse treats.

The polite young woman who sat across from me was a pale shadow of the fierce, armed-and-dangerous drama queen who'd disrupted my business and my life. But I was relieved to see the near-catatonic girl, who'd been timidly carted off to jail, was gone, too.

Face plain, sans makeup, honey blond hair tied neatly back, Carol Lynn met my curious gaze with eyes that were clear, sharp, and focused.

"I came to tell you I'm sorry, Ms. Cosi," she said firmly. "I'm ashamed of the trouble I brought you."

"No apologies necessary —"

"No, that's not true. I had no right to disrupt your place of business. It was wrong."

"I'm just glad to see you're —"

"Sane?"

"No. *Better.* And out of jail."

"The legal system was the easy part. Our producer hired a great lawyer, and refused to press charges against me over the stolen prop gun. There's a plea deal in the works that involves no prison, just probation and community service."

"That's great," I said. "You can start fresh."

"I'm required to see a doctor every week. I've had some emotional issues in the past, and I'd more or less stopped taking my medications months before it all happened. I thought I was cured, but I guess I wasn't. As part of the plea deal, my medications must be monitored by a psychiatrist, and I have to see a therapist, too."

I was glad to hear Carol Lynn was getting the help she needed, and I told her so. "I'm sorry you crossed paths with such a horrible human being. Tucker talked to me about Richard Crest, what he did to you, and other women."

"Thank you for saying that, but I've already forgiven him."

"That's very generous of you, Carol Lynn, more generous than a lot of women would be in your shoes."

"What he did was very wrong. But I was wrong, too. Now I'm glad the nightmare is over, and he and I can go our separate ways . . ."

I realized then that Carol Lynn didn't know, likely *couldn't* know, about Crest's murder.

"With so many people showing me how much they care," she went on, "I truly feel blessed and loved — and very lucky things didn't turn out worse. I have my whole life ahead of me now, and I'm seeing things much more clearly, rationally, and *in proportion!*" She laughed. "I'm feeling a lot stronger, too, like myself again. For the first time in a long time . . ."

I believed what she said about feeling stronger, but I feared the shock of hearing how Crest was shot dead might really shake her. As I debated how to tell her, Tuck arrived bearing frothy cappuccinos and a plate of Carol Lynn's favorite treats — so she said, because they brought back sweet memories from childhood.

Our big Café-Style Peanut Butter Cookies, caramelized and crispy on the outside yet moist and chewy on the inside, were the very cookies Mike was pining for in London. (Our baker delivered large batches every Sunday from my "secret ingredient" recipe.)

"I'm glad you're back, Tuck," Carol Lynn said.

"You need the coffee that bad?"

"Yes, actually, and a few of those cookies!" She laughed. "But there's another reason. Now I can congratulate you both!"

Tuck and I exchanged confused glances.

Carol Lynn blinked. "You guys don't know, do you?"

"Don't know about what?"

"The excitement about your coffeehouse. I stopped by here last evening to talk to you, Clare, but I couldn't find you in the large crowd, so I left early. Then this morning I saw the coverage. Now the whole country's heard of the Shot Down Lounge!"

SEVENTY-FOUR

"What?!" Tuck and I cried together.

"There's a huge article on *The Tablet* with tons of pics from last night and videos of your poetry slam," Carol Lynn said. "It's all about how you repurposed your upstairs lounge as a second chance for people disappointed over dating app matchups. The Village Blend is now a trending topic all over social media. On Chatter, Shot Down Lounge even has its own hashtag!"

Tuck pulled out his smartphone and went to *The Tablet,* where we discovered that the *Washington Post* reporter wasn't the only journalist at Sydney's shindig. And unlike Cinder's CEO, who thought the evening was a total disaster, the writer from *The Tablet* was amused and impressed.

The article appeared under the headline:

Hookups with a Human Face After Dating Disasters, Shot Down Lounge Provides Caffeine and Comfort

The piece opened with a summary of the storied, bohemian history of the Village Blend. Then the author launched into a vivid description of last night's event — gushing about the concept of a Shot Down Lounge, and raving about Esther's poetry slam.

There was praise for the camaraderie of the crowd, and then the author decried the fact that other dating venues didn't provide more "compassion with their cappuccinos, or community with their cocktails," concluding that "Cinder and the Village Blend have restored sanity and soul to the swipe-to-meet twenty-first century."

"Your coffeehouse is completely famous," Carol Lynn said. "And for the right reason, this time"

"This calls for a toast!" Tuck declared. "I'll grab more espressos —"

But my assistant manager found his way was blocked by two sturdy police officers in uniform, who stood on either side of Detectives Soles and Bass. The Fish Squad wasn't smiling, and this wasn't a social call.

"Carol Lynn Kendall," Sue Ellen announced. "You are under arrest for the murder of Robert Crenshaw —"

"No!" Tucker shouted.

"You have the right to remain silent, and

anything you say can and will be used against you in a court of law —"

"This is some kind of mistake," Carol Lynn cried. "I didn't kill anybody! I don't know anyone named Crenshaw!"

Quickly and efficiently, the officers lifted Carol Lynn out of her chair and cuffed her hands behind her back. Only then did she begin to struggle.

"No! This is wrong!" she yelled, squirming in their steel grip.

Customers inside my busy coffeehouse parted to allow the police to pass.

"No . . . Please . . ." Carol Lynn sobbed. Tuck followed his friend to the exit, begging the police to treat her gently.

Before Lori could follow her partner out the door, I grabbed her arm.

"What's going on?" I asked. "Why do you think Carol Lynn is guilty of murder?"

Lori broke free. "The case against Ms. Kendall is airtight. So solid we don't even need a confession —"

"How can that be?"

Lori shook her head. "You saw the video. We used street cameras to track the killer's movements after the murder. We watched her walk to the apartment at the corner of Barrow and Bedford, which is also Ms. Kendall's address. On top of that, the

430

fingerprints on the coffee cup left by the killer match the ones previously taken from Ms. Kendall during her prior arrest for *assaulting and threatening the victim* in front of witnesses. One of whom, I might add, was you."

"I know what it *looks* like, but I told you already that cup is wrong. We stopped serving coffee in those blue cups many hours before the shooting —"

"That's not all we have," Lori said. "The Crime Scene Unit found the murder weapon and the clothes the killer wore in a Dumpster behind Ms. Kendall's apartment house. The handgun was cleaned of prints, but the clothes tested positive for gunshot residue."

"But —"

"I understand your concern, but there's no reasonable doubt. We've got everything on camera, from the murder to her return home. We have an eyewitness, too. The building superintendent stated that he saw Ms. Kendall tossing a bundle of clothes and a gun into the Dumpster at approximately two fifteen AM."

The air went out of me. "I'm surprised you don't have footage of Carol Lynn at the Dumpster."

"We would have had that, too, but the

camera in the alley behind the apartment building happens to be out of order."

Lori tried to spin it positive. "Cheer up, Clare. Ms. Kendall needs help. Now she'll get it. This is the best outcome, considering what went down. We're playing down the fact that she planned the whole thing, because the DA could make a strong case for premeditation, which ups the ante all around —"

Tears of futility formed behind my fast-blinking lashes. Bad enough I lured a man, however despicable, to his execution. Now a sweet young woman was arrested, because of something that happened at my coffeehouse.

Lori squeezed my shoulder in sympathy.

"Her lawyer's smart. I'm sure he'll find a compassionate judge. But Carol Lynn Kendall is guilty, and she will be punished for the murder of Robert Crenshaw."

SEVENTY-FIVE

"I know Carol Lynn didn't kill that man. I'm certain of it." Tucker spoke while gazing morosely through our French doors at the darkening streets.

It was Sunday evening, and though the gloom of night had descended over the city, our coffeehouse glowed like a lightship beacon. Filled to capacity with human souls, our shop's rejuvenated business continued to overflow onto the sidewalks.

At this hour, Vicki and Dante were working the counter, while Nancy bused tables and Esther MC'd karaoke and comedic trivia games in our Shot Down Lounge.

Now on our evening break, Tuck and I pondered Carol Lynn's plight, and what to do about it.

"Where did she get a gun?" he asked. "It's not like you can have an Amazon drone drop one at your doorstep. And, last I checked, there is no 'Guns and Ammo' aisle at Whole Foods."

He set his empty demitasse aside. "She's innocent, and we've got to prove it."

I understood Tucker's feelings, but the evidence against his friend seemed overwhelmingly conclusive —

"Maybe a little *too* conclusive," I said, thinking aloud. "It's possible the person who cooked up this scheme put a little too much icing on the cake."

Tuck blinked. "Icing? Cake? Are you thinking about your wedding plans again?"

"No. I'm thinking about that coffee cup with Carol Lynn's fingerprints on it. It's been bothering me since I saw it on the DOT video. It feels like one clue too many — one that doesn't fit. You see, despite what the police think they know, I know my business . . ."

I reminded Tuck that Carol Lynn said she came to our coffeehouse during last night's big event. "She told us that she stopped in to apologize, but couldn't find me in that paid mob, and she left early."

"So?"

"So if Carol Lynn bought a coffee early in the evening, then she got our standard blue cup with our logo. What if someone grabbed her cup *after* she disposed of it, fully intending to frame her for murder later that night?"

Tuck's face brightened for the first time since his friend's arrest. Then almost immediately, he frowned. "Who could hate Richard Crest enough to dress up like an innocent woman, kill him, and then frame that same woman? I mean, seriously? How much can a girl hate a guy?"

I let *that* question lie, to focus on another.

"The victim's name isn't Crest," I pointed out. "It's Robert Crenshaw, and he may have a history that can give us a few leads. I say we look him up right now."

I brought my laptop to the table and did a quick Internet search. There were a dozen Robert Crenshaws on Facebook and Twitter, and a "Top 25 Robert Crenshaw Profiles on LinkedIn." But when I narrowed the search from *All* to *News,* I struck gold.

The man lying dead at the city morgue turned out to be the infamous founder of Hookster, the discredited and defunct dating app shut down by a class action suit.

I skimmed the *Wall Street Journal* article Matt had mentioned, and then hit a *Wired* piece that told the whole ugly story of the rise and fall of Hookster.

"Remind me," Tuck said. "What is Hookster?"

"It's a hookup app, dreamed up by Crenshaw when he was in college. He created it with the help of a frat house pal named Tommy Finkle. Both were named in the subsequent class action lawsuit . . ."

I then recounted for Tuck the smarmy saga of Hookster's history, which billed itself as the swipe-to-meet app with the "hottest" and "horniest" women. Only they weren't real women. The programming buried profiles of real girls, while promoting matches with fantasy profiles of girls who didn't exist.

When a man "matched" with one of these "hotties," only three messages were allowed before the app required payment for further communication. Payment was needed because Hookster was really the equivalent of a 1-900 phone sex line posing as a legit dating app.

Crenshaw and his buddy could have gotten away with their scam, too — except that Robert Crenshaw hooked up professionally and romantically with a young marketing genius named Cindy Webber. It was Webber who took Hookster to new heights, and made the company millions of dollars.

Things went smoothly until Webber and Crenshaw had a falling-out.

Cindy Webber was forced to resign. But she didn't go quietly. In a webzine interview that went viral, Webber publicly blew the whistle on Hookster's internal culture of sexually harassing female employees. She also revealed that the app's creators intended to mislead their customers through false claims, which led to the lawsuit that closed the app down.

During a criminal discovery phase, Cindy was given immunity for her testimony. But the fine print in Hookster's terms of service, which laid out its "paid entertainment" model, absolved them from criminal conviction. Generous payoffs took care of the sexual harassment charges. But the class action lawsuit, filed on behalf of duped customers, finished their business.

After digesting that history, I wasn't surprised Robert Crenshaw — the renegade web designer who *Wired* magazine gushed over as "Captain Hookster Sailing on Success" — turned into a chameleon using false IDs like Richard Crest and Harry Krinkle.

Meanwhile, Cindy Webber, with her new married name, became Sydney Webber-Rhodes, founder and CEO of Cinder, which she promoted with a passionate vow to make *real* happy endings come true for couples, especially women. Women she now lamented were so badly objectified in the Hookster app.

"It's possible that Sydney could be the killer," I said. "Or one of her loyal Tinkerbells. I don't have any proof, but it sure looks like Crenshaw had a motive to sabotage Cinder, the shiny new business started by the woman who destroyed his. And if Haley helped him, and Sydney found out, well . . ."

"You think Sydney murdered Haley, too?"

"It's possible. From what I overheard in our alley, she knew Haley had put a backdoor in the Cinder programming. Maybe she suspected it for a while and contacted Haley to wring the truth out of her."

Tuck nodded. "Then Sydney smacked Haley upside her head and killed her." He paused. "I don't know. For a genius marketing mind, murder in a public park doesn't seem like a very good plan."

"No, it doesn't. And that's why I believe Haley's death wasn't planned. I think Haley met her killer at Habitat Garden and an argument went too far. If it was Sydney who exploded and struck Haley when she realized how deeply she'd been betrayed, she probably called her watchdog Cody to help her get rid of the body."

I recalled Cody's dead-eyed stare at the Equator gym.

"Yes, Cody seems just the type to have

'fixed' her boss's problem by dumping Haley in the Hudson River — after cleaning out her pockets and valuables to make it look like a mugging gone bad."

"That could be it," Tuck agreed. "It sure looks like Sydney had motive —"

I closed the laptop. "There's a walking, talking hole in my theory, however."

"What's that?"

"More like who's that. The superintendent at Carol Lynn's apartment house told the police he saw her disposing of clothes and a gun in the Dumpster behind their building."

"He could be mistaken," Tuck said.

"Or maybe the police coached that statement out of him, in which case this witness could be as phony as the planted coffee cup appears to be."

"What do we do now?" Tuck asked. "Should we talk to the Fish Squad?"

"Eventually. But first, let's pay a visit to that building superintendent, and find out what he really saw."

SEVENTY-SIX

Ten minutes later, Tucker and I had finished a brisk walk from the Village Blend to the six-story redbrick apartment building Carol Lynn Kendall called home.

I intended to walk up to the front entrance and ring the building superintendent — until I spotted an all-too-familiar wine-colored SUV. The vehicle was parked in front of the canopied entrance to Carol Lynn's building. The driver's side door was open, the interior lights on.

"Back! Quick!" I hissed, dragging Tuck until we were around the corner again.

"Clare? What's going on?"

"That's the SUV that tried to run me down. Do me a favor. Peek around the corner and tell me if you see a man with a curly red beard."

Crouching low, Tuck peeked. "Oh, God, he's there. And a big, strapping lumberjack he is, too. Hey, wait a minute, I've seen that

guy before. He's — uh-oh. He's with someone you know."

"Sydney?"

Tuck shook his head. "You better look
yourself . . ."

I moved forward and peered around the
corner. Red Beard was on the sidewalk, having an animated discussion with a woman
out of my line of vision.

"Give me back my key," the man said
gruffly. "You don't need it anymore, right?"

The woman stepped out from behind the
SUV — and the shock of recognition made
my knees weak.

Millennial Marilyn Monroe, my ex-
husband's new love toy (and boss), twisted
a key ring in her manicured fingers, then
handed a single key to Red Beard. He
turned it in his hand and pocketed it in his
work shirt.

Marilyn Hahn ran a hand through her
sleek platinum curls. "Do you have something for me now?" she asked coyly.

"Oh, suddenly you're interested in the
perks of my new career?"

She put her hands on her hips. "You
always were a jerk, Doug, even in high
school."

"Maybe I'm a jerk, but I never ever abused
you. Treated you like trash the morning

441

after — and then forced myself on you like that total piece of —"

"Stop it, Doug." Marilyn shifted uncomfortably. "Come on. Do you have it or not?"

"I got it, I got it," Red Beard replied. "And it's the best. If you want some, get in the SUV."

He stepped aside and she climbed in. He followed her into the vehicle and shut the door. The windows were tinted, so when the interior lights went dim, I couldn't see what was happening inside.

"What do you think they're doing?" Tuck asked.

After four minutes — I timed them — the doors opened and Marilyn climbed out.

"Sure I can't give you a lift?" he asked.

"My car's coming now," she replied.

As Tuck and I watched, Marilyn climbed into an Uber car. Then Red Beard started his SUV. He was about to drive off when an elderly woman came out of the building and waved. He gave her a nod and drove away — at a *reasonable* speed, this time.

"Wait here, Tuck," I said as I half walked, half ran until I caught up with the older woman.

"Excuse me, ma'am. Who was that man who just drove away?"

She smiled. "That's Douglas. He's the

janitor of my building. He's a wonderful handyman, too. He fixed my refrigerator, and it's not even covered by the maintenance fee."

"Good for Doug," I said before bidding her a good night.

I stood in the middle of the sidewalk, the word *janitor* bouncing around my head like an Equator gym volleyball.

Why is the word janitor *vexing me?*

The answer came from the past. Greenwich Village's past to be exact, circa 1967.

On the night I found Haley's body floating in the Hudson, Mike had told me how the police had solved the Groovy Murders, a brutal double homicide that had ended the Summer of Love movement.

The key to cracking the case had been the janitor of the building where those murders had taken place. As it turned out, the man had far more knowledge of the crime than he originally told the police.

Red Beard is a janitor, too, and Marilyn handed him a key. But a key to what?

Impatient, Tuck left his hiding place and caught up with me. "Shall we ring the building super now?"

"We just missed him."

He blinked. "You mean that lumberjack is the super?" Tucker shook his head. "Small world."

"What do you mean?"

"I remember him from one of those viral videos taken at our coffeehouse the night Carol Lynn went off the deep end. After I heard what happened, I watched all eight of them."

"Eight? I thought there were only five."

"After it hit the news, more people uploaded them. Anyway, one of those videos showed this red-bearded guy actually *urging* Carol Lynn to 'go ahead' and 'finish' Crenshaw. Red Beard looked really bitter when he said it, too."

I blinked, remembering that night. I'd heard that comment behind me but never saw the person who'd made it. "Tuck, I think this building's janitor could be involved in Crenshaw's murder, right up to his furry neck."

"Really? You think he —"

"Helped frame Carol Lynn."

"But how exactly? And why? You saw the DOT video of Crenshaw's murder. There is no way on earth this big, bearded guy could have disguised himself well enough to look like my slender, pretty friend."

"No. But I know who might have . . ."

I told Tucker how I watched Marilyn Hahn's face darken when she told me how she, too, had experienced a horrible hookup with Richard Crest aka Robert Crenshaw. And I whispered what I'd just overheard between Doug and Marilyn. Putting two and two together . . .

"I think what Crenshaw did to Marilyn might have been awful enough for her to plan his demise. And if she did murder Crenshaw, she clearly had help, judging from her cozy relationship with this building's janitor. Just like the famous Groovy Murders, he knows more than he's telling the police."

"So you think Marilyn dressed up as Carol Lynn and shot Robert Crenshaw?"

"We need proof, of course. But I think we may have just witnessed Marilyn returning the key to Carol Lynn's apartment. The super would have it, of course; he has access to all the units. And they had a prior relationship. Marilyn made a remark about knowing him since high school. It's possible Marilyn went to Red Beard and asked for access to Carol Lynn's apartment —"

"Yes, I follow!" Tuck said. "Marilyn took Carol Lynn's clothes, maybe days ago, and wore them, and a wig, to commit the murder."

"And after the shooting, Marilyn would have walked back to Carol Lynn's building in full view of New York's traffic cameras. Only once she entered the building, she would have gone to the super's apartment, where she could change out of the stolen clothes, toss them into the Dumpster with the murder weapon, and exit through the alley — unseen because the security camera in the back is conveniently broken. It's the perfect crime!"

Tucker nodded in wholehearted agreement. Then he stopped nodding. "But if you solved it, how do you prove it? Soles and Bass are a pretty tough audience."

"I think even the Fish Squad would be impressed with a taped confession."

With that, I speed dialed our Brooklyn warehouse.

"Hello, Matt? I *really* need your help this time . . ."

SEVENTY-SEVEN

Two nights later, I was watching my ex-husband dress for a romantic dinner, followed — if he had his way — by a passionate seduction.

Matt was in his Brooklyn man cave, wrapped in nothing but a towel, his hair and beard glistening from the shower. He looked confident and comfortable in his natural habitat, circling a table set for an intimate dinner, complete with white cloth, crystal and china, champagne on ice, candles, and something delicious on the menu.

I was outside, in the warehouse parking lot, shivering behind the wheel of the Village Blend's panel van. As rain beat slowly on the metal roof, water drops traced curvy rivers on the windshield. With the engine off, the air was getting nippy, cold enough for my breath to cloud. So I sipped my warmth from a travel mug of coffee — with plenty of backup in the thermos beside me.

My laptop was open on the dash with the Matt Allegro Show playing on its big screen. So far, the streaming setup with Matt's phone and my computer was working as advertised, and I was recording every second of the feed on my hard drive. But since I never trust technology all that much, I'd also set up a voice-activated digital recorder in the man cave for backup. Either way, I wasn't going to miss a word.

My smartphone was activated, too, and I spoke into it.

"You are going to put clothes on, right? Marilyn's going to be here in half an hour. If you plan to reveal your true self the moment she arrives, I don't see much time to coax a murder confession out of her."

"You're breaking my concentration, Clare. I'm trying to focus."

"Don't worry, Romeo, your seduction scene will be pristine."

He checked the temperature of the champagne, then added more ice to the bucket.

"Are you finished cooking yet? I'm asking because you always say dinner's ready, and then you're ten more minutes in the kitchen. That's a mood killer, you know."

I watched Matt roll his eyes. "It's ready, Clare. The main course, the side dish, the salad — even the sauce."

"What are they serving at Chez Allegro tonight?"

Matt lit the candles. "*They* are serving grilled steaks with my Brandy Mushroom Gravy and Fluffy Garlic Mashed Potatoes, along with a simple salad."

"No dessert?"

"No *pastries.* I had a different dessert in mind when I arranged this rendezvous."

"I know, and I appreciate what you're doing. But you really should know what kind of woman you're dealing with."

"Marilyn is a lot of things, but a cold-blooded killer isn't one of them," Matt replied. "We'll know that in a little while, when you see this is all a big dumb misunderstanding."

"Well, don't forget to go for the confession before you close the deal. After she's relaxed, maybe had some champagne, start to grill her. Don't wait until . . . you know . . . Not unless you want an audience."

"And if Marilyn doesn't confess, if she laughs in my face at the very thought of murder, you'll stop watching, right?"

"I promise."

"I'm getting dressed now. Have Soles and Bass arrived?"

"*Help* is arriving any minute," I replied.

That part was true, at least. Though it wouldn't be Soles and Bass, I knew Matt was better off *not* knowing who'd be serving as our police backup tonight.

Luckily, Matt was too distracted to pursue the subject. "Before I put on my clothes, I'm going to mute this phone, so you won't distract me," he said. "It's bad enough you're watching. I don't want to hear you, too."

Before I could reply, his giant hand closed over the phone. When he pulled it away, he was grinning.

"Now you can hear me but I can't hear you, which so works for me." Chuckling, he sauntered out of camera range.

Five minutes passed. The rain increased, beating a faster drumroll on the van's roof. I drained my travel mug and refilled it from a large thermos of Wide Awake blend — light-roasted Colombian with a smattering of robusta beans for a high-caffeine kick. I would need the jolt to get through this night.

I'd just finished pouring when a knock on the window startled me.

I popped the lock, the door opened, and Sergeant Emmanuel Franco climbed into the passenger seat. Shaking raindrops off his shaved head, he flung a dripping slicker in the back. Under the storm gear, he'd dressed like the Franco I remembered — worn denims, sweatshirt, and heavy work boots, his gun and badge on his wide belt.

"Thanks for coming," I said. "Soles and Bass were called to a crime scene in the Village and bailed on me at the last minute. Mike is out of town, and I didn't have anyone else to call."

Franco detected the cold tone in my voice, but I couldn't hide it — not after the pain he caused my daughter.

"I'm always happy to help, Coffee Lady. But, I have to admit, your invitation to meet inside a van in a warehouse parking lot had me wondering about your intentions."

He'd cracked that like a joke, yet there was an uncomfortably brittle edge to it. Ignoring the awkwardness, I pressed on —

"Before I tell you what this is about, I need to know if you did as I asked and parked your car around the block and out of sight."

"Sure, how do you think I got soaked?"

"Good."

We sat in silence for a moment, tension thick between us. Finally, I spoke. "One more thing before we get down to police business."

"What's that?"

"Who's Joan?"

SEVENTY-EIGHT

"Joan?"

Either Franco was genuinely puzzled, or he had acting chops the equal of Tucker Burton's. At this point, I opted for the latter. He *was* an undercover cop, after all. Deception was his business.

"Yes, Joan!" I shot back. "The woman you're seeing when you're lying to Joy about being at work. The woman you're upscale dressing for, the one who's showering you with expensive man products and writing cute little notes. Don't play innocent, Franco. You know what you're doing!"

"Me?!"

Franco lunged for his smartphone. He reached so fast into his pants pocket that he smacked his elbow on the door handle. Cursing like the marine he used to be, he thumbed the device.

"What about this?!" He displayed the Cinder profile for Kara C — my bikini shot, of course.

"Mike's a great guy, Clare," Franco said in a tone of wounded indignation. "Why are you two-timing him? Bad enough his first wife did it. I never expected that sort of behavior from you."

"Me?!" I sputtered — then noticed movement on the street in front of the warehouse.

"Quiet!" I hissed. "Marilyn's here."

In simmering silence, we watched the platinum blonde bombshell climb out of an Uber car and hurry through the open gate. (Matt had left it unlocked for his guest, and the police backup.) Head down, umbrella rippling in the wind, Marilyn tottered across the puddled parking lot in knee-length dominatrix boots.

Matt held the door open and she raced inside.

"Truce," I said. "We'll talk this out later. Right now I need to bring you up to speed."

I did. It took a solid ten minutes, time enough for Matt and Marilyn to settle in. Despite our tension, the cop in Franco was intrigued, and he was willing to stand as a witness to a possible criminal confession.

"You're lucky this is New York," he said, sharing my thermos of Wide Awake. "This is a one-party consent state, and your ex has given his consent. And that's not your ex-husband's bedroom per se — it's a common room in a warehouse that just happens to have an Italian leather sofa and table setting that looks like he's dining at Eleven Madison Park."

I held back from asking "Fast-Food Franco" how he knew about Eleven Madison Park, where a dinner for two with drinks and wine could cost more than he earned in a week. Likely, it was "Joan" who footed the bill and played footsie with the young sergeant over dessert!

"In the end," Franco concluded, "I wouldn't expect this to be admissible in court —"

"I don't care about court," I said. "I care about the truth. And the police can certainly use a confession, or any information this woman might provide, as grounds for a further — and perfectly legal — investigation."

"Right," Franco said with a nod. He sat in silence for a moment, staring at the computer screen. Suddenly, he grinned. "I wish I had a bag of popcorn for this. I know Allegro's got a reputation as a ladies' man. Let's see how good he is at romantic interrogation . . ."

Matt was quite good, as it turned out — despite one harrowing moment. They were on their third glass of bubbly when Marilyn said, "Let's get really crazy."

She reached into her purse, and what she pulled out absolutely terrified me.

"It's called Styx," she said, "because it comes in these little straws . . ."

"More Styx," Franco murmured. "I feel like I never left work. I've been on the trail of this stuff for weeks."

"They're usually colored," Marilyn went on, "but this time the straw is clear, so you can see the pretty white powder . . ."

I tensed as she waved the cylinders under my ex-husband's ex-addict nose. *Oh, God, Matt, please don't!*

"Want a taste? It makes loving better. It makes *everything* better."

Matt reached out, and my heart stopped. Then he closed his fist around Marilyn's hand and guided it and the drugs back into her purse.

"Not interested," he said. "It's one road I avoid now, and you should, too."

My body sagged with relief. *Good for you, Matt. Good for you . . .*

"You're unadventurous for an adventurer," Marilyn chided.

"How about a nice gin cocktail instead?" Matt countered. "I've got Bombay Sapphire. It has a beautiful coriander finish."

Marilyn shook her head. "More champagne," she insisted.

They toasted two more times. Matt didn't even bring up the subject of murder until they'd finished most of the bottle. He started casually, telling her how he discovered the identity of the man in the viral video.

"Clare tells me you dated him."

"I dated lots of guys," Marilyn replied, looking more tipsy than guilty. "After small-town boys, New York was like a buffet. And I'm a girl who loves to eat."

"Not everyone is as sophisticated as you," Matt said. "A couple of bad dates, and that girl in the viral video snapped."

"She's crazy. She needs help. And she'll finally get it, now that the cops have arrested her for killing that asshole who abused her."

Matt nodded. "A little bird told me the police are looking for an accomplice in that crime. A guy with a red beard named Doug."

Marilyn didn't vacillate. "You mean my ex-boyfriend, the stalker?"

I glanced excitedly at Franco. *Bingo!*

Marilyn opened up, telling Matt how she and Doug Farthing had been a couple since middle school and moved to New York together from their small town outside of

Lima, Ohio. Her college journalism work and flamboyant blog landed Marilyn a prime position at PopCravings.com. Doug Farthing didn't fare so well.

"He dropped out of college and mostly bummed around. With no degree or résumé, the best he could do was a super's job and a windowless apartment in a basement. That wasn't for me. So I broke things off."

"You called him a stalker?" Matt said.

"He shows up everywhere I go, won't accept that we're different people now and need to go our separate ways. That's why I wanted to leave the party at your coffeehouse the other night. Doug was there and it made me feel squirmy. Anyway, the whole thing was a bore."

"Maybe you should get a restraining order against your ex."

Marilyn shook her head. "I talked things over with him Sunday night. He's feeling more optimistic about the future. He came into money and says he's getting a better job. He's doing so well that he bought my half of our shared SUV — the one we drove out here from Ohio. I gave him the key Sunday, too, and that's the last time I'll have to see that loser, unless I want more Styx, of course . . ."

Again, I glanced at Franco, this time with

disappointment. The "key" I watched Marilyn give to her ex-boyfriend was not the key to Carol Lynn's apartment. It was a key to that stupid red SUV — the one that almost ran me down a few yards away from this spot.

Now I realized what Red Beard had been doing that evening outside Matt's warehouse. He wasn't spying on me. He was stalking his ex-girlfriend — or maybe, in his mind, he was trying to "protect" her. Matt had made a date with Marilyn for dinner, but she'd canceled at the last minute. I'd shown up instead; and when I walked toward him, he sped away without looking back.

In the chilly van, Franco noticed my distracted look. "Pay attention, Clare. If this Doug Farthing is selling Styx, there's still something worth listening to . . ."

With Marilyn's next words, I realized Franco was right. She may not have killed Robert Crenshaw (aka Richard Crest), but she had a strong lead to offer in the case.

"So tell me," Marilyn pressed, "is my ex in hot water? If he is, I should warn him — because I'm pretty sure he took a bribe to set that girl up."

Matt played dumb. "What girl?"

"The viral video girl who the cops *think*

shot Richard Crest. Like I said, she was obviously unstable, and it's good that she's off the street. But she didn't kill Crest. I'm pretty sure she was framed."

"By who? Who did kill Crest?"

Marilyn curled her legs under her and held up her glass for a refill.

"Doug's new boss. Doug keeps talking about how he's getting in on a good thing, the ground floor of something big. He just had to do this 'special favor' for this new boss. As the building super, he was in a 'unique position' to do it. In exchange, Doug is getting some high-paying digital gig, which is supposed to impress me, I guess. But I think it's a crock —"

"Why?"

"Doug has no experience. He can barely work his smartphone. It's more like a payoff for the frame job he did on that crazy girl."

"And you believe him?"

She shrugged. "He said all he had to do was give a simple false statement to the cops about her, break his building's back door camera to make sure they couldn't catch him in the fib, and pick up a coffee cup with her prints on it, you know, after she threw it away. Small stuff for a giant paycheck and shiny new job."

"So who is this mystery boss?" Matt

finally asked. Franco and I leaned close to hear the answer.

"I don't know. Doug never said a name. The boss pays in cash, though. Doug is big on tax evasion, so he sees that as a plus. His boss pays with other things, too — like the Styx."

"How nice," Matt deadpanned.

"It's all good," Marilyn said, nodding. "That creep Crest is dead, which makes me happy. Crazy Girl goes to the psych ward for therapy, and Doug gets out of my hair. Win-win! Just like you and me."

"Right," Matt said. He was facing the camera and not Marilyn. When I saw his look of disgust, I knew he and Marilyn were history.

He shook the champagne bottle.

"It's nearly empty. Let me get another and we can talk some more —"

"Don't you have something stronger?" Marilyn asked. "I told you I want to get *crazy* tonight."

"I have that gin — or how about tequila?"

Marilyn shook her head. "If that's all you've got, then just bring another bottle of the champagne."

As soon as Matt left the man cave, Marilyn lunged for her purse, took out two cylinders of Styx, and poured one in each of their glasses.

"No!" I shouted and turned to Franco. "I can't warn Matt! He's muted his phone, so there's no way I can call him!"

Franco let out a string of curses as he reached for his rain slicker.

On-screen, Marilyn added the rest of the champagne bottle to their glasses and stirred them with a manicured finger.

Franco popped the door and stepped into the rain. "Get in there and stop them, if you can!"

"Where are you going?"

"To my car."

"What for?"

"Hercules!"

Franco was halfway to the gate before I jumped out of the van. As I fumbled through my purse for the warehouse key, I heard Marilyn welcome Matt back to his man cave.

"Before you pop that, let's finish the old bottle. Waste not, want not." Marilyn laughed.

"Sounds good," Matt replied. "Bottoms up!"

Seventy-Nine

By the time I got through the warehouse door and upstairs, Matt and Marilyn were unconscious. Matt was unresponsive, his pupils shrunk to pinpoints. Marilyn — a foot shorter and a hundred pounds lighter than my ex — was twitching. Foam flecked her red lips.

I finished the call to the 911 operator by the time Franco arrived with the OD antidote.

"Get back!"

Franco quickly checked their conditions. Then he injected the naloxone into Marilyn's naked thigh. Ripping Matt's pants with a switchblade, he did the same for him.

It took two doses for Matt, three for Marilyn, but Franco's "Hercules" kit pulled both of them back from the underworld. By the time they were loaded into the ambulance, Matt and Marilyn were still unconscious but breathing on their own.

As the pair was rushed to a hospital in Brooklyn, Franco and I followed in his SUV. A siren and magnetic bubble light, tossed on his roof, cleared our path.

Then came the wait, and the waiting room — a bleak space overflowing with distraught people and personal tragedy. I sat in a corner, away from everyone, sick with worry.

You'd think I'd be an old pro at the overdose game, but the last time — which was also the first time — I didn't have to notify my adult daughter that her dad was at death's door.

"I'm leaving now!" Joy said, fear in her voice as she ended the call. "I'll book a commuter flight on my phone before I get to the airport. I should be there in two or three hours."

During the wait for word, and for Joy, what upset me most was the difference between the past and the present. Matt's first OD was the result of a hundred bad decisions on his part, including throwing our marriage away for hookup games on every continent he'd visited. But this time, Matt's suffering was caused by a single bad choice — and it was mine. If Joy's father didn't survive this night, his death was on me.

After several hours, no nurse or doctor

had appeared to give me an update or a prognosis. Franco stuck close, though he'd been talking on his phone for the past half hour.

Finally, he ended the call and returned to my side.

"I contacted Soles and Bass to give them a heads-up about their Styx-dealing witness, Douglas Farthing," Franco said, rubbing tired eyes. "Turns out Red Beard is the reason they were too busy to back you up tonight. The man is dead —"

"Dead!"

"He overdosed on the same clear cylinder stuff that poisoned Matt and Marilyn. My guess? It's a bad batch."

"Or someone *wanted* Red Beard dead . . ." I turned to face him. "You heard what Marilyn said about Doug's 'new boss.' This boss bribed him to frame Carol Lynn. She also said the boss paid in cash and Styx. That's where he got the bad batch. And I believe it was intentional. Doug Farthing knew too much, and he had to die."

Franco gave me a hard look. "What the hell are you doing investigating Styx, anyway? Does Mike know what you're doing, because that's his job — and mine."

"I'm not investigating Styx. I started out trying to find out who murdered one of my customers. Now I'm trying to clear another, an innocent young woman, of a homicide charge. Along the way, I found out some pretty ugly things about a dating app called Cinder —"

"Cinder?!" Franco threw up his arms. "I'm investigating them, too!"

It took time, but I told Franco everything I knew about the "happy endings" Cinder app.

"An ending is what I'm planning for Cinder," Franco swore. "And it won't be happy."

"What are you talking about?"

"What I've been working on, night and day, Clare. I'm about to bring an end to that company. By morning I'll have an arrest warrant for its CEO, Sydney Webber-Rhodes, for narcotics trafficking —"

"What?!"

Franco finally told me what he'd been doing, and it wasn't cheating on Joy. The OD Squad confirmed that dealers were selling Styx through the Cinder app — women, because Cinder lets the ladies make the first move, and they moved toward the guys with drug codes on their profiles.

"I put myself out there as a high-rolling Cinder guy with an interest in candy. That's code for —"

"Drugs. I know."

"That mugger Quinn brought in gave us key information, and I was able to narrow down my hashtag descriptions to wanting Styx and my focus on one particular female dealer. This past Friday afternoon, we finally connected on Cinder, and made a date for Saturday night. That's why I had to cancel on Joy."

"So Mike didn't know what you were up to?"

"No, this came up after our morning briefing. I was planning on giving him a full update at our next scheduled briefing on Monday . . ."

Franco went on to describe how he met up with his female suspect, and brought her back to a luxury condo, which had been seized from a dealer last year — and wired by the NYPD for just such a sting operation.

"She made the offer, and I bit. She brought the drugs up to the condo, where backup members of our OD Squad were waiting for her . . ."

According to Franco, the intense interrogation went on all night Saturday, and most of Sunday, until finally the woman confessed.

"She said as far as she knew, she was

working for Cinder."

"Why did she think that?"

"Because her buyers never paid her directly. They deposited their drug payments in the Cinder Treasure Chest —"

"Oh, my God. Franco, your drug dealer's statement solves the mystery of the excess money in Sydney's Cinder account."

"What are you talking about?"

"I overheard Sydney and Cody discussing it. They couldn't figure out where extra funds were coming from, well over one hundred thousand dollars, and now we know — the money was payment for Styx."

"And that's exactly why we're about to arrest the CEO and shut the app down."

"But Sydney sounded genuinely perplexed about that money. It looks more like a setup to me." I thought it over. "This woman you arrested, this female drug dealer — if her buyers were paying Cinder, then who paid her? How did she get her money from the drug sale?"

"For every drug transaction, she received a cash payment from a man she described as tall and attractive. She assumed he worked for Cinder, and she couldn't tell us his real name. She only knew him as Captain Hook."

"Captain Hook?! That must have been

Robert Crenshaw. I read a *Wired* article that referred to him as Captain Hookster." I shook my head. "Franco, I'm sorry but I don't think Sydney is guilty of narcotics trafficking. I think she's been set up. This looks like payback. A vicious game of revenge played by Crenshaw — the man now lying in the morgue."

"If he's in the morgue, we can't exactly question him, although we can investigate his background."

"I've done some of that already. What I want to know is who killed him, because the clock is ticking. The police are holding an innocent woman for that crime — a dear friend of Tucker's who's been struggling with mental instability. She's now living through the worst nightmare of her life. And the only way to help her is to find Crenshaw's real killer."

"Well, Coffee Lady, you're the one who's been gathering the facts. Do you have a theory?"

"Marilyn Hahn seemed certain that Doug Farthing's 'new boss' was the killer. If I had to guess, I'd say Sydney is that boss and she killed Captain Hookster — or sent one of her Tinkerbells to do it."

"You sure it wasn't Peter Pan?"

"I'm serious, Franco. I overheard Sydney

talking to her staff the night of Crenshaw's murder. She knew her app was being sabotaged. She knew about the unexplained deposits. She even hired digital forensic investigators. If she discovered Crenshaw was behind setting her up for drug trafficking, then she had the strongest motive for wanting him dead . . . except . . ."

"Except? What?"

"The timing doesn't work. If Sydney began putting together the truth about Crenshaw's sabotage on Saturday night, how could she have the time to plan the perfect crime? In just a few hours, she would have to bribe Doug Farthing and set up Carol Lynn. It seems a stretch . . ."

Franco agreed. As we fell silent, wondering what to do next, worry suddenly clouded his face. "Clare, how much of my undercover work does Joy know about?"

"She knows about Joan. She saw the note from her. Who is she, by the way? Another undercover cop? One of your perps?"

"Joan?!" Franco rubbed his shaved head in frustration. "Joan's not a woman. It's an acronym for a multi-jurisdictional task force, Joint Operation Anti-Narcotics!"

"And all that expensive man stuff? The fancy suits?"

"Swag confiscated in prior drug busts,

used for our undercover stings."

I opened my laptop and called up the phone video that Matt sent.

"Was this Soho Lounge date part of your sting?"

Franco watched the screen in increasing distress. "Please tell me Joy didn't see this."

"She did. Matt shot the footage on Saturday night. He sent it to both of us."

Franco pounded his palm. "Now I'm wondering why I saved that guy."

"You saved Matt because he's the father of the woman you love."

Franco blew out air. "I thought Joy was too far away to be touched by any of this. I was sure I could pull off this undercover sting without her knowing. You have to understand, it was part of my job — I was meeting up with two or three women a night."

"I do understand. And you have to understand that none of this was Matt's fault. It was yours for not trusting Joy, or giving her the chance to trust you. Now she's convinced you were cheating on her. And she's devastated."

He hung his head. "Man, I really screwed up."

"To be fair, Joy did, too. She should have talked to you, face-to-face, and I think she would have, eventually. But that video wrecked her."

"I'm so sorry . . ."

"Don't apologize to me. Save it for her."

Franco looked up, just as my daughter entered the waiting room.

Their eyes met and Joy turned to flee. Franco rose and ran after her, catching her by the elevator. She resisted, refusing to listen. But soon they were talking — and finally, after several long and intense minutes, they were filling each other's arms.

I sat back in exhausted relief. Those two were in love, no question about it. *Thank goodness they figured that out!*

I thought they made a strong couple and would make an adorable bride and groom. Sure, we had a long way to go. Mike was skeptical. And Matt was nakedly hostile. But it seemed to me, Mother (that would be me) knew best.

As the pair continued their intimate talk, I finally gave them their privacy and spun the laptop to face me. The video Matt shot was on a continuous play loop, and I watched it again on the larger screen. On the tiny phone, details were harder to make out, and I wondered if another look at Franco's date might reveal a clue.

Unfortunately, Franco's female suspect

didn't ring any Tinkerbells for me. But I kept watching the video anyway.

As the pair strolled down the busy sidewalk outside the Soho Lounge, the background details were much easier to observe, including the grand glass entrance to the Soho branch of the Equator gym and the stylish crowd, some smoking or vaping as they talked and laughed with one another.

Two men in particular caught my attention — one tall, the other short — slapping hands and gripping wrists in a disturbingly familiar bro shake.

Stunned, I froze the image.

I can't believe what I'm seeing . . .

The tall man was Robert Crenshaw, just hours before his murder. The smaller man was the Critter Crawl guru himself, Tristan Ferrell.

EIGHTY

As we waited for word on Matt's condition, I channeled my worries into an online investigation of the "Critter Crawl" fitness guru . . .

Two hours after Joy's arrival, I was still searching while my daughter (*thank goodness*) was sleeping. Cocooned in Franco's big coat, her head on his warm thigh, she needed the rest, emotionally and physically, after the draining week she'd had.

Meanwhile, I was using the search engines like slot machines, and I thought I came up a winner — until I showed Franco the results.

He was less than impressed.

"I don't see anything incriminating in that handshake," Franco said, after I showed him the key part of Matt's camera phone video. "There could be a dozen reasons Tristan Ferrell said he didn't know this guy when you asked him. Ferrell was looking for

'Angels' to invest in his business, right? They could have just met Saturday night at the Soho Lounge."

"That's what I thought you'd say, so I dug deeper. I got to thinking that if Robert Crenshaw used an alias, maybe Tristan Ferrell did, too."

"Go on."

"After Hookster, Cindy started to go by her middle name Sydney. Crenshaw falsified IDs to become Crest, then Krinkle. And I found evidence that Tommy Finkle —"

"Stop. Who is Tommy Finkle?"

"According to the *Wall Street Journal*, Finkle is the other cofounder of Hookster, a friend and frat brother of Robert Crenshaw."

I showed Franco how difficult it was to find images of Tommy Finkle — the business pages mentioned him by name, but he kept out of the limelight and let the lawyers do the talking during the class action suit.

"I hit a dead end, until I remembered that Crenshaw and Finkle were in a fraternity together. I checked the archives of the fraternity's web page, and there he was —"

I turned the laptop to show Franco a decade-old picture of Tommy Finkle, a butterball with baby-fat cheeks, but clearly recognizable.

"Tommy Finkle, cofounder of Hookster, is now *Tristan Ferrell.* Franco, it all fits. When I took Tristan's Critter Crawl workout class, he went on and on about his 'painful failure in the business jungle' and how it sent him to a real jungle to regain his balance or some such. And from what I've uncovered, it's clear he found a new identity, too."

For a moment, Joy stirred and Franco lovingly stroked her chestnut hair. Then he burst my balloon by pointing out the obvious. The connections I'd found, while suspicious, were not proof of anything.

He shook his head. "Sorry, there's no evidence of wrongdoing that I can see. Even if we tried to question Ferrell, he'd lawyer up fast and that would be that . . ."

As I considered that bit of bad news, a night nurse interrupted to deliver something far more positive —

"Mr. Allegro is out of danger," she said.

I closed my eyes. *Thank you, God . . .*

"The doctor will give you an update when she's finished her rounds. *One* of you can see the patient after that, the rest of you in the morning."

"It should be Joy," I rasped to Franco. "She'll lift his spirits."

For a long moment after that, I sat in numbed silence. Then all the fears and feelings I'd been trying to ignore overwhelmed me, and I quietly broke down, sobbing into my hands.

Franco curved his big arm around my shoulders and squeezed, a silent but sweet and deeply appreciated reminder that I wasn't in this alone.

Shortly after the nurse stopped by, the doctor gave us another encouraging update. Then Joy was permitted to visit her dad.

After she left the waiting room, my mind went back to Franco's discouraging words about Tristan Ferrell.

While I had no proof of wrongdoing, I couldn't stop thinking about Haley Hartford. Ferrell not only denied knowing Crenshaw, he never answered my question about why he'd hired Haley — with a cash bonus and double her salary at Cinder.

Detectives Soles and Bass claimed Mr. Ferrell had an alibi the night Haley was killed. He was supposedly *at his place of business, with plenty of witnesses, until midnight . . ."*

But Equator was a big, busy facility with a broken security camera on its back door. If Ferrell had wanted to slip out and meet

Haley in Hudson River Park, then slip back into the club, would anyone have even noticed?

"You know," I said to Franco, "I'll bet all the evidence you would need to incriminate Ferrell is on Robert Crenshaw's phone. That might explain why the killer took it after shooting him."

"You could be right."

"And what about Red Beard's phone?"

"You mean Doug Farthing?" Franco rubbed his jaw. "Interesting. Soles and Bass told me his phone is missing, too."

"And so was Haley Hartford's. Phone snatching looks like the modus operandi for this killer — Hey . . . what if you got hold of Tristan Ferrell's smartphone? Why not get a search warrant and crack it open?"

"You're kidding, right?" Franco laughed. "Haven't you ever heard Mike Quinn gripe about the phone graveyard at the DA's office?"

I had — more than once. The Manhattan DA's spanking new Cyber Crime Lab had hundreds of phones encrypted with advanced iOS software, which made them impossible to crack without a password.

"That's hundreds of major crimes that can't be cleared, and hundreds of active criminals still walking the streets," Franco said. "So you see? Even if we got a warrant to search Ferrell's phone, it might be encrypted. Unless he gave us a password, we'd be locked out."

"What about the cloud?"

"Smart criminals don't back up their data where law enforcement can access it. They keep it in their phones."

I fell silent a minute and thought of one more option. "Mike once told me UK police found a way to get around a locked phone. They wait until the suspect is using it, then they arrest him. One officer grabs the phone while it's open, and keeps swiping until they get the device to a computer and download its contents."

"We could legally do that — *if* we secured proper warrants or had a solid reason to arrest him. With this Tristan guy, I don't see any."

Franco watched me silently deliberate.

"Spill it, Coffee Lady, what's your idea? Because I know you've got one."

"I'm a private citizen. If Tristan decides to freely give his unlocked phone to someone, who, in turn, hands it to me, then there's no civil rights issue. And if I happen to come upon evidence of a crime, I would be duty bound to report it to the police, right?"

Franco's eyebrow arched. "Okay. I'm listening . . ."

EIGHTY-ONE

The very next evening, Tristan Ferrell's Angel Party was in full swing, with help from a twelve-piece swing band. No gangsta rap here. The Critter Crawl guru knew the age range of the select New Yorkers he hoped to reel in as investors, and he'd booked accordingly.

The venue was the brand-new Anchor and Light on the Hudson, a three-story, glass-walled structure next to Manhattan's 79th Street Boat Basin. Like Pier 66 Maritime, fifty blocks south of us, this venue was built atop a floating barge. The top floor housed an elegant event space with a spectacular nighttime vista, polished teak flooring, a roaring fireplace, seafood and vegan buffets, and three open bars.

I sighed at the large, gorgeous space on the river. It was the perfect location for a wedding. Mike would absolutely love it. But we could never afford it.

It didn't matter, anyway, I thought, shaking off disappointment. I wasn't here to scout wedding locations. I was here to steal a peek at the contents of Tristan Ferrell's smartphone. It would be tricky, but I had a clever plan, and a lot of help from my friends.

Back at my bustling Village Blend, Tucker Burton was watching over the shop — and the clock, smartphone in hand.

Madame and Sergeant Jones were here at the party, prepped and ready for their roles.

As one of Tristan's Day-Glo spotters, Nancy's job as an insider was pivotal.

And just in case things went south, Sergeant Franco was parked on West End Avenue and 79th, as close as he dared get to what had to be a "concerned citizen" operation.

I listened impatiently to Tristan's presentation speech, while his Day-Glo helpers handed out packets. Inside, I found a business prospectus for the expansion of The Critter Crawl into a national brand with a premium app, line of fitness clothing, sports drinks, and sugar- and carb-free Critter Snacks. A glossy, autographed "Master of the Crawl" poster was also included. It featured the Critter guru wearing camouflage paint and little else, crawling boldly on hands and knees through a Photoshopped jungle.

A foursome of "Advanced Crawlers" soon took to the stage to demonstrate an array of Tristan's signature moves. The guru kept his tailored skinny business suit on, offering a running narration in soothing, earnest tones while his fit young pupils did the crawling.

Tristan discussed the philosophies behind each Critter pose, along with the story of his "discovery" of "Critter Flow" with phrases and ideas (e.g., "Follow your bliss") that bore a striking resemblance to Joseph Campbell's *Power of Myth* interview with Bill Moyers, circa 1988. I was only too happy to turn my attention to Madame when she appeared at my side.

As always, my elegant octogenarian employer dressed in evocative style with silk slacks matching the exact shade of her loose, knee-length cashmere sweater, "the ivory yellow hue of a George Inness harvest moon," as she put it after I complimented her outfit. She'd even accessorized with a print scarf featuring that landscape painter's masterpiece *Moonrise.*

"He was influenced by the Hudson River School of nineteenth-century artists, so I felt it was appropriate," Madame noted with a wink.

Sergeant Leonidas Jabari Jones cut a striking figure by her side. Shedding his tweeds, he'd donned a beautiful evening suit, crisp white shirt, and bright red bow tie. The black silk patch over his bad eye made him look a little dangerous as well as dashing — just the combination that continued to intrigue my ex-mother-in-law.

Though the couple appeared jovial, an angry fire burned behind Madame's violet gaze whenever she looked Ferrell's way.

"Please enjoy the buffet and bar," Tristan said, concluding his presentation. "I'll be here for the next hour, so if you have any questions, just ask!"

"I'd like to ask how he can sleep at night after poisoning my son and that poor girl," Madame hissed in my ear, cursing the man.

"It's still only a theory, so keep your cool, okay?" I warned, while crossing my fingers that this little scheme of mine would give us the proof we needed.

I made sure Madame, Nancy, and I were close to Ferrell when the moment arrived.

On cue, Tucker's call came through, and I watched Tristan pull his phone from his lapel pocket and check the caller ID. I didn't expect him to answer — he didn't need to. All I wanted him to do was unlock his phone.

As soon as he did, Madame sprang into action.

"Excuse me, young man," she interrupted. "Nancy tells me you've created a sequence of poses called 'The Madagascar Lemur.' Little furry primates have always fascinated me, and I'm disappointed your young pupils weren't able to demonstrate it."

"Well," Tristan replied as he pocketed the phone, "that's a very challenging sequence. It takes balance, strength, and unique flexibility —"

"I told you, Madame," Nancy spoke up with just the right amount of fawning awe. "It took Tristan years before even he could master The Madagascar Lemur."

"Oh, I see." Madame sighed, feigning disappointment. "But it would be such a treat to see it . . ."

Several partygoers — quietly prompted by Sergeant Jones — agreed with Madame, urging Tristan to show off this spectacular Critter creation.

Clearly flattered, the Critter Crawl Master relented. "If you insist . . ."

He removed his jacket and passed it to Nancy, who passed it to me. I made a show of draping it over a chair, but as Nancy took Tristan's designer loafers to hold for him, I slipped the man's phone out of the lapel pocket and swiftly walked away, swiping as I stepped — to keep it from locking, just as I'd discussed with Franco.

Tristan didn't notice. He was too busy finding his "Critter Center," closing his eyes, for nearly a full minute after positioning a chair just right and limbering up. Then the sequence of poses began with a kind of slow-motion backbend that flowed into an impressive handstand on the seat of the chair.

By then, I was already hiding behind the bar, searching his phone for evidence. And I started with the Cinder app.

EIGHTY-TWO

Sure enough, Tristan had an account, though the profile wasn't in his name, or even his gender.

Posing as a bisexual woman named "Tricia," Tristan had exchanged dozens of messages with "Richard Crest" and a woman named "Red," whose profile photo looked an awful lot like a young Lucille Ball.

Was young Lucy really Douglas Farthing, aka Red Beard? When I saw a reference to Carol Lynn's street address on Barrow, I knew it was!

I used my own smartphone to snap screenshots of these archived messages, including Red's agreement to work for Tricia/Tristan by making "candy" deliveries. So much for the "high-paying digital gig" Doug claimed he was getting. Red Beard's new job, if he had lived, would have been trafficking drugs.

When I saw "Tricia" traded messages with "Harry Krinkle," I knew I'd hit the jackpot.

I also discovered that my guilt over luring Crenshaw to his death was greatly exaggerated.

Robert Crenshaw hadn't come to the Village Blend to meet "Kara." It was Ferrell, using his "Tricia" account, who'd brought Crenshaw to my coffeehouse on the night of his murder . . .

Urgent news. Must meet now!
Take outside table, last one on corner.

The timing and specificity of the request convinced me. Tristan appeared to have pulled the trigger on his Hookster partner. And he'd used Red Beard to help frame Carol Lynn, which meant he was the one who'd paid him off in the deadly Styx that nearly killed Matt.

You were right, Madame, I thought. *Curse away!*

Finally, I noticed a contacts folder on Tristan's phone labeled "Hook's Crew." Opening it up, I recognized names from Franco's list of drug dealers, who were slated to be arrested within hours. He'd shared it with me in hopes of finding connections with Ferrell. Well, here they were!

Judging from the date, time, and "Hook's Crew" name of the folder, my guess was that Ferrell had downloaded these contacts from Crenshaw's phone right after shooting the man.

It looked like Ferrell had decided to take over the Styx drug-dealing business from Crenshaw. Was that the reason he murdered him? The two had been friends for years, dating back to when they were fraternity brothers. They'd gone into business together, weathered storms together, and from that warm bro shake I saw them share in Soho, I couldn't help wondering what had prompted Ferrell to turn so viciously on his old friend. But there was no time to look for more answers now. I'd already found enough evidence to have Ferrell arrested and his business investigated by the OD Squad. I quickly snapped screenshots of the incriminating messages, sent them to Franco's and Tucker's phones, and returned to the party.

Tristan was finishing his last pose as I slipped the phone back into his jacket. Suddenly, he performed a quick, unexpected flip, and faced me. I couldn't be sure, but it was possible he'd seen what I'd done.

The Madagascar Lemur demonstration ended to cheers and applause. Even Madame acted suitably impressed, and Sergeant Jones shook the guru's hand.

While Tristan donned his loafers and jacket, I hurried for the exit. I was in such a rush I even left my wrap at the coat check. There was no time to alert Nancy or Madame that I was leaving. When I hit the street, I would text Franco, telling him I was about to catch a cab to meet up with him. Then he could officially take my "statement" about what I'd witnessed at the party — as a "concerned citizen," of course.

Unfortunately, the single elevator closed in my face. My heart pounded, and my adrenaline levels went through the roof while I waited for the agonizingly slow return of the car. When the door finally opened again, I rushed inside and pounded the button.

The sliding doors were just about to close when a smiling Tristan swiftly entered, along with a few partygoers.

I thought about escaping, but before the doors closed, he subtly blocked my way and began engaging me in polite conversation.

"Ms. Cosi, right? Your boss seems quite interested in my Critter Crawl philosophy. I think she sees the potential . . ."

Thank God he was talking up his business, not asking questions. Perhaps he hadn't seen me with his phone, after all.

"I'm off to Seattle in the morning, Portland after that. I think young people in those cities will be especially receptive to my message . . ."

No doubt they'll be receptive to the Styx you're dealing, too, I thought.

Clenching my jaw into a smiling position, I tried hard to keep a pleasant face — and those images of Matt lying close to death out of my mind.

When the doors opened, Tristan and I faced two exits, one to the street, the other to the 79th Street Boat Basin.

As the other guests departed toward the street, Tristan firmly hooked my arm in his. "Do you want to see my boat? She's a Riva. You're Italian, right? You should really appreciate her sleek lines."

Before I could decline or break away, he used his jacket to shield a weapon — what felt like the barrel of a small gun was now pressing into my kidney.

"We're going on a boat ride, Ms. Cosi. I'm not going to hurt you. But I do insist you tell me why you're so interested in my phone . . ."

He led me through the door to the Boat Basin. The night air was bracing, and I shivered in my flimsy cocktail dress. I thought I might have a chance to escape, or alert some passerby to my plight, but the man's boat was moored no more than a dozen steps from the Anchor and Light.

"Get in," he commanded.

Despite his claim not to "hurt" me, I knew who this man really was. Any boat ride with him on the Hudson was going to end on the River Styx.

With a violent tug, I freed my arm to run. But before I could take a step or draw breath to shout "Help!" Tristan lashed out.

Then everything went dark.

Eighty-Three

My head throbbed, and the madly rocking cradle wasn't helping. I wanted to call my *nonna* to make it stop, but when I opened my eyes, I snapped back to grim reality.

I wasn't safe and warm in my childhood bedroom above my grandmother's little Italian grocery store. I was shivering aboard Tristan Ferrell's boat, on my way to a watery grave.

I tried to move my arms, but they were tightly tied behind my back. My ankles were bound, too — I knew because I could touch the ropes. I'd been dumped between two fine leather seats at the ship's bow, squeezing me into a fetal position. Helpless, I feigned unconsciousness while I observed the murderer, drug dealer, and kidnapper through half-closed eyelashes.

Ferrell was steering his Riva downriver. I saw the tops of several landmark buildings and realized we were just passing Midtown.

I shut my eyes completely when Ferrell hit autopilot and approached. I remained motionless while he groped me through my clothes, then under my clothes. He gave up, to rummage through my purse. When he found my phone, he tossed everything else over the side.

When I realized he hadn't tossed my phone, I felt a surge of hope.

I knew the NYPD had the ability to ping a phone and track its location, using cell phone towers. If Nancy realized I was gone, she would have alerted Madame, Franco, and Sergeant Jones.

A curse interrupted my thoughts. Tristan was poised to toss my smartphone — and my only hope of rescue — over the side. Instead, he threw the phone back at me. I stifled a cry as it bounced off my shoulder and clattered to the deck.

When Tristan took control of the boat again, I opened one eye, saw that my phone was still locked, and nearly laughed at the irony.

Meanwhile, Tristan popped a compartment on the dashboard, and a cascade of Styx cylinders tumbled onto the deck. I thought he was hooked on his own stash, but quickly learned the fitness guru had another addiction.

While he steered with one hand, Tristan used his teeth to rip the cellophane off a two-pack of cream-filled Twinkies —

Twinkies!

In a frenzy of stress eating, he stuffed them into his mouth, one after the other, grunting as he chewed. When the Twinkies were gone, Tristan went for a big bag of Double Stuf Oreos.

And I should "consider cutting out a few forms of sugar"?! Kiss my assets, guru! (Yes, despite my predicament, I silently stewed.)

After gobbling three Oreos in a row, he dropped the bag on the passenger seat and approached me again — this time to administer a designer loafer kick to my torso.

There was no faking it this time; I cried out as my body instinctively curled into an even tighter ball.

"I know you're awake," he said. "And I want to know who you're working for. You're not wearing a wire, so you're not a cop or a Fed. If I had to guess, I'd say you were a private detective working for the bitch."

I was smarting too much to make a coherent reply.

"Deny it all you want; I know you're Sydney's snoop. Too bad your boss is going down. Cops are circling her like vultures over a carcass. Of course, Sydney will still be breathing in a week. I can't say the same for you."

To ease the pain in my side, I gripped the rope around my ankle and discovered I was missing one high-heeled shoe. In a flash of memory, Haley Hartford's lost pink sneaker came back to me. I could still see it lying there, on its side, beneath that bench by the river.

After I'm dead, will someone find my shoe?

Gritting my teeth, I felt for the rope with renewed determination. Locating the knot, I began to work it. To cover what I was doing, I had to distract Ferrell —

"You know you're not getting away with anything, Tommy Finkle!" I bluffed. "The NYPD's Harbor Patrol has barge camera footage of you murdering Haley Hartford in Hudson River Park."

Tristan threw up his hands in mock surrender. "You got me," he said around a half-chewed Oreo. Then he laughed.

"I didn't kill Haley."

"So who did?"

"Robert Crenshaw — she was working for him."

"I thought she was working for you?"

He shoved another cookie in his mouth.

"I was just the front man. I needed someone to create my fitness app, and Crenshaw overpaid Haley to do it — as long as she also agreed to put a backdoor into Cinder's programming for him. He lied to her when he bribed her. She *thought* he only wanted access to Cinder's analytics — the number of users, customer demographics, that kind of crap. When she figured out what was really going on, she freaked out."

"So that's why Haley had the viral videos from my coffeehouse —"

"Haley wasn't stupid. As soon as she saw those videos, she knew Crenshaw was playing her. Some underling at Cinder was already getting suspicious with all the unexplained activity and uncovered some of Crenshaw's sabotage. The videos sent her over the edge. Turns out Haley was a true believer . . ."

"What's that supposed to mean?"

"Haley was outraged that Crenshaw used a woman-friendly app to abuse women —" Tristan raised his hands in mock horror. " 'The victims, the victims,' she kept saying. Haley told me Crenshaw's abuse, on top of sabotage, was too much, and she was going to put a stop to all of it."

"Why was Haley talking to you?"

"She thought she could trust me."

"How could she think that?"

He shrugged. "She assumed Crenshaw had lied to me, too. And she was desperate. By then Crenshaw had cut off all communications with her, and she was still technically working for me. So she demanded that I set up a meeting with Crenshaw at Habitat Garden or she'd blow the whistle. Crenshaw planned to pay her off anyway, and he offered her another ten thousand in cash to keep her mouth shut. She told him no, and the rest is history."

"Yes. Criminal history," I wheezed, my side aching from Tristan's kick.

"After he killed her — he *claimed* it was an accident — Crenshaw called me. I used Equator's blacked-out back door, went to the park, and we tossed her into the river, after I made it look like a mugging."

Another cookie went down the hatch.

"I decided that night that he had to go."

"*Go* — as in murder?"

"Please. People die every day. Sometimes they die because they make themselves *a problem* for other people. And they have to be dealt with — like you."

"But I'm not your friend. Crenshaw was."

"Ancient history. I only went along with his schemes because I needed the money, and he agreed to invest in my business —"

"So you didn't get rich off Hookster?"

"Crenshaw got richer than I ever did. He was the programmer, and he made a side bundle from the software that he'd developed, and more from his deal to distribute Styx, through a guy he knew in Scotland."

Tristan gobbled another cookie and checked the steering. Apparently, the boat was on course, because he faced me again.

"I was glad to get Crenshaw out of my life. He was the one who couldn't keep his hands off Sydney. He screwed her for a little while, then he screwed her over — like he did with all his women. But she fought back — in the press. She talked about all the crap that went on inside the Hookster offices. And when she had the gall to turn around and start her own dating app business, Crenshaw went nuts. All he cared about was setting up his ex-girlfriend for a fall. Ever hear of a website called Silk Road?"

"No, did you help sabotage that, too?"

He rolled his eyes. "Silk Road was closed for illegal activity. When you go there now, all you see is a big fat THIS SITE HAS BEEN SEIZED notice from the US government. That's what Crenshaw wanted for Cinder. He dreamed of hitting the Cinder web address and cackling over that notice, while Sydney rotted in prison. He was obsessed — so distracted that he was throwing money away, jeopardizing everything, me included. So I made my own deal with the Scotsman."

"What kind of deal?" I asked, tearing another nail as I worked to untie the ankle ropes.

"Now that the Hookster lawsuit is over, two million dollars will be released from receivership. A pathetic sum compared to what we *could* have had, but with Crenshaw finally out of the way, I get it all, and I'm going to use it to build up my fitness business — a nice, legitimate front to use while I get filthy rich distributing Styx in the USA."

He tossed the Oreo bag aside and turned his back on me.

"You really don't know anything, do you, Cosi?" he said, steering the boat. "That's a shame, because I'm about to rendezvous with a freighter beyond the Verrazano Bridge."

Part of the knot slipped, and I felt the rope around my legs loosen.

"The Scotsman sent over a batch of Styx, and I'm going to deliver you to the smugglers as a bonus. I'm sure they'll dump you overboard, in the middle of the Atlantic, *after* they're finished with you. I'll leave it to their imagination."

EIGHTY-FOUR

Ten minutes later, the tip of the Freedom Tower was receding — and so were my hopes of being rescued.

After passing Governors Island, we would motor by Red Hook, within sight of Matt's warehouse. *So close and yet so far* . . . Soon we'd be out in the open sea.

An electronic gadget mounted on the Riva's dashboard began to blink. "The smugglers are waiting!" he declared. "I just have to follow this beacon to the rendezvous point, and you can meet your new playmates . . ."

With renewed determination, I continued working the ropes binding my ankles. Another few minutes, and they finally fell away. My feet were free!

In the movies, I would then be able to slip my legs through my arms and get my hands in front of me. But even if I were that flexible — which, I'm not — I was wedged between two seats and unable to move.

Hope surged in me again when an NYPD helicopter flew directly over Tristan's boat. He peered upward, alarmed. But the chopper raced on until the sound faded. Then he tensely returned his focus to the dark waters ahead.

The beacon on the boat's dashboard continued to blink, and the boat surged across New York Bay. Suddenly the helicopter returned, flying lower this pass. A shaft of light projected from its belly, spearing the boat.

Tristan panicked and swerved out of the brilliant glow. As he jinxed the boat back and forth, he tossed the Styx cylinders overboard. I could hear his panicked breathing as he wheeled around to face me.

"Looks like you're going swimming."

When the helicopter gave up the hunt and flew away, he put the boat back on autopilot, left the driver's seat, and grabbed me. As he dragged me to my feet, he tried to loop a rope tied to several dumbbell weights around my arms.

He was interrupted by a booming voice and a spear of blinding light — this time on the water.

"This is Sergeant Jones of the NYPD. Heave to and prepare to be boarded."

As a surprised Tristan paused, I ground the one high heel I had into his loafer until he howled with pain and released me.

"Twinkies!" I yelled, kicking him in the shin. "Oreos!" I cried, delivering a second kick that knocked me and him to the deck.

Tristan was up first, and he wrapped his arms around my waist, hauling me to my feet again.

"Heave to," Jones commanded, his boat closer now.

Three lights bathed Tristan's ship in a white glow, but with no one at the controls, there was no one to "heave to." As we struggled, the Riva kept racing toward the Atlantic.

Growling like a frustrated animal, Tristan flung himself against me, and the force of that body block was too much. With only one shoe, and my wrists tied, I lost my balance. Our feet were tripped up by the weighted rope, and we both tumbled into the freezing water.

The shock of the cold was paralyzing, and I nearly blacked out. Hands hopelessly bound, I felt my body sinking fast. But as darkness closed in, a prayer rose up. Mike's prayer . . .

Angel of God, my guardian dear.
To whom God's love commits me here.
Ever this night, be at my side
To light, to guard, to rule, and guide . . .

The words steadied me, and I saw the light. *Was I dead already?* No, this light was moving. It was a *searchlight* from the Harbor Patrol boat above!

My fight coming back, I used my free legs to kick. Desperately, I tried to reach that searching light, but I couldn't. Not on my own.

As my head spun and my lungs burned from lack of oxygen, I felt myself passing out. Suddenly, strong hands closed around my waist. Then a mask was placed over my nose and mouth, and I sucked in oxygen like a suffocating newborn.

For long seconds, nothing else registered but the simple miracle filling my lungs. *Air! Beautiful air! Nothing felt better!*

Seconds later, we broke the water's surface, and I recognized the deep brown eyes of a grinning Officer Hernandez.

"Hello, again, Coffee Lady!"

He and Burns pulled me, shivering, numb, and still gasping, out of the water and aboard the *Martin Morrow*.

Hernandez dived over the side again,

while Burns cut through the ropes on my wrists and wrapped my teeth-chattering body in a blanket. Instantly, I was further warmed by Nancy and Madame, who both tearfully hugged me.

"You p-p-pinged my phone," I stammered between shivers.

"We did," Jones replied, relief on his weathered face. "Nancy found your shoe on the dock, and we knew Ferrell had taken you. I called my crew, and with Sergeant Franco's help, we tracked your mobile."

Just then, Hernandez and Burns hauled Tristan Ferrell out of the drink and dumped him onto the deck. He was still shivering and calling us "evil bitches" when they put him in cuffs and read him his rights.

When they were done, Nancy lost it. And I was reminded again how much she loved us — her Village Blend family.

"You jackass!" she screamed, lunging at the fitness guru.

It took Burns and Hernandez to pull her off, but not before Nancy found her Critter Center and delivered a swift kick to the man's *hoo-hah*.

EPILOGUE

Three days after my evening dip in New York Bay, Madame hosted a dinner party for six at her Fifth Avenue town house near Washington Square.

In a well-appointed dining room filled with fine art and antiques, warmed by a roaring fireplace, we feasted on Pork Chops Smothered in Onions from an old Jones family recipe (and rumored to be a soul-food favorite of Jimi Hendrix). We ladled the savory onion gravy over Matt's own Fluffy Garlic Mashed Potatoes, whipped up by Joy, along with a mound of succulent Hard Cider Green Beans — a popular side at the upstairs jazz supper club of our Village Blend, DC.

Dessert was provided by yours truly, my often-requested, rich and decadent Double-Chocolate Fudge Bundt Cake with a dash of espresso powder to add complexity and deepen the lovely roasted flavor of the chocolate.

After the plates were cleared, and a fresh bottle of champagne was popped, the guest of honor proposed a toast.

"To Clare," Matt said, rising. "The best ex-wife a guy could ever have, and my guardian angel."

"Please," I demurred. "I'll admit I'm a decent ex-wife, but guardian angels don't put others in jeopardy. What happened to you is on me."

Matt scratched an IV bruise on his arm. "Don't be ridiculous, Clare. That romantic dinner was set before you were ever involved. Marilyn would have slipped that poison into our drinks, and with no one watching, we would both be dead."

"Well, if that's how you feel, you should acknowledge the fact that more than one person at this table was watching over you that night . . ."

Franco tugged the collar of his dress shirt and looked away. Joy glanced at her father expectantly.

"Sure, why not?" said my ex-husband after a lengthy pause.

I held my breath, daring to hope —

"A toast, to the Angel . . . and the Mook."

Joy groaned. Franco shook his head, and we all drained our glasses. *Okay, so there's still some work to be done.*

Matt quickly sat down. He'd only been out of the hospital one day, and he still looked pale and ashen from his brush with death.

"So, Lee," Madame said, as we popped another bottle of bubbly. "Tell us what happened after you dropped us off at Battery Park."

Sergeant Jones, impressive in his NYPD dress uniform and matching blue eye patch, sent a sweet smile Madame's way.

"Well," he began, "after we located the runaway Riva doing loops off the coast of St. George, Staten Island, we boarded her and found the beacon Clare told us about. We turned it over to the Coast Guard. They boarded the smugglers' vessel, seized the drugs, and detained the crew. End of story."

"Not quite the end," Madame prompted.

"Well, I did get this a couple of hours ago." Jones touched a medal with a bronze star, flanked by blue, green, and gold stripes.

"It's a Commendation," Madame said like a proud parent. "The police commissioner made the presentation, and the mayor shook Lee's hand."

"It's a fine way to end a career," Jones said. "I'm retiring next year — forcibly, I might add. The department brass granted me extensions for years on the mandatory retirement age, but they're drawing the line at seventy."

"Sounds like you'll miss the river."

"Not hardly, Clare. I live on a houseboat."

"It's quite charming, too," Madame said. "And what a view from the bedroom!"

That revelation brought the conversation to a grinding halt. And we all took another drink.

"It's moored at the Boat Basin," Jones added, after an amused throat clearing. "Cheapest riverside rent in New York City."

Matt poured another round. "Speaking of the Hudson River. Clare, it's a shame your flatfoot couldn't be here tonight."

"Mike Quinn is stuck in London," I said. "Things went a little crazy on both sides of the Atlantic after that Styx bust. But why bring up the river?"

Joy grinned. "I know why."

"It's about your wedding venue," Matt said. "You told me you wanted something on the Hudson, so you could enjoy the sunset."

"Sure, but the cost —"

"You don't have to worry anymore. You have a beautiful location on the water, if you want it. But the place is so popular, you're going to have to wait until next

508

spring or summer before you can book it."

"What place?"

"The Anchor and Light," Matt replied. "I made a deal with the owners. I supply their flagship hotel with premium coffee at half the cost for six months, and they'll give you the top floor and all the servers, for one booking, for free."

I sat stunned. "Matt . . . I don't know how to —"

He raised a hand. "Don't thank me, yet. You'll have to pay for the catering and booze — but they'll be discounted, so it will all be very affordable. It's my wedding gift to you both." He paused to meet my gaze. "I only wish I could do more . . ."

It took several moments for me to find my voice. "Thank you."

"You're welcome! Just make sure that flatfoot doesn't leave me off the guest list."

A week later, I dined out again, this time at Veselka (Mike Quinn *finally* got me there) to celebrate his homecoming — and my hapless role in interrupting the supply chain for a dangerous new narcotic.

Thankfully, carbs were still legal, and our comfort food feast included pierogi and stuffed cabbage. But my grinning fiancé insisted on dessert at my place, because Veselka didn't serve the treat he'd been pining for — my "Secret Ingredient" Peanut Butter Cookies.

I'd baked him a special batch earlier in the day. Now we sat in front of my bedroom fireplace, a plate of those chewy-crispy-caramelized treats in front of us with a fresh-pressed pot of East Timor.

"The Brits don't know what they're missing," Mike said, taking a bite. "I love these," he mumbled around the nutty circle of goodness.

"And I love the smell of the French soap you bought me at Harrods."

"I love it, too, almost as much as these cookies."

I playfully elbowed his ribs. "Thanks. Maybe next time I'll wear peanut butter perfume."

"I suggest you don't wear anything at all . . ." He opened a button on my blouse, and then two.

"No more cookies?" I asked as he nuzzled my neck.

"I've had enough dessert. Now I'm hungry for something *really* sweet."

"So am I."

There was sweetness in the air, as well, a meaningful remedy to a past observation . . .

Before Mike had gone to London, he'd been troubled by Matt's single, forsaken rosebud that I'd saved from dying.

Sadly, I hadn't been able to save Haley Hartford from that fate. She'd taken her last earthly breath. So had the man who killed her. And the man who killed him was facing years, if not life, in prison. These weren't happy thoughts, but there was a happy ending — for Carol Lynn, Tucker and Punch, Sydney, and the Village Blend.

Grateful to be cleared of the murder charge, Carol Lynn was far from broken. In fact, her ordeal appeared to strengthen her spirit, and she said it taught her something about herself. She'd been through an awful experience — and survived. It was a New Yorker's lesson, one Madame (and I) certainly knew well.

Punch couldn't have been happier. Grits and okra were off his plate for good. Tucker finished filming his grand death scene in *Swipe to Meat* — coming to a theater near you — and the pair just held their very first *Sweatin' with the Seventies* fitness class. I bypassed my regular swim (for obvious reasons) and joined the joyous dance, letting Donna Summer and Gloria Gaynor restore my soul.

The Cinder CEO and I were on friendly

terms again. With Tristan and the smugglers in custody, my witness statement, and Sydney's full cooperation, Franco and the OD Squad quickly untangled the truth of how Sydney and her business were being framed for drug trafficking. The DA's office dropped the case against her, shifting their focus to "Hook's Crew," who did the actual selling — and Tristan, of course, for his role in the trafficking and the murders of Haley Hartford, Robert Crenshaw, and Doug "Red Beard" Farthing.

Sydney was grateful for the part I'd played in saving her business. And I appreciated her generosity after the ordeal was over. With astonishing forgiveness (and maybe a little atonement for past Hookster sins), she held a beautiful memorial for Haley Hartford, along with a fund-raiser to help Haley's younger sister through medical school.

As for the Village Blend, she donated a three-month marketing campaign of Cinder Treasure Chest discounts on our drinks and pastries.

Esther, Dante, and Nancy were happy for another reason. Though we were no longer ranked as one of Cinder's most romantic places to meet, we were now Number One in a brand-new category: Best Places for Second Chance Connections.

As for me and Mike, now that we had the perfect location, we looked forward to finalizing the plans for our wedding day.

It would be a big undertaking. But we had plenty of time to talk things over, though not tonight. We'd reached a point in our evening when neither of us was interested in any more talking.

With a private whisper, Mike pulled me into his open arms. Our friendship was long, and we'd had our ups and downs. His job was demanding and so was mine. There'd be plenty of lonely evenings in our future.

But tonight, we were together, and his kisses were warm and true, fragrant as the flowers around us. As we moved to the bed, my eyes smiled at the evidence of his feelings, all over the room.

He'd brought me roses, dozens of them, too many to fit in one vase.

■ ■ ■ ■

Recipes & Tips
FROM THE
Village Blend

■ ■ ■ ■

Visit Cleo Coyle's virtual Village Blend at
coffeehousemystery.com for a free,
illustrated guide to this section and even
more recipes including:

* Clare's Italian Cream Cake Squares
* Birthday Cake Biscotti
(*"from scratch" version*)
* Matt's Traditional Pernil (*Slow-Roasted,
Crispy-Skinned Pork Shoulder*)
* Hot German Potato Salad with Bacon

* Clare's Italian Sub Quesadilla
* Village Blend's Maple Pecan
Sticky Buns
* Clare's Double-Chocolate Fudge Bundt
Cake with Whipped Coffee Cream

SHOT IN THE DARK

"Shot in the dark" may sound like a quote from a police blotter, a gambler's adage, or even a Peter Sellers movie. But for baristas, a *shot in the dark* means a cup of drip coffee fortified with an espresso shot.

It's also known by many names. In the petroleum fields of Kansas, for instance, it's called an *oil spill,* while along the Alaskan pipeline it's known as a *sludge cup.* In Northern California, it's considered a *train wreck,* and in parts of Oregon a *stink eye.*

The name *red eye* came from the belief that the drink would provide enough stimulant to help you stay alert during (or wake you up after) an overnight "red-eye" plane trip. Variations on the red eye only get more . . . stimulating. The *black eye* is made with two shots of espresso, and a *dead eye* with three.

Whether you're game for trying these bold concoctions or prefer the creamier, sweeter, flavored beverages found in most coffee-houses, you'll need to start with espresso shots. What follows is an easy method for making those shots without an expensive machine. To see a video of this process, visit the author at her online coffeehouse: coffee housemystery.com.

THE STOVETOP
ESPRESSO SHOT

A simple espresso shot is the base for most coffeehouse drinks.

A caffè latte (the most popular morning coffee drink) is an espresso served with plenty of steamed milk, topped with a little milk foam. This is a creamy drink that coffeehouses often flavor with a wide variety of syrups. Several companies sell their coffee syrups for home use.

A cappuccino is an espresso served with a small amount of steamed milk and a generous amount of milk foam. It has a stronger coffee flavor than a latte and can be ordered "dry" (with more milk foam) or "wet" (with more steamed milk).

A flat white is a mix of espresso and steamed milk. It has a stronger coffee flavor than a latte and less milk foam than a cappuccino.

A caffè mocha combines espresso, chocolate, warm milk, and is sometimes topped with whipped cream.

An espresso con panna is an espresso topped with only whipped cream.

An espresso macchiato is an espresso marked with a spot of milk foam on top. (The Italian word *macchiato* means marked or spotted.)

A latte macchiato is the reverse — steamed milk is "marked" by an espresso shot poured on top. It has a bolder first sip than a café latte. Like café lattes, syrups are sometimes used to flavor them.

An Americano is an espresso shot topped with hot water.

To brew shots of espresso at home, you need an espresso machine. An economical alternative to a high-priced appliance is one Italian families have used for generations — the Moka Express pot.

The traditional eight-sided Moka comes in 1-, 3-, 6-, 9-, and 12-cup varieties. Note that a "cup" of stovetop espresso is not equal to a cup of regular drip coffee, which yields about 6 ounces of fluid. A Moka "cup" will give you an intense little 2-ounce jolt.

Although not the same as a machine-made espresso (there won't be any crema), the stovetop version produces a rich, satisfyingly bold jolt of steaming java. It's an excellent way to make strong shots of coffee if you're planning to mix them with steamed or foamed milk, or syrups to make a caffè latte or other espresso-style drink.

"What beans? What roast?" you ask.

Espresso refers to the method of making the coffee, not the coffee itself. The dark "espresso roasts" are certainly a traditional way to go for that bold, caramelized flavor with hints of bittersweet chocolate, and you'll find them wherever coffees are sold. But you may find a lighter roast more enjoyable, giving you citrus, berry, or floral notes, depending on the coffee's origin. Experiment with different types of coffees, blends, and roasts to see what flavors, bodies, and aromas appeal to your particular taste buds!

HOW TO USE A
MOKA EXPRESS POT

To see a video of this process, visit Cleo
Coyle at her online coffeehouse:
coffeehousemystery.com

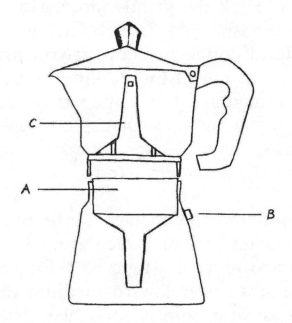

Step 1: Unscrew the top and bottom chambers. Remove the little basket (A) from the bottom chamber and fill the chamber with fresh, cold water. You want to fill it just up to the base of the steam valve (B).

Step 2: Grind the beans fine, but not too fine. You want the consistency of sand, not baby powder. Conversely, do not use coffee that's been preground for a drip maker as it is too coarse.

Step 3: Pack the grinds loosely into your stovetop basket (A). Use about 2 teaspoons of ground coffee per cup. If you prefer a stronger taste, add more. Note: You should not try to make less coffee than the pot holds. If you have a 3-cup espresso pot, then you must make 3 cups. For a 6-cup pot, you must make 6 cups, and so on.

Step 4: Screw the upper pot onto the lower one, making sure no coffee grounds are on the rim to prevent a tight seal. Put the pot on the stove over low to medium heat. If you make your espresso over heat that's too high, you may over-extract and turn it bitter.

Step 5: The entire brewing cycle takes

between 3 and 6 minutes, depending on the size of your pot. The water will heat up in the lower chamber, producing steam. Because steam occupies more space than water, it builds pressure and forces the hot water up through the coffee grinds in your basket. You will hear your espresso gurgling up through the pot's "fountain" (C) and into the upper chamber. When the gurgling slows, check the upper chamber. If it's filled with coffee, it's done! Remove from the heat, pour into pre-warmed cups. If you like, sweeten to taste, add milk or cream, and drink with espresso joy!

Quick tip: To warm an empty cup, simply fill it with hot tap water. Let it sit for a minute, discard the water, and wipe dry.

RECIPES

Homemade Caramel Apple Cider Syrup

This delectable homemade syrup is simple to make (no candy thermometer needed), but the result is complex and elegant with flavors of apple and sweet buttery caramel. Drizzle it over ice cream, baked apples, yogurt, or on the whipped cream sitting atop a slice of your favorite pie. To make Clare's **Caramel Apple Latte,** *simply add a few tablespoons of this syrup to the bottom of a cup. Stir in a fresh shot of espresso (or extra-strong coffee) and pour on steamed milk. Or use the syrup to make a Caramel Apple "Steamer" by mixing this syrup with warm milk alone. Just keep in mind that this syrup should be stored in the fridge, and it will firm up. To use, simply reheat in the microwave for about 15 seconds. Or, if storing in a chef-style squeeze bottle, warm the bottle in a hot water bath. Then drizzle with caramel apple joy!*

Makes about 1 cup

1 cup apple cider
1 cup light brown sugar, packed
2 tablespoons unsalted butter
1/2 cup heavy cream
1/8 teaspoon salt

Place the apple cider in a saucepan and boil over medium-high heat, stirring occasionally. Cook until the cider is reduced to 1/4 cup — it should take 10 to 15 minutes. Now stir in remaining ingredients and bring everything to a rolling, frothy boil, stirring frequently, for 7 to 9 minutes (do not undercook). Syrup is done when it thickly coats the back of a spoon. *It will thicken up more as it cools.* Remove the pan from the heat and allow the syrup to cool completely before pouring into an airtight container or plastic squeeze bottle and storing in the refrigerator. Once chilled, syrup will firm up. To use right out of the fridge, reheat in your microwave for about 15 seconds. Or set the container in a hot water bath, stirring the syrup as it warms.

Cooking tip: Chefs say stirring in a continuous circle is not the best way to mix ingredients. Instead, stir in a figure eight, an

S-shape, and a circle. In other words, vary the way you stir the pot to make sure the ingredients are blended well.

DARK CHOCOLATE SYRUP FOR COFFEE, COCOA, OR ICE CREAM TOPPING

*The deep, dark chocolate flavor of this syrup makes it a rich, sophisticated topping for ice cream or as a base for cocoa or coffee drinks. The Village Blend uses it to make its **Koko-Mocha Latte,** a drink Clare whipped up for Nancy the night of the Gun Girl incident. To make your own Koko-Mocha Latte, place a few tablespoons of this syrup at the bottom of a mug, stir in a fresh shot of espresso (or strong coffee), and add steamed coconut milk. It's also fantastic served warm over ice cream. Or simply mix it with warm milk for a hot chocolate treat.*

Makes about 2 cups

1 1/2 cups granulated sugar
1 cup unsweetened Dutch cocoa powder, sifted
1/8 teaspoon salt (standard table salt or finely ground sea salt)
1 1/4 cups water
2 teaspoons pure vanilla extract

Step 1 — In a bowl, combine the sugar, cocoa powder, and salt (but *not* the vanilla). Add the water and whisk well until thoroughly blended. Pour into a saucepan and place over medium heat. Stir frequently until the mixture comes to a rolling boil; continue stirring and boiling the mixture for a full 7 minutes. (You're watching for the syrup to reduce and thicken. It will also darken.) If the mixture threatens to boil over, just reduce the heat and keep stirring.

Step 2 — After 7 full minutes, remove from heat. Allow to cool a minute and stir in vanilla. Transfer to a bowl and place in refrigerator. When completely chilled, remove any skin from the top, and store the finished syrup in the fridge in an airtight container or plastic squeeze bottle. Once chilled, syrup will firm up. To use right out of the fridge, reheat in your microwave for about 15 seconds. Or set the container in a hot water bath, stirring the syrup as it warms.

HOMEMADE CARAMEL SYRUP

This easy, foolproof caramel syrup can be made on your stovetop without any special equipment (no candy thermometer needed). It has a lovely, buttery sweet flavor and can be used to flavor your coffee drinks. To make a **Caramel Latte,** *simply add a few table-spoons of this syrup to the bottom of a cup. Stir in a fresh shot of espresso (or extra-strong coffee) and pour on steamed milk. Or mix the syrup with hot milk alone for a Caramel "Steamer." Try it drizzled over ice cream, baked apples, grilled peaches, yogurt, or on the whipped cream dolloped atop a slice of your favorite pie. Just keep in mind that this syrup should be stored in the fridge, and it will firm up. To use, simply reheat in your micro-wave for about 15 seconds. Or, if storing in a chef-style squeeze bottle, warm the bottle in a hot water bath.*

Makes about 2 cups

1 cup heavy cream
1/2 cup whole milk
1 cup light corn syrup
1/2 cup granulated sugar
1/2 cup light brown sugar, packed
1/4 teaspoon salt, preferably finely ground
   sea salt
2 tablespoons butter
1/2 teaspoon pure vanilla extract

In a nonstick pan, combine the cream, whole milk, corn syrup, sugars, and salt.

Stir over medium heat until smooth and blended. Bring to a rolling boil and maintain for 8 to 10 minutes. Keep stirring (do not let it burn). After 10 minutes, stir in butter and continue heating and stirring for another 3 minutes until butter is completely melted. Remove from heat. Let stand a minute, then stir in the vanilla. Serve warm in your latte or try drizzling over ice cream, baked apples, or pie. Let syrup come to room temperature before pouring into an airtight container or plastic squeeze bottle and storing in the refrigerator. Once chilled, syrup will firm up. To use right out of the fridge, reheat in your microwave for about 15 seconds. Or set the container in a hot water bath, stirring the syrup as it warms.

CHOCOLATE-CARAMEL SYRUP

This combination of caramel and chocolate flavor is fantastic drizzled over ice cream. Try it stirred into warm milk for an outstanding twist on hot chocolate. Or follow the Village Blend's example and use it to create unique coffee drinks like their popular new **Turtle Latte.** To make the drink, add a few tablespoons of this syrup to the bottom of a mug. Stir in a fresh shot of espresso (or extra-strong coffee) and pour on steamed milk (dairy or nut milk). Top with whipped cream and a sprinkling of finely chopped pecans.

Makes about 2 cups

Use all of the ingredients in the Caramel Syrup recipe (before this one), plus:
2 tablespoons (1/4 stick) butter
1/2 cup unsweetened cocoa powder (sifted)

Step 1 — Follow the directions for previous caramel syrup recipe. When caramel syrup has finished simmering and the recipe asks you to add butter, increase the amount by 2 tablespoons — for a total of 4 tablespoons added to caramel syrup mixture. Stir until butter is melted and then stir in the sifted unsweetened cocoa powder. (Make sure cocoa is sifted or you'll be battling lumps.)

Step 2 — Remove chocolate-caramel sauce from heat and stir in 1/4 teaspoon vanilla — as per previous caramel syrup recipe. If your hot sauce is still lumpy, transfer to heat-proof mixing bowl and whisk until completely smooth. Let sauce cool to room temperature before pouring into an airtight container or plastic squeeze bottle and storing in the fridge. Once chilled, the sauce will firm up. To use right out of the fridge, reheat in your microwave for about 15 seconds. Or set the container in a hot water bath, stirring the syrup as it warms.

AMISH CINNAMON-APPLE BREAD

Growing up in a humble household in Pennsylvania, Clare learned the value of hard work and simple pleasures, including the comfort of baking, cooking, and sharing joy through food — ideas the Amish also value. No wonder "friendship bread" is an Amish tradition. While this recipe is not the classic yeast-based version of that bread, it is adapted from a recipe that originated in Amish country, and it gives Clare joy to share it with you. Some versions of this bread add apples in chunks. Clare's adaptation shreds the apples to promote better texture and includes applesauce for moistness and even more apple flavor. Take note also of her suggestion to use Vietnamese (aka Saigon) cinnamon, which will give your bread an especially beautiful flavor and aroma. This bread is a delight to toast for breakfast; try it slathered with butter. Or enjoy it in the afternoon with a warm cup of coffee and the warmth of good friends.

Makes 1 loaf

1 1/2 cups shredded apples (2 large Golden Delicious apples, see end note ★)

1/2 cup (1 stick) unsalted butter, softened

1 cup granulated sugar

1/3 cup dark brown sugar, firmly packed

1/2 cup unsweetened applesauce

2 large eggs, room temperature, lightly beaten with fork

1 teaspoon pure vanilla extract

1 teaspoon ground Vietnamese cinnamon (see end note ★★)

1/4 teaspoon nutmeg

1/2 teaspoon salt (standard table salt)

1 1/2 teaspoons baking powder

1/2 teaspoon baking soda

2 cups all-purpose flour, spoon into cup and level off

Cinnamon sugar topping (1 tablespoon sugar mixed with 1/4 teaspoon ground cinnamon)

Step 1 — Prep oven and pan: First, preheat oven to 350°F. Also, prepare a 9-by-5-inch loaf pan by lightly greasing the bottom and sides with oil. Using parchment paper, create a sling. Cover the bottom of the pan with the paper and allow excess paper to drape over the two long sides (the grease in the pan will act as glue). This sling will help you easily remove the baked bread from the pan.

Step 2 — Make batter: Peel the apples. Using a boxed grater, shred the fruit by hand into a bowl (discard core and seeds) and set aside. In a large mixing bowl, use an electric mixer to cream together the softened butter and granulated sugar. Add the brown sugar, applesauce, beaten eggs, vanilla, cinnamon, nutmeg, salt, baking powder, and baking soda, and blend well. With the mixer on low, mix in the flour until completely incorporated. Finally, measure out 1 1/2 cups of your shredded apple, lightly packing the shredded fruit into the measuring cup and including any liquid. Fold it into the batter.

Step 3 — Bake: Scrape the batter into your prepared 9-by-5-inch loaf pan and use the back of a spoon to even it out. With clean fingers, evenly sprinkle the cinnamon sugar over the top. Bake for about 60 minutes. Loaf is done when a toothpick (or long strand of uncooked spaghetti) inserted into the bread's center comes out with no wet batter clinging to it. Let the loaf cool off for 10 minutes before removing from the pan this way: Run a knife carefully between the bread's edges and the pan. Then use the "handles" of your parchment paper sling to lift the bread out. Do not slice until the loaf has completely cooled. Hot quick bread crumbles easily. Once it cools, use a serrated knife to gently slice and share with joy! To see a photo of the finished bread, visit Cleo Coyle's online coffeehouse at coffeehousemystery.com, where you can also download a free, illustrated guide to this recipe section.

* **Apple note:** Clare recommends using the Golden Delicious variety of apple for this recipe (not to be confused with Red Delicious). The Golden Delicious has a rich and mellow sweetness and good texture for baking, especially in this bread.

** **Cinnamon note:** Clare highly recommends using ground Vietnamese (aka Saigon) cinnamon for this recipe. It has a uniquely powerful flavor and aroma and will disperse more fully through your bread (and your other baked goods) than milder cinnamons. If you use a cinnamon with lesser *oomph,* consider increasing the amount in the recipe from 1 teaspoon to 1 1/2 or even 2, depending on your taste.

Birthday Cake Biscotti

When she was only twelve years old, Joy Allegro invented a basic "cake mix" biscotti recipe by adding butter, eggs, and flour to a box of cake mix. "What do you think?" she asked her mom. Clare loved the idea and used it for one of her In the Kitchen with Clare columns. In this adaptation, Clare used Funfetti cake mix (with rainbow sprinkles in the mix) to create Italian biscotti with the flavor and appearance of a child's rainbow-sprinkled birthday cake. To see a photo of these whimsical "Birthday Cake" cookies or get the "from scratch" version of this recipe, visit Cleo Coyle's online coffeehouse at coffeehouse mystery.com, where you can also download a free, illustrated guide to this recipe section.

Makes about 20 cookies (each 4 to 5 inches long)

For Biscotti

1/4 cup rainbow sprinkles*

1 stick (8 tablespoons) butter, melted and cooled

3 large eggs (1 should be separated, reserve the white)

1 package Funfetti cake mix (see note*)

2 teaspoons vanilla extract

2 teaspoons lemon zest

1 cup all-purpose flour (plus a little more
  for kneading)

For Rainbow Glaze
2 cups confectioners' (powdered) sugar
10 tablespoons heavy whipping cream
Rainbow-colored sprinkles for garnish
  (about 1/3 cup)

*Note: Funfetti cake mix already includes
some sprinkles. This recipe intentionally
adds more. If you can't find Funfetti cake
mix, simply use a white cake mix and
increase the additional rainbow sprinkles to
1/2 cup. For a "from scratch" version of this
recipe (without cake mix), visit Cleo Coyle's
online coffeehouse at coffeehousemystery
.com.

Step 1 — Form the dough: First preheat
oven to 350°F and cover a baking sheet with
parchment paper. Melt the butter and set it
aside to cool. In a large mixing bowl, lightly
beat your 2 large eggs and 1 egg yolk. (Be
sure to reserve the egg white for use later.)
Add the cake mix, rainbow sprinkles, vanilla,
lemon zest, flour, and finally the melted and
cooled butter. Using an electric mixer, beat
for a full minute. A soft dough will form.
With flour-dusted hands gather the dough

pieces together into a ball. On a floured work surface, knead the dough a little, adding extra flour if necessary, until it feels dry and smooth. Roll the dough into a long log about 2 inches wide (exact length of log doesn't matter). Transfer the log to your prepared baking sheet. Lightly press down on the formed log to flatten out another inch. The log should now be 3 inches wide (again, length doesn't matter). Generously brush the log's top and sides with the egg white. The egg white coating will help the biscotti brown and deter crumbling when you slice it later.

Step 2 — Bake the log: Bake for about 35 minutes. The log is finished when it is firm to the touch and cracking on the surface, and the middle is completely baked — to test this, insert a toothpick deep into the log's center. When it comes out free of any traces of wet batter, the log is done. Remove from oven, allow to cool on the pan for 15 minutes, and then use the parchment paper to slide the log carefully onto a rack. Let cool completely for a full 3 hours or you may have trouble with the log crumbling as you cut it. Using a serrated knife, cut the log into slices on a diagonal (use a gentle sawing motion). Slices should be between

1/2- and 3/4-inch thick, no thinner or they may crumble. Lay these slices flat on a baking sheet.

Step 3 — Biscotti means twice cooked: Preheat oven to 300°F. Bake the biscotti slices for 15 minutes on one side. Carefully turn the cookies over (use two forks so you won't burn your fingers!) and bake for another 15 minutes. Cookie sides should appear dry and lightly toasted. Remove from the oven and allow the biscotti to cool on the hot pan for 1 hour. Finish the cookies with Rainbow Glaze (recipe directions follow).

Rainbow Glaze: *Makes 1 cup.* Into a bowl, sift the powdered sugar. Wisk in the heavy cream until the glaze reaches a smooth but thick consistency. If the glaze is too thin, whisk in more confectioners' sugar to thicken. If the glaze is too thick, add a bit more heavy cream to thin it out. When you're happy with the consistency, scrape the glaze into a pie or cake pan. Gently drag the top edge of each cookie (lengthwise) through the thick glaze (you want every bite to include the icing). Immediately scatter rainbow sprinkles over the wet glaze. Allow to set before serving.

THE VILLAGE BLEND'S
CHOCOLATE SOUFFLÉ CUPCAKES

These elegant, melt-in-your-mouth Chocolate Soufflé Cupcakes are a chocoholic's dream. Light in texture, yet rich and bold in dark chocolate flavor, they pair beautifully with coffee and espresso. They're also a best-seller at the Village Blend — so popular they usually sell out before closing. Lucky for Esther, an armed woman, a potential hostage situation, and an early closure prevented all of these airy chocolate treats from flying out the door. To see a photo of these light and lovely cupcakes, visit Cleo Coyle's online coffeehouse at coffeehousemystery.com, where you can also download a free, illustrated guide to this recipe section.

Makes 12 cupcakes

8 ounces bittersweet or semisweet bar
  chocolate (60–64% cacao)*
8 tablespoons salted butter, cut into pieces
1 1/4 cups confectioners' (powdered) sugar
2 tablespoons all-purpose flour
2 teaspoons cornstarch
4 large eggs, room temperature, lightly
  beaten with fork

Step 1 — Make the batter: Break or chop

the bar chocolate into pieces and place them into a large, heatproof mixing bowl. Add the butter and place the bowl over a pan of simmering water (creating a double boiler). Stir with a rubber spatula until the two ingredients have melted together. Set the bowl aside for one full hour. Be patient — the chocolate must cool and thicken a bit. After the hour is up, sift in the confectioners' sugar, flour, and cornstarch. Add the lightly beaten eggs. Whisk well by hand for a good 30 seconds until the batter is smoothly blended.

Step 2 — Prep oven and pan and bake: Preheat oven to 325°F. Line a cupcake pan with paper liners. If your liners are uncoated, spray the papers lightly with nonstick cooking spray. Measure 1/4 cup of batter into each of the paper-lined cups. Divide any extra batter evenly among the 12 cups. Bake for no more than 30 minutes. The cupcake tops should be set (you can touch them lightly to test this). But do not overbake. They should still be moist inside when they come out of the oven. Just like a soufflé, these light cupcakes will puff up during baking and fall slightly as they cool. Serve with coffee, espresso, or a cold glass of milk and eat with joy!

*Cooking tip: Use a good-quality chocolate for this cupcake recipe and be sure to use bars, not chips. Chocolate chips often contain stabilizers, which help them keep their shape but compromise their flavor and make them more difficult to melt than bar chocolate.

THE VILLAGE BLEND'S ESPRESSO SHORTBREAD

This buttery shortbread is laced with the beautiful flavor of freshly roasted coffee. The Village Blend bakes and serves it in traditional, rustic wedges, the perfect shape for dunking into hot mugs of joe. To see a photo of these cookies, visit Cleo Coyle's online coffeehouse at coffeehousemystery.com, where you can also download a free, illustrated guide to this recipe section.

Makes 12 wedges of shortbread (for 24 wedges, double this recipe and divide the dough between two 8-inch round cake pans)

1 1/4 cups all-purpose flour, spoon into cup and level off
1 tablespoon cornstarch
1/8 teaspoon salt (standard table salt)
1/2 cup (1 stick) unsalted butter, softened
1/2 cup granulated sugar

1 large egg yolk (save the white for brushing top)
1 teaspoon pure vanilla extract
1 teaspoon espresso powder*
2 (extra) teaspoons granulated sugar (for topping)

Step 1 — Prep pan and dry ingredients: First preheat oven to 325°F. Generously butter the bottom and sides of one 8-inch round cake pan and set aside. In a separate bowl, whisk together flour, cornstarch, and salt, and set aside.

Step 2 — Make dough: Using an electric mixer, cream the softened butter and sugar in a mixing bowl until light and fluffy. Add egg yolk (reserving the white for later), vanilla, and espresso powder. Beat until all liquid is absorbed. Add dry ingredients all at once, and beat until a dough forms (about 1 minute). With clean hands, gently gather the dough pieces together and transfer to the buttered cake pan.

Step 3 — Prep for oven: Lightly flatten and press the dough to fill the cake pan. Place plastic wrap on top of the dough and use the tips of your fingers to sweep back and forth lightly, smoothing the top (or use the flat bottom of a glass). Do not press hard or compact the dough, simply try to make it as level, smooth, and even as you can. Discard the plastic. With a knife, cut the dough all the way through completely into 12 wedges. With a fork, make pricks on each wedge, pressing all the way through to the pan bottom. Start at the edge of each wedge and work toward the center, spacing the pricks out in a neat pattern. (This will prevent the dough from puffing up in the oven.) Brush the top lightly with a bit of your reserved egg white. (Do not use the entire egg white, only enough for a light coating to protect the pastry during cooking.) Finally, use your fingers to evenly sprinkle the top with 2 teaspoons of granulated sugar.

Step 4 — Bake and cut: Bake the shortbread in your preheated 325°F oven for 30 minutes. Reduce the heat to 300°F and bake for another 15 to 20 minutes (for a total of 45 to 50 minutes baking time). Remove pan from oven and gently re-cut shortbread wedges while hot. After cutting wedges, carefully run the knife around the inside edge of the pan to separate the pastry from the pan's sides. Do not remove wedges from the hot pan. Allow the shortbread to remain in the pan for 30 minutes, preferably on a cooling rack to allow air to circulate around the pan. Then remove the cooled shortbread wedges and eat (and dunk) with joy!

*Cooking tip: Espresso powder (or instant espresso) is not ground coffee. It is brewed (liquid) espresso that has been freeze dried and then ground into powder, which can be reconstituted in hot water or dissolved into the liquid ingredients of a recipe. A good-quality brand to look for is Medaglia D'oro, but whatever brand you use, make sure it's espresso. Do not substitute instant coffee. It gives a harsher and more sour flavor than instant espresso, which brings a richer, earthier note.

BLUEBERRY CREAM CHEESE SCONES WITH VANILLA-LEMON GLAZE

These scones are tender and light with wonderful flavor. The tiny bits of lemon zest in the vanilla glaze and the cream cheese in the scones perfectly balance the sweetness of the glazing sugar and nearly bursting blueberries. After Clare spent a blissful night with Mike Quinn, the pair enjoyed this traditional British breakfast treat, which turned out to be prophetic. Between satisfying bites of scone, Quinn announced an impending trip to London for the NYPD. Clare was sorry to see him go, but her own plate was more than full — figuratively speaking. After the pair started eating these breakfast scones, their actual plates were emptied in record time. May you, too, eat with blueberry scone joy!

Makes 8 scones

1 cup fresh or (unthawed) frozen blueberries (tossed with the next ingredient . . .)
1 tablespoon all-purpose flour
3 tablespoons cold heavy cream, plus a little more for baking
1 large egg, lightly beaten with fork
1 teaspoon pure vanilla extract
2 1/4 cups all-purpose flour, spoon into cup and level off
1 tablespoon baking powder
1/2 teaspoon salt (standard table salt)
1/2 cup *very cold* unsalted butter, cut into cubes
4 ounces *very cold* cream cheese (block, not whipped), cut into cubes
1/3 cup granulated sugar
Vanilla-Lemon Glaze (recipe follows)

Step 1 — Prep the blueberries: If using

fresh berries, wash and dry well. If using frozen, do not thaw. Toss the berries in 1 teaspoon of all-purpose flour. The flour will help soak up excess liquid during baking and give you a prettier result. Set berries aside in refrigerator.

Step 2 — Make the dough: In a small bowl, whisk together these three wet ingredients: 3 tablespoons cold heavy cream, egg, and vanilla extract. Set aside *in refrigerator.* (Keeping things cold is key in this process.) In a large bowl, whisk together your 2 1/4 cups flour, baking powder, and salt. Using clean hands, work the *very cold* cubes of butter and cream cheese into the flour mixture. Rub and squeeze until the mixture resembles coarse crumbs — there should be no "lumps" of butter or cream cheese left. All crumbs should be no larger than a pea. Now stir in the sugar with hands, combining well, and gently fold in the blueberries (try not to crush them). Finally, pour in the chilled wet ingredients. Gently mix with hands until a dough forms.

Step 3 — Form and chill: Generously flour a flat surface and turn the dough out onto it. Flour your hands well. Being careful not to crush the berries, very gently work with the dough, forming it into a ball. Pat the ball into an even circle of 7 or 8 inches in diameter and 3/4 inch in thickness. Use a sharp knife to slice the circle into eight wedges — do not fuss with the wedges or try to perfect the edges, handle very little. Chill the wedges in the refrigerator for at least 30 full minutes while preheating oven to 425°F. (The cold dough going into the hot oven will help give you nice, flaky scones.)

Step 4 — Brush and bake: Cover a baking sheet with parchment paper and place it into the oven to heat it. After the dough has chilled, brush the tops lightly with cold heavy cream and place the wedges on the hot pan, allowing space between the wedges for rising. Bake for 20 minutes at 425°F, rotate the pan, reduce the temperature to 375°F, and continue baking for a final 5 minutes. Cool and ice with Vanilla-Lemon Glaze (recipe follows). To see a photo of the finished scones, visit Cleo Coyle's online coffeehouse at coffeehousemystery.com, where you can also download a free, illustrated guide to this recipe section.

VANILLA-LEMON GLAZE

Makes 1/2 cup glaze

1/2 cup heavy whipping cream
1 teaspoon vanilla extract
Pinch of salt
1 1/2 cups (or so) confectioners' (powdered) sugar
1/2 teaspoon fresh lemon juice (for stronger lemon flavor, increase to 1 teaspoon)
1 teaspoon fresh lemon zest (see cooking tip★)

In a mixing bowl, whisk together the heavy cream, vanilla extract, and salt. Gradually whisk in 1 cup of the powdered sugar. Whisk in the lemon juice and lemon zest (adding ingredients in this order will prevent curdling of the cream). Now whisk in 1/4 cup more of powdered sugar. Test the glaze on a plate. If it seems too thin (and won't set), keep whisking in powdered sugar, 1 tablespoon at a time. If it seems too thick (and won't pour), splash in more cream. Finally, glaze the scones. For a drizzle effect, dip the tines of a fork into the glaze and move it back and forth over the scone top. To ice the tops completely, generously dollop on the glaze and quickly even it out with the back of a spoon, allowing a bit to drip decadently over the sides. Serve and eat with plenty of joy!

*Cooking tip: Lemon zest is simply the grated rind of a lemon. When you "zest" the lemon with a hand grater or "zester," use a light touch so you don't end up taking the bitter white pith beneath the skin, as well. You only want those tiny but flavorful pieces of bright lemony rind.

THE VILLAGE BLEND'S
BANANA BREAD MUFFINS

Another favorite of Clare's customers, these tender, slightly sweet muffins are kissed with the flavors of banana and vanilla. They can be made in any standard muffin or cupcake pan, yet they bake up big and beautiful enough to be served in a café or bakery. While amazing on their own, Clare takes them to a whole new level of goodness by crowning them with her Homemade Maple-Crunch Frosting (recipe follows). Her customers devour them in the morning for breakfast and in the afternoon or evening as a satisfying snack; and, yes, they pair spectacularly with Clare's freshly roasted coffee.

Makes 12 muffins

2 large eggs, room temperature

1/2 cup vegetable or canola oil

1/2 cup whole milk (mixed with the next ingredient . . .)

1 teaspoon white vinegar

1 1/2 teaspoons pure vanilla extract

1/2 teaspoon salt (standard table salt)

1/2 teaspoon baking soda

1 teaspoon baking powder

1/2 cup granulated sugar

1/2 cup dark brown sugar, firmly packed

3 very ripe bananas (medium to large), mash well with fork and measure out exactly

1 cup mashed bananas (see cooking tip on how to ripen bananas fast★)

2 cups all-purpose flour, spoon into cup and level off

Maple-Crunch Frosting (recipe follows)

Step 1 — Prep oven and pan: First preheat oven to 375°F. Line 12 cups of standard-size muffin (or cupcake) pan with paper liners. Coat the papers lightly with nonstick cooking spray to prevent sticking.

Step 2 — One-bowl mixing method: Whisk the eggs well. Add the oil, whole milk that you've premixed with white vinegar, vanilla extract, salt, baking soda, and baking powder. Whisk until well blended. Add the white and dark brown sugars and whisk until smooth. Now whisk in exactly 1 cup of mashed ripe bananas, combining well. Switching to a rubber spatula, stir in the flour, making sure all of the flour is incorporated into the batter, but do not overmix. Divide batter evenly among the 12 muffin cups — for exact measure, spoon 1/3 cup of batter into each cup, which should nearly fill them.

Step 3 — Bake and cool: Bake in your preheated 375°F oven for 20 to 22 minutes or until a toothpick inserted into the center of a test muffin comes out clean. Remove muffins from pan after five or so minutes of cooling. (If left in the hot pan, muffin bottoms may steam and become tough.) Finish cooling on a rack. These muffins are absolutely delicious on their own. Or try finishing them the way Clare does for her shop with her Homemade Maple-Crunch Frosting (recipe follows) — just be sure the muffins are completely cooled before frosting.

*Cooking tip: To ripen bananas fast, place yellow bananas on a foil-covered baking sheet and bake at 375°F for 5 minutes on each side (for a total of 10 minutes). Bananas will blacken. Peel right away (be careful, they're hot) and cool flesh in fridge before mashing.

CLARE'S HOMEMADE MAPLE-CRUNCH FROSTING

Clare developed this magnificent maple frosting years ago for her In the Kitchen with Clare column, which she wrote while raising her daughter in the suburbs of New Jersey. The frosting has a delightfully crunchy texture and pairs beautifully with spice cakes and muffins, including plain, pumpkin, oatmeal, zucchini, and banana. Clare shared the recipe with her baker, instructing her to use it on the Village Blend's Banana Bread Muffins. Now she happily shares it with you.

Makes about 2 1/2 cups frosting (enough to generously frost 24 muffins or cupcakes)

*For Maple Nut Crunch:

2 tablespoons pure maple syrup
2 tablespoons dark brown sugar (packed)
1 heaping cup chopped walnuts or pecans

For Maple Frosting:

10 tablespoons (1 stick + 2 tablespoons) unsalted butter, softened
3 1/2 cups confectioners' (powdered) sugar

3 tablespoons pure maple syrup
4 tablespoons whole milk
1/2 teaspoon salt (standard table salt)

Step 1 — Make the crunch: First preheat oven to 325°F. In a saucepan over medium-low heat, warm the maple syrup and stir in the dark brown sugar until dissolved. When mixture begins to simmer, pour in chopped walnuts or pecans and stir to coat well. Spread mixture evenly on a foil-covered baking sheet. Bake for 5 minutes, stir well, and finish baking for another 3 to 4 minutes. Watch carefully and do not allow the nuts to overcook and scorch. Cool these super-crunchy, maple-sweetened nuts before using them in the next step. To speed up the cooling process, transfer the foil (with the nuts on them) onto a cool pan and slip the pan into the refrigerator for 10 minutes.

Step 2 — Mix maple frosting: In a large mixing bowl, beat the softened butter until fluffy. Add 2 cups of the confectioners' sugar, half the milk (2 tablespoons), and all of the maple syrup and salt. Beat again and continue adding the rest of the sugar (1 1/2 cups) and milk (2 tablespoons). If the frosting seems too thick, add a bit more milk. If it seems too thin, add more sugar. When you're happy with the spreadable texture of the frosting, fold in the heaping cup of nut crunch. Before frosting your muffins (or cakes), make sure they are completely cool first, and . . . eat with plenty of joy!

*Cooking tip: If you double the amount of Maple Nut Crunch in this recipe, you can use 1 cup for the frosting and reserve the second cup for sprinkling on yogurt, ice cream, or salads.

CHICKEN SCHNITZEL SANDWICH WITH BAVARIAN BEER CHEESE

Clare's late-night snack on the Hudson River is a favorite Oktoberfest treat at Pier 66 Maritime. These crunchy chicken schnitzel sandwiches are served on seeded buns with mayonnaise, beer cheese, and a squirt of lemon juice. Romaine lettuce usually tops the sandwich, but iceberg lettuce works just as well with its cool crunch. The secret to great schnitzel is pounding the chicken thin and pan frying until the breading is golden brown and crunchy. Though not traditional, you can substitute panko for bread crumbs in this recipe to achieve added crispiness.

Serves 4

2 skinless, boneless chicken breasts
1 cup all-purpose flour
2 eggs, lightly beaten with fork
1 cup bread crumbs, or panko (unseasoned)
1/3 cup extra virgin olive oil or olive oil for frying
4 sandwich rolls
2 tablespoons mayonnaise
1 lemon (optional)
1 cup chopped romaine or iceberg lettuce
2 tablespoons Bavarian Beer Cheese (recipe follows)
Salt and pepper to taste

Step 1 — Prepare the chicken: Cut the breasts in half lengthwise and place pieces between 2 sheets of heavy plastic. Pound on a cutting board or other firm and solid surface using the flat side of a meat mallet until filet is 1/2 to 1/4 inch in thickness. Season pieces with salt and pepper.

Step 2 — Bread the chicken: You need 3 shallow bowls for this step. Place the flour in one bowl; the beaten eggs in another; the bread crumbs in a third. Dredge each piece of chicken in flour, dip in the beaten eggs, and thoroughly coat with the bread crumbs.

Step 3 — Frying: Heat the oil in a large

skillet over medium-low heat. When the oil is hot, fry breaded chicken in batches of 2, until golden brown, about 5 minutes per side. Drain on paper towels. You can hold the chicken in a preheated 200°F oven for 30 minutes before the chicken begins to dry out.

Step 4 — Assemble the sandwiches: Slather mayonnaise over the bottom half of each sandwich roll. Top it with 1 piece of chicken, a dash of (optional) lemon juice, and chopped lettuce. Spread a thin layer of Bavarian Beer Cheese (recipe follows) on the top half of each sandwich roll, and assemble the sandwich.

BAVARIAN BEER CHEESE

Obatzda is a classic "beer hall" spread made with a few simple ingredients that combine to create a delightfully complex flavor. Obatzda is typically served with soft, warm Bavarian pretzels, on rye bread, or with rings of raw radishes. It also makes a great spread for chicken or pork schnitzel sandwiches, or liverwurst sandwiches. It's even a great substitute for cheese on a good old American ham sandwich.

1 pound Camembert (or Brie) cheese,

roughly chopped

3/4 cup cream cheese

3 tablespoons butter

1/3 cup onion, finely chopped

2 teaspoons sweet or hot paprika (your choice)

Salt and freshly ground black pepper to taste

1/3 cup German beer (or slightly less, see directions)

Step 1 — With a fork, mash together the Camembert (or Brie), softened cream cheese, and softened butter until mixed well. You won't be able to smash all the cheese chunks, but that's okay. The lumps give the spread rustic texture.

Step 2 — Mix in the finely chopped onions, paprika, salt, and pepper. Add the beer, a tablespoon at a time, mixing well. Keep adding the beer until you reach desired consistency. It should be easy to spread, but not wet or runny. (Note: You do *not* have to add all the beer!) Let the spread sit for 30 minutes to reach room temperature. Serve garnished with a little extra paprika. Enjoy with rye bread, warm pretzels, bagged pretzels, raw radishes, or as a sandwich spread.

MATT'S CREAMY
CHIPOTLE CHICKEN

When Clare needed Matt's help to create her own Cinder profile, she went to his warehouse, where her ex-husband served up this Mexican-inspired chicken. Though based on a traditional recipe, Matt added a unique coffee-based marinade that livened up the flavor of the dark-meat chicken and complemented the creamy, smoky chipotle sauce. Warm flour tortillas are a must, to sop up the hot pink gravy. To see a photo of this dish, visit Cleo Coyle's online coffeehouse at coffeehouse mystery.com, where you can also download a free, illustrated guide to this recipe section.

Serves 4

8 pieces bone-in chicken thighs, drumsticks, or both
2 to 3 cups cold coffee
1 tablespoon cumin
2 tablespoons chili powder, divided
1 teaspoon finely ground sea salt
1/2 teaspoon black pepper
3 tablespoons butter, divided
1 tablespoon onion powder
1 12-ounce can evaporated milk
1 chipotle pepper (in adobo sauce, see note*)

3 teaspoons adobo sauce
1 tablespoon flour
4 to 6 flour tortillas

*__Note:__ For this recipe, use canned chipotle peppers packed in adobo sauce.

__Step 1 — Marinate the chicken:__ In a shallow airtight container, mix the cold coffee, cumin, 1 tablespoon of the chili powder, sea salt, and black pepper. Roll each piece of chicken in the marinade and arrange the pieces in a single layer (no overlapping) with their skin sides up. Marinate for 1 or 2 hours in the refrigerator but no more. Drain the chicken and let it reach room temperature.

__Step 2 — Roast the chicken:__ Preheat oven to 375°F. In a large skillet or sauté pan, melt 2 tablespoons of the butter and blend in 1 tablespoon of the chili powder and the onion powder. Roll the chicken pieces in the warm butter mixture and line them up on a foiled and greased baking pan, skin side up. Bake for 15 minutes, then turn the chicken over and cover loosely with foil. Bake until chicken is cooked through, about 20 more minutes. Remove from oven and let the chicken rest under the foil.

Step 3 — Make the sauce: In a food processor, blend the evaporated milk, the chipotle pepper, and the adobo sauce. Set aside. In a saucepan over low heat, melt the remaining 1 tablespoon of butter, then add 1 tablespoon of flour. Stir until a thick roux forms, about 2 minutes. Add the milk-chipotle-adobo mixture to the pan. Bring to a boil, stirring constantly. Remove from heat when the sauce has thickened enough to coat the back of a spoon.

Step 4 — Serve: Serve the chicken pieces in individual bowls and spoon on sauce. Be generous with Matt's creamy, smoky sauce, including plenty of extra for sopping up with warm flour tortillas.

BACON-WRAPPED PORK LOIN WITH PINEAPPLE

As young newlyweds, Matt and Clare first enjoyed this sweet and savory pork dish in Hawaii, during a sourcing trip for Kona. Clare loved this dish so much that she asked their hosts for the recipe. Back home in New York, Matt tweaked it with a few favorite spices. Tenderized by the pineapple, with a gentle heat, this pork serves up as a mouthwatering fusion of flavors and a truly satisfying feast.

Serves 4 to 6

3- to 5-pound pork tenderloin
1 tablespoon cumin
1 tablespoon garlic powder
1 tablespoon chili powder
1 tablespoon sweet paprika
1 teaspoon white pepper
1 tablespoon vegetable oil
6 to 8 slices bacon
1 1/2 cups pineapple juice (divided)
4 tablespoons butter
1/3 cup dark brown sugar
1 tablespoon Wondra flour (optional)

Step 1 — Prep the pork: Preheat oven to 400°F. Wash pork and pat dry; let it sit until it reaches room temperature (about 15 minutes).

Step 2 — Dry rub and roast: In a deep dish, thoroughly blend the cumin, garlic powder, chili powder, sweet paprika, and white pepper. Rub the pork loin until it is completely coated. Line a roasting pan with foil and grease the foil with vegetable oil. Wrap the bacon around the roast, starting at the front, just slightly overlapping each piece. (The amount of bacon will depend on the size of your roast, but a rule of thumb is two slices per pound.) Pour 1 cup of your pineapple juice over the meat and place the pan in the oven for 40 minutes.

Step 3 — Make the glaze: In a small saucepan, melt the butter and sugar together, then add the remaining 1/2 cup pineapple juice. Set aside. At the 40-minute mark, take the pork out of the oven, pour the sugar and juice mixture over the roast, and cover the pan tightly with foil (be sure it's sealed). Lower the temperature to 350°F and roast for approximately 1 hour and 20 minutes, basting every 20 minutes with the glazed meat juices.

Step 4 — Serve: Remove from oven, uncover, and let the juices collect in the meat for about 20 minutes, and then slice and serve. You can spoon drippings over the meat, or if you prefer thicker gravy, pour the drippings into a saucepan, heat to a boil, and make a paste from 1 tablespoon Wondra flour mixed with 2 tablespoons of the drippings. Slowly add the paste to the boiling drippings and cook for 2 to 5 minutes or until the gravy is thick.

MATT'S QUICK AND EASY
BRANDY MUSHROOM GRAVY

When you love cooking, but you live in a warehouse with no oven and a couple of hot plates, you make do. Charcoal grill on the roof? Check. Boiling ramen noodles in a coffeepot? Ditto. You do what you have to do — and one of those things is make gravy. Matt Allegro's Brandy Mushroom Gravy beautifully brightens a boring boiled chicken breast or plain panfried pork chop. The rich caramelized taste — from that dash of brandy — complements grilled meats, too, especially beef (even when cooked on a warehouse roof).

Makes 2 to 3 cups

1/2 cup (1 stick) butter
6 cloves garlic, crushed
3 scallions, sliced
1/2 pound mushrooms, sliced
2 tablespoons brandy
1 1/2 cups heavy cream

Step 1 — Cook the veggies: Melt the butter in a pan over moderate heat and add the crushed garlic, sliced scallions, and mushrooms. You can use button mushrooms, chanterelles, cremini, portobellos, or a blend. Cook until mushrooms are soft and golden brown, 6 to 10 minutes.

Step 2 — Finish the gravy: Add the brandy and cream and bring to a boil. Reduce heat and simmer for 5 minutes, or until the sauce has thickened.

Step 3 — Serve: Serve over grilled or roasted beef, pork, or chicken. Or try it over mashed potatoes. Matt's recipe for Fluffy Garlic Mashed Potatoes follows this one.

MATT'S FLUFFY GARLIC MASHED POTATOES

Matt Allegro can't help adding a dash of Italian to many of his dishes. For his famous fluffy mashed potatoes, he infuses crushed garlic into rich cream. The final perfect texture comes not from a food mill or electric mixer, but from his own elbow grease. With his pared-down kitchen, he first uses a hand masher to crush the cooked potatoes. Then he whips them into a light and fluffy cloud with nothing more than a simple fork — and you can, too; just follow his recipe.

Serves 4 to 6

2/3 cup heavy whipping cream

2 tablespoons butter
5 cloves garlic, peeled and crushed
2 pounds white potatoes
1 tablespoon salt (standard table salt)
1/4 teaspoon garlic powder

Step 1 — Into a small saucepan, combine the cream, butter, and garlic. Bring to a simmer over low to medium heat. Promptly remove from heat and set aside, allowing the flavors to mingle as you complete the next step.

Step 2 — Peel and dice the potatoes into pieces of roughly the same size. Place them in a large saucepan and toss them with the salt and garlic powder, then cover completely with water. Bring to a boil over medium-high heat, and maintain a rolling boil throughout the cooking. When the potatoes break apart after being stabbed with a fork, they are done. (Test the potatoes after 15 minutes, but the cooking may take up to 30 minutes, depending on the size of your potato pieces and the intensity of your boil.)

Step 3 — Remove the potatoes from the heat and drain well. Mash them with a potato masher and set aside. Return to the garlic-cream mixture that you made in Step 1 and strain out the garlic pieces. Add the infused cream to the mashed potatoes and whip with a fork until fluffy. This potato side dish is fantastic with gravy, but flavorful enough to stand on its own.

PORK CHOPS
SMOTHERED IN ONIONS

This down-home Southern comfort food is a Jones family tradition. Leonidas Jabari Jones prepared it every Sunday for his wife and daughters. Lee Jones's favorite musician, Jimi Hendrix, was a fan of soul food, too — and some say smothered pork chops was his favorite dish. At the special dinner Madame hosted for her son, Lee's chops were served over Matt's Fluffy Garlic Mashed Potatoes, with a side of Hard Cider Green Beans, a popular specialty at the Village Blend's up-stairs jazz supper club in Washington, DC. You can find the recipe for Matt's potatoes on page 567 of this book, and the recipe for the Village Blend's Hard Cider Green Beans can be found in the back of Coffeehouse Mystery #15: Dead to the Last Drop.

Serves 4

4 large, bone-in pork chops, well marbled,

at least 1 1/2 inches thick
1 teaspoon poultry seasoning
1 teaspoon cumin
1 teaspoon sweet paprika
1 teaspoon garlic powder
1/4 teaspoon salt (standard table salt)
1/2 teaspoon ground black pepper
2 to 3 tablespoons vegetable oil, enough to
   cover bottom of pan
3 tablespoons salted butter
2 large Vidalia or yellow onions, sliced thin
1 tablespoon all-purpose flour
1 1/3 cups chicken broth
1/2 cup buttermilk (see end note★)
Salt and pepper to taste
Mashed potatoes (optional)

Step 1 — Brown the chops: Preheat oven to 250°F. Season the chops with the poultry seasoning, cumin, paprika, garlic powder, salt, and pepper. Heat the oil in a pan over medium-high heat. When oil is hot, begin browning the chops well, about 6 minutes per side. Remove the chops from pan and reserve in preheated oven.

Step 2 — Prepare the onions: Pour the excess fat out of the pan and return it to medium heat. Melt the butter in the pan and add the onions. Sauté for 15 to 20 minutes — the onions must be caramelized a golden brown before you continue with the recipe! Stir in the flour and cook for 3 minutes.

Step 3 — Finish the sauce: Add the chicken broth and buttermilk to the pan of onions. As the mixture comes to a simmer, scrape any browned bits from the bottom of the pan. Turn the heat to low and let the onion gravy simmer for 15 minutes. Add a little water if it becomes too thick.

Step 4 — Combine: Add the pork chops and any juices (that were shed in the oven) back into the pan with the onions and coat the pork with the gravy. Cook for 8 minutes, or until the chops reach an internal temperature of 155° to 165°F. Add salt and pepper to taste, serve over mashed potatoes, and dive into soul food joy!

*Cooking tip: If you do not have buttermilk on hand, add 1 teaspoon of white vinegar to 1/2 cup of whole milk and let stand for 15 minutes before using in the recipe.

SPARKLING PEAR PICK-ME-UP

Despite the twelve-dollar price tag, Clare fell in love with this brisk and bubbly fruit drink from the Euclid — a slick juice bar in the Equator luxury gym. Since she wasn't a member, Clare decided to create her own homemade version. The drink is deliciously refreshing after a walk in the park or Clare's new favorite workout with Tucker and Punch at the McBurney YMCA: Sweatin' with the Seventies. *Madame enjoys this drink, as well, although she notes it can be greatly improved by the addition of prosecco!*

Makes four 16-ounce servings (or eight 8-ounce servings)

2 cups chilled pear nectar
1 lemon, juiced
1 cup raw honey, or 1/2 cup granulated
    sugar
2 quarts very cold seltzer★ (or 1 quart
    seltzer + 4 cups prosecco)
1 chilled, fresh pear, quartered
4 to 8 cinnamon sticks (optional)

★Note: Be sure to choose seltzer for this recipe and not club soda or mineral water. Seltzer is simply carbonated water. Club soda and mineral water include other ingredients (e.g. sodium bicarbonate) and will not give you the best results.

In a large container, combine the pear nectar, fresh-squeezed lemon juice, honey (or sugar), and cold seltzer. Cut a fresh pear into slices (4 or 8, depending on glass size). Place one slice in each glass and pour the punch over the fruit. For a garnish, add a cinnamon stick. For an alcoholic version of this recipe (Madame's favorite), simply replace 1 quart of the seltzer with 4 cups of chilled prosecco.

THE EUCLID'S WORLD FAMOUS ($18) BANANA SMOOTHIE

Renowned for its creative and beautiful drinks, the Euclid juice bar's most popular item is this Banana Smoothie. This thick dream of a drink delivers layers of flavor from banana and pineapple to cinnamon and coconut. Despite its fame, Clare felt the drink's price tag was a tad high (even with Southampton honey), so she asked Nancy to charm the recipe out of a Euclid bartender. Now you, too, can drink this famous, overpriced smoothie — and you don't even have to sneak in through a luxury gym's grubby back door to do it.

Makes 1 very large or 2 average servings

3 frozen organic bananas, chopped into 1-inch pieces

1/2 cup lite coconut milk

1/2 cup pineapple juice

1/2 cup plain Greek yogurt (Not to be confused with geek yogurt, says Nancy, which would be a typo.)

1 tablespoon raw, local honey (the Euclid sources from Southampton)

Pinch of finely ground Himalayan pink salt (or any posh sea salt)

Pinch of quality ground cinnamon (the Euclid favors Saigon)

2 ice cubes (the Euclid uses bottled spring water)

Cinnamon sugar (for glass rim)

(Clare's optional addition) Generous splash of Plantation rum!

Peel the bananas and freeze them. Into a blender, measure the coconut milk, pineapple juice, Greek yogurt, honey, salt, and cinnamon. (If using Clare's optional addition of Plantation rum, add it now.) Cut 2 frozen bananas into 1-inch pieces, and add them to the blender with the 2 ice cubes. Pulse the blender until your ingredients are smooth — no lumps. If too thin for your taste, add more frozen banana pieces (from your third frozen banana) or add more ice and blend again. To serve, pour the smoothie into a glass with a rim dipped in coconut milk and encrusted by cinnamon sugar (see below for method).

How to rim a glass with cinnamon sugar — Into a shallow bowl, mix 1/4 cup granulated sugar with 1 tablespoon cinnamon (or halve the recipe by mixing 2 tablespoons sugar with 1 1/2 teaspoons cinnamon). Invert your glass and dip its rim into a bit of coconut milk (or another liquid). Now dip the same moistened rim into the cinnamon sugar to encrust the edges. Pour your libation into the glass, carefully avoiding disturbing the pretty edges, and . . . drink with joy!

MOMMY AND ME
CHOCOLATE CHIP COOKIES

Like so many parents, Clare Cosi did her best to get her baby through all the hardships and humiliations of childhood. From bruised feelings to heartbreaking crushes, the kitchen is where they talked things over and cried things out. And sometimes, during those bittersweet talks, she and her daughter baked together. This simple yet wonderful chocolate chip cookie recipe was one of their favorites because it made just enough for "Mommy and

Me." *Easily whipped up in one bowl, in just a few minutes, these cookies truly are amazing with perfect crispy-chewy texture and buttery-caramel flavor, laced with just the right amount of chocolate.*

Makes 4 large, flat, absolutely delicious cookies

2 tablespoons butter, melted and cooled
1 teaspoon pure vanilla extract
Pinch of salt (table salt or finely ground sea salt)
1 yolk of a large egg
2 tablespoons granulated sugar
2 tablespoons light brown sugar, firmly packed
1/4 cup all-purpose flour
1/8 teaspoon baking soda
2 1/2 tablespoons *mini* semisweet chocolate chips (see end note*)
(optional) 2 teaspoons finely chopped walnuts

In a microwave-safe bowl, melt the butter and set it into the freezer to cool for five minutes while you preheat oven to 350°F. Once the butter feels cool to the touch, whisk in the following ingredients in this order: the vanilla and salt; the egg yolk; and the two sugars (white and light brown). Measure in the flour, sprinkle in the baking soda, and switch to a rubber spatula to stir into a sticky, loose dough. Finally, fold in the *mini* chocolate chips (and nuts if using). Line a baking sheet with parchment paper. Drop the dough in four equal-size mounds on the pan, leaving plenty of space between the cookies for spreading. For perfect-looking, café-style rounds, flatten the mounds *very slightly* and shape into circles. Bake for 8 to 9 minutes. Remove cookies when golden-brown but still slightly under-done. Allow to finish cooking by sitting on the hot baking sheet, outside the oven, for another 8 minutes, and . . . Eat with Joy (or your own daughter)!

*Cooking tip: For best results, use *mini* chips. If you prefer to use standard chocolate chips or chunks, chop them into smaller pieces and measure after chopping.

CLARE'S "SECRET INGREDIENT" CAFÉ-STYLE PEANUT BUTTER COOKIES

Crispy on the outside yet beautifully chewy on the inside, these sweet, nutty circles of good-ness are the very cookies Mike Quinn was pining for while working in London. Clare's secret to the outstanding chewy texture comes from a baker's trick that's been around for years. When an astringent ingredient (in this case, a small amount of apple cider vinegar) is mixed with the proteins in the egg, the resulting combination enhances the chewy texture of the cookie's interior. To preserve it, Clare warns not to overbake the cookies, and she gives you tips to get the best results in her recipe. Like Mike Quinn, the Village Blend customers have fallen in love with these cookies — may you, too, eat with joy!

Makes 28 to 32 cookies, depending on size

1 cup (2 sticks) butter, softened

1 1/4 cups peanut butter (*standard creamy, do not use "natural" separated*)

1 cup granulated sugar

1 cup light brown sugar, firmly packed

2 large eggs, room temperature, lightly beaten with fork

1 teaspoon apple cider vinegar (the secret ingredient)

2 teaspoons pure vanilla extract

1 teaspoon baking powder

1 teaspoon baking soda

1/2 teaspoon table salt or finely ground sea salt

2 cups all-purpose flour

1/2 cup (or so) granulated sugar for rolling
dough balls

Step 1 — Make the dough: Using an electric mixer, cream the butter, peanut butter, and sugars in a large mixing bowl until light and fluffy. In a separate bowl, whisk eggs with the (secret ingredient) vinegar and add this mixture to the large bowl, blending well. Now mix in the vanilla, baking powder, baking soda, and salt. Finally, blend in the flour until a soft dough forms. Cover with plastic and chill to firm up (2 hours).

Step 2 — Form the balls: Pinch off generous pieces of dough and roll into big, golf ball–sized rounds. Gently roll the balls in granulated sugar.

Step 3 — Bake: Preheat oven to 350°F. Place the cookie balls on a baking sheet lined with parchment paper, keeping the balls a few inches apart to allow for spreading. Bake them for about 17 minutes. Do not overbake. The cookies are not done until they flatten out with cracks appearing across their tops. Be patient and wait for this to happen. Remove from oven and allow the cookies to continue baking on the hot pan for another 5 minutes before moving the cookies to a rack to finish cooling. These sweet, nutty circles of goodness are especially delicious with a mug of hot coffee. And on that note . . .

From Clare, Matt, Madame, Esther, Tucker, Dante, Nancy, and everyone at the Village Blend . . . May you eat and drink with joy!

ABOUT THE AUTHOR

Cleo Coyle grew up in a small town near Pittsburgh, Pennsylvania. After earning scholarships to study creative and professional writing at Carnegie Mellon and American Universities, she began her career as a cub reporter for *The New York Times*. Now an author of popular fiction and bestselling media tie-in writer, Cleo lives and works in New York City, where she collaborates with her husband (also a bestselling author) to pen the Coffeehouse Mysteries for Penguin Random House. With well over 1 million copies of her books in print, Cleo Coyle has written 16 entries in the Coffeehouse Mysteries with the newest, *Dead Cold Brew*, now a national bestseller in hardcover from Penguin Random House. This critically acclaimed series of light, amateur sleuth mysteries has earned two starred reviews. Multiple entries have been reviewer Top Picks, chosen for Best of Year lists, and featured as selections of the Mystery Guild. Together Cleo and her husband also write the bestselling Haunted Bookshop Mysteries under the name Alice Kimberly. When not haunting coffeehouses, hunting ghosts, or rescuing stray cats, Cleo and Marc are *New York Times* bestselling media tie-in writers who have penned properties for NBC, Lucasfilm, Disney, Fox, Imagine, and MGM. In their spare time they cook like crazy and drink a lot of java. You can learn more about Cleo, her husband, and the books they write by visiting www.CoffeehouseMystery.com. Scroll down the left column of the site's Home Page and you will see links to a number of online interviews that Cleo has given.